SPEAK EASY

A KATE MARCH MYSTERY

by

LORI ADAMS

SPYHOP PUBLISHING

~For my Family~

Spyhop Publishing

Copyright © 2020
ISBN13 978-1-7371312-1-2

-CONTENTS-

"I am not at all the sort of woman you and I took me for."
~Jane Welsh Carlyle (1801-1866)

CHAPTER 1

It was the blood. That's why I couldn't think clearly. It was in my eyes and in my mouth. I had been left no choice but to spit, twice, into the spittoon next to the table. Detective Bill Cahill, special investigator with the Flying Squad, lacked a single sign of empathy. Even though I was soaked to the skin from the raging storm outside, I hadn't been offered a towel to clean up. The blood, most of which was mine but not all, was running in rivulets bound for my ear—the idea of which I found absolutely revolting.

Detective Cahill slipped a ciggy from his worn case and

1

tapped it on the back of his hand. He lit up and then pinched tobacco from the tip of his tongue, squinting as though deep in thought.

"Butt me?" I asked, offering two fingers for a ciggy. I was not accustomed to the habit but heard it calmed the nerves, which I had plenty of at the moment. Who knew, maybe a shared habit would bridge the tense gap between us?

"You want to start again?" he asked, ignoring my request and blowing a thin mean line of smoke past my cheek.

Had I known how difficult this was going to be I might have done things... no, it had to be this way. I had to explain myself. Defend myself. Before things got further out of hand. I scrambled for an idea and wondered what my hero, the intrepid journalist Nellie Bly, would do.

She would get control of her damned nerves, that's what she would do. Nellie Bly would be calm and confident and in charge of things by this time. If I didn't play things right... yes, that was it. I had to play this old stick in the mud, Cahill, before he locked me up and threw away the—

"Miss March!" Detective Cahill barked. I snapped out my musings and blinked back the self-pity brewing in my gut. I was tougher than this. Sure, things had gone sideways this evening. I mean, I was almost killed and I needed his help, but I wasn't ready to let Detective Cahill know it. Not just yet.

I took a deep breath, slouched like I hadn't a care in the world, and looked across the table. Poor Detective Cahill, he could get so furiously impatient. But who could blame him? I wasn't supposed to be this much trouble. I wasn't even supposed to be involved. He thought I was circling the fringes, begging scraps for a story and yet here I was smack dab in the middle of it.

"I told you," I drawled, putting on a show as though I had

2

better things to do than defend myself of murder. "He was handsome. A swell fella. We got along until we didn't." I shrugged and hoped he was buying my blasé attitude. Inside my nerves were snapping.

"That's why you killed him?" he demanded.

I rolled my eyes.

He sighed because I was a fool and he was tired of my games. He wasn't entirely mistaken. I had been a fool on quite a few occasions lately, but I wasn't wrong, not about everything.

"You're off the mark with those questions," I continued as cool as an electric icebox.

"Why'd you do it?" he demanded.

I fingered the cut buried within the top of my hairline. There were several to choose from, but blood from the largest one appeared to be drying into a lovely matted mess. Not for the first time I wondered just how spectacularly awful I must look. My dark hair was sticky from rain and blood. I couldn't be sure if my eye had gone black and blue. The throbbing suggested it might have. It had been one helluva night. And it wasn't over yet. I'd had the unexpected pleasure of landing exactly where I wanted to be. For the time being.

My eyes drifted to the closed door that separated me from the rest of the precinct. I would give my best hat to know what was going on out there.

"No one's coming to save you," Detective Cahill said.

I blinked innocently. "Are you sure?" I teased.

"Yeah, I'm sure. Now, why'd you do it?" he repeated with a hammer in his voice. He was having none of my games. I sighed and clenched my folded hands on the battered oak table to stop the trembling. I considered things while he breathed smoke in and out. Detective Cahill was a straight shooter and possibly the

3

most irritable man I'd ever come across. He was on the tall side with dark brown hair heavily greased with pomade to ensure it survived the apocalypse. His ramrod spine sat comfortably inside an unremarkable civilian suit while his shrewd grey eyes inventoried my every move. It was impossible to determine what lay within his hard, outer coating. Detective Cahill was the best in his profession and could hardly be happy babysitting the likes of me.

With careful and deliberate purpose, I lowered my chin, pushed out my bottom lip, and shook my head gently. Left alone I might possibly have squeezed out a tear or two. He took this as a crack in my armor, perhaps a breakthrough in the classic interrogation process?

Wear them down with repetition. Offer nothing of comfort.

As if I would give up the goods so easily. I was hardly some schmuck off the streets bumping off joes in my spare time. I had far more at stake than he would ever know. When he spoke again, Detective Cahill's voice was soothing with genuine compassion.

"Go on. It's all right, Miss March. Everything's going to be all right. Now, you just tell me what happened. Start from the beginning."

I sighed. Poor Detective Cahill...

My name is Katharine Ann March and I became involved in all this mess early on the morning of February second, in the Year of our Lord, Nineteen Hundred and Twenty-Two. I was a seventeen-year-old senior at Los Angeles High School scheduled to be a winter graduate, *God willing*. My best friend, Adelaide Wells, also seventeen and a possible winter graduate, had decided to sleep over last night. More to the point, she was determined to spy on my handsome neighbor and I happened to have the window directly across from his.

This particular morning was glorious, drenched in sun and full of opportunities. Perfect weather could make you think anything was possible, although I couldn't have imagined how the day would play out, not in a million years. But there we were, innocent as lambs that bright morning. Well, perhaps not so innocent, but, anyway, I was fairly certain there was no harm in what Addy had coaxed me into. At least no *physical* harm. The moral standard on our proclivities was up for debate.

"Is he shirtless?" Addy asked for the fifth time. We were on our knees peeking out the upstairs window and across the lawn into Nicky Masino's open window. "You said he always sleeps without a shirt. You said he always leaves his window open."

"Jeezers, Addy, have a little patience with your depravity, will you?"

We grinned like a couple of fools. Addy had staying power but I had little interest in a fleeting glance at Nicky Masino's naked chest. I'd known Nicky all my life. Surely, I had seen him shirtless over the years. I just couldn't recall a single incident at the moment.

It had been five years since Nicky went off to The War in Europe and four weeks since he'd come home to Bunker Hill in Los Angeles. I was born on Bunker Hill, in the very same Victorian home from which I now spied like an ill-bred Peeping Tom. I knew this could be the pinnacle of humiliation. If Nicky happened to look our way, he would see two of the most tragic girls he had ever known.

Addy and I notwithstanding, Bunker Hill was home to respectable citizens. Acres of lush green hills dipped and rolled around an assortment of Victorian mansions and redbrick castles. Each home proved as unique and extravagant as its neighbor. I had always found a sense of peace among the ornamental columns, towering turrets, and sweeping verandas. Parties on the Hill had been elegant if not fashionable affairs. Of course, that was before The War came along and knocked the fun out of everybody.

I suppose we had all spent the last several years licking our wounds after this thing we called the Great War. Not that there had been anything great about it. Nowadays, the Red Scare of Communism was pastel pink but most folks still suffered the loss of loved ones or friends. Myself included. The deaths of my two older brothers, Lawrence and Edward, had forever sucked their names from the air. The pain was still palpable.

I shifted restlessly on my knees at the thought of my brothers. They would not have approved of this. Nicky Masino had been their best pal. I should respect his privacy. He was one of the few in their gang who had made it out of France alive.

"Tell me again what they're saying about him?" Addy said. "The servants. What's all the gab?"

I shrugged. I meant no disrespect to Nicky but there had been talk since he'd come home. Current gossip spreading through the servants' grapevine said Nicky Masino suffered from 'black moods' or 'dark days'. I supposed Nicky had left The War but The War hadn't left him. Strange thing was, The War ended back in '18. Nicky's brother, Angelo, had come home directly after the armistice but Nicky hadn't returned until four weeks ago. Some folks were wondering where he'd been the past four years.

I lost interest and moved away from the window in search of a change of clothes. Addy made a soft sound like a dove being squeezed. Nicky was rising from bed and Addy was rising off her knees to glimpse whether his chest was bare, or possibly more. Everyone knew that soldiers returning from The War had brought back more than a few strange European customs. Addy wanted in on this one.

"Well, if that don't give you the aw-shucks," she grumbled. "He's wearing a pajama shirt. I thought you said he slept in his undershorts?"

I couldn't remember ever having said that. Honestly, I was more interested in knowing where Nicky had been during the War years and if he had any details about my brothers' deaths. The topic of Nicky's bare chest was Addy's way of keeping me out of my head and on solid ground.

"Oh Rudolf, won't you be my Valentino?" I teased, batting my eyelashes. Addy threw a shoe at me. I ducked and it hit a glass picture on the wall—a watercolor Pop had painted of Catalina Island. It crashed spectacularly to the floor, and we sucked in our breaths and stared at one another. Five seconds later a familiar thumping rose from the floorboards. It was the housemaid, Trudy Mae, and the broom handle telling us to knock it off. Addy and I had a history of rocking the kitchen chandelier below us during our many dance lessons. Ever since Pop had the house wired for electricity and installed a telephone and an electric ice box, Trudy Mae was on guard for a fire.

"Oh, golly!" Addy cried, scrambling to her feet. "I asked Trudy Mae to wake me early. Mama said I could only stay over on school nights if I had breakfast at home. She's become quite the happy little Kaiser these days. Sorry about the picture, Kate."

I picked it up. Pop's canvas was still intact. "She's afraid you won't go to school if you sleep at my house," I stated flatly and tossed the canvas onto the bed.

Addy stripped off her nightgown and wiggled into a thin slip and a long-sleeved yellow cotton dress with a white Peter Pan collar, while reminding me that her mama was justified in worrying. I held the esteemed record for most truancies in the whole student body of Los Angeles High. Even more than Freddy McElroy who was hardly ever there due to his lack of directional prowess. He got lost in his own barn once.

"Where're my shoes?" Addy asked.

"By the desk."

"Besides, Kate," she went on, "you no longer have an excuse to miss school." She stopped and stared, testing my mood against her claim.

Five years ago, I'd *had* an excuse to play hooky. Five years ago, two Western Union death telegrams arrived on the same day. *Deeply regret to inform you*...that I no longer had two older brothers. They had gone as silently from my life as if they had never been. It was also the day Mama walked out. She'd read the telegrams, packed her suitcase, and left without a word to me or Pop or my younger brother, Eugene. I was thirteen-years-old! It was insufferable and cruel what she did. And then I convinced myself that Mama only needed to grieve in isolation and that she would come back. She needed to cry out her despair with quiet discretion. Even back then I had recognized Mama as a staunch Victorian. Never one to show affection, Mama was not prone to histrionics or excessive emotions. I created an excuse for her behavior. I had imagined, or rather, I had *hoped*, she would return and hold me while I cried out my own despair. A foolish girl's notion, I suppose. Mama had never been overly sentimental. But her sons were dead. Wouldn't their deaths shatter that stubborn shell? I must have thought it likely because I refused to go to school until Mama returned. In those days of roaming the house alone I lost myself in Pop's vast library. I was eventually rescued by Whitman, Walden, Dickinson, Twain, Hardy, and Austen. I made a beggar out of Pop, "Please Kate, it's time you returned to school. Today? Please?"

I never saw Mama again.

When I finally gave in, it was for the love in Pop's eyes and the hope of putting a cork in Addy's whining. She was desperate to keep me on track for graduation. But school was never the same after that. Even now it was a daily struggle to find the desire to go. Too often it was lost on me.

Addy was sulking. She knew I was remembering, and I knew she was sorry for bringing it up.

"It's jake," I mumbled, plopping onto the bed to consider options. "Really, everything's fine. Think I'll go see what's doing with Mary. Maybe she's on the set making a new picture." I began sifting through a pile of yesterday's clothes heaped on the floor.

"Oh, yes!" Addy wailed sarcastically. "By all means, go off gallivanting with Mary Miles Minter. She may be a famous film star, Kate, but she happens to be the snootiest, most spoiled brat I've ever met! And I've met a slew of them!"

"Now Addy, you know Mary can't help the way she is. It's being in the business that makes her like that. Not to mention that vile mother of hers. But underneath it all, Mary's just like us."

Addy blew a raspberry. "You don't have to be a hen to know a bad egg." To add fuel to the fire, she flung open my armoire and pulled out the lovely butter cream dress with a white *broderie anglaise* panel down the front that she had given me for Christmas. The one I always thought would look better with her blonde hair and blue eyes as opposed to my dark auburn hair and blue eyes. The dress wasn't short enough to qualify as a Modern Girl's costume because Addy and I hadn't joined the

9

flapper craze, despite her begging. I didn't have the interest, and she didn't have the guts to take the plunge alone. Our hair was long and worn in a single braid. Our skirts were a shocking nine inches above the ground. Well, Addy's skirts were.

"How about this one?" she asked as sweet as sugar, as calculating as a snake in the grass. She knew very well I no longer wore dresses or skirts. This was Addy's way of expressing her dislike for my friendship with Mary. She was riled up for a fight.

I loved Addy to pieces but that didn't mean I would be shimmying into a dress anytime soon. I ditched my thin cotton pajama top and bottoms, and pulled on my usual clothes: a pair of slim tan trousers and a long-sleeved crisp white broadcloth shirt. Boy clothes, Addy called them. Not that she was wrong.

After the telegrams arrived and Mama walked out, I had gone into a state of introspection and shock. I shed my ruffled dresses and fashionable shoes and crawled into Lawrence's collared shirts and Edward's trousers. All I wanted was to live inside my cherished brothers' clothing. It made me feel closer to them somehow. Nothing in the world could hurt me as long as I was cocooned in the scent of their clothes.

Nowadays, I only purchased boy clothing and had them tailored to my figure. They were arguably more comfortable and functional than constricting dresses.

"You promised to go to school today," Addy insisted. "We just *have* to end our high school careers together and in good standing." She returned the butter cream dress to the armoire.

"I will. Right after I say hello to Mary." I disappeared under the bed to retrieve my shoes.

"Kate March, you made a promise! Besides, we have a French exam today, a Star and Crescent Society meeting, and Principal Housh is counting on us seniors to organize the donkey baseball fundraiser."

10

"Oh, awl' right," I moaned. The only thing worse than lying to Addy was disappointing her. I glanced out the window and grinned. "Well, I'll be darned. There goes Nicky Masino, naked as the day he was born."

"What!" Addy cried, climbing over me to reach the window. I broke up laughing at the joke.

CHAPTER 2

Detective Cahill smashed his ciggy into a nasty ashtray on the interrogation room table and pulled me from my story. There were eight others piled in the graveyard, two still smoldering since I began. I believe dear old Detective Cahill had his ciggys on a chain.

"You're not intentionally dragging this out, are you Miss March?" He judged me with those shrewd, suspicious eyes.

"Sorry if I'm boring you, Detective Cahill. You could always look the other way while I—" I clicked my tongue and jerked my thumb toward the door. I smiled as though we were school chums conspiring to play hooky. He was not amused.

"I said start at the beginning," he said, examining the length of fresh lead on his pencil. Few, if any, notations had been taken down in his little black notepad.

"I am starting at the beginning."

"I want to know what happened in the alleyway. Get to that."

I shrugged. "It won't make a lick of sense if I start there. I'll just have to backtrack and I'm sure to get it all jumbled. Besides, is that really what you want to know?"

"I'm the one asking the questions."

"And I'm telling you it's important to know what happened after I left the house that morning. I'm setting the whole scene so you'll have a front row seat." My hand drifted to my parched throat. "Trouble you for a glass of water?"

Detective Cahill lowered his chin and exhaled heavily through his nose. Double-barreled frustration. His flat expression rejected my request and put the kibosh on any hopes of squirming out of here to ask my own questions.

"Keep talking," he ordered.

As I said, it was a pleasant morning as winter had thrown back the covers sooner rather than later. The breeze had plenty of muscle and filled my bedroom with the sweet perfume of oranges from nearby groves and wild strawberries beyond the hills.

Our crisp, multi-layered Victorian home had an impressive flight of stairs, dark polished wood with thick red carpet that muffled sound and hope. The house was quiet but for the constant heartbeat of the grandfather clock in the foyer. Addy had already gone home by the time I padded down the plush red staircase. I was on tiptoes, determined to sneak up on Trudy Mae and possibly scare her for the first time in my life. Trudy Mae's hearing rivaled the canine species.

"Is that a Bushbacon from the hills or a Katie Ann trying to sneak on me?" Trudy Mae called. I had been a rambunctious child in my day. Comparing me to a wild Texas rabbit never went out of fashion.

I abandoned hope of surprising her and strolled into the kitchen where I swiped a small yellow cake cooling on the rack. It was piping hot and I juggled it from hand to hand. "What's this? Where's Pop? Is Eugene sleeping in?"

"That's Arkansas wedding cake you're poaching," Trudy Mae said. "And everyone is already up and out."

Trudy Mae was a buxom woman with brunette hair whipped into a messy bun and blue no-nonsense eyes surrounded by soft doughy skin. I smiled, tempted to explain that her Arkansas wedding cake was nothing but cornbread to folks in California. It wouldn't have mattered. Trudy Mae spoke her own language which she claimed was due to being born on a cattle drive, and being slung back and forth across the states more times than the American flag.

"You making an appearance at school today, Missy?" she asked, arching an eyebrow.

"Only if the flatfoots cut in on my dance card," I retorted, giving a half-hearted attempt at humor while stuffing a second piece of cornbread into my mouth. She reminded me that we had two flatfoots living next door, namely Nicky and his older brother, Angelo, who had been recently hired by the Los Angeles Police Department.

"Best if you don't mosey," Trudy Mae warned, sliding a glass of milk toward me.

"I'm sure I've never moseyed in my life," I muffled and forced a swallow. "Besides, they're not truant officers." I knew this because I was well acquainted with every truant officer from Los Angeles to the Hollywood Hills. I emptied the glass of milk.

"You need more than that for breakfast."

14

"It'll do."

She squinted an eye, considering me. "Well, Miss Addy says she be meeting you at the Flight 'round about now. If you ain't gonna eat, don't keep her waiting. And don't be coming home late again. You know it ain't good for your pop to eat alone."

I wanted to ask why my elusive younger brother hadn't dined with Pop but Trudy Mae plied me with another chunk of cornbread and shooed me out the back door.

I squinted up at the brilliant blue sky that arched over Bunker Hill like a snow globe minus the snow. Beyond the Masino Mansion to the left were rolling green hills that led to the Banning Mansion, the Hildreth Mansion, and the Pierre Mansion, to name only a few. It was a study in elegant verandas, soaring columns, and regal domes. Some homes were on the verge of gaudy but most were tasteful affairs. Housemaids in starched white aprons beat rugs off the sprawling balconies while uniformed gardeners pushed reel mowers or trimmed the hedgerows with clippers.

Bunker Hill, home to the Lords of Clapboard and Ladies of Brick.

I finished the cornbread, descended the steps, and rounded the corner. Our home lay in the shadows of what the neighborhood kids called the Queen Bee to Bunker Hill: the Bradbury Mansion with old Mrs. Bradbury presiding. Highest on the Hill, it was renowned for its opulence and prominent five-story tower. It had more balconies and chimneys than I could count. I heard the décor included priceless European furniture, elaborate oriental rugs, and gilded French mirrors. I was never allowed inside due to my high-spirited shortcomings as a child and Mrs. Bradbury's genteel nature. But, oh, how the old bag would scream like a banshee when we threw flour at her every

15

Halloween night! Some folks said the wrought iron fence surrounding the mansion had only been constructed to keep the March and Masino boys, and myself, off the property.

"Yoo hoo! Katherine Ann! Good morning, my dear!"

The familiar greeting wasn't the Queen Bee herself because Mrs. Bradbury never mingled with the peasants. It was old Mrs. Banning who was as sweet as cherry pie but had the habit of appearing out of nowhere. It could be downright unnerving at times. Ever since she sold Catalina Island to Mr. Wrigley and his investors, she'd been enjoying a life of leisure. Especially her morning walks with Livingston, her mostly grey and somewhat overweight cat. Mrs. Banning had been a permanent fixture on Bunker Hill for as long as I could remember.

I strolled over to pet Livingston who stood at the end of a silk tether with a diamond-studded collar. He gave me a bored, fat cat look that said he wished to God the old lady would stop coddling him.

"Morning, Livingston. Are you taking Mrs. Banning for a walk?" I scratched under his furry chin.

"A long stroll because he's been such a good boy this morning. Haven't you my sweet Livie dear?"

Brisk footsteps turned us around to Nicky Masino striding up the sidewalk. He was smartly dressed in his department-issued, navy-blue uniform, black belt, nightstick, gun and holster. His department-issued hat shadowed his eyes but revealed a square, determined jaw. Nicky looked angry and distracted. He failed to notice us standing at the corner.

"Morning, Nicola!" Mrs. Banning called, waving her plump, pale, and heavily jeweled hand.

Nicky snapped to attention, startled. He slowed his pace and seemed to contemplate whether to cross the street and avoid us, or continue forward.

I worried that he might've seen me and Addy at our worst this morning. Maybe he was considering saving me from utter humiliation. I was willing to risk it to say hello. Growing up, Nicky had been like a fourth brother to me. We hadn't spoken since I was thirteen years old, when he left for The War.

Nicky walked over and stopped abruptly. "Morning, Mrs. Banning." His voice was deep and cordial but without a smile. I hadn't heard his voice since he was eighteen.

Nicky touched the brim of his hat to Mrs. Banning and then shifted his attention to me where he frowned and gave me the slow once-over. Perhaps he was trying to identify me as someone he knew. Last time he saw me I was all knees and elbows in a dress and pigtails.

Maybe it was seeing a girl dressed in trousers that threw him, as it did most folks. I smiled and slipped my hands into my pockets, allowing him time to consider. When his eyes reached mine, there was no pleasant regard for meeting up with an old friend. No happy recognition.

A slow understanding blossomed inside me; Nicky had changed in ways far beyond his years. It was there in his eyes, that hard, jaded look no young man his age should have. I had seen men on the streets just like him. I knew The War had done it.

"'Lo there, Nicky," I murmured, losing the smile.

Something dark passed over his features, and he stiffened. "Good morning, Miss March," he snapped. Then he touched the brim of his hat and stalked past me.

Miss March? Never in my life had Nicky Masino addressed me so formally. Not to mention with such coldness.

Mrs. Banning shook her head and sighed. We were of like minds. It went back to The War. Always The War.

17

"So that was a load of malarkey, wasn't it?" Addy jumped right in when I met her at the entrance to Angel's Flight on Olive Street. "You've never actually seen Nicky Masino in his under-shorts, have you?"

Still shaken by my brief encounter with Nicky, I ignored the question and asked, "Ride or walk?" referring to riding Angel's Flight train cars or walking down the steep incline of two hundred and seven steps adjacent to the tracks.

Addy made a face and shook her stack of books at me. Of course, we would be riding down. She couldn't be expected to lug around such heavy knowledge so early in the morning. I laid two pennies on the counter and greeted Sammy the watchman as we walked through the boarding station. Addy and I ducked inside a train car and settle in.

Angel's Flight was advertised as the World's Shortest Rail-road because it was. Two, bite-size train cars passed each other on a thirty-three percent grade by cable, balance, gravity, and the Grace of God. It came in handy for housemaids from Bunker Hill who shuffled up and down to do their masters' bidding. And obviously the affluent living on the Hill liked to have a choice; should they stand or sit when going out for the day?

We lurched sideways as the train car called Olivet took off at a whopping three miles per hour.

"I mean honestly," Addy went on, "why'd I spend the night if he was going to be properly dressed?" Across the aisle and a few seats away sat a married maid and gardener combo. They gave us that *insolent youth of today* scowl so I changed the subject and asked Addy about her plans for the weekend. She was often called to do a bit of office work for her Aunt Alice down at the 77th Street precinct. Addy's aunt, Alice Stebbins

Wells, was the first female police officer in LAPD history. While at the office, Addy occasionally overheard file girls gossiping about their male friends. I believed this had fueled Addy's latest obsession with the opposite sex.

Light in the train car flickered as Olivet passed its sister car, Sinai, on the short train tracks. A minute later Olivet came to a smooth stop at the bottom of the incline on Hill Street. We climbed out and faced another option. Should we ride a red cable car to school or trek down to Pop's office where I stored my bicycle?

"Cable or bike?" Addy asked, looking left and then right down the street.

"Bike."

We scurried in front of a lumbering cable car overstuffed with patrons like a fat sausage. The irritated motorman clanged the bell, warning us to make way.

Next, we maneuvered through the open-air stalls of Grand Central Market. It was prime shopping time and the aisles were packed with people and produce. Orange crates overflowed with a rich assortment of local fruits and vegetables that bathed the air in a sweet earthy aroma.

Emerging from the shaded stalls, we hurried down Broadway and then scampered across Fourth Street through a sea of motorcars blasting ah-oogah! ah-oogah! and veering wildly to avoid us. We made it half a block when squealing laughter stopped Addy in her tracks. Across the street was a pack of Moderns, young flappers out shopping. Their arms were scandalously bare and adorned with colorful hatboxes and bags. They wore short, drop-waist dresses that were boyish yet sophisticated. At this early hour, their headbands were modest and beaded necklaces few. Chin-length hair gleamed in the sun and shimmered as they sashayed along.

"Flesh-colored stockings," Addy gushed as though the Virgin Mary herself had strolled by.

I failed to see what all the fuss was about. Los Angeles was rich with flappers, the *femme du monde*, who caroused speakeasies and petting parties waiting for something spectacular to happen. And certainly nothing compared to the lure of Hollywood and all its promises. Living in Los Angeles, I'd grown accustomed to starlets who'd risen to astronomical heights of worship. Their male counterparts often put mothers in a dead faint while enticing their daughters to drop their corsets and lift their skirts. So many naive hopefuls migrated to California with wild ambitions of starring in the picture shows and becoming famous. It was all rather dreamy, often terribly tragic. Unlike the incomparable Mary Pickford from Canada, most hopefuls would end up on the streets, in flophouses, or working in cafeterias, no better off than back in Iowa or Indiana or wherever they'd escaped from.

I looked at Addy and saw the same old story playing on her face. Each time she encountered flappers darting about town, she tried to coax me into the nearest barbershop to bob our hair. How many ways could I say I wasn't ready yet? I was rather attached to my hair and couldn't imagine lopping off fifteen inches on a whim.

"C'mon Addy, we're gonna be late for school." I gently guided her away.

We walked a few blocks in thoughtful silence and then stopped outside a glass storefront where *The Messenger* was painted in fancy white lettering. Grandad Emil's personal artistic flare when he began the March family newspaper business back in the 1800s.

Addy and I walked into a familiar cacophony of noise: clacking typewriters, ringing candlestick telephones, and arguing editors and reporters. Ours was a small office with a skeleton crew of loyal, hardworking employees.

My bicycle leaned against the wall, and Addy dumped her books into the basket. I rounded the counter and worked my way through a sea of wooden desks to say hello and goodbye to Pop. His private office was in the back near the printing room that held an ancient steam press whom everyone called Belching Bertha. Old Bertha was usually on the fritz, spewing more smoke than usable print. She was the best we could do, and her low rumble was a soothing symphony to those in the office. It meant their work was being printed and not chewed up and spit out.

Pop's office door was closed. Never a good sign.

"He's got company," called Mr. Dysinger, our assignment editor lounging across his disheveled desk. "Best leave him be."

Mr. Dysinger was waiting on the line with the phone receiver to his ear but really eavesdropping on his colleague, Mr. Waldo Fink, our assistant managing editor. Mr. Fink was thirty-nine years old and in the habit of phoning his mother to complain that he couldn't possibly work in such a chaotic environment, and would she mind sending over his favorite lunch with a thick slice of rhubarb pie. We all knew Mr. Fink's wife had him on a strict diet. I suspected Mr. Dysinger was eavesdropping to collecting munitions for blackmail.

My fist was poised to knock on Pop's door when I heard his familiar soothing voice within.

"Now Frank, you know we're good for it. Circulation will pick up. We'll get by and make that payment on time. Like we agreed last month."

"You need more advertising," came the reply.

I recognized the nasally voice of Frank Townsend. Just who

did Mr. Townsend think he was, telling Pop how to run a newspaper business? Townsend was nothing but an inky nib in a bowtie. A bank officer for crying out loud! Whereas the March family has been in business since Los Angeles was nothing but a sleepy farm town with one cattle trail meandering down the middle. The newspaper business was a tough trade, especially with the *Los Angeles Times* gobbling up the weakest of the herd and lording it over everyone else.

"We'll do fine," Pop said reassuringly. He was a hard one to ruffle, my pop, but I could detect frustration in his voice.

"Shouldn't have hired a new illustrator. It's more advertisers you need."

"Illustrations attract advertisers *and* readers," Pop explained.

"Well, I'll need something now, anyhow. As a show of good faith."

"But, we had an agreement—"

"Perhaps I made it out of haste. Perhaps it's time to, you know, think of options... like selling or—"

"Can't you give us more time?"

This was beyond my tolerance, hearing Pop beg. There was no call for making a good man grovel like that. I thrust open the door and stepped inside.

"What's doin', Pop?" I demanded.

He was seated behind his desk but stood quickly as I entered. He flustered and stammered like a sinner in church. "Oh, well, Kate. I mean... you shouldn't be here. Everything's all right. We're just discussing some new business agreements."

I glared down at Mr. Townsend who shifted in his ancient tweed suit and bowtie. He eyed me warily, perhaps recalling our last encounter when I locked him in the printing room with

Belching Bertha who was in the throes of a horrendous convulsion. How was I to know she'd spew ink all over him? The cause of his stunning rash was still up for debate, as far as I was concerned. He was such a nervous, rat-faced little man, after all. He would probably break out with hives from an auto backfire.

"I know what's doin' here, Mr. Townsend," I said. "You go back and tell the Lord of the *LA Times* that he's not putting the squeeze on us."

Mr. Townsend clutched his satchel to his chest. "Now see here, Miss March. You know very well I work for the bank, not for Mr. Chandler and the *LA Times.*"

"You tell him all the same. We know he's behind this. We know he's got the banks in his front pockets, don't we, Pop? Trying to run decent papers out of business!"

"Now Kate, please." Pop shuffled me out the door before I made matters worse. "You'll be late for school. I'll handle things at the office."

"Don't do it, Pop. Don't let Chandler make you beg. Don't let him buy us out and shut us down. Granddad wouldn't have wanted that."

"Everything's fine. Now off to school." He waved me away and closed the door with a soft click.

I stood there fuming and rubbing my stomach. I used to get these pains years ago, after Mama left. Felt like I was boiling an egg down there. Rubbing never helped but I did it on reflex. Across the sea of desks was Mrs. Hazeldine, our copy editor and my dear friend. She peered over her cheaters and shook her head. She knew I wanted to burst back in there and drag Mr. Townsend out by his mustache. Mrs. Hazeldine was probably right; I'd only make things worse for Pop.

I stalked out the front door and stood on the sidewalk. The

sun hit me like a slap in the face, and I realized I had been in the dark. Pop had been lying to me. Or, in the very least, misleading me. The paper was doing fine, he'd said. Circulation was on the rise. Pop had hardly complained about the high cost of ink or printing paper since The War ended. Things were supposed to be looking up. I had no idea he'd been taking on more loans. Loans we obviously couldn't repay.

"You all right?" Addy maneuvered the bike onto the sidewalk. Her sympathetic expression said she'd gotten the gist of things. "C'mon, Kate. Let's go to school."

I rubbed my side again and tried to control the tornado of thoughts swirling in my head. This was bad. Business must be slower than I'd thought. Something had to change. We couldn't lose the business, too. Not after all we'd already lost.

Traffic along Broadway was harried like always. Motorcars swerved around farmers who'd refused to change with the times. They steered their horse-drawn wagons right through the middle of town. I often expected to see a terrific accident.

And then one happened. Not ten seconds later, a spiffy roadster zipped around a wagon and startled the horse. The horse reared up and caused another motorist to veer onto the opposite sidewalk. The motorcar knocked over a fireplug and up shot a geyser on Broadway.

Folks were going wild and rushing over to help, but the driver was angry, not hurt. It wasn't exactly the terrific, newsworthy accident I'd imagined but it sparked an idea.

I whipped around, beaming at Addy.

"No, Kate," she said, reading my face. "Lord in heaven, whatever you're thinking of doing—don't."

"All I need is one good story! One scoop to plump up circulation and help Pop and the paper!"

"Oh, is that all?" she scoffed. "Well, it's not that easy to—"

"I'm not saying it'll be easy. Besides, if I'm going to be Modern, I might as well start taking charge of things now." That was my fail-safe way to get Addy on board, always play the Modern card and see where it falls. Trouble was, I didn't always know what I was talking about.

"No, no, no!" Addy wailed. "Now look-it, Kate, you still don't get it. Moderns don't take up a cause. They don't give a hoot about anything. Not politics or business or anything worthwhile. They want a carefree life! That's the beauty of it!"

"Okay, fine. But I'm not Modern yet. And until then, I've got a paper to save and an idea that just might do it." I flashed a mischievous grin and strolled off, looking for trouble.

CHAPTER 3

"You know the Kitchen Kettle?" I asked Detective Cahill. He nodded. Of course he knew it. Most cops and local businessmen frequented the Kettle. Just down the block from The Messenger, it was a favorite of mine but I couldn't recall ever having seen Cahill sopping up their famous biscuits and gravy.

"Yeah, so?" he urged. "If you're thinking of having dinner brought in—"

"Oh, swell idea, but no thanks." I offered a smile that belied the burning in my gut. Playing it cool was proving rather difficult. Every time I closed my eyes I was back in the alleyway, the knife glinting in the lamplight... I needed to pretend for just a while longer.

"It's just that, well, everything really begins at the Kettle. I mean, if I hadn't gone there that morning I wouldn't have gotten involved, you know?"

"No, I don't know, Miss March," he said sourly with a hint of sarcasm. "Why don't you tell me."

"Sure, if you've got the time," I said, mimicking his sour, sarcastic tone. "So, there I was..."

The Kitchen Kettle was packed with early risers that morning, the air a menu of eggs, bacon, fried potatoes, biscuits, and coffee. The gentle clink of forks against china and the hum of morning chatter was a soothing backdrop to think out my plan to help the paper. I had to find a sensational scoop that would boost *The Messenger's* circulation.

I grabbed a stack of newspapers by the door and then slid onto a barstool alongside bank officers, shop clerks, farmers, and reporters from local rags. I ordered a cuppa Joe and my favorite powdered sinker and began scanning the advertisements on pages two and three of *The Messenger*. That little rat-faced man, Mr. Townsend, had me concerned about the number of ads we ran. I counted the usual: Haines Hardware, Vandergrifts shoe store, and five others, when I sensed a presence beside me. I looked down between the barstools to a pair of cap-toe oxfords and brown tweed trousers with two-inch cuffs.

Mr. Montgomery Morgan, a *Los Angeles Times* reporter, therefore, the enemy.

I had known Mr. Morgan since he started at the *Times* roughly two years ago. In his early twenties, he was heavily invested in quality clothing and characteristically too smooth a talker for his own good. A cousin of the J.P. Morgans out of New York, he was educated back east, making him far superior to anyone west of the Mississippi. You'd think he invented the comma or something.

I had more experience with the newspaper business than

Mr. Morgan had. I knew he was a decent reporter who found me amusing, at best. Since he was the enemy, I couldn't afford to like him. Although, I would admit I found him just as amusing. He knew *The Messenger* was my family business; I knew he secretly yearned to write novels.

"She was a woman of mean understanding, little information, and uncertain temper," Mr. Morgan quoted Jane Austen as he slid onto the barstool next to mine.

Without taking my eyes from the paper, I thrust my nose in the air and perused my arsenal. "And he has a brilliant mind... until he makes it up," I quoted Margot Asquith and casually turned the page.

Mr. Morgan chuckled and ordered a cuppa from Bessie the waitress. "I enjoyed your piece on the counterfeited two-cent stamp. A first in history, quite a scoop."

His sardonic compliment referred to an article I'd written weeks ago for *The Messenger*. Pop occasionally gave me space to stretch my journalistic muscles.

I shrugged and feigned interest in an article about a railroad strike in Germany. "Crime, like virtue, has its degrees," I quoted Jean Racine, and heard his soft, playful laughter.

"Why not write something more serious? You certainly have the knowledge and talent for it. Especially for... someone your age."

I suspect he had wanted to say *especially for a woman* but knew it would land him a swift kick in the shin.

Incidentally, it wasn't my lack of interest in doing more write-ups. It was Pop's refusal and constant response, 'stay in school' that ended every conversation on the subject.

I closed and reopened the paper to another page. "What, and turn into a flat-nosed smudge writer like you boys at the *Times*?"

When he didn't respond with the usual cutting retort or clever quote, I lowered the paper and looked at him. Mr. Morgan, like so many young fellas these days, had shed the encumbering over-padded suits from prewar days for the slim and stylish silhouette of the lithe hero. Flexible collar, shorter jacket, and narrower trousers that took on a distinctly American look rather than the British and France influences of old. His blond hair was combed to perfection, brown eyes squinted with amusement, and clean-shaven face grinned like a man of great confidence. Mr. Morgan had good looks enough to charm the small clothes off a nun.

I put on my best lackadaisical expression and gave him the once-over.

"Why Mr. Morgan," I drawled. "I do believe you're over-dressed, as usual."

Didn't he know newspapermen shouldn't doll up like slick daddies in *Photoplay Magazine*? Why didn't he just become the next movie idol and get on with it already?

Mr. Morgan lowered his chin and gazed at me. Without bothering to return the once-over, he said, "And you look like you've slept in your clothes. Again. Not that I mind that early morning tousled look." He flashed his first-class smile, showing perfect white teeth. "But perhaps if you were to—" he stopped short. Mr. Morgan would not lecture me on *the proper way for a young lady to dress* because he was not a blue-nose hypocrite demanding ladies remain virtuous paragons until their marriage beds. His objection, or rather his preference, leaned toward the freedom that Modern girls enjoyed. His suggestion, before he'd stopped himself, would have been to encourage the drop waist and raised hemline. Why he should care what I wore or that I exude a softer womanly persona, I had no idea. Aside from the fact that I'd pegged him as a leg man. He had stated earlier in our budding friendship that he found my masculine attire charming and bold. To a point.

Mr. Morgan raised his hands in surrender and grinned under my narrowed stare. "Not another word I promise, only tell me... what was the *raison d'être* for sleeping in your clothes, again? All night tracking down a plugged nickel?" He winked and I rolled my eyes.

As it happened, I had been too lazy to air out my clothes last night. A few wrinkles added character in my book.

"Oh, Mr. Morgan, you know I leave the preening to you peacocks."

We smiled at each other, enjoying the harmless banter. And then a colleague of Mr. Morgan's slapped the *Los Angeles Times* onto the counter between us. Powder Pugsly, or Pugsly the Ugsly, as I called him, was a veteran reporter who sweated profusely in his too short, too tight, too smelly sacque suit. The opposite of Mr. Morgan, he wore no cuffed trousers, no vest, but always scruffy boots and a cockeyed bowler hat perched on his fat head.

Powder, named for his white hair, jabbed a finger at the front page of the *Times*. "Take a squint at what real reporting looks like, will ya?" Beneath his fat finger was his most recent column. Front page. Above the fold.

I fancied myself immune to his habitual bragging, whereas Mr. Morgan felt compelled to exaggerate a great sigh. It was no secret they hated each other because everyone hated Powder Pugsly.

"Oh, let's not be so boorish, shall we, Pugsly?" Mr. Morgan said, turning back to his coffee.

"You shouldn't concern yourself with folding newspapers, Miss March," Pugsly egged me on. "Your future will be nothing but folding diapers."

I whirled around, not entirely surprised by his insult but irritated enough to give him what-for. "Why you low-life, son of a—"

Mr. Morgan caught my arm as I was about to smash *The Messenger's* Farm Report into Pugsly's laughing face.

"That's enough, Pugsly," Mr. Morgan warned. He held me at bay while shoving Pugsly back with his other hand. Pugsly hiked up his trousers and laughed his way to the door.

I sat there for a moment, breathing heavily and watching him leave. I knew a hot cup of Joe that would love to meet his face if he cared to hang around. Pugsly pushed through the door at the same time Addy shouldered her way inside. She was breathless and wild-eyed, dragging a young boy, Rico Chavez, behind her. She spotted me and rushed over.

"There you are!" Addy grabbed my arm and then paused to acknowledge Mr. Morgan. "'Lo there," she said, throwing on a smile.

"'Lo there, yourself," said Mr. Morgan, matching the smile.

Another time Addy might've joined us but something was afoot. She dropped the smile and pulled me into a corner.

"Thought you went to school," I said.

"Never mind that, listen up. Something's happened. Go ahead Rico, tell her."

Rico Chavez was *The Messenger's* head newsboy. As a fourth generation Angelino, he had more relatives than a dog had fleas, which meant he had even better connections around town than I had.

Rico's brown eyes were high with excitement and his smile a jumbled mess of teeth. "Well, *mi tio* is a motorman for the West First-Street Red Car line. He buys bootleg from a rum runner who lives with a trombone player who dates the niece of Mr. Taylor's man, Henry Peavey."

31

I was confused but told him to keep talking.

"Word on the backstreet is spreading. Mr. Taylor was found dead this morning."

"Mr. Taylor?" I frowned.

"That director, William Desmond Taylor. He is no more."

I sucked in a breath. The news hit me like a kick in the gut. William Desmond Taylor was Hollywood's most famous film director. He was also the current infatuation of my dear friend, Mary Miles Minter.

I looked at Addy. "Oh, God."

"I know." She shook her head. As much as she hated Mary, Addy wouldn't wish this on her.

"Mary will be..."

"Devastated," Addy finished.

I glanced at Mr. Morgan stirring his coffee and talking quietly to Bessie the waitress. With Powder Pugsly gone, the few remaining reporters I recognized were elbow-deep in their scrambled eggs. No one had alerted them.

I gave Addy the eye, and then we three casually strolled to the door like nothing was doin'. Once outside, I took off like my britches were on fire.

"Where are you going?" Addy cried as she and Rico raced after me.

"To get Pop's truck!" I yelled, dodging traffic across Broadway and garnering a blast of angry horns. I found Pop's Ford parked outside the office and quickly lifted the hood. After priming the engine, I threw open the door and climbed behind the wheel. I leaned out the window as Addy and Rico caught up. "Rico! Tell Pop to save two columns on the front page of today's Extra Edition! You hear me? And fetch that fella Pop just hired. I heard he has a new Kodak. Tell him to bring it and meet me at Mr. Taylor's!"

"But he is the illustrator!" Rico wailed, caught up in my excitement.

I waved him on and then started the truck. It sprang to life with a loud rumble and backfire. Addy climbed in and slammed the door.

"What are you doing?" I demanded, anxious to be on my way.

"What are *you* doing?"

"Going to Taylor's home."

"Then I am, too."

"You should go to school."

"So should you."

We stared at each other.

"Do you think Mr. Taylor's death will give you that scoop you needed?" she asked.

"No, but he is famous and famous people make good copy, especially when they die unexpectedly. I think we have the jump on this one. If I get enough for a short column, it might help."

"You asked for the Kodak. You're not thinking of putting photos in the paper?"

"I want to add them alongside my column. A few papers are doing it these days. It might not matter but it's something different." I sounded even less confident than I felt. This wasn't the sensational scoop I'd hoped for because every news reporter in town would hear about Mr. Taylor's death within the hour. And then the Associated Press wire service would send it across the nation. But for me, it was a damn good start.

"I know you want to help your pop, Kate. I know the paper's in trouble but—"

"I've got to do something!" I snapped and then closed my eyes and sighed. Addy was only trying to help. That's why she'd searched me out in the first place. But I wasn't handing this off to one of our reporters to kick around the office all day.

"Well, if you think being the first to write William Desmond Taylor's obituary will help, then I wanna be there for you." She squeezed my hand. "I can't bear for you to lose the only thing left that has any meaning. I reckon there's only so much loss a person can take before they crack."

Not for the first time, I felt a rush of gratitude that Adelaide Wells was my friend. My honest-to-goodness friend.

"What about the French exam, the Star and Crescent meeting, and organizing the donkey baseball fundraiser?"

Addy shrugged and grinned. "Those jackasses will just have to take care of themselves."

The truck chugged with hiccups as we bounced along to a chorus of horns blasting from surrounding motorcars. We veered through traffic as though the steering wheel was loose even though Eugene said it wasn't. I couldn't understand it. I was an excellent driver. Even Eugene said there wasn't any more he could teach me after our second lesson. At fifteen, Eugene spent most of his time driving or tinkering with Ford's machines. He could disassemble one and reassemble it to run faster, which was exactly the point, he always said.

Addy's voice vibrated from the bumpy ride as she asked where we were going. I explained that we were headed to the Westlake Park district where Mr. Taylor lived. Then I tooted the horn at a farmer with a load of chickens slowing traffic.

"Not to Mary's first?" she asked.

I felt a pinch of remorse. I *should* go to Mary's house. I should be the one to tell her about Mr. Taylor. It was cruel to let her read about it in the paper or hear it from some tactless society reporter. But Mary's house on Hobart Street was in the opposite direction.

"I hope to reach the scene before the coroner arrives or I'll never get near the house."

"How can you be sure Mr. Taylor died at home?"

"Where else would he die at seven in the morning?"

"But, shouldn't we stop and call Mary's mother? Someone should be with her when she hears the news. I know I'd want someone with me if... well, you know."

I scoffed and gave Addy a sideways glance. "Not Mary's mother. Not Charlotte Shelby. You know what Mary calls her mother? The Monster. How's that for a lovely pet name?"

It was true that Mary despised her mother. It was that unique commonality that had drawn Mary and me into friendship; I despised my mother, too.

"Besides, I don't think the Monster cared for Mary spending any time with Mr. Taylor, even if he was a renowned gentleman." I pushed the pedal to the floor and rounded the corner onto Alvarado Street, throwing Addy against the door.

"Well, gosh Kate. You know Mary is only nineteen and Mr. Taylor is—well, he *was*—in his late forties. It wouldn't seem right to me either." We clipped a pothole and bounced painfully up and down on the seat. "Are you sure this is the right road?" Addy grimaced.

"I'm sure. Mary and I drove by here one night. She'd gotten that new roadster and wanted to show it off to Mr. Taylor. He is, he was, partial to fancy machines. Mr. Taylor wasn't home then but I remember where he lives."

"Did you ever meet him?"

"Once. He was very polite. Sharply dressed. The perfect British gentleman. I understood why Mary liked spending time with him but..."

"But what?"

"Well, I had hoped she would end this infatuation. Probably

came from her not having a father around." I yanked the wheel to the right and then hit the brakes at the curb. We were the only auto on this side of the street. Addy and I peered through the windshield.

Alvarado Court was a stylish U-shaped arrangement of two-story pseudo-Spanish bungalows. Red tile rooftops blazed over bright white stucco houses. The U sported a lush tropical landscape with a pergola heavy with vines and a few white benches. The bungalows were home to movie folk of Mr. Taylor's caliber. Even if I hadn't known which bungalow belonged to Mr. Taylor, the crowd gathered at the foot of the stairs was a dead giveaway. No pun intended.

"You stay here," I said. "When the photographer arrives, bring him to me. I'll be at 404-B." I rifled under the seat for the notepad Pop stashed there for emergencies like this.

"But, Kate, do you think... could Mr. Taylor really be there? I mean the *body* be there?"

I sat up with a start. I had never seen a dead body before. The thought of actually seeing Mr. Taylor's lifeless corpse hadn't occurred to me until now.

How bad could it be? A pale waxy figure? A blue-faced lumpy form under the bedcovers? What if he was crawling with worms? No, probably too soon for that. How about the smell? I wrinkled my nose at the thought.

"If those worthless smudge writers at the *Times* can take the hard knocks, so can I."

"Atta girl," Addy mumbled, chewing her fingernail and staring out the windshield. She was more than happy to wait in the truck.

I climbed out with my heart hammering and my hands clutching the pencil and notepad. I'd never done a write-up like this before so I arranged my thoughts carefully, focusing on what I knew—get the facts: cause of death, surviving relatives, details of his profession, birthplace, and personal history if possible.

Taking a deep breath, I strolled up the walk to the bungalow in the left corner of the U. Henry Peavey, Mr. Taylor's valet and cook, stood in the courtyard with his black eyes flashing and his black head gleaming under the morning sun. He was flailing his arms dramatically as he repeated to the neighbors how he had walked in and found Mr. Taylor dead. I checked my new stylish wristwatch and wrote down the current time: seven fifity. Several truths I'd picked up from the family business. First being that details make the story.

My eyes swept the area like a searchlight. I took mental notes and jotted things down as chicken scratching. Lordy, but I was nervous!

Some neighbors were still in their dressing gowns. I recognized Douglas MacLean, Mary Pickford's co-star, standing next to his wife, Faith, who was shaking her head in disbelief. The beautiful Edna Purviance, a famous actress discovered by Charlie Chaplin, was also there but the rest were strangers to me.

I mounted the stairs that led to a small porch area, stepping cautiously through the open front door of 404-B. I stopped cold and gasped.

Mr. Taylor was laying just a few feet away, face up, eyes closed. Seeing how this was my first dead body, I was shocked to see the dignified director laid out so still and perfect as though asleep. I thought to find him in bed at this hour.

There was commotion on the porch as the neighbors trickled in. Someone bumped my shoulder, jolting me into action. I stepped aside and took in the place with an untrained eye. Nothing looked disturbed but for the corner of the carpet flipped over at Mr. Taylor's feet. The room was simply furnished with an upright piano in the corner, and a brown peanut bag perched on top. A cushy chair sat near a tailored sofa that took up the far wall, and a small desk littered with an open checkbook and several bank checks was nestled under the window. Mr. Taylor laid face up before the desk.

I moved through the adjoining dining room which held a small wooden rocker and a polished table with a single chair. Two curio cabinets flanked the walls, and various framed pictures dressed the overhead shelf that bordered the room. I turned a full circle. Every nook and cranny was filled with books on philosophy, sociology or the like, war mementos, high-end bric-a-brac, and autographed photos. A few quick steps brought me to the kitchen doorway. A peek inside confirmed my suspicions: typical and clean. I moved back into the living room, satisfied that everything looked in order. Well, almost everything.

A tray with two empty glasses and a cocktail shaker full of curious orange liquid was arranged on the table next to an open book. I had the overwhelming sense that Mr. Taylor had been interrupted.

By now there was a handful of people hovering inside the small living room. A woman remarked that Mr. Taylor looked to be asleep.

"Pity, he was a fine man," another replied.

"Heart attack?" someone suggested to which we all leaned over the body as if to verify at a glance.

"Must be," a gentleman muttered sadly.

Fearing Pop's photographer wouldn't make it in time, I scribbled down a quick description of Mr. Taylor, noting something curious. He was wearing evening attire, not pajamas. But, as I wasn't in the habit of knowing how successful film directors dressed in the early morning hours, I moved on to other details. Mr. Taylor's head pointed toward the east wall while his legs were directed toward the entry door. Then something caught my eye. A large diamond ring sparkled from Mr. Taylor's hand. It was beautiful, and I wanted a closer look but raised voices from outside brought everyone around to the door.

Mr. Taylor's chauffeur, Howard Fellows, stepped into the room. A few years my senior, Howard appeared dumbfounded with shock and stared down at his dead boss. Within moments, Howard's older brother, Harry, walked in. I remembered Harry had been Mr. Taylor's chauffeur before he was promoted to assistant director at Paramount Studios. Harry ushered in a short woman in blue who seemed familiar to everyone but me. The crowd parted, allowing her a view of the body.

The woman stifled a cry, and then, showing tremendous fortitude, blinked back tears and collected herself. She went to the phone closet where Mr. Taylor apparently stashed his bootleg liquor. Young Howard and I stared at each other while Harry and the Woman in Blue removed all the liquor. No one said a word as they hauled it outside and returned minutes later to disappear up the stairs to Mr. Taylor's bedroom.

Howard had gone pale and stared at Mr. Taylor. Assuming we were both in the company of our first dead body, I walked over and touched his sleeve.

"Sorry about your boss," I said quietly.

Red eyes swollen from unshed tears lifted to mine. "I-I just left him last night... but I phoned him like he asked. 'Round seven thirty but he don't answer, and I... never spoke to him again." He choked up and left the room to presumably cry outside.

Harry Fellows and the Woman in Blue returned with arms full of boxes and coat pockets bulging with God only knew what. They marched by without a word. Curiosity got the better of me so I dashed after them.

"Excuse me, sir? Ma'am? Who are you? And what are you taking from Mr. Taylor's bedroom?" I was ignored without a backward glance. The pair packed up the car and sped away.

"That was Julia Crawford Ivers," Edna Purviance's soft voice answered behind me. I swung around, surprised the actress had addressed me. "She's the Chief Scenarist at Paramount. Mr. Taylor's very good friend." She sniffed and dabbed a cloth to her eyes. "*Was* his good friend," she corrected.

I nodded sympathetically and jotted down the name. So much was happening, I couldn't trust my memory.

"Did you know him?" Miss Purviance asked.

"I did. Through a mutual friend. He was a swell fella."

She tamped the delicate cloth under her nose and nodded. Hiding a fresh batch of tears, she turned away, and I found myself facing Faith MacLean. I smiled tentatively and walked over. After introducing myself, we struck up a conversation. Mrs. MacLean said she knew Mr. Taylor from the business and that she lived next door. She and her husband shared the duplex with Mr. Jessurun, the landlord, who had been the first neighbor to rush outside when Henry Peavey fled into the courtyard bewailing the state of his employer at the top of his lungs.

And then, as conversations often tend to trail along, Faith MacLean casually revealed something that drained the blood from my face. My heart all but stopped and I took a moment to collect myself.

"How interesting," I managed calmly before asking her to elaborate. Once she'd summed it up, I excused myself so as not to appear overly excited and then frantically scribbled everything down to ensure no detail was lost. It was at this time the first patrol car pulled to the curb on Alvarado Street. The passenger climbed out and I groaned. Detective Sergeant Ziegler, a far cry from my favorite human being.

Sergeant Ziegler and I enjoyed a mutual dislike for one an-other dating back to my junior year when his overenthusiastic son, Zachary Ziegler, tried unsuccessfully to grab my left breast. Addy and I had been sitting at the soda counter in Galco's Italian grocery store when the unprovoked assault was perpetrated. My elbow promptly gave Zachary a black eye for his troubles. An involuntary reflex on my part but Zachary's father, being a virile police officer, refused to believe his son's shiner had come from a girl. Zachary was forced to concoct a story that he'd been jumped by thugs in an alleyway. Addy had found the whole thing hilarious and recited a blow-by-blow description of the truth dur-ing lunchtime at school the following day. Suddenly I was Jack Dempsey knocking out Georges Carpentier in the fourth round all over again. Zachary was humiliated twice over.

I met up with Sergeant Ziegler and matched his pace as he headed to 404-B. "Morning, Sergeant," I said, checking my wristwatch. I'd beaten the first officer to the scene by almost thirty minutes.

"What the hell are you doing here, Miss March? Why aren't you in school?"

"Time off for good behavior." I smiled amiably.

"I doubt that. Now beat it or I know an officer who'll take you for a ride." He jerked his thumb toward his patrol car where an officer was climbing out of the driver's seat.

Nicky Masino.

"I have a right to be here. I'm working for *The Messenger* today," I said, hoping to avoid another truancy charge. The ser-geant would hardly take time to verify my lie with Pop. Not with a famous film director lying dead.

Sergeant Ziegler stopped at the bottom step and jabbed a finger in my face. "You are not allowed inside!" Then he marched up the steps with a trail of nosy neighbors in his wake.

I was a little shaken by the level of hostility but not altogether surprised. Some people can hold onto a grudge like it was a hip flask full of hooch.

"Well, Miss March, you do get around," Nicky said, casually strolling up.

I shrugged and perused my notes. "Since when are you playing chauffeur to the charming Sergeant Ziegler, *Officer* Masino?" If he wanted to continue speaking formally as though we hadn't chased each other all over Bunker Hill, not to mention every baseball field in town as kids, it was fine by me.

"I go where I'm needed. And you should be in school, Miss March."

"That right?"

I was fully prepared to repeat my white lie but Edna Purviance stole Nicky's attention just then. With Nicky busy, I slipped back inside the crowded bungalow and stuffed myself into the phone closet.

Sergeant Ziegler was too busy conducting interviews to notice me. With a captive audience, Henry Peavey repeated for the umpteenth time how he came in that morning about half past seven and found Mr. Taylor lying dead on the floor. He then ran screaming into the courtyard, rousing the neighbors. Someone rang the police, and here we all were.

The crowd nodded but no one mentioned that studio executives had preceded the Sergeant's arrival. I couldn't risk pointing things out because Nicky had stepped inside, obviously looking for me. I pressed against the wall of the phone closet to no avail. He spotted me and began making his way over but was interrupted by a man pushing into the room. He seemed familiar to the neighbors who made room around the body.

"Mr. Eyton," Sergeant Ziegler said, clapping him on the shoulder. "I'm afraid it's true. He's dead."

Oh yes, Charles Eyton. I had heard the name but didn't know the man's face. Mary once remarked that Charlie Eyton, the manager of Famous Players-Lasky Corporation, was Mr. Taylor's closest confidant. Poor Mr. Eyton appeared in shock—but only for a moment.

He dashed upstairs to Mr. Taylor's bedroom. After a minute of rummaging around, he swept downstairs, concealing something bulky beneath his overcoat. He left and returned moments later without a word of explanation. I was baffled. What on God's green earth was everyone removing from Mr. Taylor's bedroom? If I keeled over dead this very moment, there wasn't a single thing of interest to secret out of *my* bedroom.

"Excuse me." An elderly gentleman shouldered through the crowd. "I'm a doctor. Do you need assistance?"

"The coroner is on the way," Sergeant Ziegler informed him. The old man bent over the body and adjusted his cheaters.

"Hmm. Blood at the mouth. Stomach ulcer. I should say he died of a hemorrhage in his stomach." Everyone leaned toward Mr. Taylor to have another look.

I found it curious that the doctor should make such a conclusion without examining the body.

A bevy of questions I should have liked to ask swirled through my mind but Nicky was making his move toward me. No doubt I was to be promptly kicked to the curb where I would miss all the pertinent information. As the sole reporter on the scene, I felt it my duty not to waste such a valuable opportunity.

"It was murder!" I blurted out.

Several people gasped and then the entire room swiveled around to face me. Heat flared in my cheeks. I must have looked just as shocked as they did.

"Jesus Christ, Miss March!" Sergeant Ziegler yelled. "I told you to stay out! Officer Masino, remove her!"

"Wait!"

It was Charlie Eyton. Sergeant Ziegler may have had the scene but Charlie Eyton seemed to have the authority.

"Who are you and why do you think Mr. Taylor was murdered?" Mr. Eyton demanded.

"She's nobody. Not even a real reporter," Sergeant Ziegler barked and then scribbled onto his notepad, "Died of natural causes."

"Well," I began somewhat hesitantly. "Faith MacLean, right over there, said she heard a gunshot last night." I sounded far less confident aloud than I had in my head. What Mrs. MacLean had so nonchalantly revealed in the courtyard was that she'd thought she heard a gunshot last night. Never mind that she'd also said it could have been a car backfiring. For better or worse, the idea had stuck in my head. "And... and Mr. MacLean heard it, too. And, so did their maid, Christina Jewett."

Faith MacLean, who hadn't realized I would take her at her word, grew flustered and embarrassed. The room fell silent and everyone looked again at Mr. Taylor perfectly laid out as though he had decided to nap on the floor.

The thin line of blood at the corner of his mouth gave me doubts. Had I jumped the gun? Had the doctor's diagnosis been right after all? More importantly, had I doomed myself as a serious reporter?

Mr. Eyton knelt down and opened Mr. Taylor's jacket and vest. "No wound," he announced. "Better turn him over." He and the sergeant rolled the body over and revealed a pool of dark blood that had saturated the thick carpet. The neighbors whispered disbelief and hovered closer. Carefully, Mr. Eyton lifted the jacket and shirt. He gasped. The crowd gasped.

"A bullet hole!" Mr. Eyton said. "He's been shot in the back! Good God! He *has* been murdered!"

CHAPTER 4

"So, you were the one in the phone closet," Detective Cahill said, jotting something down. "I heard about that. Should have known it was you."

"Yes, I'm happy to enlighten you on what happened next, but first..." I touched my throat and grimaced. "Do you mind? I'm so parched."

Detective Cahill relented and left the room for a glass of water. He had closed the door but hadn't engaged the lock. This might be the opportunity I had been waiting for. I wasn't necessarily trying to escape the precinct, not yet anyway. What I needed was information, or at least contact with someone who knew if my plan had worked.

After a moment, I quietly open the door and poked my head outside. I faced a hallway lousy with distant voices, clacking typewriters, and ringing telephones. If I struck out to the left

45

I'd find a large open room packed with desks just past the Night Officer's station. I knew this because I had been paraded through the garden of patrol desks when I arrived. It was the central hub of all the noise. The hallway on my right led to a black door with a frosted window marked W D Doran: Deputy District Attorney, otherwise known as a dead end. I adored a challenge, but not to the tune of confronting the Deputy DA.

I looked back to the left and caught a glimpse of Mrs. Wells walking by. My heart leapt. Addy's Aunt Alice could help! I raised my hand and just caught her eye as Detective Cahill appeared around the corner. He had a glass of water in one hand and a cuppa Joe in the other. A startled scowl flashed across his face. I ducked back inside.

Detective Cahill slammed the door behind him. "I should stick you in a cell and finish this tomorrow!" he yelled with sudden rage. "This is no game, Miss March! You try to escape here and they'll shoot on sight! They won't care who your family is! Is that clear? Or shall I repeat myself?"

"I was only saying hello to an old friend," I said.

"Nobody is coming to save you!" he barked. "Nobody!"

I smiled, secretly happy to know that Nicky had kept his word and not provided Cahill with details of my attack this evening. Nicky must have trusted me to handle things in my own way.

With that, I took a long drink of water and then continued.

It was quite a shock, the murder of William Desmond Taylor. After my outrageous claim had been confirmed, Officer Masino, Nicky, took me by the arm.

"Out of here. Now!" he snapped, pulling me from the phone closet.

I tried to wrangle free but Sergeant Ziegler announced that the area was now a crime scene and everyone should return to the courtyard for questioning. I was swept away in the current.

"Go to school, Miss March," Nicky ordered once we had settled back on the lawn.

"I'm on assignment. A *murder* assignment," I said calmly. "I've gotten the jump on this and I'm not leaving." Despite my bold declaration, I was terribly conflicted. This *was* the sensational story I had wanted, but it was Mary's Mr. Taylor shot dead on the floor. It was awful. Brilliantly awful.

"Just for curiosity's sake," Nicky said, "how did you know it was murder?"

I shrugged. "I don't know, really. When Mrs. MacLean told me she thought she'd heard a gunshot last night, I immediately thought of Mr. Taylor lying dead in his nice suit. Not in his robe and pajamas. I just thought it sounded reasonable."

"Reasonable? Murder?"

"You know what I mean. And that's why I'm staying to—"

"You're not. Staying. Do as you are told and go to school before you—"

"Why should I?" I asked, not particularly caring to hear his response. I was overcome with annoying feelings of nostalgia from the life Nicky and I had lived before this one. The faint faraway life where I begged to play first base and he tried to send me away with the constant refrain: *Go home before you worry your pop.* It hadn't worked then and it wasn't going to work now. Honestly, you'd think he didn't know me at all.

"Miss March, this is a murder scene with a murderer on the loose."

"I realize you're a cop now, *Officer* Masino, but I've been around enough to know you can't legally make me leave."

Nicky contemplated, possibly recalling how stubborn I could

be. It was a war of attrition between us and I simply wouldn't relent. Luckily for Nicky, Sergeant Ziegler called him away.

With a final warning to remove myself, Nicky returned to the bungalow to stand guard at the entrance. Meanwhile, the sergeant disappeared into a neighboring home, presumably to telephone the station for backup now that the situation had changed. The neighbors mingled anxiously in the courtyard, absorbing the second shock of the morning. Interesting conversations began to arise, curious antidotes about Mr. Taylor and disbelieving outrage as to how this could have happened to such a nice man.

A cursory inventory suggested that none of the heartbroken neighbors could have done in the poor director. And why should the killer hang around anyhow? He'd have to be a complete moron, really. He would know the police would be called and people would be questioned. Far too great a risk, if you asked me. Unless the killer wanted to get nabbed.

I moved about leisurely and made perfunctory notes, adding details from earlier observations. I scrutinized Mr. Taylor's bungalow, particularly the upstairs bedroom window. I was itching to poke around up there. I'd give my eyeteeth to see what had been overturned by Mr. Taylor's friends. I'd once considered Mr. Taylor a mild-mannered film director. Now, the possibilities of his indiscretions seemed endless, if not as mysterious as his death. If only I could get inside.

I scoured the bungalow with a thief's eye. The cypress trees on either side were too flimsy to master. The entry was flanked by two ornamental columns that supported a slim, pseudo second-story balcony with a decorative iron railing encasing double doors. It was climbable and no more difficult than scaling the trellis beneath my own bedroom window, from which I had vast experience. But reaching Mr. Taylor's second-story window would be tricky without footholds. It might take a few, unortho-dox attempts but I was more agile than most girls I knew. Plus, I had the advantage of wearing trousers.

I was being watched. Nicky, who appeared to be reading my mind, was deliberately shaking his head no.

"Suppose he does know me after all," I murmured and strolled away. I found Mr. Taylor's valet, Henry Peavey, by the pergola, and more than eager to talk. He had gone through something of a metamorphosis in the last few minutes. His sim-pering demeanor had changed now that he was the former em-ployee of a famous *murdered* director. Spine straight, shoulders squared, head tilted just so, Henry generously reenacted the previous night when he left Mr. Taylor's home and returned in the morning. Twice, he stopped to verify that I had the correct spelling of his name.

I smiled patiently. There was nothing so contagious as a public spotlight, and Henry Peavey had caught the bug. I took few notes throughout Henry's lengthy oration. Most useful was the identity of the last person to see Mr. Taylor alive, apart from the murderer. Mabel Normand. Miss Normand was a famous film star at the height of her career. I knew her work in the comedies with Fatty Arbuckle and the Keystone Cops.

"That so?" I interrupted Henry's exhausting list of duties performed for the deceased, the least of which was the time-consuming technique of dry brushing Mr. Taylor's expensive suits. "And, have you any idea what those people removed from Mr. Taylor's bedroom this morning?"

"Uh, no, ma'am."

"Any idea who would want your boss dead, Henry?"

He stared down at his shoes and shuffled around a bit. "Why, there ain't nobody not like Mr. Taylor."

I hadn't the miles of experience required to work a murder

story but I'd spent countless nights across the dinner table as Pop shared stories of his early reporter years. As a young fella out to make a name for himself, Pop had become a prolific writer and investigator; he could sniff out a story, gather details, and then bam! A feeling would ignite, something he called his 'reporter juices'. Whenever someone dropped a detail or perhaps a lie, Pop's reporter juices would start flowing and he knew he was on to something. Possibly, I had it as well, because for the second time today, I felt a surge in my veins. The first happened when Faith MacLean mentioned hearing a car backfire the night before. The second surge hit me just now, the moment Henry Peavey lied.

Unfortunately, my interview was cut short and I hadn't time to probe deeper. Two motorcars raced up the street and stopped along the curb. Sergeant Ziegler had alerted the Flying Squad, the department's newest crime fighting division. My enthusiasm sank like the Titanic.

Five dark suits with overcoats flapping in the breeze and fedoras slung low moved in unison across the manicured lawn. They marched past me with all the confidence and cockiness their positions afforded. The Flying Squad was composed of prime detectives who only investigated high-level crimes, the kind that happened in the dead of night when the vilest creatures slithered from under rocks to commit heinous monstrosities. The Death Squad at the OK Corral, killing my chance to sneak into Mr. Taylor's bedroom.

If I came in short on details, Pop would hand over the story to a more seasoned reporter, of which we had one. Mr. Handle was capable, at best. I would have to be resourceful and drum up my own information.

I raced back to Addy and filled her in on Mr. Taylor's murder. She slumped against the seat and stared in shock. About this time, a string of Tin Lizzies whizzed along the street and screeched to a stop. A nest of Johnny-come-lately reporters poured out and scattered across the lawn. I laughed and felt my spirits lift.

"I've beaten all those lollygagging cake-eaters to the scene of the biggest story in town!"

Addy snapped out of it. "Well, don't stop now!" she ordered, shoving me out of the truck.

I returned to the pergola and checked the time. Nine-fifteen and the place was lousy with reporters: *Los Angeles Record, Los Angeles Examiner, Los Angeles Express*, and what seemed like a horde from the *Los Angeles Times*. Even Pugsly the Ugsly was creeping about. Reporters shouted questions, which the Flying Squad shot down like hunted quail.

Mr. Montgomery Morgan sidled up to me with a sheepish grin. His fedora sat back on his handsome blond head and a toothpick dangled precariously from the corner of his mouth.

"Well now, Miss March, fancy meeting you here."

"Why Mr. Morgan, this is a murder scene. Whatever are *you* doing here?" I teased.

"Oh, yes, murder," his eyes flashed and he spoke in an ominous tone. "I love the old way best, the simple way of poison where we, too, are strong as men," he quoted Euripides as though this was all a game and not a horrible act that had ended a man's life. I wondered if there was anything he took seriously.

"Shameless," I said, shaking my head.

He grinned and then began act two where he played the bashful little boy still in short-pants hoping to steal from the cookie jar. "Trouble you for the details?" He bumped his shoulder playfully against mine.

I gave him a sideways look; he couldn't care less about the details. He was a reluctant reporter with the attention span of a child. How he stayed on the *Times'* payroll was a mystery to me. But Mr. Morgan was sweet and fun so I put on a show of hopeless resignation.

"Well... 's okay, I suppose. You see, somebody opened a window on Mr. Hollywood." I wanted to remain respectful but my high praise for Mr. Taylor had recently plummeted to unknown depths. Not only was I curious as to what he'd been hiding in his bedroom, but I'd recently overheard a few snippets of something unbelievable from those closest to him. Snippets that, once verified, would blossom into full blooms in my column.

"So, he was shot," Mr. Morgan mused. "How many times?"

"Suppose after the first one it doesn't really matter how many follow."

"Suspects?"

"Yeah, the guy who pulled the trigger."

He laughed and slid an arm across my shoulders. "Well played, my dear."

I backed away and inclined my head by way of a curtain bow. "And now if you'll excuse me. I'd like to say hello to an old friend."

I walked away with a reckless grin. Mr. Morgan was the kind of wolf you could distinguish at a glance. He said hello like other men said I love you.

The old friend I had spotted happened to be Deputy Coroner Dr. MacDonald. He must have snuck inside the bungalow while I was talking to Addy. It appeared he'd finished his work and was trying to escape the scene unnoticed.

"Dr. MacDonald!" I called, jogging to catch up. He didn't hear me so I tried again. Still nothing so I hollered, "Hey, Alfred!"

He paused on the sidewalk and glanced around nervously. Doc was a blustery old man, always fidgeting and shifting and often caught mumbling to himself. He wore spectacles perched on the end of his nose, and his salt-and-pepper hair was in constant shambles as though he'd peed on an electrical wire. His train of thought was no more organized than his hair style. I'd known Doc since I was five-years-old. He was a long-time friend and poker buddy of Pop's.

"Oh, it's you, Kate. How are you this morning? How's your father?"

"Did you find the bullet?"

Doc twitched as though the question had poked him in the ribs. I suspected he wasn't allowed to talk about the case before the inquest but I knew how much he loved his work. As a child, I'd enjoyed numerous fireside chats enthralled by the morbid details of his latest autopsy.

"Well, you know," he whispered as though we were co-conspirators. "When I didn't find the exit wound I traced the entrance path from his back up toward his cervix. It, well, you know how bullets are. Doggone, but they don't always want to come out. They could hit a bone or—"

"And you found it? What caliber?" I smiled encouragingly, poised to extend my lead on the story.

"Oh, yes, well, it was, uh," he scratched his head. "I mean no, we haven't found it yet. It's still in the body. A thorough examination isn't usually done at the scene, Kate."

"Oh," I murmured, feeling my cheeks warming. A rookie reporter's mistake. "But you'll let me know what caliber? As soon as you know, you'll let me know, right, Doc?"

He nodded vaguely, his attention already shifting to something important he shouldn't forget. Doc shuffled away mumbling under his breath.

Addy was making her way over with *The Messenger's* newest employee. A snappy dresser in sports attire: plus fours, a light sweater over a slim waistcoat, and bow tie. According to Pop, he was originally from the San Fernando Valley and a recent college graduate specializing in illustrations and photography. He claimed to be plenty eager to learn the newspaper business. In other words, he had a bucket full of debt and came cheap.

"Name's Buddy Randal," he said, shaking my hand. "Call me Bud. Don't mind my costume, I figure photography is a kind of sport, anyhow." He smiled affably and I decided I liked him immediately. Buddy's other hand clutched a Graflex Speed Camera. I recognized it from the latest Eastman Kodak catalogue. Bud broke into an even wider smile when he caught me gawking at it. "It's the Speed Graphic with a top handle. Real swell. Even included a crosshair folding optical finder."

"Well, color me green with envy, this *is* swell," I said, examining it. "You know how to operate it?"

"Oh, sure I do." He opened the camera, allowing the tapered bellows to extend. "So, where's the stiff?"

"As it happens," I said delicately. "Mr. Taylor was a friend of a friend. He's... still inside his home."

"Aw, shoot. Stuck my foot in it, didn't I. Sure sorry about that Miss March. Don't mind if I'm a bit jumpy. First crime scene and all."

I explained the overall situation and most of what I'd already seen this morning. The Flying Squad had split into groups, some gathered around Nicky at the foot of the steps while others had disappeared inside the bungalow. "They won't let you near Mr. Taylor, you understand, but here's the perspective. I want you to humanize this. Think of the headline: "Hollywood's Been Murdered", and shoot accordingly. Cut your angles with his friends, there, in the foreground and the bungalow in the background. Get their expressions, their reactions, if you can. Another headline might read: "William Desmond Taylor's Last Audience." Get the idea?"

Bud nodded. "Say, that's pretty swank. I know just what you mean." He strolled up the walk muttering the headlines to himself.

At half past eleven Bud had enough photos, and I had written my notes into a sensational story. I sent Bud and my column back to the office with strict instructions. He was to deliver my story to Mrs. Hazeldine, the copy editor—and not Mr. Handle—Pop's top reporter. Mrs. Hazeldine would ensure the article was ready for print. I would discuss my truancy and any subsequent punishment with Pop later.

Sometime after noon, the body was removed. Most of the reporters gave up trying to pilfer stories from the neighbors who were returning to their homes. Sensationalizing the death of their murdered friend suddenly seemed uncivilized if not un-nerving. Some locked their doors. The uniformed officers left in their police cars with the exception of one guard who had re-placed Nicky outside the bungalow's front door. No one would be allowed to enter the murder scene. Nicky and Sergeant Zieg-ler left without a glance in my direction.

With the front door guarded, Addy and I strolled between the buildings and milled around Mr. Taylor's back door. What I hoped to find, I had no idea. Certainly, the detectives had combed over the area, possibly looking for an easy exit route the killer might've taken. The alleyway led to the garages and then to the street be-yond where a number of autos were parked, probably local ten-ants who hadn't paid extra for garage space. It was a decidedly easy exit route if ever I saw one. The killer would have had ample room to park his car along the street in either direction.

"Now doesn't that strike you as odd," I said to Addy as we retraced our steps to Mr. Taylor's back door. A messy pile of gold-tipped cigarette butts had been tossed in the dirt not five feet away. "According to Henry Peavey, Mr. Taylor liked things neat and tidy inside. Why would he allow Henry to dump the ashcan so near the house?"

"Unless he didn't dump them," Addy said. We leaned over the pile.

"You're right. These have been smashed into the dirt. Someone had been smoking like a chimney back here. Have you ever seen gold-tipped ciggys before? Me neither."

Addy suddenly clutched my arm as the sound of hurried footsteps grew louder. They were accompanied by soft wailing emanating from the front of the bungalow.

"Mary!" I said, suddenly stricken. "I forgot to phone Mary!"

We rushed through the alley and just met Mary as she stopped at the bottom of the bungalow's porch steps. The guard blocked her way.

"Sorry, miss. No one is allowed inside."

"But I must see him!" Mary shrieked. Tears streamed down her pale child-like cheeks. Her blond curls, usually spiraled to perfection, fell in disarray around her pretty face. I called her name and she whirled around, and then rushed over to grab me by the shoulders.

"Is it true, Kate?" she sobbed, digging her nails into me. "Is he dead?"

I nodded and then supported her as she swayed forward.

"No, no, no. I can't believe it," Mary whispered in a daze. All the animation and color drained from her face. Her pale blue eyes drifted out of focus. The light had gone out.

Addy and I exchanged looks of wonder. Had I been wrong? Had Mary's feelings for Mr. Taylor been more than just a young girl's infatuation?

Mary had become so pale I feared she might faint. Her eyes closed and her head tipped forward as I held onto her. "I-I have to see him," she murmured. "Where... where is he, Kate? Do you know?"

"Oh, Mary, I'm so very sorry." I pulled her into a hug. "You can't see him," I said as gently as possible. "They've taken Mr. Taylor to the mortuary. Please, let me drive you home and—"

"No!" she snapped, pushing me away. "Where, Kate?" she demanded. "Tell me where they've taken him!" Her sudden outrage startled me. Her chest heaved furiously and a look I had never seen before burned in her eyes. In a matter of seconds, Mary's utter devastation had whipped into pure anger. What would come next, uncontrollable grief?

"Oh, Mary—"

"Tell me!" she yelled. She shook my shoulders until I grabbed her wrists and held her at bay.

"Mary, please! Calm down! Now, let me think. Yes, I believe if Dr. MacDonald performed the preliminary that would mean... they probably took Mr. Taylor to Ivy Overholtzer's Mortuary. But they won't let you—"

Mary tore away and fled down the sidewalk to her roadster parked recklessly in the street.

"Should we follow her?" Addy asked.

"I'm sure Mary has no idea where the mortuary is. We'll go there directly and wait. If she shows, I'll take her in to Dr. Mac-Donald."

We arrived in a few minute's time at Ivy Overholtzer's Mortuary at Tenth and Hill Streets. Mary took nearly half an hour, and she was in no better shape.

I asked Addy to remain in the truck while I handled things. There was little chance they would allow Mary to see Mr. Taylor before the inquest so it shouldn't take long.

I caught Mary at the door. "Please listen to me. You must understand how things work. They won't let you see him. Not before the inquest because... Mr. Taylor was murdered."

Her fury abated only slightly. The news of his murder did not seem to penetrate her consciousness. Her mind was set. I began to wonder if Mary truly believed Mr. Taylor was dead.

"They *must* let me see him!" She pushed me aside with surprising strength. Dr. MacDonald was just leaving the examination room when Mary and I burst into the lobby.

"No, no, and definitely no!" Doc smacked his fist into the opposite hand to punctuate each NO upon hearing our request. "Kate, you know better than this. Now take Miss Minter home and put her to bed. She's hysterical and... and very upset."

Mary wailed and sobbed into her hands. That anger had finally turned into anguish. My heart nearly broke for the poor girl. I pulled her into my arms and let her release it against my shoulder. Through the blubbering she slurred, "But I must see him. I must. I must..."

I dug a hanky out of Mary's wrist purse, which she took and pressed to her nose. I let her sniffle and hiccup and blow her nose. Then I stroked her hair and asked her to wait a moment while I spoked to Doc. I pulled him aside.

"What harm could it possibly do, Doc? Can't you see how distraught she is? She just wants to say goodbye. Wouldn't you want to say goodbye if anything happened to your Martha?"

Sympathy washed over Doc's face, his fuzzy salt and pepper eyebrows crunching together. "Oh, yes, well, yes I certainly would. By all means she can—now wait just a doggone minute, Kate! I'm a man of science. I have work to do! I have to, I have to..." He glanced around and then lowered his voice confidentially, "I have to find that blasted bullet."

"Okay, Doc, you dig out the bullet and we'll come back to-morrow." I took Mary by the shoulders and quickly guided her to the door.

"Fine, you come back—hey tomorrow? No, that'll never do. The inquest hasn't been set."

"Tomorrow. Around noon? Thanks Doc, you're the bee's knees!"

He smiled at the compliment and waved goodbye. "Okay then, around noon— hey, wait a minute!"

The emotional upheaval had left Mary too exhausted to argue about leaving without seeing Mr. Taylor. She thanked me, snif-fling and sobbing, for securing a visit for the next day. I ex-plained, in no uncertain terms, that she had been afforded a great privilege in this. It was unorthodox for anyone but family members to see the deceased before the inquest, much less the autopsy.

Mary agreed to do as I asked and drive straight home to Mama's house—her beloved grandmother's home on Hobart Street. Charlotte Shelby occupied a palatial estate on New Hampshire Street. Mary needed rest, not an interrogation from the Monster. With Mary safely on her way to Mama's, Addy and I returned to the office.

I parked at the curb, cut the engine, and checked the time. "Huh, that's funny. It's exactly two twenty-two, on February second, nineteen hundred and twenty-two."

Addy sighed. "Huh, that is something funny. Think I'll walk home from here. I'll be lucky if Mama don't take a switch to me for ditching school." She grabbed the door handle and paused. "Is it always this exciting when you play hooky?"

I smiled. "Thanks for coming, Addy. I mean it. And I hope your folks aren't too sore."

"You know what, Kate? It was worth it. See ya tomorrow." We hugged goodbye and then she climbed out. I stared into the storefront of the Messenger, contemplating my approach to Pop. In all likelihood, he would be disappointed in me, which was akin to a knife in the heart. Then again, he had the business in his blood; perhaps he would understand my chasing down a lead and turning it into a sensational scoop.

The rapid clacking and chaotic chattering that usually greeted me upon entering the office died the moment I stepped inside. Heads lifted and swiveled as the staff ignored their Underwood typewriters and candlestick telephones to glance from me to Pop.

Just outside his office door was a spare desk, an acre of oak scored with pits, burns, and indecipherable doodles from past reporters. Pop liked to work there when he wasn't cloistered in his private office. It was his nature to be in the trenches as much as possible. He didn't look up when I entered.

"We did it!" Buddy Randal declared, unaware of the tension in the room. He thrust our Extra Edition into my hands. My write-up was on the front page! Above the fold!

I clutched the paper as a smile spread across my face. Take that Pugsly the Ugsly, I thought.

Everything looked in order as I devoured each line. Only a few minor changes. Then came the shivers along my spine. I'd given our readers something no other paper could, a detailed description of the deceased—down to his evening attire and the large diamond ring on his pinky finger. I'd also painted an accurate picture of the crime scene from furniture to bric-a-brac—an intimate view of how a successful Hollywood film director lived, modest though it was. And the topper was a full depiction of the possible murder suspect leaving the scene of the crime! Thanks to Mrs. Faith MacLean's nosy nature.

Upon hearing what had sounded like a gunshot around eight o'clock the previous evening, Mrs. MacLean had gone to her door at which time a figure in bulky clothing stood on Mr. Taylor's porch. He reached in, closed the door, and then turned toward Mrs. MacLean. He then walked calmly down the steps and into the alley between the houses. The exact path Addy and I had taken less than an hour ago. Fortunately for the murderer, his cool demeanor had raised no further suspicions in Mrs. MacLean. He left without being questioned.

Next to my story was a crude drawing of a body lying below a desk, precisely as I had seen it. I noticed Bud's artistic handiwork, adding depth and proportion to my mediocre scrawl. I thrilled at the sight of it. No other paper would have that kind of detail. Below the illustration was a spread of Bud's photos to complement the text. I gaped in wonder.

"Bud! How'd you get the film developed so quickly? I figured you'd have to send it to the company in New York. Have them develop the photos and send them back. It should have taken at least two weeks!"

Bud grinned. "Well, I figured we needed these in a hurry so I rang up my old professor from UCLA. We cooked up a batch of chemicals in his kitchen and then developed the film in his basement. They're not perfect but near enough. Don't you think?"

"And how! It was more than I had hoped for. Thanks, Bud."

I tossed the paper onto Pop's desk and flopped into the chair opposite him. I held my breath and waited. Pop lowered the copy he'd been studying and gave me a long stern look over his cheaters.

"The cat who ate the canary," Pop finally said as the corners of his mouth twitch into a smile. I bit back a giggle. "First on the scene, I take it?"

"Yes!" I leaned over the desk and choked back my excitement. "I want so badly to gloat, Pop, but, how can I? The whole thing was a fluke! It's not as though I knew Mr. Taylor had been murdered and raced over to prove it. But I learned a thing or two about the newspaper business, sometimes just being in the right place at the right time is enough to get a sensational story. Right, Pop? Sheer dumb luck. That's all it was."

Pop rocked back in his chair, chuckling softly. I loved to make his old blue eyes sparkle with pride. To bring out the time-worn dimples in his tired smile. It was the least I could do considering the grey I'd put in his hair.

"You should have seen me, Pop. I was two feet from the dead body while those news-hounds from the *Times* were stuffing their pie holes at the Kettle."

Pop's smile teetered a bit. I shouldn't have added the part about the dead body.

"As much as I like getting the scoop," he said, sounding weary. "I'm not overjoyed to have my daughter involved with dead bodies, especially dead bodies with bullet holes in them." He fogged his cheaters and cleaned them with a hankie. "But I like the use of photos and the angle you were after. I wouldn't have thought of it. I'm asking Bud to sketch out your description of the suspect leaving Mr. Taylor's. That should complement the next column."

Next column? My hopes soared.

"Well, it was a lucky break, like you said," Pop mused. "A nicely written piece, Kate."

There was a finality in his tone that raised my hackles. I scooted closer so as not to be overheard groveling. "Listen, Pop, this is my story. It's big, I know. But I was there first. You can't take it away."

"Now, Kate—"

"Just hear me out," I jumped in. "I've got the inside dope on this." I glanced around and lowered my voice. It didn't help to see our top reporter, Mr. Handle, waiting in the wings. I called him a scratch reporter because he was always scratching his head at the typewriter in search of the appropriate word. Mr. Handle was a decent fellow, doing the best with what God gave him, but I didn't want him taking my story.

I explained about Mary Miles Minter and how she was close to Mr. Taylor. She would give me inside information on the film industry because we were close friends. Truthfully, I had no idea if Mary would do any such thing but it was the best card I had to play.

Pop considered me. He pursed his lips and fiddled with the chain on his pocket watch. "Your bio on Mr. Taylor, that bit about his past. I don't remember hearing that before. It's true? You checked your facts, I assume?"

I nodded. "It was no secret to his closest friends, just the general public."

It occurred to me that I'd been so caught up with the story and Mary's emotional state that I had forgotten to tell her about that snippet I'd overheard. The one that bloomed in my column upon verification from Mr. Taylor's neighbors. With Mary at Mama's house and away from reporters, I had time to work on a subtle way to reveal Mr. Taylor's little secret.

"As awful as it sounds, Pop, the paper needs a story like this. And with Mary's insight, I'm the one to write it. So... what do you say?"

Pop rubbed the back of his neck. "This is about this morning, isn't it? Mr. Townsend's visit?"

I shrugged. "Well, anyhow, you know I've been asking to write more serious copy."

"But you're so young... and then there's school—"

"Did my story sound too young?"

"Of course not, Kate. It's not your writing. I'm very proud of your talents. You've always been an exceptionally gifted writer but this is a case of murder, not the rising cost of scripto ink."

"I can handle myself just fine, Pop. I always have."

His eyebrows fluctuated, and I hoped he wouldn't call me on my outright exaggeration. I'd gotten into more trouble than a Dumb Dora in a rumble seat. Only half of which he knew about.

"Well," Pop conceded with a heavy sigh. "Just interviews. You can report on official statements and conduct a few interviews. No exaggerations. Nothing fabricated."

"Of course!" He needn't tell me twice. I hated yellow journalism like communism. I jumped out of my seat and hugged him. "Thanks, Pop!"

"And you must attend school, Kate. If your marks fall—"

"They won't. I promise." I turned to leave and then flashed a smile. "We'll discuss my salary over dinner."

It was later in the day, after Rico and Bud had delivered our Extra Edition to all corners of Los Angeles, and I'd finalized my list of questions for Mable Normand, that I noticed Eugene hadn't been around the office today. He should have helped with deliveries. It wasn't often we had a sensational Extra Edition. His lack of interest in keeping the family business afloat had always put a fight in me. I asked Pop his whereabouts and he shrugged with his nose in a stack of papers.

"You know Eugene. He's a man of his own. Said he was taking this machine he'd been tinkering with down to the Long Beach Pike to race against some other fellow's machine." Pop and I couldn't understand Eugene's fascination with motorcars.

"When was this?"

"Oh... Monday? Or was it Tuesday?"

That was three days ago!

"And you haven't seen him since, that right? Playing hooky, is he?" I was spitting mad at Eugene's thoughtlessness. At least when I played hooky I didn't disappear for days at a time. The last thing Pop needed was the added burden of a vanishing, vagabond son.

"He's a man of his own," Pop said, shuffling through his stack.

"He's fifteen!" I snapped.

"Now don't judge him, Kate. He was born independent."

I rolled my eyes. "You want I should find him, Pop? Drag him back here and—"

"No, no, let it alone. And as far as I know, he has been to school. Which is more than I can say for you." He gave me pointed look. I was prepared to retaliate but just then the phone on my desk rang. I snatched it up and held the earpiece to my ear.

"Kate March speaking at *The Messenger.*"

"Kate!" Mary squealed.

"Mary? How are you feeling?"

"Kate, you must come over right away! You won't believe what she's doing!"

"Slow down. What who's doing?"

"The Monster. She's making me do an interview with the *LA Record!* Please get over here. I'm at the house on New Hampshire!"

"But you promised to go to Mama's—"

"Hurry! Please! I can't do this alone!"

"I'm on my way, Mary." I jumped to my feet, struck by a horrible thought. "And don't talk to anyone until I get there, you

understand? Please, Mary. There's something you should—"
The line went dead.

I jammed the receiver onto the hook, explained to Pop, and then dashed out of the office. I had to reach Mary before the reporters did. Mr. Taylor's shocking little secret would hit her the hardest.

CHAPTER 5

"I saw that headline," Detective Cahill said quietly, thinking back. "I read your article, the first one on the scene and all that. You know I was with the Squad at Taylor's place that morning? I saw what you described."

I nodded, remembering Detective Cahill among the Flying Squad.

He exhaled and sat back with a resigned expression. "We're not going to get off track here, Miss March. You're in here on a murder charge but... I know what you've been up to. I mean, I've read some of your recent columns on the Taylor case—"

"This evening's Extra Edition?" I asked, my heart quickening. He shook his head and frowned. I breathed easy again. It was a fine line I was walking here and I didn't want Cahill suspicious of my underlying plan. I was safe as long as he was unaware of my latest story.

"I've been a little busy," he said bitterly as though he would rather be anywhere else but here interrogating me. "You and your paper have stirred up a lot of trouble, which I'm sure you're aware of. Unsubstantiated bull, if you want my opinion. You know DA Woolwine was spitting mad when your description of the suspect changed?" He waved me away when I opened my mouth to argue. "Can't say as I blame him for that—"

"There was a compelling reason for that," I said hotly. "If you've read—"

"I've read plenty. You and your wild imagination. All's I'm saying is it's not good for your credibility."

"My credibility? Are you even interested in hearing how I came to my own conclusion about the Taylor case?" I asked, crossing my arms tightly. My unrest about the murder tonight had suddenly shifted to anger. As far as I was concerned the accusation that I had murdered someone was perfectly justifiable. In theory. But to accuse me of being unprofessional or inept was completely out of line.

"I'm interested in what happened in the alley tonight."

I rolled my eyes. "Aw, you're just sore because I did your job for you."

"With that hysterical headline of yours a few days ago?" he said, chuckling and lighting another ciggy.

Inside, I was fuming. Cahill saw me as nothing but a female busybody playing games in a man's world. I gave him a simpering smile. I could play games until the cows came home. He wanted information? Fine. I'd bury him in the details.

"You don't like my headline? I'll tell you all about it and you'll eat your hat when I'm done..."

I left the office after Mary's call that day and drove down Broadway and then rounded the corner onto Grand. I eventually turned south on Flower and then west on Wilshire Boulevard. Wilshire took me several miles out to South New Hampshire Street. As I motored toward house number 701, I wondered what the Monster was up to by letting the *Los Angeles Record* interview Mary. Mrs. Shelby could be so insensitive at the most inappropriate times.

I stopped at the curb and cut the engine. Across a crisp green lawn parked on a corner was an enormous mansion with three stone arches, white columns, and a pair of white stone lions flanking the long steps leading up to the veranda and front door. It was stately and regal and very suitable for a successful Hollywood starlet, never mind that it belonged to the starlet's mother. Eager reporters swarmed the veranda like flies on stink so I slipped around back where Mary occasionally sneaked me in. I heard arguing through the back door; Mary and her older sister, Margaret, were not happy. I knocked and the door opened. It was Mary, flushed and out of breath.

"'Lo there Mary, how's—"

"Sh-sh-sh!" She yanked me into the kitchen. "Mother's letting the leaches in the front," she whispered. "What should I say, Kate? They're going to ask all sorts of personal question about me and Mr. Taylor." She spotted her reflection in the china cabinet's etched glass and tidied her curls. They were shiny and blonde and bounced against her shoulders. She pinched color into her cheeks and then peeked through the swing door that led into the parlor. Mary had obviously recovered from her devastating grief of this morning. I couldn't begin to guess why she'd come to this house when Mama's was tranquil and homey. If I were Mary I'd never step foot in the same room as her mother, Charlotte Shelby.

I glanced at Margaret who was leaning against the counter in an ordinary brown frock and plain brown hair piled in little ringlets atop her head. She had a glass in her hand and by the dull look in her eyes, I guessed that big sister was making good on the cooking cherry again.

"Just say as little as possible," I warned Mary. "Tell the truth, of course, and repeat as little as possible. That's the quickest way to get rid of them."

Mary began pacing and wringing her hands. "Oh, you know that never works with those prying degenerates. They have nothing better to do than snoop into people's private affairs."

As usual, it never occurred to Mary that I considered myself part of that profession by way of the family business, and now as an official reporter handling the Taylor story. I knew what she meant, though. Movie folks didn't seem to have private lives anymore. Especially when they've invited the press into their own homes.

"Well, after all, Mary, there has been a murder. People have a right to know—"

"People have rights!" she sneered in a spoiled tone. "Well, I have rights, too! A right to love whomever I choose without someone making it dirty!"

"Who's making it dirty?" I frowned. Margaret snorted into her glass but said nothing. I pulled Mary aside and whispered, "Listen here. There's something you should know. It'll be in all the evening papers and—"

The kitchen door swung open and Charlotte Shelby marched in. A petite woman, she was draped in a black lace Paul Poiret dress with black stockings and black patent one-strap shoes trimmed in black alligator. A very stylish ensemble, no doubt acquired on her latest holiday in Europe, but I wondered where she had parked her broom.

Mrs. Shelby shot me a frosty glare. "Who let you in?" she demanded and then turned without waiting for an answer. "It's time, Mary." She tried to adjust the ruffles on her daughter's virginal white bodice but Mary twisted away.

"Mary, wait!" I said, reaching for her. "I have something to tell—"

"There is nothing you need to say to Mary," Mrs. Shelby retorted. "Why don't you scramble back to that pathetic little news office and let the real reporters do their jobs." She guided Mary to the parlor door. "Now settle down and we'll get through this. The world wants to know our distress about this shocking news." She paused a beat or two, took a deep breath, and then pushed the door open. Mary followed with a stiff spine and a celluloid smile.

Forgotten Margaret drained the last drop of numbing nectar and walked out the back door. I went to the parlor door to eavesdrop.

"No, I was never engaged to Mr. Taylor, I regret to say," Mary said "No, I was not at his home on the night of the murder. I was at Mama's house, er, my grandmother's home. But you know I loved him, dearly..."

I peeked through a slit in the door and watched the tenderness play on Mary's features. She was seated next to the Monster on the sofa, directly opposite the reporter. Mary continued sweetly and innocently, so different from moments ago. I realized Mary really did love Mr. Taylor. In her own way.

"He thought of me as a child, more or less," Mary lamented softly. "But I saw a great deal of him before I went to Europe—"

"He was a hard worker," Mrs. Shelby cut in sharply. She patted Mary's knee mechanically in a feeble attempt at compassion. "He was interested in business more than anything else." Her voice, like her manner, was crisp and decisive. She gave Mary a tight, apologetic smile.

71

"And, do you know where his wife and daughter are?" The reporter asked with a greasy grin. I could almost hear the explosion of Mary's heart. She gasped and her eyes flew to mine.

There it was, the sole purpose of the reporter's interview, to shock Mary with Mr. Taylor's secret. To splash the headlines with her stunned reaction. And where was I, the only friend who could have prepared her? Hiding behind the door and failing miserably. Mary's greatest agitation was prying reporters, and now I understood why.

I felt like a louse. Why hadn't I stood up to Mrs. Shelby and demanded to be heard? I hated how she bullied me. I hated how she allowed this. And I hated how she hurt her own daughter.

"Why, he had no wife!" Mary found her voice, trembling though it was. She gave herself away by fidgeting unbecomingly. "He-he was never married, I'm... positive of that."

The reporter was scribbling frantically while my mind was screaming at Mrs. Shelby. *For chrissake, end it! Now! Mary will only make a fool of herself! What's the matter with you? What kind of a mother are you?*

Mrs. Shelby was performing act two of her maternal pretense by patting Mary's white-knuckled fists lying in her lap. "Maybe he just didn't tell you he was married, Mary dear."

Mary snatched her hands away. "But I knew him so *well*, Mother. I'm sure he wasn't married." She was seething. Fighting for control. And the reporter was lapping it up. Mary looked beseechingly at me but I had my attention on the Monster. Mrs. Shelby had blanched upon learning of the director's marriage. Perhaps she was realizing the error of her arrogant ways? Perhaps now she would end this ambush?

The reporter continued, all but smacking his lips and rubbing his greedy little hands together. He was taking candy from a baby.

"And, what of the affair between Mr. Taylor and Mabel Normand?"

Mary looked at him vacantly and then shook her head. "No, no," she stammered, weakly. "I don't think there was anything to that rumor. Mabel is a big-hearted girl with sterling qualities." Her eyes dropped to her hands. I sensed she was collecting herself, sorting her thoughts. When she looked up again, Mary had found that celluloid smile and recited her answers as if scripted. She described how wonderful Mr. Taylor had always treated her. How kind he was when directing her in *Anne of Green Gables*. How everyone thought the world of him and that he couldn't possibly have any enemies. And no, she had no idea who could have ended his life in such an ugly manner.

Several minutes later the interview mercifully ended. As Mrs. Shelby showed the reporter out, Mary marched straight into the kitchen and right up to me. She demanded to know everything I'd learned about Mr. Taylor. She was deadly calm, a new kind of hysteria. I couldn't blame her, learning about the marriage in such a cruel way and all. I hated myself for letting it happen.

Mary dragged me out the back door, away from her mother and eavesdropping servants. The backyard was small and square and shadowed with trees. We stopped at a bench beneath a pepper tree and sat down with a hard flop. Mary's eyes were blazing.

"Start talking," she ordered.

I debated my approach. I wanted to tell Mary everything, but I didn't want to hurt her further. Plus, I needed to know if she were willing to share information with me. I had to be subtle. Mary was temperamental, but not stupid. She had thirty-four movies under her belt and was a millionaire at nineteen. She had ways of getting what she wanted. I decided to be gentle with her, after all, she was grieving a terrible loss.

"Did you truly love him, Mary?" I asked tenderly. "I mean, was it real love?"

Her scowl dissolved. Emotions slowly played on her face. She'd been ready for battle but the question tugged at her heart. Her shoulders eased and a melancholy smile spread across her pale face.

"I think I did love him," she murmured, fingering the lace on that ridiculously frilly thing she wore that made her appear years younger. She looked all of twelve-years-old, not a woman of nineteen. "He was... so kind to me. So much a man, you see."

"Yes, I could tell that about him. But Mary, was he, you know, ever improper?" I think we both wondered where that question came from. Mary's demeanor changed and I regretted my impulsive nature. Slow and gentle played better with Mary.

"Why, Kate March, are you... trying to interview me? On the record?"

"What do you mean?" I asked, innocent as a fox in a hen house.

"I thought you were my friend but even I can hear that investigative tone in your voice. Just like that weasel from the *Record*. So, what, now you're one of them?"

"Now, Mary—"

"Oh, don't be like them, Kate! I so need a friend." She squeezed my hand. "We're true friends, aren't we, Kate? You're the only one I can trust to tell me the truth."

"Okay, Mary, here's the truth." I stood and began pacing. "Every paper in town—maybe in the country—is going to be after this story. The murder of Hollywood's most beloved film director will feed the rags for weeks, perhaps even longer depending on how long it takes to nab the murderer. Everything you do and say from this point on will be fodder for them, however insignificant or innocent. They'll twist your words to stir the pot, you know, to sell copy. But I can make sure your true story is out there; I won't make your feelings for Mr. Taylor dirty or inappropriate. I mean, you just have to trust me. 'S okay you trust me, Mary, honest."

Mary chewed her thumbnail, mulling this over. She might've been working the angles or might've been contemplating asking the gardener to toss me. It was so hard to read Mary. Her moods could swing like monkeys on a vine.

"It could be a give-and-take situation," she mumbled, contemplating the idea blossoming in her head. "I'll answer your questions and you'll tell me what the police are doing, who they suspect and all that business." She sat up beaming as though it had been her idea all along.

I breathed a sigh of relief. I had made some rather grandiose promises to Pop. The last thing I needed was coming up with the dry end of the lollypop.

"And you'll answer my questions, honestly and completely, right, Mary?"

She looked quizzically at me. "Why, Kate, I never do lie. You must know that."

I nodded. Yes, I must know that.

Unlike Addy, who couldn't tell a lie without a slew of tell signs, Mary had been raised on the stage in New York and on the screen in Hollywood; she was trained to say things that weren't true.

"Fine, Mary, let's start with why that reporter from the *Record* thought you and Mr. Taylor might've been engaged."

Mary sucked in her cheeks and flared her nostrils. "No, Kate! First, you will tell me about Mr. Taylor's w-wife and... daughter." The catch in her voice pulled at my heart. She was trying desperately to be brave. The last thing I needed was Mary bawling herself into an hysterical fit.

I returned to the bench and clasped her hands. "Her name is Ethel May. They were married back east about twenty-two years ago. They have a daughter, Ethel Daisy. She's twenty-one now and—"

Mary broke away and sobbed into her hands. I wrapped my arms around her and rocked us under the sad drooping branches of the pepper tree. I murmured condolences and kindnesses, none of which helped, this I knew from experience. There really was nothing to be said when one was deeply grieving.

When Mary finally came around I realized I had no handkerchief to offer. She reluctantly wiped her nose on her sleeve and whimpered, "If you're going to dress like a boy, Kate, the least you could do is carry a handkerchief in your pocket." We laughed quietly.

We remained for an hour or so as Mary recalled her professional relationship with Mr. Taylor, what a wonderful director he'd been, how gentlemanly he'd always behaved and so forth. Nothing vaguely inappropriate. As for the rumor about their engagement, Mary reminded me that the papers had accused her of engagements with no less than eight gentlemen since she'd arrived in California. None of which were true.

"Will this go in the paper?" Mary asked for the fifth time.

"I'll decide what's relevant for my story but you must tell me everything. No surprises."

Mary smiled sweetly and toyed with her curls. "No surprises," she repeated.

I shared my thoughts on the police activity thus far and details of my interview with Henry Peavey and other residence of Alvarado Court. I had no theories to offer as to who might have killed Mr. Taylor. Finally, when we were satisfied that an equal exchanged of information had been shared, we stood.

"One last thing," Mary took my pad and pencil and wrote down Mabel Normand's address. "Here, in case you don't know."

"Thanks, Mary. Now, you get some rest. You look exhausted."

I felt the day catching up with me as well but rather than skip back to the office with my notes, I persevered. Mary's statements lacked the weight needed for the next column. The importance of interviewing Mabel Normand as quickly as possible was paramount. I refused to let my story come up short or appear redundant. Another thing nagging me was the inconvenience of tomorrow being Friday. While other reporters gobbled up relevant leads and statements, I would be forced to make an appearance at Los Angeles High School. Not for the first time I'd come to the conclusion that my high school career was getting in the way of more important matters. That got me wondering if I was clever enough to maneuver my way out of school altogether.

Mabel lived just down the block from the Monster at 3089 West Seventh Street. Sobering thoughts of school tomorrow had put my mind squarely on my assignment and I drove there straightaway. Not being a seasoned, hard-nosed reporter did little to stop me from operating like one. Confidence was key.

The front lawn of Mabel Normand's apartment house was overgrown with newspapermen in a variety of blue, brown, and cream suits topped with fedoras, bowlers, and panama hats. It was a scene similar to the mob outside Mr. Taylor's bungalow with one exception, *I* was the latecomer this time.

Poor little Mabel Normand stood on the top step, her big brown eyes swollen from crying. She was a petite brunette but a giant in her own right. Paired with Charlie Chaplin or Fatty Arbuckle, she could hold her own on the screen. At twenty-nine, she was a successful model, actor, and director. I just hoped she'd give an honest interview and not an acting demonstration.

Miss Normand was already speaking when I approached. "No, Mr. Taylor and I were never engaged. He was a dear, dear, friend. A kind, gentleman who perhaps loved me as a friend, as I loved him. But then I don't know anyone who didn't love Bill Taylor."

Hmm. If I wasn't mistaken, those were nearly the exact words Mary had used in our private interview.

An array of placating questions regarding their professional relationship was tossed around but I wasn't interested in that angle. I waited patiently for someone to put meat on the bone. Three more insipid, flattering inquiries came and went and I became restless, tapping my pencil on my notepad. The next question regarding Miss Normand's favorite Taylor picture sent me over the edge. I squirmed to the front of the male-infested throng and raised my pencil.

"Miss Normand," I called. "Exactly what time did you leave Mr. Taylor last night?"

A sea of hats swiveled in my direction, along with more than a few gaping mouths and flustered scowls. I wondered if the question had already been asked. Or perhaps their reaction came from my being a woman? Maybe a *young* woman? Dressed in pants? Oh, the possibilities seemed endless and tiring. I sighed. The crowd shifted and there was Mr. Morgan, his wide smile aimed squarely at me. His fedora sat back on his head and his hands rested casually inside his pockets. It was safe to say he hadn't taken down a single note.

"I believe I went there around seven o'clock and stayed a short while," Miss Normand answered. "He had some books for me, you see, and I should say I left about a quarter to eight."

"You left him inside? Was he alone?" I followed up, aware

that every reporter, save one, scribbled down her reply.

Miss Normand gave the questions some thought. "No, Mr. Taylor walked me to the curb where my car and chauffer waited. His valet had already gone for the night, as I recall. Then Mr. Taylor and I said goodbye, that he might call later that evening... but he never did." She swayed against her maid, Mamie, and succumbed to tears. Mamie, a large black woman, informed us that Miss Normand needed her rest and then led her frail employer inside. Three uniformed officers blocked the entrance; no one would disturb Mabel Normand further.

I jotted down a few notes and curious observations and returned to the truck only to find Mr. Morgan casually leaning against it, legs crossed at the ankles. His smile said a lot more than hello.

"And, where might you be headed with those questions?" His tone was playful but probing.

I shrugged as though I'd left all my cares at home. "Just wondering. You know, to round out my story."

"Round out your story," he mused rubbing his chin. "Sure you're not trying to solve the whodunit?" We exchanged secret smiles. "Ah," he chuckled. I hoped I hadn't committed some novice journalistic blunder, trying to play detective instead of collecting and reporting the facts objectively. All my bragging to Pop aside, I was fully aware of my lack of experience.

"And, what might be *your* story?" he asked.

"You wanna know my angle? Is that it?"

He shrugged as though he was just making small talk. I couldn't help but wonder if he were truly lazy and trying to pilfer facts. Or perhaps there was something more sinister involved. Perhaps he was spying for Mr. Chandler. Trying to get a jump on *The Messenger's* take because I had been first on the murder scene.

If I had been alone, I would've laughed at my own audacity. The *Los Angeles Times* had top-drawer reporters; they wouldn't give two bits what *The Messenger* might write. So, what could Mr. Morgan want with me?

"How are you making out with your novel?" I asked, tossing my notepad through the open window.

Mr. Morgan inhaled and rubbed the back of his neck. "Oh, struggling, I'm afraid. I've some colleagues in New York who're trying desperately to offer assistance. It's demoralizing, if you must know." He pursed his lips thoughtfully. "Now, let me pose a question, if I may. I heard there was an inordinate amount of foot traffic through Mr. Taylor's bedroom prior to police arriving this morning. Have you discovered what was removed?"

I considered alternative answers and decided to be honest. I shook my head. Mr. Morgan stepped closer and lowered his voice to an intimate tone.

"You would tell me if you knew anything, wouldn't you, Miss Kate?"

Good Lord, was he trying to seduce information out of me? The idea produced a nervous giggle.

Mr. Morgan's brown eyes were practically dancing with amusement. "We *can* share *some* information, yes?"

"Meaning?"

"Meaning… all those I've interviewed or heard interviewed shared one common belief. Everybody loved Mr. Taylor."

"Save one," I said, growing uncomfortable with his overfriendly tone and close proximity.

"Yes," he whispered. "Save one. And the secret marriage hadn't particularly shocked any of his closest friends?"

I thought of Mary's reaction. Shocked was an understatement. "Mary and the Mon—er, her mother hadn't known. Why?"

He gave me a sly grin. "I don't know about you but I've

been in more than a few bedrooms, and my imagination is running wild with ideas of what might've been taken from Mr. Taylor's bedroom. Wish we could find out somehow."

We?

Where was he going with all this? I only had seventeen years under my belt but I knew enough to know when I was in over my head.

"Well, I *can't* imagine," I murmured, reaching for the door handle.

Mr. Morgan stepped back, readjusted his fedora, and bowed slightly.

"It's been a pleasure, Miss Kate."

"Has it?" I asked, arching an eyebrow. He strolled away, chuckling to himself.

CHAPTER 6

"After I left Mr. Morgan that day, I handed in my column for the evening edition," I told Detective Cahill. "You know the one? It stirred up some controversy about Mable Normand being the last person to see Mr. Taylor alive."

"I remember," he said dryly, lighting another ciggy off the last one. "And you were warned to stay away from her, if I recall."

"That was later. But yes, Nicky, excuse me, Officer Masino warned me plenty. But I was having doubts about him by that time. I didn't know who to trust." I thought of all that had gone on with Nicky. He was living proof that you never really knew someone, no matter how much you think you did.

Detective Cahill stopped and looked up. "What do you mean doubts?"

Ah. I smiled on the inside. So, Detective Cahill was curious about Nicky Masino.

"Oh, the same doubts you've probably had about him."

"Don't play games with me, Miss March. What has Officer Masino got to do with any of this?"

"Don't you find his authority here at the station a bit odd?" I pushed. "I mean, Nicky Masino hasn't got a tenth of the experience you've got and, yet, he—"

"That's enough."

"Did he leap frog right over you?"

"Miss March—"

"Do you take orders from him, Detective Cahill?"

"I said, that's enough!" he barked and then smashed his dead ciggy into the ash tray with more force than necessary. "Now answer my question. What has Officer Masino got to do with any of this?"

I chewed my lip, contemplating the best way to navigate forward. I felt I'd won a tiny victory against Cahill; he was now interested in more than just the tragedy in the alley. I didn't know how much to tell him so I kept rambling on...

Late Thursday afternoon, the day the body was found, I finished my column regarding Mabel Normand and went home. It was a comfortable evening and I had the window open. But I was restless and couldn't sleep. It was late when I finally went under but not for too long. Something roused me a few hours later.

I sat up and gazed around my bedroom. We had a three-quarter moon and everything was grey and black. I focused on what had woken me. *Voices.*

A light glowed from Nicky's bedroom across the lawn. His window was open and he was standing toe-to-toe with Angelo. Nearly equal in stature, Nicky was only slightly taller and Angelo a breadth wider. Angelo's brown hair was laced with burnt gold and gleamed in the lamplight. Still donned in their blue uniforms, both looked a bit hostile under the influence of an intense argument. I leaned out the window, catching the tail end of their conversation. Nicky's voice was deep and gravely.

"I don't *want* back in," he said, to which Angelo snapped, "You were never out!"

How interesting. Was Nicky saying he didn't want to be a cop anymore? Was Angelo trying to make him stay on the force? And why should it matter either way?

The next couple of exchanges were too muffled to clarify. Angelo said something and jammed his finger into Nicky's chest. Nicky knocked it away. Could this be one of Nicky's notorious 'black moods'? Not that I hadn't seen the Masino brothers argue before. They'd gone after each other plenty as kids. It was mainly your garden variety rough-housing. Nothing too serious. Nicky had always looked up to Angelo who was like their father, aggressive and loud. Nicky was rather quiet and patient with an intelligence that could sneak up on you. Deep down, they shared certain qualities with my older brothers, mainly they always watched out for each other.

Nicky suddenly burst out, "No! You can't ask me to do that!" He shoved Angelo in the chest and sent him reeling out of view. I gasped and nearly crawled out the window to better see the fight.

Angelo returned cautiously with hands raised. His voice was low and calm with no effect. Nicky was shaking his head.

"Forget it!" Nicky yelled. Angelo dropped his hands and stared wearily at his brother. I took this as an old argument. Angelo seemed fed up with trying to convince Nicky. He eventually retreated and walked out.

Nicky was boiling. His chest heaved and his hands clenched as though they wanted to strangle someone. Then he snatched the phone from his bureau and dialed a string of numbers. Long distance operator, by the look of it. I glanced at the clock on my desk: three-thirty. Who in blazes was he calling at three-thirty in the morning?

Nicky mumbled into the mouthpiece, much too quiet for an eavesdropping neighbor to hear. He was getting himself riled up again. His voice rose until I could make out phrases.

French. Nicky was speaking French. My eyebrows rose. Angry French, at that. Nicky spoke Italian fairly well due to his father's heritage, and an occasional French phrase stemming from his mother's roots in *Les Orme*. But Mrs. Masino's attempts to teach her sons the French language in their youth had been futile. Or so I'd thought. And this was no clumsy tête-à-tête I was overhearing. Somehow, Nicky had become fluent in French and wielded it like a weapon.

I suddenly regretted ditching so many of my own French classes. A casual understanding would have come in handy right about now.

Nicky jammed the receiver into the cradle and braced both hands on the bureau, breathing erratically. He seemed to be fighting for control, a battle he lost moments later when he grabbed the phone and hurled it across the room. Glass shattered and the lights went out.

"Miss March!"

I jerked to attention at my school desk. My mind had been recalling Nicky's unprovoked destruction of his innocent telephone and lamp, not on Mr. Grime's impromptu essay on Napoleon Bonaparte. Our history teacher, with his inflated self-adoration, liked to flout his mistaken superiority on the unsuspecting youth of Los Angeles High. It was Friday and I was

85

cranky to boot. It was a waste of my time, sitting here listening to this drabble when I could be out in the real world hunting down leads for my next column.

"Could you repeat the question?" I mumbled, checking the time on my wristwatch; it was almost noon. I was due to meet Mary at Ivy Overholtzer's Mortuary in twenty minutes, which meant I needed to devise an escape plan, and quickly.

Mr. Grime toddled around his desk and leaned against it to face the class. With short, thick fingers laced over a portly belly, he looked down his nose at me as I was seated in the front row.

"Now, Miss March, as elated as we are that you have generously graced us with your presence today, we would expect you to pay attention." His eyes swept the classroom as if to gather everyone behind his insult. "My inquiry was... what did you find most interesting about the essay question?"

It wasn't enough that we had to listen to his superfluous lectures but we were forced to analyze the genius of his insightful questions. I sighed heavily and forced a smile. "Well... it was most enlightening, ever thought-provoking, and a real philosophical gem, if you asked me. Which I guess you just did." I glanced sideways at Addy. She was scowling.

Mr. Grime's lips curled into a sardonic smile. "You know, young lady, just because you rarely attend school and somehow maintain high marks, does not give you the privilege to behave in such a pompous manner. Now, I'm sure you're aware that my question was not an opportunity to stroke my ego."

Do *what* to his *what?* Jeezers, that sounded highly inappropriate. I looked at Addy again. She was making the face I was feeling.

Ah well. Enough of this. I've got a date with a starlet and a dead body. Clearing my throat, I began, "Fair enough, Mr. Grime. I believe these egregious essays you continually pop on

86

us are a pathetic attempt to embarrass your students and bolster your declining individuality with unsubstantiated theories
about far greater men than yourself. Your hypothesis that Napoleon Bonaparte plowed through countries with his 'slash and
burn' policy because he was fueled by an insatiable bitterness
from being born abnormally short is preposterous. His actual
height is undetermined due to a difference in the French pounce
and British inch. Upon his death, Napoleon was recorded as 5'2—
in French measurement. The Imperial equivalent is somewhere
around 1.7 meters or about 5'7, which made him just taller than
the average Frenchman at the time. Regardless, his height, or
lack thereof, offers no insight into his military genius or reputation as a formidable tyrant. Sir." I smiled pleasantly, and then
mouthed to Addy, "See ya later." I laid my exam on Mr. Grime's
desk and headed for the door amid a rash of whispers.

"Miss March!" Mr. Grime called, flabbergasted. "You have
not been excused!"

"Shall I discuss the split infinity in your essay question or
perhaps your annoying habit of persistently dangling your... participle in front of everyone?" I was being quite an ass because
deep down I believed Mr. Grime and his highfalutin attitude deserved my smart mouth, and more. The pleasure he took in
habitually humiliating students, and not just *moi*, had ignited
my last nerve. It was just my good fortune that it happened on
a day I needed to get tossed from school, that's all.

While the color rose in Mr. Grime's face, I stormed out like
Mary Pickford leaving Douglas Fairbanks.

I pulled to a stop outside Ivy Overholtzer's Mortuary and cut the
engine. I admit I felt like a louse. It wasn't in my nature to speak
so rudely to adults, and I made a solid promise to apologize to

Mr. Grime at my earliest convenience. In the meantime, I had spotted Mary climbing out of her car. She was quiet and strangely subdued. We exchanged polite greetings on the sidewalk and then she clutched my hand as we headed inside. Mary was led into the back where she could spend a few last minutes alone with Mr. Taylor. I coaxed Doc MacDonald into explaining the results of his exam.

"I did it. Well, I mean to say that I assisted Dr. Wagner. You know, Kate, he was in charge and in my assisting him, I, er, helped him out. With a portion. Of the autopsy. He found, I mean, we, found the bullet."

"Yes, go on, Doc."

"It was a .38 caliber, steel-nosed bullet." Doc MacDonald shook his head and tapped his chin thoughtfully. "But I just don't understand it, Kate."

"Understand what?"

"Well, it was his clothes. Yes, his shirt, and his... his, uh." He flapped his hands around his mid-section.

"Vest?"

"Oh, yes, the vest. The shirt and the vest. Yes, that was it." His spectacles slid to the end of his nose as he looked down, rubbing his chin again. "Well, see, they didn't match."

I lowered my notepad and smiled. "I'm sure his tailor will forgive him."

"Oh, yes, his tailor will—what? No, not that—"

Mary burst through the door in a fit of tears. Her hand was clutched to her mouth and her face streaming with tears. She shook her head at me and rushed outside.

"I'd better go, Doc." I hurried to the door. "Thanks for letting Mary in before the inquest. Mums the word. And, don't worry that Mr. Taylor's clothes didn't match. I'm sure he'll be properly dressed for the funeral."

"Yes, I'm sure he'll—hey, wait. That's not what I meant. Of course, that's not what I meant. I meant his clothes didn't match up; the bullet holes didn't align properly."

I slowly retraced my steps. "Repeat that, please."

"Why, that hole in the vest. It was slightly lower than the hole in his shirt."

"What are you saying, Doc?"

"I don't know, Kate. But something doesn't... it doesn't..."

"You're right, something doesn't," I murmured.

After I helped Mary into her car and was assured she was calm enough to drive, I returned to *The Messenger* with my mind stuck on Doc's observation. My hands hovered over the typewriter keys but my mind couldn't conjure up anything to write. What did it mean if the bullet holes didn't align properly? Was it a clue? If so, did I have another lead?

My heart was pounding but I wished to heaven it was my fingers on the keys. Maybe this reporting business wasn't so easy. How was I supposed to decide what information was relevant? And more importantly, who should I ask?

I glanced at Pop but he was heading for the door. Something in his walk suggested he was sneaking out.

"Hey, Pop," I called, wading through the sea of desks to catch him. "What's doin'?"

Pop whirled around with a nervous look.

"Why, Kate, I didn't know you were here. Aren't you supposed to be in school?" He made a vague attempt to check his timepiece but fell short. He opened the door, edging out. I was in mid-sentence about my next column when he said, "All right then. See you at home." He turned and left me standing there with my thoughts hanging out.

Pop was usually up to his elbows tracking the curious appointments of President Harding. If that were the case now, he would have said so. Was he headed to the bank? Was he off begging Mr. Townsend for more time? I rubbed my burning stomach for a moment and then went after him.

Tall grey buildings blocked out the sun and turned the sidewalks of Broadway into concrete shadows. It was just as well. If I was going to stalk my own father it was fitting I should do it in dim lighting. Pop rounded the corner, hurried through the alley, and arrived on Sixth Street. He entered a two-bit coffee shop set back from the curb where bootleggers and bums from Pershing Square scurried inside to escape a thumping from the beat cops. It was a cruddy old building jammed between a hardware store and a giant grey bank that overshadowed the entire block. A forgotten place to all but the desperate and abandoned. I couldn't imagine why Pop would go there, a shiny penny dropped in cow dung. I waited a moment before peeking through the grimy window.

Filthy tables with chipped paint and broken chairs were scattered about. Yellowed photos sagged on the musty wall behind a dilapidated serving counter with three missing stools. Bullet holes riddled the far wall, and a menagerie of patrons huddled in twos and threes. My stomach clenched in anguish. Most of the men looked to be homeless veterans from The War.

Pop had joined two men at a small round table midway back. He blocked one man from view but I recognized the second one immediately—unkempt brown hair and a five o'clock shadow just past noon. He had the peculiar habit of wearing a crumpled grey overcoat year-round. The man was an old family friend, which didn't mean much on its own. But this old family friend was Ed King, a detective for the Los Angeles Police Department. My curiosity was piqued.

I slipped quietly inside. The smell of urine hit me like a frying pan and I faltered, forcing down the need to gag. On the floor to my right was a derelict high on something and mumbling to himself. To my left was a young fella in a ratty uniform. He had the shakes and was stroking an empty pant leg. Pity welled inside me as I shuffled toward Pop's table.

The light was dim in the back and grey with smoke. As I approached the table, the second man came into view and stopped me in my tracks.

Nicky Masino looked up, startled. His eyebrows rose and then crunched together in an unwelcome expression. This brought Pop and Detective King around.

"Kate!" Pop yelled, twisting in his chair. He started to rise but changed his mind. "What are you doing here?"

Nicky and Detective King eyed things behind me as though I'd been followed.

"Pop, what are *you* doing here?" I asked.

"You should leave. Now," Nicky said. His voice was low and tense as though someone in this rat hole would give a nickel I was here.

I looked at Detective King. I didn't know him well but the scowl on his broad face told me that Special Investigator Edward C. King was not fond of surprises.

"Miss March, didn't know you were joining us." He gave Pop an irritable look.

"She's not," Pop and Nicky said in unison. I bristled. Whatever they were up to felt too covert and dangerous for Pop to be involved with. I stared directly into Nicky's dark blue eyes and slowly pulled out a chair and sat myself down.

"Kate, we're just having coffee," Pop said, shifting uncomfortably. It wasn't often, if ever, that Pop lied to me. All that bank business aside, we had a close relationship and I adored him like no other, but I was the one who rolled out the fibs without compunction, not Pop.

"Nobody comes to a dive like this for coffee," I said, matter-of-fact. The man behind the counter looked up from the Want Ads. He and his week-old scruff gave me a nasty look. My eyes drifted toward the homeless men in the front.

"Look-it, Pop," I said, scooting closer and lowering my voice. "Things are different now that I'm writing for the paper. You have to trust me. I don't know what's up in your attic, but I don't like you hanging in a joint like this. I have a right to know what's doin', see?"

"What did she just say?" Nicky asked.

Detective King leaned over the table and looked me square in the eye. "What's doin', young lady, is that I owe your father a favor. I called him with some information that—in the hands of a Lucy Loose Lips—just might get him plugged, see?"

"Now, Ed," Pop soothed. "No need to frighten her. I'm sure that was a gross exaggeration." He tried to smile but couldn't put the cherry on top of his second lie. I looked at Nicky for reassurance. Surely, he wouldn't let Pop in on something dangerous. Surely, Nicky had some residual loyalty to the father of his best pals.

Nicky's blank stare only boiled the fear brewing in my gut.

"I'll walk Miss March out," he said, standing.

He seemed in an awful hurry to get rid of me, which only inspired me to plant my flag a little deeper.

"Listen, I've been raised with a certain amount of manners but my father is sitting in a stinking rat den on the corner of Filth and Suspicion. I'm not going anywhere." I reached over and squeezed Pop's hand. "Don't you think it's time to trust me?"

Pop covered my hand with his. I could see the uncertainty

in his eyes, the hesitation. After a moment, he motioned for Nicky to sit down.

"It's alright, Nick, Ed. Kate is already involved in a manner of speaking."

Detective King reached inside his overcoat and pulled out a crumpled pack of cigarettes. After fishing one out, he tapped it on the back of his hand and lit up, taking a long draw. He pinched tobacco from the tip of his tongue, his eyes squinting through the smoke. Nicky, who had reluctantly returned to his seat, was quiet and pensive, running a finger over a chip in his coffee cup. Pop may have allowed for my presence but the others were mulling things over. I was loaded for an argument should they try to toss me and then the strangest thing happened. Nicky gave Detective King a faint nod, like a go-ahead gesture of authority.

I stared at each one in turn, wondering if I'd imagined the whole thing. Had a special investigator been granted permission to continue—from a desk cop? The pecking order was obvious, and yet...

"Understand something," Detective King began. "I'm taking a big risk here. People depend on me. I'm not doing anything but following orders."

"What orders?" I glanced at Nicky. He sat emotionless like he had cotton in his ears and hadn't heard a thing. Detective King went on, speaking directly to Pop.

"Early this morning, District Attorney Woolwine calls me into his office. Assigns me to the Taylor case. To represent his office in the murder."

"This is about the Taylor murder?" My mind was buzzing like a beehive missing its queen. "I thought the Flying Squad was handling the case. Why would the district attorney step in and change things so quickly?"

Nicky frowned with a look that said, 'stay quiet'. I slumped back in my chair.

"Woolwine was piggish with the evidence but I took a look," Detective King said. "I see what direction he *wants* the investigation to go, but...well, I don't know. Let's just say I'll be trusting my own instincts."

I gaged Pop for a reaction. He was harder to read than a Penny Dreadful but my reporter juices were starting to flow. A special investigator for the LAPD didn't trust the DA? This case was in its infancy and already there was a whiff of dishonesty from Woolwine's office? This could make an already sensational story skyrocket!

"What direction is Woolwine heading?" Pop asked. "What's this evidence?"

Detective King leaned back in his chair and considered. "I'll give you what I can, Thom. When the time is right. Let me see how this plays out first. I'll check the relevancy of some items collected and get back to you. Meantime, keep my name out of it."

"What kind of items?" I asked but King shook his head.

"And you'll be careful, Ed?" Pop asked. "I wouldn't want you to jeopardize your job."

"Sure," he gave Pop a half-cocked grin. "Running down my own leads first—"

"What leads?" I asked again. He refused that, too. As far as I was concerned, if Detective King promised to supply pertinent information he might as well start now. "Well, at least give me your theory for the bullet holes not matching up."

I doubted he had that information just yet but I hoped if I shared a secret, he'd understand I wasn't sitting back twiddling my thumbs. I was up to my ears in this story.

Nicky cocked his head. He might've been intrigued by my

insight or irritated that I couldn't keep quiet. So hard to tell these days.

I opted for intrigue. I hadn't wanted to impress Nicky since I tried to decipher the password for the boys' clubhouse. Jeezers, that felt like a lifetime ago.

"That bone you just tossed out there," Detective King said. "Mind putting some meat on it?"

I explained my meeting with Doc at the mortuary, omitting Mary's visit with Mr. Taylor. No point in getting my reliable source in hot water.

Detective King toyed with his ciggy and mulled things over. He and Nicky exchanged a telling glance that sparked my suspicions back to life.

Why was Nicky here? Why was he involved with King and the Taylor case? Shouldn't he be shuffling papers and prisoners around? For a desk cop, he kept showing up at the oddest places. Hadn't he told Angelo he wanted off the force only last night? Or had I jumped to the wrong conclusion?

Detective King blew out a stream of smoke. "Don't know if I'm more irritated that the Deputy Coroner squawked about the case before the inquest or what he spilled. Can't say as I know anything about bullet holes in his clothes not matching up. My first guess would be that Taylor had his arms up when he was shot. Clothes tend to move when the body does."

"That makes sense," Pop mused, "if Mr. Taylor were being robbed."

My eyes shot to Nicky and then Detective King. They were staring at their coffee cups. A couple of lousy poker players if you asked me.

"But we know he *wasn't* killed by a burglar, don't we?" I said with as much authority as I could muster. Official statements had already been insinuating as much. There'd been a string of robberies in the area, but I couldn't connect the dots. Not with Mr. Taylor's diamond ring being left behind. Besides, robbing a man was one thing, shooting him in the back was something altogether evil.

Detective King jammed his ciggy into his mouth, grabbed his hat, and stood. Everyone took the cue and joined him.

"I'll say this, Miss March. Don't believe everything you read in the papers. Thom." He nodded at Pop and then stalked out. Pop dropped some coins onto the table and practically flew out the door without a second thought for me. I tried to follow but Nicky grabbed my arm.

"Not yet," he said. "Give them a minute. Seems like your Pop has something on his mind."

Pop caught Detective King outside the window where they continued their conversation. I was itching to follow but stayed put. Most likely, Pop would fill me in later. I was peeved all the same, being left out like I didn't belong or couldn't be trusted. Then an idea by way of Mr. Morgan came to me. I leaned against Nicky's shoulder and smiled up at him.

"So, tell me, Nicky. What's a cop like you doing on a case like this?"

He looked me over real good and repeated something he'd said earlier outside Mr. Taylor's bungalow.

"I go where I'm needed." His voice was as flat as a pancake.

I rolled my eyes and stepped away. Apparently, Nicky Masino was immune to my flirtatious overtures, which I chalked up to being necessary in his line of work. You had to respect a guy for that.

The men up front had been arguing quietly but their voices were on the rise. Nicky and I watched until I couldn't take it another minute. I went to the counter and ordered several cups of coffee from the barkeep. Carefully balancing them on a tray,

I maneuvered through the tables and served the men one at a time. The fella in the ratty uniform with the missing leg saluted me. Another smiled warmly and winked like we were old pals. The others eagerly took their cups with shaking hands and devoured the contents. I gave them every cent I had and returned to Nicky. He stared at me until I spoke.

"I don't like Pop involved in this case. Tell me he's not in danger."

"That's funny coming from you, Miss March. You should be in school, not working angles on a murder."

"I'm a reporter now, Officer Masino. I go where I'm needed." I looked at him without an ounce of humor. His eyes were the darkest blue I had ever seen and doing a great imitation of a pair of glass marbles. Was he on some sort of drug or medication? Or maybe he was holding back tears? But why? And why here and now of all places?

"Leave it to your Pop or someone on his payroll," he said, blinking quickly and looking away. "And to answer your question, yes, anyone poking into a murder investigation is in some amount of danger. Especially inexperienced young ladies in over their heads." Nicky walked out and left me alone on the corner of Filth and Suspicion.

CHAPTER 7

For the past hour Detective Cahill had been staring at me as though I had been cracking bad jokes. It must have been a revelation for him, learning that Detective Ed King, a respected special investigator, was skirting around District Attorney Woolwine and working with a local rag like The Messenger. As far as I knew, Pop never paid King a dime for his troubles. No moral codes broken there but the implication that Detective King didn't trust the DA was significant. Woolwine had been embroiled in plenty of scandals regarding bribery and what-not over the years. Even had himself quite a temper which, on more than one occasion, caused him to sock opposing counsel in the eye. Still, that didn't necessarily mean Woolwine would tamper with a murder investigation. I understood Detective Cahill's reluctance to believe me because I hadn't even gotten to the disappearing evidence part of the show.

"Go on," Detective Cahill said, sounding somewhat distrustful and suspicious.

Like it or not, what he was about to hear wouldn't sit well. Detective King was a fellow officer after all. Maybe even a pal, for all I knew. At this stage in my illustrious journalism career, I knew cops could buddy up to each other if they were of like minds about things such as taking bribes or looking the other way on occasion. But they were just as likely to turn on each other if some goody-goody wanted to play by the book. No monkeying around, I mean, strictly by the book. I had no idea which camp Detective Cahill sat in. It occurred to me that I could be making a huge mistake by talking. On the other hand, I could be gaining a much-needed ally. It was a risk I had to take, considering my present situation. The Messenger's latest Extra Edition had been circulating long enough to reach my intended audience. Now more than ever I had to time things just right. I had to convince Cahill that I was telling the truth. And the only way to do that was to keep talking...

It was early evening and I was lying on my stomach on a rug before the fireplace. A fire crackled and shed soft light around our cozy library. It had been a pleasant February day but promised to turn chilly by sunset. Beneath my fingertips was a mess of notes about the Taylor case. Pop was standing by his desk talking on the telephone, having answered it moments ago. The Victrola played "Toot, Toot, Tootsie" by some fella named Al Jolson, and I was humming along and tapping my heels together behind me.

"I see," Pop murmured into the mouthpiece. "Of course. Anything else? My apologies again. Goodbye."

"Was that Detective King?" I asked, rolling onto my back

and holding my notepad above my face. "Does he have any new leads? You know Pop, I don't think he really shared much information with us today."

"No, Kate, that was Principal Housh." Pop sank into his worn leather chair and picked up his pipe.

I sat up and prepared for battle. "Now just listen, Pop. It's not as bad as it sounds. Mr. Grime has a way of demoralizing students and—" Pop deflected my barrage with a brisk wave and a disappointed scowl. Excuses fell out of my head like dead birds. It wouldn't serve anything good to insult Pop's intelligence. "How long did I get this time?"

"One week, which is generous, considering." He gave me a pointed look over his cheaters. "You will offer both a written and verbal apology."

"Yes, Pop." I had the good sense to appear remorseful and appalled by my own behavior, which wasn't too far outside the truth. On the other hand, I was dancing proud of myself. I had gained a whole week to devote to sleuthing! Just what I'd hoped for. It must've been that added bit about Mr. Grime's dangling participle. I'm sure it had the English department gabbing.

"So, I was studying my notes here," I said, flipping a page. "And I think I need more information from Mabel Normand. She was the last person to see Mr. Taylor alive. And that circus outside her apartment house the other day, boy-oh, what a joke! Do you know if Detective King plans to interview her?"

Pop clenched his teeth around his pipe stem and tapped tobacco into the chamber. After lighting up, he took a few puffs and then went to his bookshelf. "Yes, I believe sometime this evening." He selected *The Conduct of Life* by Ralph Waldo Emerson and settled back into his chair. "They'll let us know if anything substantial comes from it."

"But, I should be there! Pop, I should—"

"No, Kate. We think it's best for you to wait here. You should be tackling the pile of schoolwork you'll be missing. It won't do to fall behind so close to graduation."

"Who's *we*?"

He grunted distractedly and slid a finger between the pages.

Nicky. I had no doubt Nicky Masino was behind the *we* not wanting me involved. He couldn't possibly share the same views toward women as Pugsly the Ugsly did. Could he? And why should I care if he did? Why should I care if the thought made me sick? And angry.

"Sure I can't go?" I asked, gathering my notes and pencils. Once Pop had hunkered down with Emerson there was no reaching him. I told him I'd be upstairs tackling all that school-work and he shouldn't expect me for dinner. He nodded vaguely and turned a page.

I made a concerted effort to do as I had said. Ten minutes saw me at my desk dutifully making headway on my next English essay. But who was I kidding? I had no intention of sitting back and waiting for Detective King to throw us the leftovers. I wasn't afraid of hard work and I certainly wasn't as trusting or as patient as Pop could be. Those two may have an agreement but that hardly meant I had to sit on my hands.

What would Nellie Bly do?

I grinned. I knew exactly what she would do. So, with a light heart and a bit anxious excitement fluttering in my stomach, I stuffed my notepad and pencil into my back pocket and quietly opened the window. With practiced ease, I crawled out and shimmied down the trellis to land softly on the lawn. It had just reached the magic hour, the sky fading to soft blue, so I strolled away nonchalantly; as long as I played like nothing was doin', no one would suspect I was on the lam.

I took Angel's Flight down the hill and a red cable car over to Mable Normand's apartment house. I was halfway up the sidewalk when Nicky and Detective King came strolling around the far corner of the building. Detective King was finishing a ciggy, which he dropped and smashed with his shoe. Nicky halted abruptly upon seeing me. His eyes flicked open in surprise and then narrowed.

Smiling seemed rather presumptuous of me so I just stood there expectantly. What I should've done was make for the apartment building before they could stop me. If I thought Miss Normand or her maid would welcome me inside without proper representation, I would have.

Detective King looked up. "Jesus, Miss March!" he said in surprise. "Where the hell did you come from?"

"'Lo there, gentleman." I put on my newly acquired professional expression hoping to keep things civil. After our brief conversation at the rat hole café, I wanted to convey a serious reporter's attitude. Somehow speaking crisply and thrusting my nose in the air were requirements. "I heard we were interviewing Mable Normand this evening."

Nicky cocked an eyebrow but said nothing.

"I thought to sit in and jot down a few notes." I waggled my notepad and took a step toward the building.

Detective King's chosen course of action was to ignore me altogether. He smoothed down his lapels and fiddled with his tie. Nicky murmured, "Go ahead. I'll meet you inside."

As I had noticed before, the unnatural chain of command came from Nicky to a special investigator. It just didn't jive. Unless Nicky was working directly for District Attorney Woolwine. If so, why would Detective King openly share information in front of him if he didn't trust the DA? Or had Nicky been promoted? So why the copper's clothes and not civilian garb as Detective King or other detectives wore?

I'd have to work that out later. Tonight was all about this interview. I followed Detective King up the walk until Nicky barred my way.

Once King had entered the apartment house, Nicky stepped back. "I believe I had an agreement with your father," he said.

"That so?"

"I agreed to supply him with information about the case and he agreed to keep you from intruding."

Never mind the cruddy feeling of Pop's betrayal rolling around in the pit of my stomach, I was stuck on Nicky's determination to exclude me. I had my suspicions as to why he was so adamant but none of them went down easy. Yes, I was young. Yes, I was a woman. Get over it or step aside!

"I am not intruding, Officer Masino," I said, firmly. "I wonder if you would be so persistent if I were a *male* reporter?" I had no intention of wasting my time debating his answer, mostly because I couldn't bear the idea of Nicky repeating any vulgar old-fashioned insults that spewed from Pugsly the Ugsly. I may have been too young to be a true suffragette but that didn't mean I wanted to be treated like a second-class citizen.

I had a surprising amount of anger raging inside me. Maybe I expected more from Nicky, my brothers' best pals and someone I had considered a close family friend.

Nicky didn't answer or even rise to the challenge. He could be stalling to keep me from the interview.

"I also had an agreement with my father," I said, edging up the walk. "I, alone, will work the Taylor story for *The Messenger*. We need this story."

"By *need* you mean the paper is in trouble?"

The last thing I wanted was to make public our financial struggles. Pop would be humiliated.

"That explains why Ed's been wanting to help your father,"

Nicky said, coming to his own conclusion. He removed his department-issued hat and wiped his forehead. "But we had an agreement that you wouldn't get involved." He adjusted his hat back in place and then looked at me with fresh understanding. "Your father doesn't know you're here," he said matter-of-fact. I shrugged. "Did you attend school today?"

"Mostly."

Nicky scowled. "Did you or did you not attend school today?"

"Briefly."

"Played hooky?"

"Work appointment."

"Played hooky," Nicky concluded. "I could have a truant officer tail you."

"Oh, that's sounds just lovely, but, unfortunately, I've been suspended."

"Not surprising. Duration?"

"One glorious week!" I flashed a satisfying smile. Nicky knew very well what it meant. I had strategically maneuvered myself into a full-time reporter's role, temporarily.

"Very well, Miss March, you may sit in on the interview, but I want to see your notes when we're finished."

I laughed lightly. "And who are you, William G. Harding? I don't think so, Officer Masino. I'll happily sit in on the interview but you may not see my notes." He opened his mouth to object so I hurried on. "You won't mind, I assure you. *The Messenger* has a strict policy against yellow journalism, if you've been paying attention all these years. This is a sensational story that *will* be told, one way or another. We don't print fluff or make up things to sell copy like those other rags. The story *will* be written, Officer Masino, and I would think you'd want the truth out there."

"Are you trying to test my patience, Miss March?"

"No, I am trying to write a damn good story here!" I barked out and then forced a deep breath. "Look, Officer Masino, I don't feel the need to test your patience. Just as I don't feel the need to share my notes. They are mine, or will be mine, and the property of *The Messenger*, once I write my story."

His mouth twitched into a smirk. "Fine, Miss March. You may sit in on the interview and you don't have to show your notes. But your story will *not* reveal that you were privy to an official police interview. And, you *will* keep quiet inside. Not a single question. Not a single word."

"But... how am I supposed to conduct a proper interview if I can't ask questions?"

"*You* aren't. Detective King is conducting the interview. You'll remain silent or you'll remain outside. Those are the terms. No negotiating. I want your word that you'll keep quiet, Miss March."

I rolled my eyes. "How's about I promise to try?" I muttered, feeling all of ten- years old.

"Your word," he demanded.

"Alright, alright! Don't have kittens."

Detective King and Miss Normand were seated in the living room when Nicky and I entered. Her maid, Mamie, poured a fresh batch of tea while introductions were made. Nicky took the second chair in the grouping next to Detective King and left me to sit on the sofa. Miss Normand sat at the opposite end, her legs curled under her and draped with a lovely crocheted blanket. She held a crumpled handkerchief in her hand, her big brown eyes red and swollen.

"Books," Miss Normand continued to Detective King. "As I told the police yesterday, Mr. Taylor had some books for me so

I stopped by to pick them up. He offered supper. I declined. He had already eaten. I had dinner waiting at home. His valet, Henry Peavey, served drinks and then left."

Detective King and I began writing in our notepads. "But you came with a bag of peanuts," he said. "Why did you leave the bag?"

Miss Normand covered her face with her hand and moaned. "Oh, why does it matter? The other detectives didn't care. I don't know why I even brought the stupid bag. It was a joke. I was teasing Bill that I had something wonderful hidden behind my back and it was nothing but a stupid bag of peanuts."

"Did he laugh?"

She smiled softly at the memory. "Yes. He always laughed at my jokes."

"Did you put the bag on the piano?"

I looked at Detective King. Where was he going with this?

Miss Normand frowned thoughtfully. "No, I should say Bill set the bag of peanuts on the piano."

"Why? Why there?" Detective King pushed.

Miss Normand looked uncomfortable under the pressure. I realized he was forcing her through the mundane trivialities, walking her through that evening, step by step.

"Well, he put the bag on the piano because... he was on his way to his desk. Yes, that's it. He took the chair at his writing desk. Then he pulled up his rocking chair and told me to sit down by the desk so I did."

"Why the desk?"

"He wanted to show me some checks."

"What kind of checks?"

"Gosh, I'd forgotten that part. Bank checks. Forged bank checks his old driver had stolen."

I was scribbling as Mabel spilled her story. She had been so distraught about Mr. Taylor dying and what time she had arrived and departed that she'd forgotten the meat of their conversation. Forgotten because no one had asked her. It could mean absolutely nothing, then again, who knew?

I had to hand it to Detective King, he didn't ask ordinary questions. Then again, I had never witnessed a murder investigation before. I imagined I could learn a great deal from him.

"His previous driver," Miss Normand continued, "Edward Sands had forged some checks and stolen some of Bill's clothes and a car. Some time ago. Last year. Bill filed a report but nothing ever came of it."

"Why did Mr. Taylor show you the checks that night, Miss Normand? Why then when you were talking about books?"

She mulled this over and then recited everything as it came to her. "He'd gone to his desk to get the book for me. I noticed his bankbook open. I asked what he was doing. He said, 'preparing my taxes'. Then he mentioned the forged checks and showed them to me. We compared the signatures and I tell you, I couldn't distinguish Sand's writing from Bill's."

"Then what?"

"I left around seven forty-five."

"No," Detective King said patiently. "Tell me what you did after you put the checks down."

She rearranged the throw to better cover her legs and then gathered her teacup. "I commented that he'd moved the furniture or something, that things looked different. He said I hadn't been there in a while and the Victrola was a newer model, that was all." She took a sip.

"And then?"

"And then Peavey came with drinks."

"What kind of drinks?"

Miss Normand blinked rapidly and took another sip of tea.

She eventually shrugged and went about folding her damp handkerchief with great care.

I lowered my eyes and smiled. I had recognized the concoction at Mr. Taylor's bungalow. Thanks to Addy and the file girls down at the 77th Street precinct, I was learning all about assorted libations.

"Miss Normand," Nicky said smoothly. "This is a murder investigation. We are not concerned, beyond the scope of the investigation, about illegal bootleg. If that has you worried."

Miss Normand sighed congenially and said, as though we were all terrific school chums, "Now, don't go and print this but...do you know what an Orange Blossom is?"

Bingo!

I jotted down gin and orange juice, the newest postwar rage. Nicky glared at me.

"Did you accept the drinks?" Detective King asked. "No, Peavey set them on the table and left."

"Did he say anything?"

"No, Bill said he could go after he removed the dishes from the dining room table, and he did."

I had already gotten this information from Henry, so while Detective King took note, I watched Miss Normand's reaction. She had a secretive smile that had me curious. I hoped King would notice but he was thumbing through his notepad, unaware.

I tapped my pencil nervously against my notepad. Nicky gave me a 'stop fidgeting' scowl. I cocked my head at him.

"What's going on?" Miss Normand asked, looking at us in turn.

"She wants to speak," Nicky answered dispassionately. I felt like a pet begging for attention.

"I don't mind," Miss Normand said, smiling uncertainly. I grinned at Nicky.

"You may ask one question, Miss March," he said, crossing his ankle over the opposite knee.

I turned my attention to Miss Normand. "What were you thinking. Just now? When you recalled that Henry Peavey had left for the evening."

At first, she shrugged off my question. Then she laughed to herself and toyed with a piece of loose yarn on the blanket. "Oh, nothing, really. Well, I mean... it really was nothing. You see, Peavey had gone somewhere in the house and returned a few minutes later—" She pressed her lips together. "He'd changed out of his white serving coat and had on the funniest clothes. Bright green golf stockings, yellow knickers and the ugliest purple tie I'd ever seen!" She shook her head with genuine pity.

Nicky gave me a humorless smile. Detective King sat back and made himself comfortable. He wasn't the least bit interested.

"You see, nothing, really." Miss Normand shrugged again.

"Why was Henry Peavey wearing golf clothes at night?" I asked.

Miss Normand snorted. "I have no idea, but I told Bill—" She stopped abruptly, blushing.

"Continue, Miss Normand," Nicky said. "What did you tell Bill?"

"Well, I... I told Bill that if he'd let Peavey play golf more often he wouldn't get into trouble... in the park."

"Trouble in the park?" Detective King frowned.

"You know." She lowered her voice, "Peavey leaned *that* way. You see, he was arrested not too long ago for soliciting favors from men in the park. Well, Bill felt so badly for him, he bailed him out and promised to appear in court on his behalf, you know, to testify as to his character or something like that. Why, he even paid two hundred dollars for the bail."

Jeezers, soliciting men in the park! According to Addy and the file girls, there was one taboo in this town worse than murder—being a homosexual. Poor Henry. But why would a man of Mr. Taylor's stature risk an appearance in court for a homosexual employee?

Detective King and I were of like minds; he asked Miss Normand that very question.

"Oh, it was just like Bill to do something like that. Always for the underdog, helping anyone in need. That's how he met Edward Sands, you know. A fellow soldier from The War down on his luck. He offered Sands a job, but the poor bastard was rotten, if you ask me."

"Where is Sands now?" Nicky asked.

"Long gone, according to Bill. And he didn't expect to ever see him again. Sands could be arrested, you know, if he ever showed up here. On account of those items he stole."

"And what time did Henry Peavey leave that night?" Detective King asked.

"Around seven twenty."

"And yourself?"

"I'd say seven forty-five."

"Anyone call or come by?"

"No, no one. I couldn't stay long, you see. I had an early studio call in the morning and Mamie was serving me dinner in bed. So, I left somewhere round seven forty-five and Bill walked me to the car."

"Did he leave the front door open?"

"Yes, I believe so."

"It was chilly last night." Detective King looked up from his notes.

"Bill liked the crisp air. He certainly wasn't worried, if that's what you mean."

"Anyone outside? Did you see anyone?"

"Just Davis, my driver, cleaning peanut shells out of my car. Bill had a good laugh at that, too. Funny, I never realized until you asked me that I had left the bag inside. Maybe if I'd gone back to..." Her eyes welled up and she pressed the hanky to her nose.

I made a concerted effort not to react. I was well aware of the 'maybe if' game, having played it for years with The War, the deaths of my brothers, and Mama. It was a cruel game that never ended. In spite of my efforts I found myself rubbing my stomach. The familiar pang burned inside.

I wondered if Nicky every played the game. His flat expression gave nothing away. I envied him that.

"How did the night end?" Detective King asked.

"I hugged Bill goodbye," Miss Normand said around the lump in her throat. She took a moment to collect herself and swallowed hard. "He said he'd call later but I said I'd probably be asleep. Then I got in the car."

"That was the last time you saw him? On the curb?"

She nodded. "Yes, I... we blew kisses to each other, just being silly, you know, as he walked toward his house."

"And no one else was there but your driver?"

She nodded. "Does any of this help, Detective King?"

"We'll see. But tell me, Miss Normand, is there anyone you know who would want to kill or hurt Mr. Taylor? An angry actor? An old boss? Did he have enemies from The War he spoke of?"

"I can't think of anyone," she said, looking away and blinking rapidly.

Miss Normand may have been a celebrated actress but it was obvious she had just lied. As far as I was concerned.

"Well," Detective King breathed heavily and pushed himself to his feet. "That'll be all. For now. You'll be around if we think of anything else?" It wasn't so much a question.

111

"Of course." Miss Normand stood, clutching the throw in her arms.

Detective King and Nicky headed for the door, which Mamie had opened. I followed slowly as something was nagging me, a forgotten follow-up question.

"Oh, one more thing," I said as I remembered. Nicky shepherded me toward the door.

"That'll be all, Miss March," he said.

I fidgeted in his grip and called over my shoulder. "When was Mr. Taylor due in court on Henry's behalf?"

"What?" Miss Normand called. "Oh, well, I think it was, oh, yes, he said the second. February second. Why?"

"That was yesterday," I said. "The day Mr. Taylor was murdered."

CHAPTER 8

"You shouldn't have been allowed in on that interview," Detective Cahill said sourly. "You're a civilian."

"I printed the truth," I said defensively.

"So, Detective King is the source of all those crazy headlines you pumped out? He was behind all that?"

"Of course not," I said. "And they weren't crazy. I collected evidence and came to my own conclusion so—"

"Like I said, you're a civilian. Certainly not an investigator. I'm sure King will catch it when his involvement comes to light. Woolwine won't like it."

"See, that's the thing, isn't it? Woolwine. He's tried to push the investigation in his direction for his own purposes. Tell me he gave the Flying Squad free rein to go where the evidence led. Tell me you don't have doubts about him. Go on."

Detective Cahill glared at me. He wouldn't commit one way

or the other.

"Okay, then, tell me why Woolwine shifted the investigation from the Flying Squad to King? Did he think to control him? Was he concerned about what you and the Squad might discover? Who added Officer Masino to the case? You?"

He fell quiet, pondering things. "We... the Squad has never officially been off the case. We've been... look, I don't see what any of this has to do with you and that guy in the ally."

"What about Officer Masino?"

"You tell me, Miss March."

"Sure," I said, settling back into my chair. "Sure, I'll tell you all I know about Officer Masino."

After the interview with Mabel Normand I laid awake for hours, puzzling out everything she'd said. I found myself looking for clues where there weren't any. It was enough to give me a headache. When I finally drifted off in the wee hours, I had one of my unfortunate dreams. Unlike the nightmares when Mama lurked in the shadows as a menacing figure emanating scornful judgements without uttering a word, this dream involved my brothers.

It was just the three of us, me and Lawrence and Edward in our early years before Eugene came along. The boys were racing around the back lawn and I was stretching out my little arms, begging them to stop and carry me. And then Nicky was there. At eight-years-old he scooped me up and set me in the little wagon to pull me up the path to Mrs. Banning's garden. I wanted strawberries and my brothers had promised me some. They'd gotten distracted with an ant hill so Nicky would take me. There was a breeze whipping laundry on the lines and a soft melody floating between the houses. Tender and mournful, the song made me cry. I wanted the devastatingly sad music to stop. I tugged Nicky's shirt and begged, *please make the sadness stop!* Nicky put a finger to his lips and shook his head, and I knew instinctively that the sadness would never go away.

I awoke feeling feverish and sticky, my thin white nightshirt clinging to me. I sat up and cupped my moist hot cheeks. Over the years I had learned to manage such dreams, a routine of slow breathing and forced happy thoughts.

Tonight was difficult. I dropped my head into my hands and breathed. Deep, deep breaths. It was no use so I kicked back the covers. Maybe one of Jon Held's cartoon antics could take my attention. I glanced around for a *Life* magazine. No such luck. I swung my legs over the edge of the bed, gripping the bedsheets. Maybe a glass of warm milk?

As I contemplated options, a strange awareness took hold. I was awake and yet I heard the mournful sound from my dream. It swam in my head and nearly swept me back to the visions of my brothers. I turned slightly and listened. The sound was seeping through the half-open window, and a vague memory rose from the depths of my mind. A lifetime ago, Nicky Masino played the saxophone. He would practice in the evenings during his high school days. What an age it had been since I'd heard that sound floating around the Hill.

The window moved easily beneath my hands. Once fully opened, I leaned out and gazed past Nicky's darkened bedroom window and across the rolling slopes of Bunker Hill. The moon doused everything in shades of blacks and greys. High-pitched rooftops and block chimneys jutted against the night sky. Sounds could echo up here but I was sure the hum of a saxophone emanated from the Masino property.

I fell back on the pillow and told myself to go to sleep. I breathed and focused, and failed. I was exhausted but wide awake. Sleep would never come and besides, I was getting curious as to what Nicky had on his mind, playing such a sad melody at this hour.

I slid into a robe and then shimmied down the trellis and padded across the lawn between our houses. Maybe I simply felt drawn to the music. Maybe I was drawn to the sadness it evoked. Maybe I was a glutton for punishment.

My bare feet grew cold and slick in the moist grass. The night had turned chilly, and I shivered in my thin robe. Ethereal mist, drifting between the homes as though searching for lost loved ones, nearly smothered the familiar scent of sweet citrus. This time of year, farmers lit smudge pots to keep frost from destroying produce in nearby fields. The thick, smoky scent created a pleasant, heady mixture in the air.

I strode past Mrs. Masino's clipping garden and slipped around back. A wide veranda complimented the Masino mansion and featured a sitting area filled with elegant wicker furniture, an Italian rug sent from relations in Sicily, and potted palms from a trip across the Mexico border. Nicky was reclined atop the far railing with his back against the house. He was naked from the waist up and wore pale blue pajama pants. His long legs were balanced on the flat railing and his tan feet crossed at the ankles. With hooded eyes clouded by some distant memory, Nicky played the saxophone cradled in his hands.

Suddenly embarrassed by his near nakedness, I was tempted to flee. Nicky noticed me at once but hadn't reacted. His gaze was unflinching and he continued playing, seemingly lost in his mood. Was it one of those mysterious dark moods? I couldn't fault him for that, having been awakened by a heartbreaking dream myself. Maybe it was best to leave him be. I stepped back.

Then again, maybe that's why he was out here in the first

116

place. He was in The War again, or *it* was in him. I knew as well as anyone the need for distraction when ghosts came calling.

I alighted the first few steps slowly. Nicky played on, that tender sorrowful melody that seemed to dig a hole in the heart. I wondered how much suffering he'd endured during The War. I wondered what haunted him as I had wondered so many times what haunted those poor souls walking the streets of Los Angeles, their eyes unoccupied. I heard it said that pain could travel far deeper than the imagination could. Listening to Nicky play, I guessed it must be so.

Nicky's lashes were moist and spiked together. He'd been crying. Somehow the thought of a guy as big and strong as Nicky Masino crying made life all the more miserable.

I stepped onto the porch as the music slowed and the last agonizing note died quietly in the night. Nicky laid the saxophone across his lap. The Hill was quiet again. I held my breath and waited. It was understandable if he gave me the bum's rush after today. I'd certainly been a pest.

Slowly, Officer Nicky Masino turned and looked at me. His midnight blue eyes were black as coal and heavy as a broken heart.

"What's doin', Katie Ann," he murmured.

I closed my eyes and pressed my lips together. Sweet nostalgia rushed through me. The clock reversed the moment he said my name in that old familiar way. I could almost feel Lawrence and Edward with us. They would be lounging there on the loveseat and chair, a leg thrown over the armrest as they batted complaints of boredom back and forth. Lawrence would suggest baseball while tossing a ball into a mitt. Edward would concoct a plan to break into Mrs. Hildreth's mansion and rearrange her furniture. I could feel them so close to me. They were right here.

And then they weren't.

117

I opened my eyes and breathed deeply. I searched Nicky's sad face for a moment and then asked, "Are you back?"

"Are you?" he challenged softly. We shared forlorn smiles, and then he looked away and fiddled with the saxophone. "I see the trellis still holds you."

I swallowed the painful lump in my throat. "Can I help you, Nicky? Can I do something? Anything?" I had no earthly idea what I was asking but it felt natural to offer. You see a wounded animal, you try to help. Problem was, I had my own wounds. What good was my help?

He pursed his lips and shook his head. He would spare me the ugliness. I didn't blame him for that. My brothers would have done the same, if only...

I cleared my throat and made a valiant effort to rearrange my thoughts. I had questions about my brothers and their deaths. Once I finally found the courage, I asked Nicky what he might know about it. He stared at me for a long thoughtful moment until I wondered if he hadn't heard they were dead. Then he began to speak in a low monotone voice I hardly recognized.

"It was during the Battle of Belleau Wood. In France, near the Marne River. They call it the German *Spring Offensive*, the move to control the Wood. We were aiding the French and British forces. The First Battalion, Fifth Marines attacked Hill 142 in early June. No scouting party had been issued so they walked into a nest of German machine guns and artillery." He paused and ground his teeth on the rest. "Our men advanced in waves across an open wheat field. Over a hundred men and all five junior officers were mowed down, including Lawrence."

I felt him looking at me but I had been staring at my feet the moment he began. I had just enough time to envision Lawrence twisting in pain and falling to the ground when Nicky continued.

"The second wave with the Third Battalion, Sixth Marines was sweeping the southern end of Belleau Wood. They took heavy machinegun fire. Sharpshooters and barbed wire were everywhere. Edward got tangled in the wire. He was cut down by machinegun fire."

I sank into the nearest chair and clutched the armrests. I had imagined, or rather convinced myself, that my brothers had died peacefully in hospital beds all the while knowing it couldn't have been true. Their bodies had not been returned home for burial. Thanks to the orders of General John Pershing, Commander of the American forces, no fallen American soldier would be returned home. Instead, they would be buried as quickly as possible wherever they had fallen. It was for logistics, lack of available space on ships, and sparing families the horror of seeing their mangled loved ones.

"They didn't suffer," I told Nicky as a matter of fact. I wouldn't allow it. Not my brothers.

"I'm sure they didn't," he murmured without emotion.

"They didn't! It was instant! Painless! They never suffered!"

"Yes."

My heart pumped furiously beneath my nightshirt. I stood and paced, rubbing the burn in my stomach. I had mistakenly believed answers would fill the gaping hole inside me. But I was on the verge of crumbling all over again. Imploding. I couldn't let that happen. A second stint in Pop's library, alone and miserable, was not an option. I was no longer a frightened little girl. I was a grown woman for chrissake! Sure, I lost my brothers and my mother abandoned me, but I was still here! Heartache hadn't done me in!

I forced myself to breathe slowly. When the screaming in my head abated, I looked at Nicky. A hint of compassion showed in his soft expression. He genuinely felt bad for me. And

I suddenly felt terrible for not realizing he had lost his best pals in the bargain. Probably more friends than just my brothers. Friends he'd made in The War. Nicky seemed to have lost so much more than I ever had, having experienced it firsthand.

"Were you there? With Lawrence and Edward? In France?"

He shook his head. He had been miles away and hadn't heard the death count until weeks later. Names weren't available until weeks after that. Mail was practically nonexistent. He eventually heard the news from Angelo.

"What about you, Nicky? What happened to you over there?"

His eyes turned dead as headstones. He was a stranger again. The most familiar stranger I had ever known.

I couldn't guess what he'd been through in The War. I couldn't guess what he thought of himself now. All I knew was who Nicky had been before it all changed. Maybe a reminder would loosen him up.

"I'll tell you what *I* know," I said gently. "Your name is Nicola Gianni Masino. You were born July 4, 1899 upstairs in this house. Your father died when you were ten. You have a scar on your right knee from an accident with a carving knife. You fell out of that tree over there when you were twelve and broke your left arm. You and your brother are best pals. And every year you give your mama a new rose bush for her birthday."

"That's not me anymore. People change, Katie Ann. Don't think for a minute they don't."

"I know that, Nicky. I know you've changed. We all have. But we've got to move on, and I just thought, I mean, I don't know really. Maybe I could help? If you'll let me?" For all my probing, I knew I was deeply afraid to hear Nicky's story. More than anything I wanted to help but something in his eyes frightened me.

Nicky looked out across the lawn, considering things. "You remember that scruffy old dog you found limping around the baseball field? That black and white mutt with a broken leg? You begged your pop to keep it."

"Sure I do. I remember."

"That's not me, Katie. I'm not some stray dog you can try to fix."

"But I *did* fix him. We had to give his leg a clean break so it would heal properly. But it did. Remember?"

"Not everything can be fixed. Don't fool yourself by thinking it can. You don't know me. And it's better that way."

"I'm not fooling myself. About anything."

"That so? How long have you been wearing boy clothes? Are you clinging to your dead brothers' memories or are you still rebelling against what your mama did to you?"

I stood very still. No one mentioned Mama to me. Not Trudy Mae, not Addy, not Eugene. Not even Pop anymore.

"I don't talk about Mama," I said flatly. It took every ounce of strength I had not to lose control. I had an arsenal of names and accusations I could let loose against Mama. Always on the tip of my tongue. "What's done is done. I can't change the past. I can't make her come back. I can't ask her why she left or where she ran off to. And I don't care to anymore."

"Like I said, people change. You're not the same little girl in pigtails and I'm not me. You won't talk about your mother but I'm supposed to talk about The War?"

I looked away. He had a point. I couldn't go a month without having nightmares myself. Whatever I was trying to bury wouldn't stay down. No more than what haunted Nicky.

He sighed. "I suppose it's better to have had something done *to* you than to have been the one—" he broke off, his eyes sweeping past me into the night. "Sometimes... the past doesn't stay in the past." His eyes had gone vacant again. His body slacked as though life had slipped right out of him. I noticed several odd scars along his right side, one between his ribs and two below that. When had he gotten those? During that downhill bicycle accident? No, that's when he'd hurt his collarbone. Maybe that summer when the boys ambushed the ice truck? Funny, these scars looked new. I couldn't remember ever having seen them before.

"Nicky, where'd you go *after* The War? I mean, when you were released? Did you stay in Europe?"

His body tensed. I was maneuvering through a mine field.

"For a while," he said tightly.

"And, when you came back to the states? I heard you were working somewhere in the Midwest? Or was it the plains? Farming or something?"

"Farming," he murmured with a faint smile as though that was some funny joke. I knew it hadn't sounded like an occupation Nicky Masino would take up. But what then?

"You certainly have the makings of a fine reporter," he said without humor. "You ask a lot of questions, which I believe I've already said I wouldn't be answering."

"I'm not trying to pry. I was just wondering..." I paused to consider another angle. "You like working on the force? How do you know Ed King?"

Nicky mulled this over. He seemed to be selective about which questions he would answer. "I've known Ed for a while now. Which reminds me," he gave me a pointed look to mark his seriousness. "I don't want you on the Taylor case."

"No kidding."

"I'm serious. Tell your pop to give the story to someone else."

I flopped back in the chair and sighed. "There you go again, sounding like the savage of the Sahara. Prince Hassan bossing around Lady Diana."

He frowned. "Speak English."

"You know, the film? *The Sheik?*"He still didn't get me. I rolled my eyes. "With Rudolph Valentino?" I had only seen the film five times because of Addy. She fancied herself in love with Valentino and I was dragged along to witness his perfection. Nothing was ringing on Nicky's register.

"Oh, never mind," I said. "Tell me why you're so keen to have me off the case. 'Suppose it's because I'm a girl."

"What?" Nicky frowned like he didn't get me. I felt a measure of relief. "You're not *on the case*, so just do as you're told. For once."

"I'll do no such thing. Like I said, it's a great story and we could use a great story just about now. And I'm the one writing it."

"I could make it difficult for you."

"You already have."

"You haven't seen difficult yet." His eyes flicked with amusement and a hint of a smile played at the corners of his mouth. His mood seemed to be lightening.

"Tell me something, Nicky. Does Detective King take orders from you?"

His smile fell off and he sighed like I was boring him to pieces.

"How's about this?" I pushed. "You tell me what happened to you during The War, and I'll quit the Taylor case."

"I'm not in the habit of bargaining with children but I admire your effort. So, how's about *this*... you won't be asking me about The War again. Ever. You'll be telling your pop to give the Taylor case to someone else. You'll be attending school every day. I won't be catching you intruding on another interview. You'll be a good little girl, and I won't be sending truant officers to track your every move."

"Well, well, Kaiser Wilhelm right here on American soil." I stood up and nodded. "Challenge accepted, Officer Masino."

CHAPTER 9

"I didn't know about your brothers," Detective Cahill said softly, looking uncomfortable for the first time. "My condolences."

I crossed my arms and looked away before the tears welling in my eyes spilled. For the life of me I don't know why I went into such detail about Nicky and my brothers. Well, perhaps I did know. It was important for Cahill to understand our relationship, even though I couldn't quite understand it myself. Nicky and I became tangled in Taylor's murder but also with the man in the alley. Cahill wasn't the only one who wanted answers about the dead man. In my retelling of events, I've come to suspect that Nicky hadn't been honest with me. Maybe if I combed through the specifics I might find my own answers.

The inquest for William Desmond Taylor was scheduled for ten o'clock in the morning and it was raining pitchforks. The room was packed with restless sinners before an angry God. Or was it just me?

I was sandwiched between Addy, whom I had dragged here on a Saturday against her will, and a reporter from the *LA Record* whose name I had forgotten. He was a nice enough gentleman cologned in cheap cigars, Rexall hair tonic, and bootleg whiskey. Since I had nothing to lose and everything to gain, I hadn't seriously considered skipping the inquest, as I was sure Nicky would have preferred. I would continue hunting down leads while Pop collected information from Detective King. Nicky, I would avoid like the plague. Simple enough strategy, execution being a bit tricky.

"Well, what the futz are we waiting for?" Addy asked, fidgeting in the pew.

We garnered a few of those *insolent youth* scowls that had been flying around rather freely these days. It was getting so bad I wondered if our generation was getting *everything* wrong. But we had as much right to be here today as any of these flat tires, maybe even more. I was working a story; they had come to gawk. Still, it was nothing to get in a lather about and I didn't want trouble or attention. I elbowed Addy and whispered,

"Shut your pie hole, will ya? You can't talk like that in here. You wanna get us tossed?"

Addy pulled a face. "Oh, these bug-eyed palookas don't know from nothin'." She started humming, *"In the meantime, in between time, ain't we got fun."*

I scanned the room for Nicky or Detective King but hadn't seen hide nor hair of them. Addy wasn't the only one bored; rows of spectators and reporters had grown restive. We had been waiting some thirty minutes or so. The coroner, Dr. Nance, stood aside talking with the Deputy Coroner, my old pal Doc MacDonald. First-officer-on-the-scene, Sergeant Ziegler, was there along with the entire Flying Squad, which had me curious. Hadn't the Flying Squad been pulled off the case when Detective King and Nicky came on board?

Facing us in a line of chairs down front were thirteen witnesses waiting for their chance to state-for-the-record everything they knew. Most of them I had seen or talked to on the morning the body was found but I jotted down their names while waiting for something to happen. Absent was Miss Normand. A side door opened and Detective King walked in followed by Nicky.

"Well, good gosh and golly," Addy murmured. "Get a load of him." She nodded at Nicky looking trim and spiffy in his dark blue uniform. "If he ain't the cat's meow."

"Prince Hassan," I grumbled.

"And how!"

"What? No, not like that. I mean he's... oh forget it."

Nicky and Detective King met up with Dr. Nance and Doc MacDonald. They chatted while waiting for things to begin. Every so often, Nicky gazed across the sea of spectators, and I scrunched in my seat to go unnoticed. I had no intention of getting the bum's rush before things got started. Every paper was represented by at least two newspapermen. I was sitting solo for *The Messenger*. As long as I remained inconspicuous I should make out fine.

The main door in the back of the room opened and closed, and then footsteps tapped along the tiled floor. Mr. Morgan's overcoat and cockeyed fedora were dripping wet. He deposited his hat and coat on the coat rack and then adjusted his fancy eastern tie while nodding pleasantly to colleagues. As he moved up the aisle, he shook an occasional hand and threw out a wave across the room. A real cake-eater, Mr. Morgan. He certainly had a way about him, comfortable being the center of attention. Probably his usual habitat.

An attractive woman in a pink cloche and smartly tailored pink skirt and matching jacket made room for him along the bench. Mr. Morgan hesitated, having somehow spotted me across the room.

"Morning, Miss March," he called, flashing that dazzling *Photoplay* smile.

"Oh, for crying out loud," I muttered, slouching further down. "Don't come over. Don't come over."

He came over.

Nicky watched Mr. Morgan walk directly to my row.

"Hells bells," I mumbled.

"So much for disappearing in the crowd," Addy said.

"Morning all!" Mr. Morgan greeted the line of people seated along our pew. He began wedging his way between the mortuary parishioners on his way to me. People twisted and turned to make room. "Sorry there," he called after smashing a foot. When he reached the gentleman next to me, he clapped him on the shoulder. "Do you mind, old sport?" He jerked his chin toward a narrow slice of real estate along the side wall where a few reporters were allowed to stand. The nice gentleman from the *LA Record* glanced at me and then smiled knowingly at Mr. Morgan. He gathered his umbrella and notepad and squeezed out of the pew to stand along the wall.

"Miss March," Mr. Morgan said as he made himself comfortable. His knee and shoulder pressed against mine. "Lovely day for an inquest."

Addy leaned around me and beamed at him. "'Lo there, Mr. Morgan. Remember me from the Kettle?" She was wide-awake and bushy-tailed now.

128

"Oh, but you have me at a disadvantage... Miss?" Mr. Morgan threw on a devilish grin.

"This is Addy Wells, best friend," I muttered, trying to let light in between us. He was sitting so very close.

Mr. Morgan slid an arm across the back of the bench and leaned over me to shake Addy's hand. "Pleasure, Miss Wells, Best Friend."

I gave Mr. Morgan a sideways look. He was too close for polite company and he knew it. Giving me a cockeyed grin, he lowered his voice.

"Hello beautiful," he said.

"Smile's crooked," I said.

"Crooked smile, straight talker," he quoted without missing a beat.

"Who said... you just made that up," I charged, and he laughed and relaxed against the bench.

"Almost had you with that one."

I gave him a smile that said, 'oh, but you'll never have me'.

Dr. Nance called for attention, and all eyes shifted forward. Things were finally getting started. Nicky and Detective King had taken seats along a bench that faced the crowd. Nicky stared straight ahead with a soldier's expressionless gaze. You wouldn't know he was facing a sea of curious onlookers. Detective King, on the other hand, fidgeted with his ciggy and stared down the line of witnesses like he'd rather be anywhere but here.

Dr. Nance called the first witness. Curiously enough it was Mr. Eyton, almost the last person to arrive on the scene that morning.

Directed by Dr. Nance, Charles Eyton stated his name for the record followed by his address and occupation as being the General Manager of Famous Players-Lasky Corporation.

"Mr. Eyton," Dr. Nance continued. "Have you seen the remains of the deceased in the adjoining room?"

"Yes, sir."

"Do you recognize them as one you knew in life?"

"Yes, sir."

"Who was it?"

"William Desmond Taylor."

Mr. Eyton confirmed much of what I already knew. Mr. Taylor was born in Ireland, forty-five years of age, was married, and had died at 404-B Alvarado Court, Los Angeles. He detailed the timing of Mr. Taylor's assistant's call, about eight o'clock Thursday morning, to inform him of Taylor's death. There were questions about Taylor having a small revolver in his upstairs bedroom drawer, the caliber which did not match the murder weapon. Dr. Nance failed to ask Mr. Eyton what *he* had removed from Mr. Taylor's bedroom that morning. The one question I was looking to answer. But he did ask Mr. Eyton what Faith MacLean had heard the evening before. The sound of an auto backfire or possibly a gunshot, around eight o'clock or thereafter.

This may have been my first inquest but the line of questioning didn't add up. I whispered to Mr. Morgan. "Why would the coroner ask Mr. Eyton what Mrs. MacLean had said? Shouldn't he ask Mrs. MacLean herself? Second-hand accounts are hearsay. Why not get it directly from the horse's mouth?"

Mr. Morgan returned his arm to the back of the bench and whispered, "That's very astute of you, Miss March. I suspect the coroner is trying to establish some consistency in the story. But I agree with you, he's got the witness and should wait to get the MacLean woman's statement directly."

A few heads turned and gave us the quiet down frown. Mr. Morgan withdrew his arm and put a finger to his lips. We grinned like naughty school children.

Mr. Eyton went on to describe how he rolled the body over and found a pool of blood and the bullet wound. To answer Dr. Nance's question he said, "Yes, the body was stone cold and very stiff and rigid."

Mr. Taylor had been dead many hours and he was wearing the same clothing that Mr. Eyton had seen him wearing the day before. No one doubted that the murder happened the previous night, before the deceased had a chance to change into his bedclothes.

According to Mr. Eyton there had been no sign that Mr. Taylor, or his home, had been tossed.

No one said it outright but burglary didn't seem likely.

Mr. Eyton verified those at the scene the following morning including neighbors and Sergeant Ziegler. No mention of a girl in the phone closet. Mr. Eyton was excused.

After being duly sworn in, the autopsy surgeon, Dr. Wagner, relayed his post-mortem findings. Entry was on the left side, six inches below the left armpit. The bullet, a .38 caliber, traveled slightly upward and passed inward through the space of the seventh rib, straight in and out of the left lobes of the lungs, across the right collarbone, settling just below the skin in the neck. All remaining organs were disease free. Cause of death, gunshot.

Those in the crowd unaccustomed to grisly autopsy details stirred in their seats. Reporters kept their heads down, scribbling details. My pal, Doc MacDonald, had shared the basics with me but I fleshed things out a bit. Which had me wondering if the killer might be left handed, considering how the bullet entered so far left of the spine. Or maybe the killer was right handed and Mr. Taylor had turned just before being shot. Perhaps Mr. Taylor heard the killer behind him and simply moved. Rather than risk being identified, the killer had fired quickly. That might explain the holes in the clothing not matching up.

When Mabel Normand's name was called, heads swiveled around in question. She was absent from the row of witnesses up front. Oddly enough, Miss Normand appeared through the side door, escorted by none other than District Attorney Woolwine himself. There was no other reason for this beyond plain old favoritism. Miss Normand was famous. She deserved special treatment.

It rubbed me the wrong way, an elected official kowtowing to the rich and famous. The rash of whispers in the crowd said I wasn't the only one. Regardless, Miss Normand's account remained the same as I'd heard it—she had arrived around seven o'clock and left around seven forty-five on the evening of the murder. Henry Peavey had left somewhere in that timeframe. When Mr. Taylor walked Miss Normand to her car, there'd been no one outside the court but her driver who was cleaning peanut shells from the car. Mr. Taylor promised to call later that evening but never did.

Next came Henry Peavey. Soon into the questioning Henry became distraught, sobbing and hooting loudly. After wiping up with a silk hankie, he eventually talked about the timing of the evening, of Mr. Taylor's impeccable attire, and his partiality for a tidy home. He discussed jewelry, bank checks, and an identification stamp for Mr. Taylor's bank checks, which were found at the scene. All the windows in the bungalow had been locked and so forth. The back door had been locked as well, the key left in the lock. Henry left through the front door, confirming Miss Normand's account. No new information for me, and no mention of Henry's personal troubles in the park.

Sergeant Ziegler took his turn and accurately recounted what I had witnessed while hiding in the phone closet. He had questioned the neighbors about hearing a gunshot the night before. Only Faith MacLean, her husband, and their maid claimed to have heard something sounding like a gunshot or auto backfire between eight and eight-fifteen that night. Mrs. MacLean told me it might've been a little later. The Mister and Missus hadn't agreed on the timing.

Sergeant Ziegler reconstructed the vague description of the man leaving Mr. Taylor's bungalow about the time Mrs. Mac-Lean had looked out her front door—a man dressed in bulky clothing reaching in and closing Mr. Taylor's front door. The man then walked through the buildings, exiting toward Maryland Street.

Dr. Nance asked about finding the gun in Mr. Taylor's upstairs room. The sergeant confirmed that it did not match the murder weapon, which he believed to have been a .38 caliber, although he had not seen the bullet himself.

And then Dr. Nance abruptly announced, "That's all the evidence we'll take in this case. All but the jury will be excused."

The room erupted in confused chatter.

"What just happened?" Addy asked, yawning.

I checked my wristwatch. "Only forty-five minutes!"

Mr. Morgan and I looked at each other, dumbfounded. The remaining witnesses seemed just as mystified. They should've been called to testify, particularly Faith MacLean, the only eyewitness of the murderer.

The entire crowd slowly got to its feet. I clutched Mr. Morgan's arm as a thought struck me. "If Mrs. MacLean didn't testify—"

"Her eyewitness description of the murderer leaving Taylor's home can't be officially verified," he finished, seemingly amused. I was alarmed. This wasn't passing the smell test in my book. I stood on tiptoes and searched the mayhem for Detective King and Nicky. King's face was blistering red. He was viciously mining through his pockets for a fresh ciggy. Nicky was talking quietly to him with a stoic demeanor that made him impossible to read.

"Looks like it's letting up," Mr. Morgan said, drawing my attention toward the back doors. They had been flung open and reporters were rushing into the grey haze no doubt anxious to get their next pieces into print. Exactly what I should be doing.

"Headed to the office?" Mr. Morgan asked. "I could drop you." His offer was friendly enough but I had noticed Rico pushing his thin frame between the fleeing throng. He was dripping wet from the rain and hiding something beneath his coat. While Addy happily accepted Mr. Morgan's offer, Rico found his way to me.

"What are you doing here?" I asked.

Rico pulled out a hidden newspaper. "Your pop thought you'd want to see this."

"What is it?" Mr. Morgan asked, peering over my shoulder as Addy and I stared at the front page of the *Examiner*. In a large black-and-white display was a crude drawing of a butterfly with an M traced along its wings and a handwritten love note below. I groaned while Addy read aloud.

"Dearest-
I love you—I love you—I love you—
X X X X X X X X X
XO
Yours always!
Mary"

Addy let out a rude snort. "My, oh my, the secrets we keep."

The caption below stated where the love note had been found: the home of William Desmond Taylor.

"Mercy me. Isn't she something like... nineteen-years-old?" Mr. Morgan said. "And the old boy in his mid-forties?"

I sent Rico back to the office. Then I rolled the paper tightly in my fist and went in search of Mr. Eyton. Addy followed, and to my surprise, so did Mr. Morgan.

"Well, kids, what shall we do now?" He seemed awfully cheerful considering we were at a murder inquest gone awry.

"You wanted to know what was removed from Mr. Taylor's bedroom?" I asked as we shouldered our way upstream. "Well, they have the answers." I pointed out Mr. Eyton, and the Woman in Blue, Mrs. Ivers, whom I'd recognized from Mr. Taylor's bungalow. They were trying to slip out a side door.

Mr. Morgan rushed ahead and caught them before they could escape. He asked Mr. Eyton about his escapades that fateful morning but the General Manager feigned innocence. Then his eyes fell on me.

"'Lo there." I smiled politely. "Remember me? From Mr. Taylor's home? The morning his body was discovered?"

Mr. Eyton whispered to Mrs. Ivers, no doubt explaining that I'd seen him at his worst—or best—that morning. She appraised me, and then whispered a response.

"Letters," Mr. Eyton said as though granted permission to speak. "We took letters, documents, anything that might prove inappropriate or embarrassing for Mr. Taylor, his friends, or colleagues. Nothing to do with his death, you see. I'm sure you understand. We informed the police."

I flipped open the *Examiner*. "Did you forget Mary's letter? Or did you leak this to the press on purpose?"

They studied the paper with appropriate shock. Okay, perhaps they hadn't leaked it. But someone had.

135

Mr. Eyton confirmed they had no knowledge of Mary's letter.

"Guess I'll have to ask Mary why her letter, among all of Mr. Taylor's papers, would be taking up space on the *Examiner's* front page," I said, practically accusing them of lying. I was being rude but Mary's little love note had thrown me. She had promised no surprises. If there were to be surprises, they should be constructive, in my paper, with my byline. Not that I would've printed something so tawdry as a love note to the deceased. That would only serve to humiliate Mary. It would offer no aid in finding the murderer. Journalism as yellow as a daisy.

Mrs. Ivers bristled. "Mary has nothing to say on the matter. You will leave her alone. She is in mourning. Have some decency."

"Of course, no one will disturb Miss Minter," Nicky said, coming up behind us. He shook Mr. Eyton's hand and then Mrs. Ivers's. "Sorry for your loss," he said. In one fail swoop, he had ended the conversation. The pair dashed off, thankful to escape.

Nicky tucked his hat under his arm and looked down at me. "A word, Miss March." It was not a request.

I crossed my arms over my chest. Addy shuffled her Mary Janes and Mr. Morgan extended a hand, introducing himself.

"Don't believe we've met, old boy. Montgomery Morgan here."

Nicky ignored him. Mr. Morgan's hand dropped to his side, and he leaned against me in that too-close-for-polite-company way.

"Shall we go to the office then?" he asked softly but not so low that Nicky couldn't hear. Mr. Morgan could have been inviting me back to a love nest the way he spoke.

"Miss March is being detained for questioning," Nicky said sharply.

"Says you," I said, remembering last night's conversation. "Everything's jake here, Officer Masino. Simply jake. So, if it's all the same to you, I have a column to get out." I walked away grinning from ear to ear. Had Nicky really thought I'd give up that easily? Just because he'd ordered me to? Naw, Nicky Masino knew me better than that.

CHAPTER 10

"Tell me you weren't surprised by the sudden end to the inquest," I challenged Detective Cahill. "You were there. With the Flying Squad. You saw the abrupt way Dr. Nance stopped the questioning."

Detective Cahill ignored me and perused his notes.

"You say that inquest was on the up and up, and I'll say go chase yourself," I pushed.

"We're not talking about the inquest. We're talking about you. How we got you on a murder charge. Mind telling me why that doesn't concern you, Miss March?"

"Who said it doesn't concern me? Believe me, I'm getting to all that but I have to unload the more important stuff first."

"More important?" he asked incredulously. "You'd better pray the Lunacy Laws work in your favor, Miss March, because your mind is gone."

I grinned.

"Being flippant is not helping you and I'm not interested in your thoughts on the inquest," he said. "Tell me—"

"How I found out about the mystery suspect?" I said, widening my smile. "Yes, I was just coming to that."

"You mean the man in the alley?" he asked, trying to clarify. I waved him to hush and then cleared my throat to continue—

Addy's mama, being of the old-fashioned type who refused to take up the odd job now and then, was in the habit of hiring her out for extra dough. Addy liked to complain but was having a ball most of the time, not to mention skimming off the top for herself. So, that was how it came about that Addy and I parted ways after the inquest, her mama had arranged for her to work a few hours at the Palace Theater on South Broadway, the heart of the theater district. Between vaudeville acts, the Palace showed movies. Addy was hired as the organist for the afternoon movie crowd, and her little brother, Ricky, was hired as the page-turner.

I returned to the office and whipped up a new column. It explained what was *not* stated-for-the-record at the inquest of William Desmond Taylor. Mrs. Hazeldine, being a copy editor, had fallen in love with a crafty new invention, one of those artistic red colored pencils. I could see her across the office playing surgeon to my piece, slicing through clever phrases and cutting out colorful descriptions. I couldn't bear to watch my hard work bleed so I picked up the *Hearst* paper. According to their reports, police had gathered *evidence* from Mr. Taylor's home in the form of a lady's undergarment with the initials MMM.

Hmm, I wonder who those could belong to. And, just how could a lady's undergarment be evidence in a murder?

I had moved on to the *Los Angeles Times* when Pop walked through the door, followed by my elusive brother, Eugene.

Eugene wore workman's overalls decorated with lovely motor oil spots and patched holes. Two wrenches clanged in his back pocket, and a red rag dangled from his front pocket. A Bakers Boy hat covered most of his disheveled auburn hair. Smeared grease across his smooth chin made up for his lack of facial hair. Eugene tipped back a bottle and downed the last drop of phosphate cola. He flopped into the chair across from my desk and belched.

"Hey, sis, what's doin' with the dead guy?"

"What, no explanation for your whereabouts for nearly a week? Just business as usual?" I gave him a perturbed look.

"So, who d'ya think dunnit?" He snatched the rag from his pocket and cleaned grease from his fingers.

"Not sure. Mr. Taylor doesn't seem to have any enemies."

Eugene snorted. "Enemies are like lousy haircuts. Sooner or later everybody gets one." He grinned like in the old days when we would break the wishbone from Sunday night's chicken dinner and he got the good end. "I'll tell ya what I know. Those movie folks, they're a ruthless bunch. There's more double dealing and backdoor bargaining than down at the tracks in Tijuana."

Pop looked up at the mention of gambling across the border, a point of contention between the two. Eugene hunched over the desk, lowering his voice. "Down in Long Beach, south of the Pike, there's these caves where bootleg is hid when ships unload after dark. The other night, me and the boys was camping on the beach and watching empty boats head out to the ships and come back *loaded for bear*. Come morning, we sneaked into the caves to see what's doin'. There were crates stacked four high and five deep."

"Swell, Eugene. You just discovered how bootleg gets across the border? Why do you think the twelve-mile line out at sea is patrolled by the coastguard?"

"I know, I know, but listen. I'm not talking toilet tea from down South. It's Canadian whiskey. The good stuff. And it's traveled a helluva long way. These shipments were *allowed* through. I'm telling ya. And, who do you think unloaded the goods? Uniformed police officers swinging by while on duty."

"But that can't be—"

"And these crates had names scrawled on the sides, you know, specific destinations. They aren't just hitting the streets or random blind pigs. They already had homes."

"Names like what?"

"Like Paramount and Metro. One said, 'Wilshire district'. I'm telling ya, they're orders already filled, and the cops are playing the delivery boy shuffle."

Bootleg ordered for the studios wasn't so surprising but cops in on the assembly line rubbed me the wrong way. "Yes, well, that's just another can of worms," I said pensively. "What's it got to do with the Taylor murder?"

"Aw, that's just the cake, here's the icing. See, there's this sheba I know—can't give her name—but we were killing some pints at a local when she started yapping like she was somebody. Turns out she works for Mac Sennett, you know, the one who started the Keystone Comedies? The one who was engaged to Mabel Normand once upon a time?"

It was bad enough that my younger brother had gotten into a speakeasy before I had, but he had better not be wasting my time.

"Everyone knows who Mac Sennett is, Eugene."

"But do you remember around the time they were engaged, when the hospital reported that Miss Normand was injured on the set?"

"Vaguely."

"Well, this sheba gave me the inside dope on that. Turns out Miss Normand wasn't injured on the set. She walked in on Mr. Sennett playing sheik-of-the-sheets with some betty. The women went at each other. Miss Normand was hit on the head and staggered to a friend's house who took her to the hospital. The studio made up a lie to explain how she'd come to have an ostrich egg on her forehead. The hospital docs turned a blind eye." He shrugged. "Anyway, this sheba who works for Sennett does filing and whatnot. She says the movie folk have a lot of influence like that; they watch out for each other. Everybody is dirty so you can't rat on anyone without ratting on yourself, see?"

I nodded. I'd witnessed the parade of movie folk removing potentially embarrassing material from Mr. Taylor's apartment. Miss Normand had been escorted to the inquest by the district attorney himself. And Mr. Eyton and Mrs. Ivers were thick as thieves, ordering me to stay away from Mary.

"And they get plenty dirty, let me tell you," Eugene went on. "Why, the parties this sheba has gone to. Huzza! The booze. The fornication. The drugs. All that depravity we hear about. Saturday night sinners and Sunday morning repenters. But she says it never fails that some dolly leaves a clip-joint boiled as an owl and introduces her motorcar to a light pole. Or, say she's a hophead and strolls into traffic. She gets a new set of bracelets and a ride in the paddy wagon. Next day, she's back at work, nothing doin'." He sat back, satisfied with his offerings.

I blinked. "Did I miss something?"

"Hey, you're the investigating reporter now, you tell me."

"Are you talking about someone in particular? An actress got arrested and no one knows? I hardly think that's possible with the way the newspapermen hound—"

"Oh, it's not only possible, it happens all the time."

"And how does this help me?"

"Don't know if it does but how do you think it plays out? This sheba who works in Sennett's office says that when a particular call is put through to the back office, she's instructed to take a certain amount of cash from the office safe and put it in an envelope. She leaves it for a man in a dark suit. This man leaves with the envelope and returns with Miss Can't Hold Her Liquor. Life goes on like this at all the studios."

"Out on bail."

"Nope. No arraignment. Charges dropped."

"You're telling me the movie moguls are not only paying off the police, they have a prearranged system?"

"You said it, not me."

My mind was spinning with a hundred possibilities. Did that explain how the muckety- mucks arrived at Mr. Taylor's bungalow before the police? And why Mr. Eyton took charge over Sergeant Ziegler? He was a civilian and yet he was allowed to examine the body.

If Eugene was right, then somebody with the authority to remove arrest warrants, erase records, and control the process from start to finish was on the take. The studios had deep pockets; the payoffs were making a couple of somebodies awfully rich. I wondered if Nicky or Detective King were aware of this, or possibly in line with their hands out. And would they admit as much to me?

Did that account for Nicky's involvement on a murder case? Was he on the take and ordered to keep an eye on Detective King, who was not? Had this anything to do with Nicky's fight with Angelo the other night? And what about the abrupt inquest that left witnesses off the record? Just how long was the assembly line of corruption?

It was after one o'clock and Pop hadn't taken a break all

143

day. "Listen, Eugene, Pop looks tired, why not take him home? Make him eat a nice lunch and lie down for a bit. I've got some things to do."

"Naw." Eugene stood and stretched. "Pop brought me in to look at the printing machine. Belching Bertha's too slow or something's jamming her real good."

"Is that how it is? You're not around until Pop hunts you down for help?" I wondered if he'd been caught gambling down south again. Besides, I caused Pop plenty of worry myself and it irked me that Eugene should, too. Especially when he seemed so casual about it.

"I've been around for three days which is more than I can say for you," Eugene quipped. "Trudy Mae says you haven't had a decent meal since that guy got plugged."

I shrugged. "Trudy Mae has always been overly attentive to my eating habits."

Eugene lowered his voice. "And everybody knows you've been sneaking out at night."

I glanced at Pop. "What do you mean everybody?"

"No, not Pop. It's enough that we let him work hard all day, he doesn't get the pleasure of knowing what his offspring are really up to. You know how the servants on the Hill gossip. Some housemaid from the Bradbury mansion saw you climbing out the window the other day. Not for the first time, I'm guessing. Trudy Mae won't worry Pop about it but she tells me in case I'm needed to haul you out of a ditch somewhere."

"Now, that *is* interesting," I said, coming to a new thought.

"What, finding you in a ditch?"

"No, gossiping servants. And not just those working on the Hill."

"Yeah, so what's it mean to you?"

"Let me take care of that. You've got a date with Belching Bertha."

I riffled through my notes regarding Christina Jewett's statement. As Mrs. MacLean's cook, Christina had not only heard the gunshot that fateful night but claimed to have heard someone walking between the houses approximately thirty minutes prior to the shot. She had described the sound as men's shoes crunching on gravel as though someone had been pacing. Perhaps waiting for someone, or something, to happen? After the gunshot, the pacing had stopped.

Not forgotten was that nasty pile of gold-tipped ciggys Addy and I had seen near Mr. Taylor's back door. If I connected those dots, they might lead to someone pacing and smoking and waiting. Someone nervous? Someone preparing to murder Mr. Taylor once he was alone?

I combed over Henry Peavey's statement. No one had asked him about the dead pile of ciggys or the sound of pacing shoes between the houses. A trip to Henry's was in order.

It was late in the evening when Addy and I exited the house by way of my bedroom window. I had planned ahead and dressed us in black from head to toe in hopes of avoiding the gossip grapevine. We had made an appearance at the dinner table with Pop and Eugene, and then excused ourselves for some good old-fashioned study time upstairs. Pop was still sore that I had intruded on the interview with Mabel Normand. It put him in an awkward position with Detective King, but not so awkward as to withhold my column from the front page.

"It's a fine line you're walking here, Kate," Pop had said sternly. "There's plenty reporting being done on this murder by newspapers across the country but there's only one with my daughter involved. If the killer is getting nervous—"

"He's probably high-tailed it out of town," I had argued. Pop hadn't necessarily agreed but it gave him something to think about. Would the killer hang around after committing such a highly publicized crime?

With Pop worrying about my involvement, I elected not to ask permission to track down Henry Peavey at this late hour. Why burden someone with the task of rejecting a sensational idea?

Addy and I reached Angel's Flight but the train cars were done for the night so we began the slow process of walking down the long precarious stairway adjacent to the Flight. It was dimly lit and we were wise to watch our step. Addy had been babbling on about some boring new picture show playing at the Palace.

"German!" she snarled. "Can you believe the bloody thing was in German?"

"That so?" I was mildly shocked myself. Sure, The War had ended nearly five years ago but featuring a German film in the heart of Los Angeles showed quite a bit of hutzpah. "What's it called?"

"Oh..." she shook her head, thinking. "Dr. Mus, Dr. Mab. Oh, yeah, Dr. Mabuse the Gambler."

"Any good?"

"How the hell should I know? It was in German, for chrissake!" she scoffed. "It's about some doctor of psychology who's a master of disguise. He goes out gambling—in disguise of course—and hypnotizes the other players so he can win at cards. The big cheat." She scrunched her face. We reached the sidewalk on Hill Street and headed for Broadway where Pop's truck was parked outside the office. Pop rarely drove the truck home, preferring to ride Angel's Flight so he could stop and say howdy to folks on the walk home.

It was a chilly night and Pop hadn't used the truck all day; the engine would be cold. Addy walked around to the front and waited for me to climb in. I found the key in the off position and then hollered the go-ahead. Addy pulled the primer knob and gave the crank a half turn, priming the engine.

"'S okay," she hollered. I set the brake to neutral and turned the key to the on position and hollered back. Addy cranked another half turn and the engine sputtered to life.

"Where're we meeting Henry Peavey?" she asked, hopping in beside me.

"Henry's not exactly expecting us. We're stopping by his place. I'm playing this off-the-cuff."

I navigated easily through town, encountering little traffic at this late hour. We arrived at 127 East Third Street in no time at all. The front of the apartment house was a checkerboard of light and dark windows. Most folks were in bed for the night. We found Henry's apartment number on the mail box in the foyer and trooped up to the second-floor landing. After copious amounts of banging it became evident that Henry was not home, but the noise had roused Henry's neighbor across the hall. An elderly woman in a headscarf and a long nightgown thrust her head out the door and ordered us to stop the racket or she would call the police. I explained our urgent need to see Henry Peavey. She squinted a suspicious eye and gave us the once-over.

"Might know where he be, if I's made to feel generous," she said rubbing her fingers together.

"Thank you," I said and quickly dropped two bits into her hand before Addy could spout the insult on the tip of her tongue and ruin our only chance for help. Addy never understood that information wasn't free.

The old woman explained that Henry had gone plum crazy for dancing lately. Sometimes, he danced all night on the weekends and she would meet him coming in on her way going out to Sunday morning services. At least, she hoped it was dancing that kept him out until the wee hours. Beyond that she didn't care to know.

"Mostly, he be talking about some joint called The Night Owl," she said. "Cain't rightly say he's there at this moment but could be." She pulled a face like she was smelling something bad and moaned. "Yup. Could be."

I had never heard of The Night Owl but had a good idea where to find it. If Henry loved to dance, then downtown along Central Avenue, better known as the Avenue, was a cinch. Some folks called the stretch between eighth and twentieth streets the Negro Belt or Brick Block. I was familiar with the area due to Pop being friends with Charlotte Bass, a real nice lady who owned and operated the *California Eagle Newspaper*, one of the few black-owned newspapers in town. Mrs. Bass called the Avenue 'the Black Belt of the City'. It was considered middle class and quite respectable with black-owned businesses, churches, banks, pharmacies, and whatnot. During the day, all was jake along the Avenue, but nighttime offered an assortment of dancehalls and clubs hosting jazz players who had come from the Deep South in great migratory waves. One afternoon I'd given Rico a ride to the Avenue. He'd had a calling to learn jazz music and Jelly Roll Morton was teaching kids to play New Orleans style swing. Rico's calling faded, however, when he got wind that Morton was associated with a side business—trafficking prostitutes for the Pacific Coast Line.

Addy and I chugged along Central Avenue, crossing Forty-First street where the *California Eagle* had an office on the corner. A few blocks later we heard the low thumping of music but couldn't find the source. Addy stuck her head out the window and listened.

"Right there, I think. There's a sign on the door." She turned around. "Yeah, we just passed it. But, Kate..." her voice faded and she stared at me. Addy had never been on Central Avenue before. White folks didn't often frequent Black nightclubs. Addy was justifiably concerned. Would we be welcomed?

The sidewalk was lined with tin lizzies, farm trucks, and a few depot hacks. Working folks were out for some whoopee. I wheeled to an open space, killed the engine, and turned to Addy. She was bug-eyed scared and I didn't blame her. This wasn't exactly what I had in mind when I said let's jaunt over and ask Henry a few harmless questions.

"Look-it, we'll just take a squint inside. If he's not there, we'll leave," I said.

"I should hope so!" Addy clambered down from the truck and slammed the door. "This had better be worth it, Kate."

"You ain't talkin' hooey," I mumbled, wondering if Nicky hadn't been right. Should I be investigating this case? It was a murder, after all. What if the killer was lurking around the Avenue, planning to knock off Henry Peavey next? What if the killer heard I was poking into his business, asking too many questions?

I was having serious doubts, but Addy was already at the door. She may have been petrified but she was also a curious little thing.

"Now, if we were Moderns," Addy said, turning an ear to catch the low thumping beat seeping through the door. "We'd sashay in like we owned the joint, right?" She looked at me with a face full of encouragement.

"You're asking me?" I blinked.

We considered ourselves for a few moments, no doubt coming to the same conclusion. Neither of us had the equipment or pizazz to fool anyone. But that didn't mean we weren't prepared to try. A sign on the door read, *No Alcohol!* in big angry letters.

This wasn't a typical juice joint. It was right on Central Avenue, not hidden down some dark alleyway where we'd be forced to give the wrong password and get thumped for our troubles.

Addy took a deep breath and slowly pulled the door open. Blaring music walloped us in the face. Dixieland jazz! We grinned like a couple of fools.

The Night Owl was all smoke and sound. Airborne sweat layered with musky cologne and tangy perfume engulfed us as we squeezed inside and quickly closed the door. My eyes adjusted to the dim light and brought dark figures into focus. They huddled at white clothed tables in suites and ties, shimmering flapper dresses with beads, and sparkling tiaras. It was a classy joint. I threw a glance around. We were fish out of water, the only white folks in the place.

We moved further inside and pressed against the back wall. The dance floor, surrounded by tables on three sides, was a wild mass of bodies bobbing and contorting from a concoction of the Charleston, the Blackbottom, and something in between. Stage lights illuminated the band that was pumping out raw Dixieland jazz. The accompanying sign read, *Kid Ory's Creole Jazz Band*. Far to the right was a bar where barkeeps in white jackets and black bowties served phosphates and coffee. A second *No Alcohol!* sign dangled from a hook behind the bar, mostly to appease any coppers poking their noses inside. Just for show. Customers were adding their own kick of juice from hidden flasks at their tables.

By now we were garnering attention. Men gave us the once-over while women threw aggressive looks that stuck like insults. I was feeling about as comfortable as a frog in boiling water. Addy, on the other hand, started tapping her feet. Pretty soon she was smiling and clapping and singing along with the band.

"Hot feet! Fire in the middle! Hot feet! Fine as a fiddle!"

She was infectious and I leaned over laughing. Nothing like swell music to chase away your fears. If Addy could do it then so could I. It was a matter of relaxing as though I had stuffed all my cares in my back pocket. I nodded to the rhythm and tapped my feet. Jeezers, but I loved music and this was the bee's knees. If we hadn't been working, I wouldn't mind exercising my Animal Dances. It's been an age since our last school dance.

"You okay?" I shouted to Addy over the music.

She nodded emphatically and hollered back, "Do you see him?"

I searched for Henry and came up empty. It was too dark and smoky to see clearly. I waylaid a young kid in a white collared shirt and black bowtie. His sleeves were rolled up and he was carrying an empty tray.

"Hey, we're looking for Henry Peavey!" I shouted. "You know him?"

The kid's jaw dropped, and his big dark eyes shifted back and forth between me and Addy.

Addy yelled, "Okay, yeah, we're white! Don't crack your eggs over it! Do ya know Henry Peavey or not?"

"Yessum, I know, Henry. He's here." The kid searched the crowd and pointed him out. Henry was dancing up a storm in his glad rags—a bright orange shirt and striped green trousers. Don't know how I could've missed him in that get-up. He was gyrating and flopping like his arms had come loose. Some wild distorted blend of the Turkey Trot and the Grizzle Bear. The kid said Henry came here a lot and often danced till closing. If we wanted to talk to him, we'd best drag him from the dance floor.

Addy and I elected to wait it out. Nearly twenty minutes went by but Henry kept on dancing. Sometimes he danced with himself on the crowded floor. After a while, I realized Addy had been playing a tennis match with some fellas at a table in the corner. Back and forth she glanced, throwing out her best smile. Three gentlemen in suites and ties were smiling back. It was hard to say but they could've been laughing at us. Addy waved and the suit in the middle beckoned us over by way of lifting a flask.

I elbowed Addy to cut it out. "What are you doing?"

"He's got hooch," she said about the man grinning around a fat cigar clenched between his big white teeth. "As long as we're here... might as well enjoy ourselves. Just act like a Modern."

Addy sashayed over with her hips rocking like a boat. I followed in her wake.

"Howdy, y'all," she said loudly. The men stood and the cigar man gestured to the two empty chairs. We sat down and everyone settled back into their seats. After an awkward pause, the big man with the cigar tipped a flask into a tall glass of orange juice, filling it to the brim. He stirred it twice with a long knife and then slid it across the table to Addy.

"Try this, ladies," he said with a wide friendly smile. Addy sipped, coughed softly, and then handed it to me with a challenging look that said, 'Moderns never turn down a drink'.

Sure, why not. I can toss back a quick swallow same as anyone. I gulped two mouthfuls right off the top. Fire hit the back of my throat and shot up my nose. The back of my eyeballs stung and I coughed until I got the hiccups. The men broke up laughing. One of them slapped me on the back so hard I fell forward.

"Attagirl!" he said, barking with laughter.

I rubbed my burning eyes. "Holy smokes! I could use that to start my auto!" I said. Addy kicked me under the table. The men had a good laugh at my expense and then the guy with the cigar introduced himself as Wallace Ory. Folks called him

Boon. The others were Edgar and Rix. They were nattily turned out in spiffy suits with bright fashionable ties.

"That's my own brew," Boon said. "You like it." It wasn't a question but a certainty. I had to admit that, after the initial fire bolt shot through my system, I felt pleasantly warmed.

"You know Henry Peavey?" I asked over the music. Addy risked another sip of Boon's concoction and then slid the drink back to me.

"Not really." Boon leaned forward so I could better hear him. "I seen him around. Thinks he's some big shit now that his famous boss got plugged. The Pride of Central Avenue. Tells the story over and over." He shook his head and stuffed the cigar between his choppers. Edgar and Rix had lost their attention to a couple of ladies at the next table. After a polite nod to us, they left and pulled the women onto the dance floor.

I took another sip. It went down considerably easier than the first one so I took another.

"Y'all got guts coming in here," Boon said. "There's some clubs 'round here for white folks digging on the jazz but this ain't one of them."

"Guts or lack of common sense?" I asked, smiling politely. "You must think we're off our nut, huh?" He grinned. "Well, I gotta talk to Henry so..." I looked back at the dance floor which hadn't thinned in the least.

"Might be a while," Boon said. "The joint's hopping tonight on account of the music. That's my cousin up there, Kidd Ory and his band. They's top drawer. Recorded the first black jazz record on the West Coast. Just last year. Y'all can get your hands on a copy at Spikes Brother music shop down the block. Yeah, if some two-bit band was playing, the folks would get restless and lit out, but the Kidd's got it. You get me?"

No argument from us, the Kidd was hitting on all six cylinders. The waiter circled around our table, laying out more glasses and pouring them half full of orange juice. Boon topped them off with his concoction. We sat back and enjoyed. I drank slowly, letting the gradual warmth spread to all parts. Addy and I were feeling mighty fine. She and Boon struck up a conversation about the migration of jazz music while I shifted on the hard, wooden chair and kept a loose eye on the dance floor should Henry opt for a break.

Time was flying by and then the main door opened and I did a double take. Mr. Morgan strolled in looking as cool as an icebox. I thumped Addy and nodded in his direction. Mr. Morgan headed straight for the bar. Addy, who'd grown increasingly goofy for him since the inquest, hiccupped and squealed with delight as though he was a puppy come to play with us. Mr. Morgan had other ideas.

She was slender and stylish, a flapper in a blood-red dress, a sparkling headband with a twelve-inch white plume, and bronzed satin for skin. Sliding gracefully from the barstool, the woman moved seductively up to Mr. Morgan who greeted her with open arms. They kissed on both cheeks and then Mr. Morgan whispered in her ear. The woman swatted him playfully, making them both laugh. He whispered again and her pleasant smile turned serious. She crunched her thinly arched eyebrows, and then, with some obvious frustration, pointed toward the dance floor. I followed their line of sight.

"Oh, no you don't!" I said, jumping up far too quickly. Something unnatural rolled through my brain and I swayed.

"What?" Addy blurted unladylike over the music.

I clutched the back of her chair to steady myself. The epiphany arrived too late, as sometimes happens with epiphanies. I had meant only to enjoy a sip or two of Boon's bathtub gin to calm my nerves and fit in with the crowd. Presently, I felt as though I had jumped in fully clothed.

"Mr. Morgan's... here for... I'm not... letting him steal Henry out from unner us," I slurred and then grabbed Addy's arm, urging her to stand. She must be the pillar to my crumbling tower. Addy didn't budge. She was ossified, her eyes rolling around like two lost buoys. "Aw futz. Juss stay here," I mumbled and staggered through the blur of tables and patrons. I was more than a little disgusted with myself. I had tried so hard to embody a hard-nose reporter's fortitude and here I was, blotto on the job. How could I possibly extract pertinent information from Henry when I had just swallowed my tongue?

I stopped at the edge of the dance floor, my stomach rolling in syncopated rhythm with the room. I caught sight of Henry and stifled any urges to vomit. Henry, in his bright orange shirt and green trousers, was flapping his arms and strutting across the floor like a wild bird. I couldn't help but laugh. Had a Mad Rooster been added to the list of Animal Dances?

"Hey, Henry!" I shouted when I had caught my breath. I waved and waved. "Henry! Henry Peavey! Over here!"

Henry jerked to a stop and stared. A light slowly dawned in his face, and he threw his hands in the air, hollering,

"Oh, my heavens! Miss March? Is that you? What on earth is you doing here?"

I clutched his forearms and drew him from the crowd. He would do nicely as my pillar. I leaned heavily against him and shouted in his ear. "We need to talk! About Mr. Taylor!"

"Oh no! Not until we finish this dance! C'mon on, girl!" He pulled me onto the floor. Henry flapped and bounced and made me do the same. We went awkwardly into the Grizzly Bear, me with my chin balancing on his shoulder and his on mine with our arms out wide. We seesawed around the floor as much as the tight crowd would allow. Thoughts of upchucking returned.

I was zozzled and making a fool of myself. It was for the story. Anything for the story. The last thing I'd expected on my secret jaunt this evening was to be demonstrating an Animal Dance with Henry Peavey at the Night Owl. But I jigged and jammed, hopped and flapped, gyrated and slapped my knees. We did the Charleston, the Turkey Trot, the Maxixe, the Black Bottom, and made a sad attempt at the Boston. The floor was too tight for the Castle Walk which was just as well. Never much cared for it myself. Truth be told I was having a ball. There are few things in life that gave such unadulterated, carefree pleasure as dancing. I felt uninhibited and unencumbered by the prejudices I'd been feeling since throwing my hat into the reporter's ring.

Through the haze of contorting figures, I glimpsed Addy along the edge of the dance floor. She was laughing her fool head off. Henry was an insatiable hoofer and I was a real Oliver Twist, only by comparison to some of the heelers around me. When I'd had enough, I tried to pull Henry away but some fella half under slammed into me from behind. I dominoed into Henry, knocking him into someone else. The crowd closed in, jostling us around. The music had become primitive, a complex polyrhythmic beat that sent my internal metronome spinning. There was no solid measure to hang your hat on. They fooled around with the rhythm, changing on a whim, and then there were the drums—so many drums. A choir of drums. My old music teacher often said that the gods spoke through drums. If that was true, I'm fairly certain they were yelling.

The more skilled dancers flowed with the changes, stomping, flapping, and gyrating. The tight confines and blasting barbaric composition created a juggernaut. I was feeling lost in the sudden upswing in tempo when a sharp elbow slammed into my side and nearly separated my ribs. I spun around ready to confront the guilty party. It was a spiffy sheba snarling at me, her face glossy with sweat. She rushed at me and I had no choice but to shove her into the nearest dancer.

She whirled and attacked as a wild cat, claws out and black eyes flashing. The night became a blur of fists and elbows after that: shoving and smacking, and pounding outside as well as inside my head. The dancers had become hostile, taking vengeance upon anyone who bumped into them. Miss Wild Cat pummeled me, pulling my hair and scratching my face. I was horrified by my own behavior but when one is in the throes of a cat fight, one can hardly remain subdued. I gave as good as I got.

Henry was screaming like a girl, and then suddenly Addy was there. She smacked Miss Wild Cat as though tamping out a flame. Slap! Slap! Slap! Slap! Miss Wild Cat rounded on Addy but her elbow caught me squarely across the right eye. I flew backwards, my head exploding with pain. Tiny pinpricks flashed against the back of my eyelids. I doubled over and covered my face, howling beneath the violence around me. And then two arms wrap around my waist and lift me off the floor. I flopped like ragdoll, cupping my aching eyeball.

The back door was kicked open, and I was suddenly outside in the cool night air. Dumped roughly onto my feet, I was spun around to face my rescuer.

"Aw, don't," I groaned, grabbing my head as my brain slowly came front and center.

"You all right?" Mr. Morgan's voice registered a pleasant sort of panic. He brushed hair from my face and lifted my chin. I gently peeled back my eyelids. Mr. Morgan frowned at the bump I could already feel taking shape around my right eye.

"That woman packs a wallop," I slurred and then winced as I fingered the rising bruise. The heat and fight seemed to have stimulated the raw alcohol swimming in my bloodstream. I was ten times the drunkard I'd been half an hour ago.

Addy and Henry were leaning against the building, panting and groaning. Addy's eyes were at half-mast and her head was swaying like a street car. She was grinning from ear to ear.

"Our firsssh-peakeasy rumble!" she slurred proudly.

"Technically speaking," Mr. Morgan corrected. "This isn't a speakeasy. But your enthusiasm is commendable. Next thing I know I shall find you naughty young things smoking in public." He smiled affectionately. Addy giggled. I didn't give a whoop-tee-do.

Henry, who'd been inspecting his clothes, gave an outrageous wail. "Aw! My shirt! Brand-spanking new! And they gwahn and ripped it!"

Then, the back door burst open and a young man was flung into the alley by two burly dockworker types. The men turned in the doorway and tossed out another troublemaker.

"Let's get you out of here, shall we?" Mr. Morgan took my arm and then quickly snatched Addy as she began to meander rudderless in the wrong direction. We careened down a side alley, heading toward the Avenue.

"Henry!" I hollered sloppily over my shoulder. "'S okay you come with us. We're giving ya a ride home." My brain may have been unmoored but I had not forgotten my purpose here. After all the fuss I'd gone to, I figured Henry owed me.

When we reached the sidewalk, Mr. Morgan propped me against Pop's truck and gave me the once-over. "Unfortunately, Miss Kate, you don't look fit for driving. May I ensure you ladies safely home?"

"Ah, ah, ah." I wagged my finger at him. "You're not schwiping Henry out from unner my nose." I tried to click my tongue reproachfully but it just laid there.

"Ah, so that's the reason I find you here," he said, grinning.

"Henry'll drive," I said, to which Henry shook his head.

"Why, I cain't drive, Miss. I don't know how."

"And there you have it," said Mr. Morgan cheerfully. "Rest assured I wouldn't think of stealing Henry." He opened the truck door in a grand gesture. "I shall feel privileged for your company."

"So, you drive while I queshon Henry? Zat it?" I blinked hard as Mr. Morgan's image had multiplied into a crowd under the lamplight. I felt terribly sleepy all of a sudden.

"Yes, I drive while you queshon Henry," Mr. Morgan confirmed. "I don't mind if you don't."

My main concern, aside from the whirling dervish in my head, my stinging eyeball, and Addy's general health, was talking to Henry. The last thing I needed was Mr. Morgan's next column mirroring mine.

"But you're the enemy," I whined. Mr. Morgan bristled, genuinely startled by my choice of words.

"Aw, you gwahn and done it, now," Addy said, giggling. She'd been fiddling with Henry's torn collar and he'd been slapping her hands away to do it himself.

Somehow, hearing Addy mimic his speech so fluently got Henry's funny bone going. He mimicked her mimicking him, slurring and swaying, and then he laughed and slapped his knee.

"Why, Miss Kate," Mr. Morgan said, affronted. "Surely, you don't think of *me* as the enemy."

I had no doubt Mr. Morgan was being facetious. Embalmed or not, I knew up from down. His sad, puppy dog expression slowly morphed into a devilish grin that I imagined opened many a bedroom door. I didn't trust Mr. Morgan any further than I could throw him.

Addy groaned and doubled over, contemplating giving back

all she had imbibed. She tried to spread her feet with her hands to avoid upchucking on her Mary Janes. Watching her sway precariously from side to side and then puke onto the street was not something I enjoyed. My expectations for this evening hit rock bottom.

I had no idea what or how much we had consumed, how bad the effects would get, how late it was, or in what general direction I lived. Driving around in search of a giant hill in the dead of night seemed an awful bore.

"Well..." I said blinking slowly. "I suppose you're not the enemy so mush as a tassy driver right now." I punctuated this sentiment with a lovely hiccup. "But no stealin' my quote... es... es. 'S okay?"

"'S okay." Mr. Morgan chuckled and helped me into the truck. "I do know how you love good quote... es... es."

Mr. Morgan drove Pop's truck while I tried to get comfortable between him and Henry. We had mopped up Addy's face, which she was hanging out the window like a bloodhound. Her long brown hair had come loose and became ears flapping in the wind. She was gulping fresh air and staying quiet which was a general benefit at the moment. Despite my insistence on questioning Henry, I was having a devil of a time concentrating. Mr. Morgan must have taken pity on me; he kindly prompted me to focus on what had brought me out this evening. Henry hemmed and hawed about being interviewed again, claiming he'd already told the police everything.

"But you didn't tell them 'bout the incident in the park," I said. Henry dropped his head into his hands and moaned that I should know his private business. "Henry, I don't care 'bout that. I just need to know if the, uh, other gentleman in queshon was someone powerful. Someone who'd wanna hurt Misser Taylor for knowing 'bout it?"

Henry wiped his nose on his new shirt and sat back. "Aw, no. Nothing like that. It weren't nobody. A fellow my age—I mean, it weren't nobody." He fiddled with his sleeve, embarrassed. "I was, uh, relieving myself on some bushes." He looked sideways at me. "Well, anyhow, there was this cop smoking nearby and, well, he took me in on a morals charge." He fidgeted like he was trying to crawl out of his own skin. "I don't wanna talk 'bout it no more."

I patted his knee, feeling sorry for Henry, and a little disappointment. That curious angle had come to a dead end. "Henry, you know Christina Jewett? The neighbor's maid? Yeah? Well, she said she heard shoes crunching on gravel between the houses the night before the murder. You hear any?"

"I don't recall hearing any."

"Well, what 'bout that pile of gold-tipped ciggys outside Taylor's back door. You dump the ash can there?"

"I ain't never!" Henry said, offended. "'Sides, Mr. Taylor don't smoke no gold-tipped ciggys."

Mr. Morgan gave me a look that said he was also connecting the dots with the person pacing and the pile of ciggys. I hoped I wasn't stocking his next column with my ammo. There was little to be done about it due to our close proximity and my need to question Henry.

"The morning Misser Taylor was found, I asked if you knew who'd wanna kill him. Remember?"

"I dunno," Henry grumbled. "I've been asked so many questions by ever-body. The police. Them reporters. I cain't say."

"You said you couldn't think of anyone. That's what you told me." The truck hit a rut and I grunted, my brain sloshing around a bit. "You lied, didn't ya?"

"Why, I don't never lie!" he wailed, highly aggrieved. "I mean, I cain't say who dunnit. I wasn't there."

"But, if you had to guess," Mr. Morgan spoke up. "Who comes to mind first?"

I gave him a pipe-down look and then winced. My forehead hurt too much to frown. The skin around my eye was tight and sensitive. I couldn't imagine what color it might be.

Henry sighed. "Well, I'd have to say Miss Normand."

Mr. Morgan grunted with mild curiosity. "Why Mabel?"

Henry yelled, "turn left here!" and we all slid against each other as Mr. Morgan wheeled around the corner.

"Well," Henry said, smacking his lips. "She curses something awful. Bet y'all didn't know that. Miss Normand looks like a proper lady and all, but she curses. Some words I ain't never heard before. And, she was cursing that night, before I left. They argued a bit and—"

"Whoa! What?" I snapped alert.

"Who argued?" Mr. Morgan jumped in.

"Miss Normand and Mr. Taylor," Henry said. "They was arguing the night he was murdered. Don't know 'bout what, exactly. I was coming and going."

"Why didn't ya say this before?" I demanded. "You should've said something at the inquest!"

"Ain't nobody ask me at the inquest!" Henry wailed. "Them two argued a lot. 'Sides, they don't figure her for the killing."

"Who do they figure?" Mr. Morgan asked.

"They's after Edward Sands."

"The entire city knows the police are looking for Edward Sands," Mr. Morgan said.

I slumped in my seat, disillusioned. Mr. Morgan wasn't wrong. Every newspaper had been running the story of Edward Sands as the main suspect. My gut said it was a dead end, and I had no intention of jumping on that bandwagon only to contradict myself in a later column. This night was turning out to be a dry run, in a matter of speaking.

"But *I* knows *why* they's looking for him," Henry said, smugly.

"Because he stole stuff from Misser Taylor," I grumbled through a yawn. "That was ages ago."

"Nothing was stolen from Taylor the night he was killed," Mr. Morgan stated. "Sands is a thief first. If he came back months later to kill his old boss—which is highly unlikely—he'd surely have taken Taylor's jewels and money. No thief could've resisted that diamond ring on his finger."

"Nope. That ain't it. It's cause of Jimmy Valentine. Y'all know 'bout Jimmy Valentine?"

Mr. Morgan and I looked at each other. My eyes were doing the tango trying to stay focused, and he was frowning. Addy, I could hear snoring against the door. As we headed toward Henry's apartment house, he kindly unraveled a mystery new to us all.

Sometime last year, after Taylor was robbed, a letter arrived at the bungalow. Taylor read it and became enraged. When he left, Henry took a squint at it. The letter was something of an apology for the inconvenience of the forced sale of assets, a cheery Christmas greeting, and then signed off by Jimmy Valentine. Two pawn tickets for the stolen articles were inside the envelope.

"What does that prove?" Mr. Morgan asked. "Sands obviously didn't want to reveal his real name. If it was Sands."

"Oh, it was Sands," Henry said, his eyes growing bigger. "Y'all know what the kicker is? That envelope weren't addressed to no William Desmond Taylor but William Dean Tanner. Them pawn tickets was made out to one, William Dean Tanner!"

The sophisticated gentleman born in Ireland and educated in England wasn't exactly who he claimed to be. Only a few reasons I could think of for a fella to change his name. He was ashamed of it or he was hiding from those who knew him.

"A secret marriage and a secret name," I said, contemplating what it all meant.

"The police want Sands for more than suspicion of murder," Mr. Morgan concluded. "They want information on Taylor's secret life."

Henry pointed out his apartment house, and the truck slowed and came to a stop near the front walkway, idling in the street.

We woke Addy and she fumbled with the door handle, letting Henry out. He stepped onto the sidewalk and thanked us for the ride. Mr. Morgan wheeled the truck around as a forgotten question resurfaced in my soggy brain.

"Wait!" I yelled. Mr. Morgan hit the brake. I crawled over his lap and stuck my head out the window.

"Henry! One more queshon!" I yelled.

Somehow, I had remembered reports that Mr. Taylor had been talking to his tax accountant, Mrs. Berger, on the phone before Miss Normand knocked on the door that evening. I wanted to know if there had been any trouble or arguing.

"With Mrs. Berger?" Henry called doubtfully. "Why, no ma'am. That was earlier."

"Earlier?"

"That afternoon," Henry said, walking backwards toward the apartment house door. "Mr. Taylor, he was arguing with someone on the telly-phone. Don't know who."

Another interesting tidbit. I wiggled around to gauge Mr. Morgan's reaction. His eyes were glued to my backside and he was sporting a surprised but pleased expression.

"One thing I do know, Miss March!" Henry called out. "And that be who Mr. Taylor was talking 'bout. Angry as blazes, too."

I may have been in unsuitable proximity to Mr. Morgan but some things had to be weighed for importance. Namely, the reputation of my bottom against the betterment of my story.

I ignored Mr. Morgan and thrust my head back through the window to holler down the block. "Who was Misser Taylor arguing 'bout, Henry?"

He reached the top step and turned dramatically as though in a musical theater production.

"Why, it was Mary Miles Minter!"

CHAPTER 11

Detective Cahill leaned back in his chair, staring pensively at me. I could almost hear the wheels in his mind churning with questions about Jimmy Valentine. Or perhaps he wanted to chastise me for the uncouth way I had chased information.

"Yes," he began, "I know about Jimmy Valentine and the discovery of Mr. Taylor's real name. People change their names all the time. Especially when they enter the movie industry."

"Or, try to hide from a wife and daughter they abandoned?" I said. He nodded.

"Possibly, but... if you're thinking this is a revenge killing... no one in their right mind thinks Mrs. Tanner or the daughter had anything to do with killing Mr. Taylor. If that's what you're leading up to."

I tilted my head, pondering things. "But it is a curious angle, isn't it?"

"No," he barked dismissively.

"I mean the motive. See, I've been having a time of it, finding the true motive and all."

"Not interested," he said briskly, sitting forward and tapping his open notepad. "I'm only interested in the man in the alley. Now are you saying that he was Edward Sands? Or Jimmy Valentine?"

"What? No, of course not," I said, sighing and rolling my eyes. "I'm not talking about the man in the alley."

"Well, you're supposed to be," Detective Cahill snapped irritably.

"Aren't you the least bit interested in why Mr. Taylor was arguing about Mary on the day he was murdered?"

He glared at me and then looked away. I grinned. Try as he might, Cahill couldn't resist. He was a detective involved in a sensational murder story that had stalled. It must be driving him mad. Especially when he was stuck in here with me and not out investigating. Maybe he had finally realized I was the goldmine he'd been searching for.

"Now, where was I?" I said lightly, relaxing back in my chair. "Oh, yes, the motive..."

How I managed to make it home after the Night Owl fiasco and wake fully clothed in my own bed was a mystery. Addy woke beside me, smacking her lips and complaining about a horrible aftertaste that rivaled her mama's liver pie. We both shared tremendous headaches. Trudy Mae had roused us at the unconscionable hour of seven o'clock because Addy's mama had phoned, demanding her daughter be sent home at once. Somehow, Trudy Mae had had the foresight to bring in a tray laden with two glasses of water and two packets of headache powder prepared in advance. I was too grateful to question her shrewd, knowing look and I had no intention of hearing the sordid details of our late return, of which, thankfully, I drew a blank. But I did wonder where Pop's truck had ended up.

After crawling from bed and bidding Addy farewell, I went into the dining room with a juicy raw steak in hand. Pop came down for breakfast and found me draped over the table. I had the steak on my swollen eye and was attempting to write my column with my head resting on a napkin. Sitting erect had been awfully painful.

"Trudy Mae tells me you were assaulted on a dance floor and not in a dark alley somewhere," Pop said, sternly. "I suppose that's preferable, but, Kate, this sneaking out has *got* to stop. It's simply not safe for a young woman your age to go out alone at night."

"I'm hardly ever alone," I said, looking at Pop's sideways image. "Addy is usually with me."

"That's nearly the same thing in my book. And besides, it's just not necessary, and—"

"Would you tell Eugene the same, if it were him?" I sat up and plopped the steak onto my plate.

"Now, be fair, Kate. I only want you to be safe."

"I think it *is* necessary, Pop. This story has helped the paper. You can't deny that copy has been selling like hotcakes since Taylor was murdered." I felt a twinge of guilt. It wasn't as though the rest of the staff hadn't been working hard on their stories, especially Pop with his pieces on President Harding.

"I want my daughter to be safe," Pop repeated forcefully. We stared for a long thoughtful moment.

"I'm sorry, Pop. I do understand. Really. I promise not to take any unnecessary risks. Okay?"

Later at the office, I phoned Mrs. Hazeldine at home and asked her to stop by after church services to perform the necessary autopsy on my column. I had relied too heavily on my sketchy memory as I had only a few notes jotted down. As she went to work, I sat back drinking a phosphate soda and combing through the local papers.

"Hmm, interesting," I murmured after scanning their lead stories. Nice thing about having an inside source was ringing her up when the occasion called.

I snatched the phone and clicked for Irene, the operator. "Hello! Hello! Irene? Yes, it's me, Kate. I'd like to... just fine, thank you. I'd like... he's fine, too. We're all fine. Now, Irene, I need Miss Minter's house on Hobart Street. The number is... oh, you know it? Yes, I know I've been calling there frequently, but... well, she is a good friend and... yes, thank you. I'll wait."

I chewed my thumbnail while the maid took her sweet time answering. I asked for Mary and waited again.

"Why, hello, Kate." Mary's voice was sweet and unassuming and made my temperature soar.

"Mary! What's all this about? This hooey in the *Times* and the *Record*!"

Mary launched a diatribe about the papers reporting on Tom Dixon, an old flame of hers. The papers reported that she and Mr. Dixon had once been engaged. They claimed he was a man of suspicion in the Taylor murder. The police were looking for him. Mary was furious about being dragged into this mess.

Thirty minutes of rambling and I felt sorry for Mary. After all, she couldn't help what the papers printed about her. She had no privacy and no control over her own reputation.

"But Mary, what about that 'I love you' butterfly letter in the *Examiner* the other day?"

Mary squealed with sudden delight. "Oh, wasn't it wonderful that Mr. Taylor kept my letter?"

I groaned and dropped my head onto the desk. "Well, what about that pink nightgown with the initials MMM the papers are hollering about?" This was supposedly among the items the police had confiscated from Mr. Taylor's apartment. I'd had my doubts. It seemed unlikely Mr. Taylor's friends would have left something so scandalous behind to taint his reputation.

"Well, my goodness, you know mother buys all those personal items for me. And her putting my initials on a pink nighty! Heavens! What will she say when she hears about that?"

Mary must have suspected Irene was listening on the line. Mary didn't give a fig what her mother might think.

Flipping open my notepad, I dared to translate my own scrawl. "Tell me, Mary, what reason would Mr. Taylor have to be arguing about you on the afternoon he was murdered?"

There was a long pause before her voice finally came on the line, soft and innocent.

"Why, Kate, I don't know what you mean. Mr. Taylor wouldn't have any reason to argue about me. On any day. At any time. Ever."

If she had only said she hadn't known. Once. I might have bought it.

"Mary," I ventured carefully. "Just when did you last see Mr. Taylor?"

Another long pause. "Oh, months ago. Around Christmas. Don't you remember? I told you we had seen each other in our autos on the street. Mama was with me and we just waved as we passed by."

"And, when were you at his home last?"

"Kate, why are you asking me these questions? Didn't I tell you everything already?"

"Did you?"

"Now don't be silly, Kate. This nonsense about finding my unmentionables at Mr. Taylor's, and the police looking for Mr. Dixon... why, it's just fluff to sell papers. You told me yourself that newspapermen will invent whatever they want—"

"Some, Mary. I said *some* will. It's called yellow journalism, but I hardly think—"

"Yes! That's it! I knew it was a color! All this yellow-belly talk. Not a bit of it's true or important to the murder. Why, Mr. Dixon wouldn't hurt a fly!"

"Okay, Mary," I sighed rubbing my temples. She was giving my headache a headache.

"It's my turn, Kate," Mary said sternly. "What can you tell me about the goings-on with the police? I heard they were combing the streets for any manner of criminal from drug pushers to strange men in the park."

"And, just how would you have heard that? Nothing about men in the park has been mentioned in the papers so far."

"Oh, j-just talk. Gossip down at the studios. You know how it is. Now stop asking questions. It's my turn."

"Well, besides your Tom Dixon, I heard they were actively looking for Edward Sands," I said flatly.

"Yes, Mr. Taylor's old chauffeur. Have they found him?"

"Not yet. Now, Mary, think one last time. Could there be any reason Mr. Taylor might exchange words about you *with anyone* on the afternoon of?"

"Ohhh!" Mary growled into the phone. "I've already told you, Kate. Now, I'm due at a costume fitting so I've just got to run. You'll let me know if anything important pops up, yes? Good! Cheerio!"

I slowly hung up the receiver, thinking. I hadn't believed the connection between Mary and the nightgown left at Mr. Taylor's when I first heard the story so I pushed that nonsense aside. But Mary had lied just now regarding Mr. Taylor arguing about her. The fact that she would lie so forcefully revealed plenty. Eugene hit it on the nose when he said movie folk stick together. Mary was hiding something. She must know with whom and why Mr. Taylor had argued about her, but why hide it? For whose benefit? Was it for Mr. Taylor's reputation or her own?

* * *

Trudy Mae was standing over my bed in her starched white apron with her hands on her broad hips. I cracked open my good eye and squinted. The sun was up, indicating I had slept through Mrs. Hildreth's crowing rooster, which was fine by me. So, what in blazes was Trudy Mae going on about so early on Monday morning?

"You heard me. Rise and shine, Missy," she repeated. "You's going to school today."

I grunted and rolled into my pillow. "For the love of God, I've been suspended, remember?"

She tutted and pulled back the covers. "We got a call this morning. Your suspension's been lifted on account of the apology you're gonna write to that teacher."

"What! Who called?"

"Don't rightly know. Principal Housh or his secretary, I suppose. Your pop picked up the line before he left for work."

"But that's impossible. I've been suspended. Why would they do such an asinine thing as commute my sentence?" I sat up and kicked back the rest of the covers. "Who has the power to influence Principal Housh? Pop wouldn't interfere, would he?" Trudy Mae made a noncommittal noise and collected soiled clothes strewn around the floor. "No, he'd never intrude like that. He might complain now and again but never go so far as to lighten a well-earned sentencing." I climbed from bed and opened the wardrobe with deep consternation. I stared vacantly into the abyss as my mind ran over a few unsavory choices. It had to be Nicky. Aside from Addy, who would never cross such a dangerous line with me, there was no one so determined to have me back in school as Nicky Masino. But how on God's green earth could he have any influence at Los Angeles High School?

Playing judge and jury, and finding Nicky resoundingly guilty, I refocused on the needs at hand, suitable clothing. Trudy Mae had swept out the door with most of my outfits since I'd been too lazy to bring them down to the washroom myself. As I trained my attention on my wardrobe I noticed my clothing options had expanded greatly since yesterday. I smiled and parted the hangers, revealing several new blouses. I had selected these the day before the murder at Mr. Bullock's department story on Seventh and Broadway and had forgotten all about them. They must have arrived yesterday while I was out.

I sorted through soft blues, dark blues, peaches, pinks, and creams. There was a fashionable middy blouse with short sleeves and a Peter Pan collar. Another middy pullover with buttons down the front, a pointed collar, and long sleeves. Another with geometric shapes that were so in vogue these days. A few peasant blouses and a lovely sheer, pale blue blouse made from *crepe-de-chine*. It was far too delicate for the rough and tumble schoolrooms. I eventually selected the deep blue middy pullover that was typically paired with a skirt for a true separate ensemble. Instead of the skirt, I opted for my smooth tailored trousers, which highly aggrieved the faculty at Los Angeles High, and my patent leather Mary Janes. Satisfied with the look in the mirror, black eye notwithstanding, I whipped my hair into a braid and then dutifully occupied my desk, and penned an award-worthy apology. Then, I collected all relevant school books and departed for my incarceration.

Addy was elated, not only about my new fashionable blouse but about my commuted sentence. Dearest Addy, hell bent on keeping me on the winter graduation schedule, which, to my surprise, was only two weeks away! My, how time flew when you rarely attended school. You missed things like preparations for your impending graduation.

I had dutifully served Mr. Grime my apology letter which he dropped unread onto his desk. He wouldn't look me in the eye so I repeated how sorry I was for my rude behavior. He was only slightly appeased. After offering the class my apologies as well, I spent the remainder of the morning dodging questions about my eye. Addy and I refused to explain the circumstances under which I'd gotten my face made over. Speculation was high. Zackery Ziegler, the boy I'd given a black eye only last year to stop his roaming hands, was especially annoying. He yammered on about how I must've earned a beating from sticking my nose where it didn't belong. A real wind-sucker if you asked me.

When history class ended, Addy and I trooped outside for lunch. She tossed away her mama's tuna fish sandwich and opted for whatever the vendor wagon offered. Since I had come empty handed, we bought a couple of those new folded tacos called burritos and then joined the gang at a table under the pepper trees. The six board officers of the Star and Crescent Society, our preeminent school club, were discussing the approaching donkey baseball fundraiser. It was serious business for a great cause. Directed by the school administration board, the goal was to earn money to build a memorial for our local boys lost in the Great War.

Addy and I weren't officers in the club but diligent members. She was over the moon about the memorial but I found the subject painful. Never a meeting went by without someone recalling their own personal loss. It cut fresh wounds that I wanted to heal. Besides, I had something else on my mind. More than just selling papers, I wanted someone to pay for what they had done to Mr. Taylor.

No matter how many indiscretions Mr. Taylor might have committed, getting shot in the back was such a cold and heartless way to die. A coward's killing, plain and simple. I wanted someone to pay. No one had paid for what had happened to my brothers. No one had been held responsible, in my eyes, for destroying our family. Nothing had been fair from start to finish.

I wanted something that resembled fairness in the mad world I lived in. But this story was a riddle I couldn't solve. An itch I couldn't scratch. What must it be like for Special Investigator Detective King, someone trained to do this for a living? I had been at it for less than a week and I was nearly ready to check into the local sanitarium.

"How could a *man*... with no *enemies*... get shot in the *back*... in his own *home*?" I pondered aloud while staring at the burrito in my hands as though it was stuffed with the answers.

"What'd she say?" asked Dewey Deets, president for the boys' side of the Society. A swell guy but a little young for a stuffed shirt, if you asked me. Certainly not someone you would stumble over at a speakeasy. He was set on law school or politics, or some combination thereof. Dewey wore his hair parted smartly down the middle and his bowtie tucked importantly beneath his chin.

I looked up to find everyone staring. "Sorry," I said, shrugging.

"I should say so!" said Leigh Hastings, secretary for the girls' side of the Society. "That is hardly suitable conversation for the lunch table." Leigh's blonde curls were so tightly wound I often wondered if they accounted for her narrow-mindedness.

"Aw, go chase yourself," Addy said before biting into her burrito.

"He can't," Dewey answered.

"What?" I asked.

"To answer your question, I say, he can't. A man with no enemies can't get shot in the back in his own home. It's not plausible."

"But he was," Addy insisted, staring down the picnic table. "That's not in question. He was shot, and Kate, here, was the one who discovered it!" She beamed at me and then took another bite.

"We're talking about that director fellow you're writing about?" Dewey asked. "I sometimes read your paper when I'm not perusing my father's law journals. But I tell you he couldn't have been a man without enemies." A few of the board members nodded thoughtfully because they generally agreed with anything Dewey said.

"The problem is simple," said Abner Felts. As the vice president, he used a highfalutin tone to disguise his underlying insecurity for never measuring up to his father's expectations. Abner had light brown hair and cheeks as soft as a baby's bottom. He liked to be included in things but rarely had much to offer. "Everybody is over-thinking the situation. If you ask me, I'd say keep it simple. Uh, isn't that right, Connie?" We all looked over at Constance Bigelow, the girls' prosecuting attorney.

Connie was quiet and pensive but sharper than a Gillette safety razor. I had always respected her because she was happy to learn more from listening than talking. A virtue I strived for.

Connie set her book aside, tucked a stray brown hair behind her ear, and considered things while sipping her phosphate.

"Get the facts is all," she said flatly. "The when, the where, the how, and the why. When the first three are established, it'll be that fourth element that's key. The why. That'll lead you to it. Sure as I'm sitting here." She smiled politely and returned to her book. Her services were no longer needed.

Always so calm, that Connie. She hadn't been running herself ragged chasing the story as I had, and yet she laid things out as easily as making a bed. The why!

Of course! The why!

I'd been so consumed with the timing and the comings-and-goings of everyone who knew Mr. Taylor that I hadn't given the why enough consideration.

"Well, isn't that what I was saying," Dewey muttered sourly. "Get your facts and you'll get your man."

"I should say it wasn't burglary," Leigh threw in now that the topic had become suitable since Connie had participated. "I mean, Mr. Taylor wasn't robbed that night, right?"

"No, he wasn't," I confirmed.

"Somebody needed him out of the way," Abner mused.

"Has anyone in particular benefited from Mr. Taylor's death?" Dewey asked.

The whole table looked at me, every board officer plus Addy with a bean burrito protruding from her face. I opened my mouth and then shut it. I had no idea who might've benefited from Taylor's death.

The table conversation explored different motives: anger, betrayal, jealousy, revenge, greed. Everyone had differing opinions, all sound and reasonable. But it was Becky Wade, the girls' president, who made a fine point about jealousy.

"I mean, you never know who'll be jealous of what," she said. Her blue eyes flashed like she knew from experience. I remembered back when Becky had a sweetheart last summer.

For no good reason, this cuddle cutie had worked himself into a fearful state that someone might woo her away. He began following her every move and serenading outside her bedroom window. Every night. It got so bad the neighborhood dogs would howl and her folks had to call the police.

Tom Dixon came to mind. Perhaps he had been enamored with Mary and gotten himself jealous of Mr. Taylor. Jealous enough to kill? But that would mean Mary and Mr. Taylor had been seriously involved and others knew about it. No, I just couldn't believe it. Mary was so young and Mr. Taylor was Father Time. Even if Mary had been unreasonably aggressive towards him, I truly believed he was a gentleman, of sorts.

And by gentleman I meant a man with a questionable past and a bedroom full of suspicious material that needed to be confiscated by his friends. Hmm.

Lunch ended and classes resumed. I became anxious about the case, wondering what leads the smudge writers from the *Times* were tracking down while I was shackled to a school desk. I hardly remembered a single lecture the rest of the afternoon. My school day ended with a lovely knot of frustration taking root in my stomach.

The cool February day brightened our cheeks and made for a pleasant walk home. Addy and I had a light load of books but heavy minds. I was all about the news business and she was all about graduation. We turned onto Broadway which was busy with working stiffs out for their midday coffee breaks, folks rushing to do their business, and Moderns sashaying to a petting pantry to catch an afternoon movie. Local farmers hauled flats of luscious red strawberries in their truck beds that you could just smell over the motor oil clinging to the air.

"It's not your job to solve the murder," Addy said. She was fed up because my mind was elsewhere and she had failed to lure me into a conversation about graduation prep. "That's a job for the police. Remember, Kate, you're only a reporter. Maybe it's time to write whatever the police divvy out."

I stopped in my tracks, preparing a stump speech regarding the ineptitude and untrustworthiness of the LAPD. Never mind the suspected corruption. I had only just begun when I heard the distinct chopping sound of an Indian motorcycle.

These motorcycles, like the Harley-Davidsons which produced a similar sound, weren't like any other machines around. Both had been employed in The War and now cluttered the streets with clatter and chaos. They appeared far too dangerous for the common civilian which meant I was itching to take a spin on one. Officers of the LAPD motor division rode Indians or Harley-Davidsons. The officers had significant training whereas most civilians paid for their licensing and went on their way. They were inexperienced novices no better equipped than some auto drivers to handle the quick maneuvering in and around traffic, which seemed to be multiplying like Catholic rabbits. Accidents were far too common and sometimes deadly. I had seen a crack-up myself where the motorcycle driver flew through the air like a circus acrobat and then plopped to the ground. Deader than a dollar bill. It was awful, and the memory, like seeing Mr. Taylor's dead body, caused an internal shiver.

Addy and I watched the Indian draw closer. Low and behold, it was Nicky Masino in the saddle. Dressed in his blue uniform and hat, Nicky wore a pair of those glasses the flyboys had brought home from The War, Albex eyeglasses with the gold rims and dark lenses that shielded their eyes from the sun.

"Wonder why he's driving a motorcycle?" I asked. "Didn't know he was part of the motor division."

"He's not," Addy said. "He should be driving a patrol car." Then again, Officer Masino wasn't so much a desk jockey as a high-ranking officer without the rank. "When he's on duty he practically runs the place."

It was a puzzle to both of us.

Traffic on Broadway was always lousy with autos. Just now, they veered toward the sidewalks as a red cable car came barreling down the middle of the road. Nicky slowed the Indian and caught sight of Addy and me among the pedestrians. I had no proof he'd been instrumental in my reinstatement at school but when I shook my books at him, he flashed a wide smile.

"Bingo!" Addy said. "Case closed."

"Yeah," I said, glaring at him. "And now for his sentencing. A long walk off a short pier."

The traffic light changed and Nicky slowed to a stop. About that time, a flock of fashionable flappers spotted Nicky and put on a show, calling out and inviting him to some juice joint where a party was jumping. The nerve! Trying to lure a police officer to an illegal party! In the middle of the afternoon! Right on Broadway! It was outrageous, but I guess that was the point of being a flapper.

Despite their efforts Nicky failed to react. When the light changed, he tipped his hat to Addy and me, and zipped around the corner. The flappers burst into chatter about the handsome young officer. Addy broke up laughing.

"What's got your funny bone?" I asked, continuing up the sidewalk.

"I dunno. I just like the way those girls didn't give a hoot that Nicky was a cop. And, he didn't give a hoot that they were Moderns trying to lure him into breaking the law. It all kinda works out, huh?"

The flappers went on their way, looking so carefree and happy. I couldn't remember what that felt like, and it prompted me to take a good hard look at myself. Here I was, rubbing the ache in my belly because I was an anxious mess trying to solve a murder to write copy that might save our paper. Was I taking life too seriously? I was only seventeen, for chrissake.

"Do you suppose I'm taking life too seriously?" I asked Addy. She shrugged.

"Sure, I do. But don't worry, I've got our futures all mapped out. We'll want to keep focused on where we're headed and all, because we'll go Modern, at some point. It's inevitable. Right now, we're just distracted on account of the paper and Taylor's murder. As soon as that's all buttoned up, we're not gonna care about anything. We're gonna be in it for the laughs and good times. First, we'll graduate, and then, well, as far as marriage goes, it's a prison sentence so none of that. Oh, we might take up with a Good Time Charlie now and again, you know, to make a woman out of us and all. But it'll be on *our* terms. And then later on, well, who knows?"

"What if I don't want to be Modern? I mean—"

"Oh, it's unavoidable. Aunt Alice says we're the new breed. She's not Modern, per se, only practical. It's gonna happen sooner than you think. Like I said, when the timing is right, the choice will rear its beautiful head and you'll have to decide. Will I follow the cookie-cutter life of my Victorian mother and grandmother? Or, will I be a Modern girl, rollicking down immoral paths on the bandwagon of live-free-today-for-tomorrow-we-may-die mantra? Or, will I hitch my wagon to the League of Women and dive into all that sordid business of politics?"

It certainly seemed to be the crossfire so many of us girls were caught in. If I paid close attention, I could see the battle lines right there on Seventh and Broadway. On one side of the street were the pillars of our feminine history, those Victorian mothers and staunch supporters of decorum and conformity.

Their sandwich board signs warned against the evils of an unsuspecting generation. Flesh-colored stockings, longhaired men, shorthaired women, and alcohol would be our downfall if we didn't hold fast to our moral righteousness and matrimonial obligations. But, I knew that every now and again, the middle generation had a bone to pick, too. Folks like Pop and Trudy Mae, for instance. They'd been let down by the effects of The War. They recognized that change was inevitable, even necessary, in this cruddy old broken-down world they were passing down to their offspring.

On the other side of the street *were* those offspring. Those anti-political, anti-rule, pleasure seekers vowing to live it up and burn life at both ends. Was that what lay ahead for Addy and me?

What about the League of Women with the suffragettes' ideals? They were as heroic as anything I'd ever seen the way they brandished their civic duties like weapons. It was those brave women who Addy and I would be thanking come Election Day when we had the right to step up and vote. All those dreamy promises of independence and equality were just as alluring to me as anything else.

Maybe Addy was right. Maybe we should keep dancing to our own drum until fate changed the tune. And then... who knew what we would get ourselves into.

Addy and I parted company at Angel's Flight. Her mama had pressed her into working at the precinct tonight for extra dough. As usual, Addy groaned and complained that her mama was breaking the Child Labor Laws but I knew Addy really didn't mind so much, not with all the nice young officers strolling around.

Pop and I had a nice quiet dinner together, the first in a long time. Eugene was out working on a pal's machine somewhere in Long Beach. I suspected he was really across the border betting on the bangtails down at the tracks. To my relief, but not surprise, Pop had not interfered with my school suspension. He had always respected my independence and encouraged me to handle things in my own way but there was no excuse for being rude. I could hardly disagree. Pop refused to confirm or deny that it had been Nicky's handiwork. After seeing Nicky's wide knowing grin this afternoon, I had little doubt.

"I'd bet my best hat that it *was* Nicky Masino, but how could he have any influence with my principal?"

Pop and I had drifted into the library where he took up his nightly routine of pipe, chair, and reading material. He filled his pipe as a pensive scowl creased his forehead. The pleasing aroma of spices and wood soon came tripping through the air. I had come to love that scent. It was my childhood and represented bygone days when the boys were home and we were a family. We would gather around Pop's leather chair as he read aloud from Dickinson or Emerson. Back before it all came apart.

I paced along the rug, thinking. Nostalgia was a bitter sweet tonic that could make my skin itch. I caught myself rubbing the ache in my belly and quickly stuffed my hands into my pockets.

"Nicky seems to have some unspoken authority," I mused. "With everyone. Even Angelo, which is strange. Don't you think it strange, Pop? I think even Detective King takes orders from him. I can't figure it."

Pop puffed his pipe and relaxed in the arms of his soft leather chair. "Lots of these young fellas have returned home with more worldly experience than nature should permit. War makes men out of boys. In a hurry. I suppose that kind of hardened familiarity is desirable in law enforcement."

183

"How so?"

"Oh, discipline, perhaps. Strong work ethic. Training to push a man to his limits. The drive and ability to get a job done, at any cost. Those are rare qualities these days. Too many young folks have turned wild and rambunctious."

"What about Lawrence and Edward? Do you suppose they received the same training as Nicky?"

Pop pursed his lips and frowned thoughtfully. "The basics, yes. But your brothers were foot soldiers in the army. I understand Nick was sent somewhere else. Both he and Angelo were selected for special assignments. Something to do with their Italian and French backgrounds. We haven't spoken about it specifically but that's what I gathered. You understand some men find it difficult to talk about The War."

Boy, did I.

The telephone rang just then and Pop turned to Whitman, leaving me to answer it.

"Kate! Kate! Is that you?" Addy yelled before I could say hello. I held the earpiece out and winced.

"Jeezers, Addy, you don't have to scream into the mouthpiece anymore. They fixed that problem ages ago."

"Oh, don't be a boob! Now listen up, will ya?" There was rustling noise and then she came on again, whispering loudly. "Kate, you gotta get down here. They just hauled in a guy on suspicion. It's all hushed up, see?"

"A guy! Who?"

"Some dewdropper named Red Kirby. They figure him for the Taylor murder!"

"Can you get me in?"

More rustling erupted and then Addy grunted. "Um, no. Apparently he's higher than Franklin's kite. Looks like they're taking him to special lockup. Sorry, Kate, I tried."

"Wait! Wait! Lemme think, will you?" I snatched the receiver and paced. One glance at Pop said he and Whitman were in deep. No doubt he would advise me to wait for an official statement from the DA tomorrow.

"Hey," Addy broke in. "I can't stay late tonight so this'd better be quick. I got that essay to work on and tomorrow night I'm back playing at the Palace." There was a crashing noise in the background and Addy yelped.

I stopped pacing at the mention of the Palace. A latent memory surfaced. Days ago, Addy had complained about a movie playing at the Palace. It was a German production about a doctor who went out in disguise to cheat at cards...

"I believe I have a way in," I said. "Just trust me and stay there as long you can. Watch for something big and that'll be me."

"Something brilliantly stupid and overtly scandalous I should hope."

"Nothing but."

"Oh goody! Be careful, Kate."

CHAPTER 12

"So, at that point, I had shifted my attention to the motive, thanks to my savvy classmates." I said to Detective Cahill who was reclined in his chair with his arms crossed and smoking a ciggy. He hadn't interrupted once in the past thirty minutes. I believe I finally had is full attention. He told me to go on, so I did...

By ten o'clock Monday evening I was strolling down Broadway dressed fashionably for Halloween in February: black trousers, black tunic blouse tied at the waist, and black kid boots. All I lacked was a cape and vampire teeth. I had Pop's fedora cocked at a wicked angle over my right eye in hopes of adding an air of mystery and authority. Rico strode beside me. He had the backstreet connections I had needed and was always eager to earn extra dough. Two bits got me an escort to a mobile speak-easy that changed locations as often as I changed socks. It was run by two brothers who had previously filled miners' lunch buckets with moonshine for a nickel each. When prohibition took effect, they went underground and called themselves the Bucket Boys. Booze and gambling topped the menu.

Rico's second cousin's fiancé's brother gave him the inside dope, and here we were standing outside a storefront off Broadway. It was a rundown nickelodeon not yet converted to a movie house as so many had been. Set back from the curb and inhabited by street kids and hopheads, it was long and narrow and noisy. Buster Keaton's film "The Saphead" was flickering on the back wall but nobody was watching. The kids were huddled in groups on the floor playing cutthroat marbles for pennies. An occasional squabble broke out.

Against the wall to my left was the black box I needed. Tall like a phone box, it was windowless and had a long black velvet curtain for privacy. Inside, you could pay a penny to see Edison's fifteen minute film of *Frankenstein* or, if you were in-the-know, you could slide back a wooden panel on the wall and step into a secret hallway.

I bid farewell to Rico and then stepped inside the black box, followed the directions, and then took a moment to allow my eyes to adjust to the darkness. At the end of the hallway loomed the door to the Bucket Boys' mobile speakeasy. I found in myself a certain fear that came from being completely alone in this venture. The courage I'd had when entering the Night Owl had come with Addy. I always felt a little braver with her at my side.

I knocked too hard and had to rub my knuckles.

"For chrissake, don't let this be another version of the Night Owl," I whispered over the nerves boiling up my throat. "My poor face can't take another beating."

I flinched as a rectangle window in the door snapped open and the top half of a face appeared. His bug eyes squinted, and then his mouth appeared in the opening.

"What'd ya have for breakfast?" asked the lower half of the face.

The eyes reappeared.

I cleared my throat and repeated Rico's instructions. "Blinky John."

Why anyone would have sour milk for breakfast was beyond me but who was I to argue. The window snapped shut, the bolt slid back, and the door opened.

I found courage in passing the test and put confidence on my face by way of a lazy smile. Mary wasn't the only one who could play act.

"Thanks. You're a doll," I told the burly gatekeeper as I strolled in like I owned the place. He grunted and bolted the door behind me.

It was not a large room but windowless with a low ceiling and acrid smoke hanging around like disoriented ghosts. Perhaps it had been a storage room in its previous life. If my directions were accurate, the back door across the room faced an alleyway for deliveries. It appeared to be nailed shut.

The Bucket Boys' latest location was not as flashy or rambunctious as the Night Owl and certainly lacked the dangerous vibe. A handful of musicians pumped out a lazy, sad attempt at ragtime. The few dancing couples were draped over each other like finalists in a marathon dance. A makeshift bar lining the far wall was crowded with patrons and served anything from Yak Yak Bourbon to Pumpkin Wine. As my first official speakeasy, it was far from the swanky bash I had always imagined. But it was exactly what the doctor ordered.

Three poker games were in action and, thanks to Rico, the table at the far right had a place for me. I strolled over, said,

"Hiya," and showed my wad of cash to prove I was good for it. I pulled out a chair and sat with my back to the alley door. Two gentlemen at the table were considerably old, probably crowding forty. The first wore a fine, single-button dinner jacket and appeared to have escaped a fancy occasion he hadn't cared for. The second sported a fashionable stripped suit with a cockeyed pocket square. Both men seemed far too wealthy for their current surroundings. And they were both sufficiently drunk. They smoked like a chimney and could barely see through the fog they'd created.

The third fella was only a few years my senior but had acquired a twitchy constitution. He wore a second-rate tweed suit that had seen better days and a plaid golf hat. I caught him staring. His eyes quickly shot around the table to gage any objections from the others. It wasn't so strange to find women in speakeasies but one sitting at a poker table could cause a stir. The two gentlemen booze hounds gave me slow, sly smiles. They took me for easy prey.

"Seven stud?" I asked the twitchy fella. He began to deal.

We played three hands which I promptly lost. It wouldn't do to exhibit the skills I had learned from Pop back when we played for matchsticks. The first hand went to one of the gentlemen drunkards I had mentally named Hooch One. Not to be confused with his sidekick, Hooch Two, who was nearly too tight to remain upright in his chair. Hooch One took the first game because he had an ace in the hole, literally.

"Say, this on the up and up?" I had asked after the showdown when we turned our hole cards face up. Hooch One had been sitting on a pair of aces with one faced up while I'd been tossing out puny bets on a pair of kings. The second and third hands went to Mister Twitchy. I had dealt one of those hands so I couldn't complain.

189

I checked my wristwatch, feeling a bit twitchy myself. I had timed things as best I could but hadn't counted on running low on dough this quickly. We were on the sixth hand, betting on the flop when the trouble began. The band was playing "Toot, Toot, Tootsie" when the first loud bang hit the alley door behind me. After a moment's pause the door burst apart, spraying wood everywhere. Chunks of splintered debris littered the floor around us. Then the secret door from which I had entered burst open. Cops poured in. The music had stopped and the screaming had started, mostly women on the dance floor startled into sobriety. It was utter chaos as blue uniforms with billy clubs took over the room. We were fish in a barrel. Most of the patrons, wailing and scattering, quickly found themselves thrown against the walls and cuffed. No one at our table had moved; the Hooch Hounds were too stupefied to react with any sort of surprise, and Mr. Twitchy was paralyzed with fear. I pulled my fedora lower over my eyes and waited.

One of the officers strolled to our table, thumping his club into his palm. "Well, well, who do you suppose we got here, Frank?" he asked his partner.

"It ain't Mathew, Mark, Luke and John. Now is it, boys?" Frank replied.

Mr. Twitchy tried to shove some lettuce into his pockets. His hands were trembling. The officer-not-Frank knocked my fedora off and bent the rim. It landed on the table, scattering our meager pile of dough.

"Hey!" I whirled on him. "What's doin' with—" I stopped and stared. The cop, a hefty fella with ruddy cheeks and peach fuzz clinging to his chin, squinted down at me. We knew each other. He'd been a schoolmate of Lawrence's. "Ronald Hicks, didn't know you were a cop."

"I'll be damned. Kate March. Didn't know you were a criminal."

"You mean all this?" I scoffed and waved a hand at the table. "Aw, Ronnie, you wouldn't have the guts to arrest me. After all, I'm just an innocent lamb led astray by these corrupt gentlemen." I smiled sweetly just about the time Hooch Two slid off his chair and crumpled to the floor. "So, how's your mama?"

"Swell. How's your pop."

"Can't complain."

"Aren't you still in school?"

"Occasionally."

"Uh-huh. Well, you've stepped in it this time." Ronald Hicks lifted me from the chair and slapped a pair of cuffs around my wrists.

The paddy wagon was full to the brim with late-night carousers, meaning it was slower than an ice truck in August. Mr. Ford had yet to perfect the power of the wagon's engine, and a few officers had to climb down and push us up the hill. One of the regulars in irons said it was typical. We eventually rolled up to the 77th Street precinct, and we weren't alone.

A horde of cops had gathered around the first paddy wagon to arrive. A second wagon had parked just ahead of us. By the looks of the passengers staggering out, more than a few speakeasies had been raided.

I gingerly climbed down and fell in line with my fellow sinners from the Bucket Boys. A loud commotion down the walk had the cops in a fluster to maintain control. The drunkards from the first paddy wagon vehemently protested their innocence. They were garish flappers and slick dandies decked out in brightly colored party hats and speckled with confetti. Most likely someone's birthday. Then again, it could be just another Monday night. Noisemakers blasted and horns tooted. Bawdy laughter punctuated their cries of innocence. Some made lurid accusations at the folks stumbling from the second paddy wagon who were just as boiled and flamboyantly turned out. There was a brief battle of tawdry remarks between the belligerents, and then several officers blasted their whistles, pushing through the crowd. They knocked the noisemakers to the ground, quieting the party by degrees.

"What's going on out here?"

It was the officer in charge shouting from the precinct steps. I recognized Angelo's voice and ducked behind a burly musician from the Bucket Boys.

"We hit a speakeasy," Officer Hicks announced, puffing out his chest. "Got a dozen on gambling, too."

Angelo took in the madness and shook his head. "We've already booked two wagons and have two more on the way. Never had so many hot tips in one night. I'll get the night officer and we'll start processing your group."

He returned a moment later with the night officer and a handful of rookies. We criminals were ordered to start the slow shuffle toward the doors. The rookies drifted alongside us in case someone got wise and tried to make a break for it. Not a chance I would take. Everything had worked perfectly. In a few moments, I would be sitting pretty in the same lockup as Red Kirby, the murder suspect in the Taylor case.

I relaxed in my cuffs. There was nothing more satisfying than a well-laid plan coming to fruition. If I hadn't been cuffed I'd have patted myself on the back. I was just going over my list of questions for the suspect when I was abruptly jerked to a stop by a hand on my shoulder. The fellas behind me bumped together like a clumsy chorus line.

"Miss March?"

I grimaced. What lousy luck!

Nicky pulled me from the line, sparking an uproar from the walking embalmed who thought I was receiving special treatment. Angelo blasted his whistle. The rookies thumped a few shoulders with their clubs and hollered threats involving loose kneecaps. The ruckus petered out. Meanwhile, I was marched back to the paddy wagon and out of earshot.

"Where do you think you're going?" Nicky demanded. Officer Hicks, who had been as equally curious as my fellow sinners, had followed us.

"She's being arrested for gambling," Officer Hicks stated importantly. "This is one of my arrestees. We got a dozen in a speakeasy off Broadway. She was gambling, no doubt about it."

"A speakeasy, huh?" Nicky cocked an eyebrow at me. "And, what led you there, Officer?"

"Well, we got a call. You know, one of them anonymous tips from a concerned citizen."

"Yes. It seems we've received an unusually large number of anonymous tips this evening. Don't you think?"

I smiled and shrugged.

"Release her," Nicky ordered.

"What!" I snapped.

"Go home, Miss March," Nicky ordered.

"Now see here—" Officer Hicks began. Nicky turned and looked him squarely in the face. Hicks assessed the name on Nicky's badge and blanched. "Oh, s-sorry, sir," he stammered. "I didn't know who—".

"That's fine," Nicky replied coolly. "Now, uncuff her."

"You can't do this!" I said. "I was arrested, fair-and-on-the-square! I was gambling! And I was cheating for chrissakes!"

Officer Hicks fished out his key but Nicky suddenly changed his mind. "Hold up there. Leave her cuffed. You have a patrol car?"

"Huh? Well, yeah. I mean, yes sir. Over there. Number thirty-three." He pointed toward the motor division parking lot on the side of the building.

"I'll need it to escort this juvenile delinquent home where she belongs." Nicky took my arm again.

Hicks handed over the car keys. "You want my cuff key?"

"Have my own." Nicky pulled me away.

"What are you doing?" I hissed, trying to wrangle free.

"Saving you from another black eye." He frog-marched me toward the motor pool.

"You're interfering! Again! I know you had me reinstated at school!"

Nicky halted in the middle of the sidewalk. "Miss March, are you going home without a fuss or should I announce that *you* were the anonymous tipster who had everyone arrested just to create confusion and slip inside yourself?"

"I haven't the faintest notion what you are referring to, Officer Masino," I said haughtily. Inside I was burning with anger. What harm was I actually doing, anyway? Just trying to get a story. The good thing about Nicky, despite sticking his nose into my business, was that he wasn't the sort of guy to rub your nose in it. I detested people who tripped you up or ruined your plans, and then rubbed your nose in it. Nicky was bending the law by letting me go, no doubt there, but he was only trying to protect me. It was sweet and all, but I just wished he'd leave me alone and let me do my job.

"At least tell me this," I said. "You do have a guy in on suspicion for the Taylor murder?"

Nicky blinked at me.

I looked behind me at the chaos I had created. The walking embalmed were staring in our direction. Whether they could actually see me or not was debatable. "Not a single newspaper-man around. Would I have gotten a scoop?"

He sighed and stuffed his hands into his pockets. "*If* there had been a suspect in custody, someone *might* have gotten a scoop, *if* she'd been allowed inside. But how you knew he was here, and what you did to get inside..." He shook his head in sheer disbelief at the lengths I would go to. "It was a worthy effort, but don't ever do anything like that again. Those folks you ratted out wouldn't take it lying down, if you know what I mean."

I'd been soundly defeated and it didn't sit well with me. I had no time to feel sorry for myself as I'd caught movement out of the corner of my eye. Across the parking lot, a couple of swells stepped from between the patrol cars. I wouldn't have given them a second thought if they hadn't been staring so intently, and if they hadn't been wearing such peculiar clothes: high-wasted, wide-legged trousers, boxy suit coats, and no ties beneath knit vests. The evolution of men's fashion trends could be slower than molasses in a whiteout blizzard at the North Pole, but these rags were positively... foreign. That was the word, not just outdated but foreign.

They had clean shaven faces, dark hair fashionably styled, and pasty complexions. Too pasty for Southern California, if you asked me. Even for February. They were sweating in the cool night air. I could see it shining off their foreheads and noses. One was talking while the other was writing in a notepad.

"Say, you know them from the local rags?" I asked defensively. If I were being removed because the cops had promised the *Times* or the *Examiner* or any other competitor a scoop on the arrest, there'd be hell to pay.

Nicky slowly turned, looked in the direction I was pointing, and then froze. His jaw tightened and the color drained from his face. He yanked me against his side and scanned the area as though expecting to find more men lurking between the autos. It was the craziest thing. All that authority vanished; Nicky looked scared.

"What is it?" I asked, trying to pull away. His arm became a steel trap.

Nicky waved for Angelo who had remained on the sidewalk, supervising the mayhem. Angelo spotted the two fellas in the parking lot and then slowly pulled the whistle from his lips and mirrored Nicky's stone-cold expression.

"Hey!" I snapped. "Are they here to bust out Red Kirby?" It was a grand idea and would've made for a sensational headline, but somehow it didn't jive with Nicky's reaction. If those pasty-faced dandies were jail breakers, I was Clara Bow.

Nicky dragged me toward patrol car number thirty-three. The rambunctious arrestees burst into protest, pointing and hollering after me. My brilliant plan to sneak inside had been thwarted, but it was all jake. Buried within the crowd of criminals was my gambling pal, Mr. Twitchy, in the plaid golf hat. Buddy Randal, our new illustrator, smiled at me and then lifted his cuffed hands and strolled inside the precinct.

CHAPTER 13

"Should have known you were the cause of that nightmare on Monday," Detective Cahill said. "Me and my crew walked into that mess and couldn't get a blasted thing done that night. Do you have any idea how much paperwork you created by that stunt?"

"Oh, now really, Bill," I said overly friendly all of a sudden. "Can I call you Bill? Well, I'm sure you've seen worse—"

"No, Miss March! You may not call me Bill! I am Detective Cahill and you damned well know it!"

I bit into my smile, taking pleasure in his outburst. Somehow these little fits of anger seemed to put us on equal footing. And, this one shifted his attention from possibly adding another charge against me.

"So, what has this got to do with Mr. Taylor arguing about Miss Minter on the day he was murdered?" he asked.

"Absolutely nothing, I assure you," I said lightly.

"You... then what the hell are we talking about?"

"Well, you asked about the man in the alley." I grinned, letting him put it together.

"You mean... he was there? He was—"

"One of the pasty-faced fellas. Standing in the motor pool. Yup, that was him."

Detective Cahill sat up and thumbed through his notepad. He jotted down a few more details. *"Tell me more. About the men,"* he ordered. *"The ones in the motor pool."*

"I've described them as best as I remember. I'll say I was accurate because they looked quite different the next time I saw them."

He looked up. *"How so?"*

"Their clothing. They had updated their wardrobe considerably. Of course, we were attending quite the fashionable affair so the occasion had called for it."

He frowned. *"So, you and these gentlemen attended a party together?"*

"I wouldn't call them gentlemen unless you know something I don't. We were at a party. Yes."

"Together?"

"No."

"And where was this party?" he asked. I sat up excitedly.

"Oh! You wouldn't believe me if I told you!" I said, tapping his hand. *"It was the most wonderful thing, in the strangest sort of way!"*

He sat back with a blasé expression. *"Go on, Miss March. I can see you're dying to tell me."*

The first thing I heard when I return home from the station that night was Pop yelling,

"Kate! What have you done!"

I strolled into the parlor as he hung up the telephone with a resounding clatter.

"'Lo there, Pop. Kind of late for you, isn't it?" I tried the casual approach, collapsing onto a chair as though I had been all night dancing the tango.

"Don't be flippant, Kate. I've just been informed that my daughter was the mastermind behind a flood of anonymous tips bombarding the police station. You sent officers to every speak-easy, pool hall, and gambling den in the city just to sneak inside the precinct?"

"Who informed you?"

"What? Never mind that."

"Angelo," I muttered, wondering if Angelo knew enough to recognize Bud. All would be lost if Angelo got wise, or if Addy failed to get Bud into the same lockup as Red Kirby.

"But, Pop, aren't you interested in knowing the cause for my ingenious plan?"

"I'm very aware. It was that Red Kirby fellow. Angelo explained everything. But did you have to call in so many tips? You've made such a mess. Even the Bradbury Mansion, Kate?"

The Bradbury Mansion was for old times' sake. Mrs. Bradbury was a crotchety old fart who should have been nicer to us kids, especially when wayward baseballs were involved.

"Well, jeezers, Pop. It's not like I had the Mayor arrested."

"Mayor Cryer was *at* the Bradbury Mansion!"

"Oh. That was unexpected." I laughed lightly, imagining Mrs. Bradbury entertaining the Mayor and his cronies only to have the cops banging down her front door. "I take it they hadn't believed the hot tip about the mansion doubling as a storage house for the cocaine trade? Oh, to have been a fly on that wall!"

Pop didn't share my humor. In fact, he was looking rather pale so I sat him down and repeated the brilliance of my scheme.

"But you tried to get arrested!" he said, exasperated. "Did you imagine what an arrest record would do when applying to a university? You have to think of the future."

I sighed. How many times had I told him I had little interest in a second incarceration on the university level? "Well, Pop, if I didn't know better, I'd say tonight was chock-full of higher learning."

"You don't know better," Pop grumbled.

"I outsmarted the coppers," I teased.

"You got an employee arrested!"

"Yes, that was the brilliant part. Just so you know." Pop moped his forehead with his handkerchief. "Well, anyway, it worked," I said. "Bud strolled right through the doors and is probably talking to Red Kirby as we speak."

"Poor Bud," he muttered sadly as though he had failed to protect a fellow human being from the wild antics of his daughter.

"Aw, he was willing. 'Sides, it's his first offense. I've raided my piggy bank for the bail money. Ready for first thing in the morning. I'll be at the station by five o'clock and—"

"No, no. That'll never do." Pop went to his desk and rummaged through a long mahogany drawer where he pulled out an envelope stuffed with money. "First offense is $250 but I think I can talk them down. Maybe nothing at all if Angelo is still there."

"You? But Pop, Addy and Bud and I have it all worked out and—"

"Yes, I've seen the way you've worked it out," Pop said. He slammed the drawer shut and braced his hands against the desk, thinking. I hadn't seen him this upset since Shoeless Joe

200

Jackson was banned from baseball. Had I finally pushed Pop too far? I'd never forgive myself if I gave him a heart attack or something.

"What's more," Pop said. "You didn't give me time to change the morning paper if you plan to have a scoop on the front page."

I grinned.

"No, now don't go thinking I approve of your behavior," Pop said sternly. "It was completely outside the boundaries in which I work, but, if Bud is already there, well then..."

"Oh, sure, since he's already there and all," I said, shrugging nonchalantly.

"Now, seriously Kate, that old machine is taking longer and longer to warm up. I'll go back around midnight to fire it up and ready the type. You'll have to get the goods from Bud through the phone. Perhaps Addy can arrange it. Write it up here and then phone me at the office; that'll be the quickest way. If there's a story here, we'll be ready."

I waited until a quarter of twelve and then called the precinct's back line. A flustered file girl put Addy on the line.

"Jeepers Creepers, Kate! You almost made it!" Addy cried in her boisterous whisper. "You should see the joint. Chaos! Confusion! It's wonderful! They even raided the Bradbury Mansion. Mrs. Bradbury—that ol' face stretcher—and her so-called cribbage games! Whew, I'll say! Anyway, this place reeks of hooch!"

I couldn't help but laugh. There was a rash of noise on the line and I had to yell to be heard.

"What about Bud! Did he find Red Kirby?"

"And how!" Addy shouted. "Hold on, Kate!" She set the phone down and it crackled like she'd tossed it under a Southern Pacific train car. Just when I thought we might lose the connection, Bud came on the line.

"Kate, listen good," he yelled in the same forceful whisper as Addy's. "I don't have much time on the phone! That man, Red Kirby, was picked up in a rooming house off West Washington. A hophead with a big mouth. He started bragging like he knew something about the Taylor murder so the police nabbed him. Now, nobody thinks he knows anything. Can you hear me? Just arrested on suspicion with nothing much to go on."

I slumped, deflated but somehow not surprised. I didn't know Red Kirby from Adam and couldn't imagine what connection he had to Mr. Taylor. So, I'd have a scoop about a dead-end suspect and the cops chasing their tails. At least it would be more than anyone else had.

"Yeah, I heard you. Thanks for the sacrifice, Bud. You okay in there?"

"What?" He sounded annoyed. "Of course, I'm okay. Now just wait. There's more. Something's happened here tonight, think you'd better hear about it. I don't know if it's important or not."

"Go on." I sat up and gripped the receiver.

"While I was being processed, I overheard two officers talking; one told the other that earlier this evening the DA's office received a mysterious letter over at the Hall of Records. DA Woolwine is meeting with his detectives first thing in the morning about it. That's all I know but it sounded urgent and it was definitely about the Taylor case."

"That's great, Bud! You did great! I'll get this to Pop, and we'll get you out as soon as possible."

That was the angle I was looking for, a mysterious letter. If Woolwine hadn't planned on sharing it with the general public, we'd make sure our readers damn well knew about it.

Early the next morning, I sat on a barstool at the Kitchen Kettle leisurely enjoying a cuppa Joe and a powdered sinker. Bud had been safely retrieved from the station, all charges dropped due to overcrowding and it being his first offense. Our morning edition had the scoop about Red Kirby *and* the mysterious letter. Pop pretended not to be overjoyed. After all, he was an ethical man living in an unethical city. And, the paper was selling like peanuts at the World Series. Belching Bertha could hardly sputter out copies fast enough while Rico and his newsies sold out as quickly as the stacks hit the pavement. The whole town was itching to know who, if anyone, would fry for killing their beloved director.

The regular newshounds at the Kettle had accosted me when I entered. They had playfully demanded details about the mysterious letter from the DA's office. Some even proffered a reward if I were in possession of such a letter. Still, some doubted my credibility but not enough to ignore my reporting altogether. I was slowly gaining a reputation as a tenacious investigative reporter. Red Kirby had been absent from my competitors' morning editions. And if this mysterious letter actually existed and proved important to the case, they would have to answer to their editors.

"Aw, go write your own letter," I had said when they demanded proof it existed. "Better yet, try naming sources on these alleged interviews you all have had with Mr. Taylor's friends."

Every major newspaper had published quotes directly from Mr. Taylor's friends about his generosity and good companionship, his loyalty, honesty, and high moral character. It sounded more than suspicious but downright scripted. The muckety mucks at Paramount wouldn't give anyone a direct interview about Mr. Taylor but I had the distinct feeling they had been orchestrating what everyone else said about him, as though scriptwriting his life. Everything was picture perfect, only this picture had a dead body and a murderer on the loose they seemed to have forgotten about.

"The man who reads nothing at all is better educated than the man who reads only newspapers." Mr. Morgan casually quoted Thomas Jefferson as he took the barstool on my left. A smile sprang to my face. I hadn't seen Mr. Morgan since the Night Owl and had wanted to thank him for escorting Addy and me home.

"I should say I owe you a big one," I said after thanking him profusely. Mr. Morgan forced a smile but eventually caved.

"Miss Kate, your eye," he said, grimacing. "Has it gotten better or worse? It's hard to tell."

"Oh, this?" I laughed lightly. "Battle scars. You know how it is. I've looked worse after a round of lawn tennis."

"I had no idea. Was it that woman on the dance floor?"

"Only the elbow end of her."

"If only I had found you sooner. I feel just awful."

His genuine concern for my well-being was touching. I swallowed the smart-alecky retort on the tip of my tongue and squeezed his hand.

"You saved me just in time, Mr. Morgan," I said softly. "I'm very grateful."

He laid a hand over mine and leaned closer, his soft brown eyes probing mine. "Anything for a friend. We are friends, aren't we, Miss Kate? You would have done the same for me, wouldn't you?"

"Well, of course. Sure." I withdrew and fiddled with the paper as heat rose to my cheeks. Why his declaration of friendship should make me so uncomfortable, I had no idea. Against all common sense, I felt giddy inside.

Bessie the waitress grinned while refilling my coffee cup and then moved on to take an order. The voice beside me ordering a cuppa was deep and familiar. My lighthearted mood took a nose dive. Nicky Masino was the last person I had wanted to see this morning. After all the chaos of last night, I felt certain that lying low for a while was a grand idea. Then again, I had a few choice questions for him about the two pasty-face fellas lurking in the motorpool. Nicky had refused to speak about them on the drive home. Something about those men had turned him off like a water spigot. Little chance he would offer an explanation now with Mr. Morgan within earshot. Perhaps Mr. Morgan would take the hint if I disappeared inside the pages of *The Messenger*. Then I could broach the subject to Nicky.

I deliberately buried my face within the first few pages of *The Messenger*, going so deep that my nose nearly squashed into Menihand's new and improved arch-aid shoe with snake inlay on sale at Vandergrift's Shoe Store. Mr. Morgan ordered breakfast. I sighed and lowered the paper. I would have to put the screws to Nicky later.

As far as things went, Nicky Masino hadn't even thrown a friendly howdy-do in my direction. I guessed he was still sore about last night. He stirred his coffee with his teeth clenching and his jaw muscle twitching as though he was chewing on a storm. He must've been waiting on someone because a few minutes later, Detective King stepped inside. A few newshounds clinging to their biscuits like life preservers threw out questions about the mysterious letter. Detective King tossed back scowls, which had them scribbling in their notepads. Apparently, silence was good enough for print.

Detective King stomped to the counter and plopped down with a sour greeting to Nicky. Customers began whispering like ladies at a church bazaar.

"How in the hell did they know about the letter?" Detective King groused. He waved Bessie over and received a steaming cup of tar black coffee.

"You can thank me," I said cheerfully across Nicky's coffee cup. I was suddenly as chipper as the day was long. Nicky and King stared, speechless. If I had grown two heads, their expressions wouldn't have altered.

"Well, the suspense is terrible, I hope it will last," Mr. Morgan quoted Oscar Wilde with heavy sarcasm. I snorted a laugh.

"You haven't been writing anonymous letters to the police department have you, Miss March?" Detective King demanded.

I held up our front page. "You mean this letter sent to the DA late last night?"

He startled. "How in the Sam hell—" he bit off his question and flushed. After shifting uncomfortably, he threw a scathing glance behind him and then lowered his voice. "Yeah, all right, Woolwine got an anonymous letter last night. He showed us this morning."

"Anything reliable?" I asked eagerly. "What'd it say? Who wrote it?"

"If she has written a letter, delay not an instant but burn it," Mr. Morgan drawled. He was leaning on his elbow, head in hand, and openly eavesdropping. He looked positively bored.

Nicky glared at me as though my wayward child was misbehaving in public. I muttered, "Kipling," by way of explanation and then smacked Mr. Morgan on the leg.

Detective King went on to explain the mysterious letter. It suggested that Woolwine should send a detective to Miss Mabel Normand's apartment house and search her basement. They could expect to find the .38 caliber revolver used to kill Mr. Taylor.

"How interesting," I said. "So, Sands hid the gun at Miss Normand's." I eyed their reactions. It was one of those times when I didn't believe the words coming out of my own mouth.

"How's that?" Detective King frowned.

"Well, word on the street suggests that the police make Sands for the crime. He must have hidden the gun and then written the letter."

Nicky gave me a *what are you* up to look.

"I don't figure it that way," Detective King muttered uncomfortably.

"But, the letter could be analyzed and compared to other handwritings by Sands. Say... the Jimmy Valentine letter? You find the gun in the basement and bam! Case solved."

They were taken aback that I had knowledge regarding Sand's alias, Jimmy Valentine.

I was appropriately annoyed. "Haven't either of you read my columns?"

Detective King scratched his day-old beard. "We don't need to have the letter analyzed, Miss March. We know Sands didn't write it. We've seen the Jimmy Valentine letter that Sands sent to Taylor. The handwriting doesn't match. No one in their right mind would think they matched. I'm sure like I'm sure of my own name."

Of course they don't, I thought smugly.

"Well, at least we know the killer just excluded Miss Normand from the list of suspects," I said. "She wouldn't write a letter saying, hey all, come look in my basement, see what I've done."

"Unless we do find the gun," Nicky said without any real conviction.

"We won't," I said.

"We? No, Miss March, you're not going anywhere near Miss Normand's apartment house."

I stood and laid two bits on the counter. "Oh, I wouldn't

waste my time. Somebody's playing you, boys. So, you can count me in on staying out. At least on this one."

"Can I drop you at school?" Mr. Morgan asked, eagerly climbing to his feet.

"But your breakfast—"

"Forgotten."

"Okay, then. See round, fellas. Oh, and you will let us know if you find the gun?" I smiled and strolled out.

CHAPTER 14

Detective Cahill was studying me intently. He remembered reading the mysterious letter and attending the meeting with Woolwine that morning. "I don't mind saying that letter threw us for a loop," he said. "King was assigned to the Red Kirby angle while the Squad and I hunted down Sands." He paused, mulling things over. "Woolwine was so sure Sands was our man but that letter—"

"Didn't add up?" I asked, already knowing why it hadn't made sense. I waited, hoping Cahill would offer more. It would be nice to hear someone besides myself admit it out loud. That letter had stumped the investigators but it had solidified my own theory about the murderer. Cahill wouldn't believe me if I told him now. No, I had to keep talking. He had to understand how things unfolded if I wanted him to believe me. Strange thing was, I realized that I did.

The donkey baseball fundraiser was in full swing. Gates opened at noon and the cash box had been growing like a lettuce patch. The memorial for our lost boys was as good as gold. The game itself was another story.

It was deep in the third inning when Addy and I climbed the bleachers and wormed our way into the crowd which was sizable considering folks had given up their lunch time for a bunch of jackasses. No Ty Cobb here, but it was full of entertainment.

Abner Felts maneuvered his donkey to home plate where he promptly hit a solid fly into left field. He then proceeded to kick his stubborn donkey toward first base. We cheered him on as he huffed and puffed, cajoling his ride down the line. Dewey Deets was straddling a donkey named Blackie whom we all knew as a veteran from the fire department back when they used wagons to respond to fires. Nowadays spiffy new fire trucks arrived on the scenes. Dewey and Blackie left first base and headed toward second. Blackie took a sudden right turn when he spotted a patch of clover in the outfield. Dewey flailed and hollered and tried to rein Blackie on track. The spectators roared with laughter.

Addy cupped her hands and hollered for Dewey to take him by the bit, prompting another swell of laughter. Next came a hard grounder through the shortstop that sent the infield donkeys and riders scrambling and the outfield donkeys and riders into a frenzy. When Abner's donkey sat down between second and third base, he rolled off the backend. Fans booed and launched peanuts at him.

The game was a nice distraction but only temporarily. I had my mind on the contents of that letter implicating Mable Normand. I had finagled a phone call from the school secretary,

Miss Brown, and gave Pop the details I'd extracted from Detective King at the Kettle. I earned points with Pop for denying my urge to tag along in the search at Miss Normand's apartment house and sticking to my school schedule instead. How could they possibly find the murder weapon at Miss Normand's when common sense said she wouldn't have killed Mr. Taylor? Her grief had been too genuine. I believed she truly loved him, in her own way. Perhaps as a good friend, despite the fighting that allegedly went on. I saw no evidence that she had benefited from his death. The *why* was stuck in the forefront of my thoughts.

Whoever had benefited from Mr. Taylor's death had tried to pin it on Miss Normand. I reasoned that if the muckety mucks at Paramount knew Mr. Taylor had been killed by one of their own they were likely to cover it up. It was highly doubtful they would point the finger at one of their most valuable assets. Not with Taylor's murder on the heels of the Fatty Arbuckle scandal. The movie industry needed that kind of publicity like a fish needed a bicycle. That was assuming they knew who had bumped off their director.

"Too bad no one at Paramount is talking about the *real* Taylor," I mused aloud. "The one they don't want the good citizens of our fair city to know. Lots of secrets were revealed on the days following his murder but now things have positively dried up. I'm guessing Paramount has gotten control of their stable of actors and threatened their livelihood should they talk."

Addy cracked open a peanut and popped it into her mouth. "How about we make them?"

"What?"

"Make Paramount talk."

"How are we supposed to do that? We're not one of *them*. Mary's our only inside man and I think she's being too selective with her information. I should tell you I'm having doubts about her honesty."

"Naw!" Addy said sarcastically and then laughed. "Okay, so don't rely on Mary anymore. All the more reason to get on the inside. I mean, literally. Say!" She sat up as though she'd been poked by an idea. "How about we sneak into Paramount studios? Seriously, Kate. If we can infiltrate the 77th Street precinct, why not Paramount?"

Why not, indeed. If I could get some working stiffs to talk, or better yet, some lesser film stars that the muckety mucks didn't have their hooks in yet, I might get the real inside story. Nothing scripted. Nothing planted to bolster Mr. Taylor's sterling reputation. What I needed was some good old-fashioned gossip. As the saying went, *where there's smoke there's fire*.

I turned Addy to face me and looked her square in the eye. "We could do it but it would be dangerous. The film industry is taking a hit from all this bad publicity. You know their reputation, all that depravity and debauchery that goes on at their parties? And, now they have Taylor's murder to deal with when the Fatty Arbuckle scandal hasn't gone away. His third trial is set for next month and the whole thing stinks to high heaven. Never mind that he's probably innocent, being accused of rape and murder of a young girl at a wild party has soured the public's stomach for the movie folk." I shook my head. "The Hearst paper up in San Francisco has been reporting on hop parties and orgies *financed* by local film studios. And Pop tells me the morality mobs have been campaigning Washington to shut down the studios. All across the country, folks have been boycotting Arbuckle films and tearing up screens that show them. When's the last time you saw an Arbuckle film in a movie house? Some believe the whole film industry is in shambles. So, Addy, there is a very valid reason why the movie folk aren't talking to reporters. Too much pressure from concerned citizens and the industry could collapse. They certainly won't want us poking around their private sets."

"Well, we'll need a plan, of course," she said, cheerfully undaunted, which made me love her all the more. "They won't let us stroll right in, you know. We'll need disguises and a distraction."

We turned back to the game, thinking things over. Just about that time, Blackie lifted his tail and dropped a load of poop onto third base.

It was as simple as that, a foolish idea set in motion with Pop's funeral coattails and an old bowler hat. A cane and black oversized shoes we borrowed from Addy's grandfather completed my disguise. Addy stuffed herself into her brother's sailor suit with knee-breeches and her father's golf hat. The next day we were strolling up Melrose Street headed toward the Paramount Studio's gate.

"Stop fidgeting," Addy said. She was determined we act as natural as any other actors heading to work on a movie set.

"It tickles," I complained, pressing down the stumpy black mustache Addy had swiped from the school's drama department and pasted to my top lip. It was a tiny square of horse hair but had large possibilities of producing a sneeze that would send it airborne. "How do men put up with these things?"

"Theirs are real, you idiot."

I practiced swinging my cane and waddling like Charlie Chaplin of whom I was a great admirer. We slowed as we approached the entrance marked by giant stone pillars with *Paramount Pictures* etched across the archway. I had passed by here numerous times over the years but never with the intention of entering the gate. It seemed larger somehow, more impressive and imposing now that my purpose was to sneak inside. There was a high percentage of power behind that gate. Power and a sort of magic that seemed to hang in the air. All the make-believe that went on. And I wasn't just referring to the picture shows.

A long line people snaked down the sidewalk. Hordes of movie extras and workmen had answered the second call of the day. The afternoon shift. Quite a few more than I had expected.

"You know, Addy, I'm starting to think the Holy Trinity of the land isn't the Father, the Son, and the Holy Ghost but the Paramount, the United Artists, and the First National."

"And how!" she said, staring wide-eyed at the mountain we had decided to climb.

Thanks to Adolf Zukor back in 1912 who decided nickelodeons catering to working-class immigrants weren't the be-all end-all. He wanted full-length feature films with real theatrical players to entertain the middle masses. Along came Lansky, De Mille, Goldwyn, and a fella from Utah with a distribution company called Paramount. Over time, they all got in bed together, so to speak, with Paramount Pictures heading distribution nationwide. I couldn't imagine the size of their payroll now. Young Hollywood businessmen had turned into movie moguls overnight. Roustabouts, milkmen, and farmers became sheiks, pirates, and bandits. Maids, schoolteachers, and store clerks were now damsels in distress. It was proving to be a viable trade. The folks in line seemed happy enough but something occurred to me as I watched them shuffle past the guard shack and through the gate. Not a single person was dressed in a movie costume.

"I suppose they have a costume department on the inside," I said quietly to Addy. We stood out like a couple of sore thumbs.

"Make like we belong," Addy whispered. She tugged my sleeve and led me to the back of the line. Autos and delivery trunks in line for the gate began to clog up the street that ran alongside the entrance. Regular folks passing in their autos were having a time of it. Horns blared and drivers shouted. Three rough-looking security guards in black uniforms with whistles and billy clubs manned the gate. Another gatekeeper in a tan security uniform was checking the identification cards of anyone trying to enter. The guards in black had their eyes on a gaggle of newspapermen gumming up the works on the far side of the entrance. The reporters would occasionally step into traffic and holler questions about the Taylor case to the guards. If a known celebrity happened to pull up to the gate the newshounds would pounce, demanding information about the true nature of Mr. Taylor's relationship with Mabel Normand. I stood on my tiptoes, hoping to spot a side door or secret walk-through gate. No such luck. Anyone entering, on foot or on wheels, had to pass all three guards, the gatekeeper, and the giant gate. No two ways about it.

Commotion up ahead brought our line to a halt. The gate-keeper alerted a security guard who jerked a young fellow in ragged overalls out of line.

"Your identity card!" the burly guard shouted. The fellow mumbled something, which prompted the guard to kick him in the seat and send him sprawling into traffic. "And don't try it again or I'll break your kneecaps!" the guard yelled, wielding his club.

Addy and I exchanged nervous looks. There wasn't a single identification card between us.

"Lordy, Kate, are we in a pickle?"

"Not yet," I said as our distraction arrived.

It came in the form of Bud wheeling Pop's truck into the auto lane in front of the gate. Lucky for us Buddy Randall had

215

an adventurous appetite and hadn't hesitated to play chauffeur when duty called, even after his short stint behind bars. His first love remained his Kodak but I suspected Bud might harbor dreams of acting. This was the second performance I had offered him in a week and he practically jumped at the chance. With him, Bud brought the sharp, unmistakable stench of manure hovering around the truck. A black cloud of flies buzzed over the heap, adding sound to stink. Our diversion was a giant mound of donkey fundraiser poop put to good use. The plan may have stunk to high heaven but I thought it was one of my more ingenious ploys.

Several newshounds had started a quarrel with the guards in black, even going so far as to call them Red scourges and union dupes for not allowing them entrance to do their jobs. The thick-headed guards, who were not entirely clear about the insults, shouted and waved their clubs. A dolled-up sheba broke from the line and tried to pry open the gate and sneak inside. The guards seized on her and, to her credit, the sheba gave them what for! She kicked and scratched and wailed about needing to see Rudolph. She was going to marry Mr. Valentino, or die trying.

While the guards brawled with the future Mrs. Valentino, the newshounds roared with laughter. The driver in the auto ahead of Bud was busy exchanging heated words with the gatekeeper. The driver was eventually denied entrance. He wheeled hard to the right, nearly bowling over the distracted reporters. It was Bud's turn next and he jammed the gearstick around, grinding awkwardly until the truck lunged up to the gatekeeper.

"Scheduled for delivery," Bud announced importantly. The gatekeeper checked his clipboard and shook his head. Bud repeated, rather loudly, that he was scheduled to deliver his 'goods' to the back lot. The gatekeeper wasn't buying it.

I had a death grip on the cane while Addy dug her nails into my arm. We had to make it inside. This was our only chance.

The gatekeeper complained that he had no such order in his paperwork.

"It's for that new Western!" Bud railed on him. "Look Mister, I don't deliver this load of shit, it'll be *your* job not mine!"

At that moment, a magnificent Rolls Royce Silver Ghost limousine rolled up behind Bud. It was an open-top number in varying shades of grey. I had never been this close to one before but I would say it lived up to its name; it was as quiet as a ghost. In the plush back seat, under a wide-brimmed hat, sat an impatient starlet. I couldn't identify her as her face was hidden but she squirmed and complained that she was late for a meeting with 'the boss'. Her white-gloved chauffeur tooted the horn incessantly while she smacked his hat with her fan. Her other hand pinched her nose as she was overwrought by the stench wafting from Bud's load.

Bud kicked up his threats about his job and the possible failure of the picture show awaiting his smelly prop while the starlet's chauffeur laid on the horn. The gatekeeper grew flustered. The three guards in black sent Mrs. Valentino on her way, sobbing and sniffling, and then came to assist. I grabbed Addy and we darted between the autos to hide on the far side of Pop's truck. The starlet stood up in the backseat and hollered something to the gatekeeper, calling him by name. Her thin, squeaky mouse-of-a-voice pierced the cacophony and nabbed the gatekeeper's attention. He recognized her at once and fumbled to opened the gate. Bud throttled through first, followed by the starlet in the Silver Ghost. Addy and I ducked alongside the truck and scurried inside while the newshounds wailed that stowaways had breached the castle. Since they had firmly established themselves as pests, their warnings were ignored.

Addy and I had beaten the odds and stood on sacred ground.

Paramount studios was a far cry from the horse barn on Sunset and Vine where Cecil B. De Mille first filmed *Squaw Man* back in '13. I liked to think it was fitting that Bud should dump a pile of manure here. Coming full circle, as the saying went. Addy and I thanked Bud and sent him on his way. He was to drive around in hopes of finding a fictitious backlot awaiting his pile of poop while we got our bearings.

In a word, it was chaos behind the gates. A motley crew of gypsies, cowboys, Arabs, and soldiers scrambled in every direction across an open common area. The backdrop to all the bedlam was an array of white fluttering tents as far as the eye could see and plywood box stages crammed with movie folk. Various directors in tan jodhpurs, starched white shirts, and black boots shouted into megaphones while actors and actresses flung themselves about. An occasional Victrola scratched out music to set the mood.

A man with a monkey on his shoulder was feeding treats to a yapping dog that walked on its hind legs. Workmen laden with façade storefronts nearly collided with lighting crews and their poles and wires. A pack of trained German Shepherds barked at a brown bear being led from its cage. Horses reared at the commotion and caused a handful of bank clerks-cum-cowboys to hide behind wagons piled with breakaway tables and chairs. Labor men in overalls carried ladders and buckets and trudged through the pandemonium on their way to repairing something.

Addy and I fell in step with the labor men and followed them toward the center of the lot where filming was in progress in a giant three-sided tent. A cameraman cranked the tripod camera while the director yelled orders.

"Now, look at each other! You are afraid! Show me fear! Show me fear! Hey, bring me a coffee and roll, will ya?" He'd caught an errand boy on the fly and then, without missing a beat, continued his verbal assault on the actors. "Fear! I say! Show me fear!"

Addy and I dissolved into laughter and then hustled away amid stinging looks from the crew; the scene was clearly not meant as a comedy. I gave Addy her first acting job. She was to nose around the costume tents in hopes of overhearing any curious conversations regarding Mr. Taylor. My part involved securing a box lunch from the kitchen detail and joining the extras at a group of picnic tables. Lunchtime at school was always a boisterous harmony of anecdotes, and I hoped this might prove the same. We made plans to meet back at the gate in thirty minutes.

In spite of the peculiar glances I received, I blended in with the crowd at a row of tables and opened my box lunch. A meat sandwich, grapes, and a pickle awaited. I gingerly munched on the grapes and tried not to chew off my mustache. My tablemates consisted of an Indian chief in full headdress and war paint. He was as pale as a bottle of milk, smoking Lucky Strikes, and griping about work conditions in a thick accent straight from the Bronx. Beside him sat Little Bo Peep who got the hiccups from her phosphate soda. Further down, sitting apart from the others, were a couple of pirates with painted on tattoos arguing in Russian. Over the next ten minutes, a grab bag of characters ebbed and flowed. Eventually, bits of conversation captured my attention.

"He was such a decent fella..."

"A gentleman, if ever I've seen..."

"Why, I remember one time..."

Such sympathetic nostalgia brought to mind my own first impression of Mr. Taylor. The only time our paths had crossed, I'd felt the same as these folks: Mr. Taylor was a decent, honest fella. Sometimes you don't say more than hello to someone but you get a sense of their character. Mr. Taylor had a calm demeanor and came across as someone not easily rattled. He had a smooth, tranquil voice. Probably a great listener. I imagined him as someone you could tell your troubles to, and someone who would offer sound, practical advice.

Then I thought about all that fussing Henry Peavey had overheard the day Mr. Taylor died. Particularly that argument on the phone about Mary. I wondered what had Mr. Taylor and Mable Normand at odds. Henry said they fought a lot. Being a swell fella, or even a renowned gentleman, didn't mean you were immune to losing your temper now and again.

"Well, no more late-night rendezvous for the little Miss. She'll have to pick another buck from the herd."

I snapped out of my analysis and looked down the table. The source of the comment was an old lady dressed in a calico dress you'd see on an Oklahoma prairie. A black shawl was draped over her shoulders and a sunbonnet hanged down her back.

A few sniggers and angry looks flew around the table, to which she replied, "Well, we're all thinking it, ain't we?"

More grunts and nods. The speaker shrugged and bit into her sandwich. As the lunch crowd eventually thinned out, I was left alone with the old lady. Thinking it was now or never, I scooted closer and was astonished to discover the old lady's hair was a grey wig and her wrinkles had been painted on. She couldn't have been more than thirty years old.

"Why, you're not an old timer at all!" I blurted out.

She chuckled in a rough sort of way and removed the grey wig, revealing soft brown hair. "And you ain't Chaplin."

We smiled, and then I leaned over the table, speaking quietly. "Don't mind if I say that your colleagues didn't care for your table talk."

"My colleagues! Well, ain't that something." She sat up importantly. "I like that word. Think I'll borrow it myself. Anyhow, this Taylor business... well, I tell it like it is, see? As my dead husband, Harlow, used to say, 'If it ain't the truth it ain't worth squawking about'." She pushed her box lunch aside and pulled a worn cigarette case from her bosom. She flicked it open, offering one. I stared at the ciggys. They had gold tips like the pile of dead ciggys Addy and I had seen outside Taylor's bungalow.

I refused the offer and watched her light up. She had the effects of a younger version of Trudy Mae so I took to her right away. I relaxed and folded my arms on the table.

"Who were you talking about anyway?"

She pinched tobacco off the tip of her tongue. "That little thing, Mary."

My stomach clenched. "Mary?"

"Minter," she said. I closed my eyes and inhaled a deep breath before opening them again.

"But, I-I thought Taylor was jake. A real gentleman and all. How could he and Mary have late night..." I couldn't finish the horrible thought. Mary was so innocent and pure. Sure, she was hot-tempered and celluloid at times but she would never be indecent with her infatuation with Mr. Taylor. Of that I was sure.

"That's right, Taylor was jake. Lots of women liked him because he was genuine. Not a skirt chaser like a lot of these directors." She pointed her cigarette toward the movie sets. "I'm not saying he was ever improper with Mary because I don't know. But that wouldn't stop her from trying."

"You know Mary?" I asked, feeling strangely protective of her. Mary was a handful, to be sure, but I knew her. I could say such things. Just who was this old prairie bird and what gave her the inside track on Mary?

221

"Yeah, we worked together before. Even back when she was on the stage. See, I come from the vaudeville side of things. Then I hit the big stage in New York. After a while, Harlow and me come out west for the picture shows. I first worked with Mary back then."

"Oh," I mumbled. Sounded like the old bird knew her stuff after all. "I know Mary, too. And her sister. Well, the whole family, really. Her mother is some piece of work. Zero at the bone, ya know? Doesn't like me much."

She chuckled. "Shelby don't like nobody. I heard her once say she don't have no use for men, except the dead ones. You get me? The Franklin, Jefferson, and Washington type." She rubbed her fingers and thumb together.

"That so?" It didn't take much imagination to believe Mrs. Shelby had said such a thing. According to Mary, her mother had negotiated contracts like a lawyer and made the family very wealthy. Wealthy with Mary's money. "We all knew Mary was sweet on Mr. Taylor but what's all this about a late-night rendezvous?"

She hesitated, sizing me up through smoky eyes. Something in my tone had drawn her suspicion. I picked at my sandwich like all this small talk was putting me to sleep.

"Gossip goes 'round, ya know?" she said quietly. "Folks love a good scandal. Especially on the lot. There's always talk 'bout who's parting sheets with who. Now, take Mary, she's a wild little thing, always working an angle to rile up her mother. They go around caterwauling at each other like a couple of tomcats, but that's the biz. Like I said, Mary probably ain't never slept with Taylor. But she's been known to show up at his place late at night a time or two. Among other places."

I hated believing this about Mary but I could hardly disagree. I'd been with Mary on one of those late-night jaunts to

222

Taylor's home, for chrissakes. She had claimed she wanted to show off her new roadster. Mr. Taylor had a penchant for autos. Certainly, Mary would never have done anything scandalous with me along. But there had been other visits. The gossip wasn't far from the truth. If Mary had asked for 'it', then Mr. Taylor would have answered. I could only hope the answer had been no.

"You okay, kid?" she asked. I must've looked ill. I certainly felt it.

"May I ask your name?" I forced a weak smile.

"Fannie Baker," she announced robustly and then reached across the table to vigorously shake my hand. "It's mighty nice to meet you, Mr. Chaplin." She winked and I scoffed.

"Oh, well, I'm not really an actor."

"Naw." She clucked a funny sort of laugh but I didn't care. I liked her. She wasn't one to beat around the bush.

"My name is Kate March," I said confidentially. "And I... work for the papers."

She frowned. "No offense, kid, but ain't you the wrong sex for the newspaper business?"

"I have as much right as anyone else."

"Okay now, don't bite your mustache off. I hear ya. Tough working in a man's business, huh?" She curled her lip with dis-approval and cemented another bond between us. Mrs. Baker opened up like a clam, elaborating on some 'mighty strange doings', as she put it: overheard conversations, secret meet-ings, and several trips to Mr. Taylor's bungalow in search of mysterious items.

"But listen, kid, if you really want the inside dope, be at the Ambassador Hotel this Friday night. There's a big shindig hap-pening at the Cocoanut Grove. A private party. Only the cream of Hollywood allowed. I got friends who got me on the list. That's where you'll get the goods." She stood and spilled the rest in a rush. "Get yourself dolled up. Arrive after seven. Bring a date. Ask for Fannie Baker's party or they'll turn you out. Got it?"

"Yes, but—"

She cut me off with a sharp nod over my shoulder. I twisted around. Two security guards were marching toward us with billy clubs firmly in hand.

"Oh, I don't think they're after me." I grinned with confidence and adjusted my bowler-hat-of-a-disguise.

"Yeah, you fooled me too, kid. Problem is, Charlie Chaplin don't work for Paramount." She threw her head back, laughing at my shocked expression.

"Jeezers and dammit to hell!" I said, scrambling clumsily from the picnic bench. I hiked up my britches, and took off running with Fannie Baker's throaty laughter following me around the corner.

Tripping and stumbling, I struggled to gain a lead in Addy's grandfather's oversized shoes. I clumped frantically down one path after another. The middle of the compound was dotted with more stages crammed with props, lighting poles, and actors. I raced deeper into the maze and then ducked under the wall of the nearest tent. I suddenly found myself immersed in a crowd of extras facing brilliant lights that nearly blinded me. It was one of those three-sided tents with the director and his cohorts sitting just outside, watching the scene. A large wooden camera on a tripod was situated next to the director's chair. A man behind the camera was slowly cranking a lever. The director yelled into a megaphone. "START YOUR ACTION!" and then everyone in the tent began mingling and laughing as though they were in a swanky Paris nightclub. I crouched and wormed my way around, desperate not to be noticed. The director yelled for the starlet to see her uniform clad true love amongst the crowd. The actress threw on a magnificent smile, tossed her hands in the air, rushed on her tippy toes across the nightclub and launched herself dramatically into her sweetheart's waiting arms. The extras began dancing and hollering as though something wonderful had just happened. To blend in, I clapped and went hog-wild alongside them. The security guards must have noticed Charlie Chaplin out of place in all this French hubbub. They raced to the director and pointed in my direction.

"Uh-oh!" I plunged through the mob, stomping on toes and shoving pretend Parisians aside. The actors yelled and complained but kept performing because the cameraman was still cranking the box. I tripped over an angry extra in a black-and-white striped shirt and red beret. I flailed backward and snatched his shirt for support. The shirt gave way, knocking me into a lighting pole which fell against the tent and made a tremendous ripping sound all the way down the canvas. The entire tent gradually collapsed on top of the actors in great billowing waves. Laughter turned into shrilled cries for help. A symphony of obscenities punctuated the air. I was thrown to the ground in a heaping dog pile that rivaled my brothers' rough housing. The air left me and I struggled to cough the dust from my lungs. I grunted and pushed the wiggling weight off me and then crawled out from under the heavy canvas on my hands and knees.

Once I had cleared the catastrophe I sat back, panting. All that remained was a giant white canvas rolling with waves and wiggling lumps. To my surprise, something Mama had often repeated to me as a child came flooding back. *You have an unnatural thirst for rebellion and can turn any idea into a qualified disaster!* The memory added salt to the wound. I never saw myself as Mama had. The present moment notwithstanding, I thought I was inventive and precocious with unabashed vigor.

Next to the unfortunate wreckage stood the flabbergasted

director and stunned cameraman. The security guards flanking them had spotted me and blasted their whistles. I scrambled to my feet, high-stepping it like a circus clown.

Paramount studios was truly a dizzying labyrinth. Endless rows of tents were mostly stuffed with people but some were overflowing with props or animals or costumes. I veered between a utility shed and a make-shift cook house and then rounded the corner and ran smack into Addy.

"Kate! Oh, Kate! They're after me!"

"Me too! Which way's the gate?"

We didn't have time to consider. Whistles blasted and the guards appeared around the corner. Addy yanked me forward. We raced headlong toward the steps of a giant grey building adorned with overstated baroque architecture. Several yards behind us, the security guards met up with a couple of men in snappy three-piece-suites and shiny shoes. They spotted us and came running.

"Jeezers, Addy, it's the muckety mucks!"

Addy hauled me up the steps and into the building. We mounted a flimsy staircase and then raced down a long corridor where we eventually slid to a stop. An extraordinary realization set in as we turned a full circle to take in the place; the building wasn't real. It was fabricated. A movie prop. We tried a row of fake door handles along the flimsy walls but none would open. One handle even came off in my hand. We were at a dead end.

"Lordy, Addy! Now you've done it!" I snapped, throwing the fake door handle aside.

"Now *I've* done it?" she wailed.

We swung around, frantic for an escape. Addy spotted something leaning against an open window and raced to the end of the hallway. "A ladder!" She slung her leg onto the ledge and maneuvered out the window. The security guards appeared at the opposite end of the hallway, blasting their whistles.

The fear of billy clubs dislodging my kneecaps overshadowed my fear of climbing down an uncertain ladder in oversized shoes. Had I the time, I would have removed the shoes. As it was, I had just enough time to straddled the widow's ledge and climb through.

Once outside I looked down. Three stories high and windy. My hat blew off and my hair came loose. I couldn't see a blasted thing. A guard appeared at the window, grabbing at my arms. I yelped and smacked his hands.

Addy yelled. "Push away!"

I screeched back, "Push away? Are you nutso?"

The guard at the window yelled threats involving Alcatraz. Down below, more guards blasted their whistles, and somewhere the bear roared and the pack of German Shepherds barked and barked and barked.

And then we were suddenly free, drifting backward away from the building. I gasped and clung to the ladder. The guard at the window flung his arms toward me, his mouth gaping and his eyes bulging in horror. The ladder came center, teetered, and finally pitched backward with our weight. The ladder floated one way and Addy and I fell the other. I heard myself scream. I heard Addy scream. Screams from folks below seemed to surround and swallow me whole. I spread my arms and stared up at the brilliant blue California sky. Wind ruffled my clothes like dry laundry, and my loose hair danced around my face. I fell and fell and fell.

CHAPTER 15

"Was it worth it?" Detective Cahill asked. "Sneaking into Paramount and almost getting yourselves killed?"

I shrugged, reluctant to say just how terrifying the experience had been. Mostly, I'd felt bad for Addy. "In a way. See, if we hadn't gone to the studios, I wouldn't have gotten the invite to the Grove."

"Yeah, so you went to a party with fancy swells," he said sourly. "You don't seem the sort to care for—"

"Oh, I don't. Not usually. But this wasn't just any run-of-the-mill party. It was a Hollywood industry party and it became crucial in the events that led up to this evening."

"How so?"

"Well..." I said thoughtfully, considering options. "A few things happened before the party that set my investigation in a different direction."

"I'm not interested in—"

"Yes, yes, I know," I said waving my hand to stop his customary objection about my take on the Taylor murder. "Now stay with me on this part, will you? I promise I'm leading you right up to the man in the alley. As a matter of fact,..." I tiled my head, reflecting back. "I remember thinking, after we left Paramount...

There was a certain amount of humiliation and utter embarrassment one should face during our precious time on earth if only to add spice to life. A boring life was not worth living. Mama would have stridently disagreed which is perhaps why I embraced this philosophy wholeheartedly.

So, there we were, Addy and I, strolling down Hollywood Boulevard steeped in our newly added spice. Unfortunately, it came in the form of donkey poop, and it was oozing down my coattails and dripping from my sleeves. My entire backside—Pop's funeral coat with tails—was smeared with thick healthy chunks of fundraiser poop. I had lost one of my oversized shoes and walked up-squish, down-squish, up-squish, down-squish. The cane and bowler hat were lost causes.

"I thought you said *push away* from the building," I said, offering Addy a sympathetic smile. During our fall from grace, she had twisted around and landed face first on the heaping, smelly pile. Someone might think she had slithered from the depths of a Florida swamp.

"Push away from the building!" she shrieked while digging manure from her ear. "Are you nutso! Why would I say push away from the building? I said push *him* away! *Him*! That security guard trying to pull you up!"

"Ah." That did make better sense. But I hadn't exactly

pushed us away from the building; I had just gotten flustered. First from the grabby guard and then from Addy shouting and all the whistles and barking and screaming from below. Not to mention I thought I was about to meet my Maker and not a pile of poop.

"But wasn't it terrific luck that Bud unloaded the truck right behind that fake building?"

Addy wasn't buying my *let's look on the sunny side* shtick. We squished onward in relative silence for another block or so and then I asked if she had anything interesting to report. She stopped so abruptly a brown glob fell from her shoulder.

"Are you joshing me right now, Kate March? We almost *died* and you're asking if I discovered anything to help your story?"

"I know, I know. It was shitty of me to ask," I said, watching her lips twitch into a grin.

"S'okay," Addy said. "I'm sorry I lost my temper." She grabbed me for a big, squishy, gawd-awful hug. I grimaced and took it. Then she stepped back and rubbed extra helpings on my suit front.

"All better?" I asked. She nodded and smiled.

"We sure do stink," Addy said as we continued homeward. We swapped stories about what we had seen and heard behind Paramount's pearly gate. I had a few leads that pointed toward Mary but I didn't want to give them any weight. Having an affair with an older man, which I couldn't confirm, wasn't motive for murder. Addy heard gossip about Mr. Taylor visiting hop houses for work. Apparently, actors often made use of drug dens for character research. Or so the rumors said.

And that was extent of it. An hour behind Paramount's pearly gates hadn't amounted to much. Not compared to the life-threatening circumstances we had faced.

"I really am sorry for almost getting us killed," I said, shaking my head. "I should have known better. I should have—"

"Hey, don't go second guessing yourself now. It doesn't suit you. And don't feel sorry for us either. I'd do it again, if you asked."

"Thanks," I murmured, but it hadn't made me feel any better.

Addy could always read me. She got my ups and downs and especially when I went sideways and started doubting myself. She threw an arm around my shoulders and tried to lift my spirits with some lame jokes. She could be a real crackpot when she wanted. Pretty soon I was laughing at her jokes. Shitty jokes. Stinky jokes. Defecating donkey jokes. We fell against each other, laughing mostly from pent-up emotional energy but a little from her whacky sense of humor. While Addy wiped tears and poop from her face, I noticed Pop's truck stopped dead center in the road. It wasn't Bud behind the wheel, but Nicky.

"Aw, swell," I said, thinking this was the last thing I needed. "Make like we don't see him."

Addy turned and waved like her house was on fire. "Lo there, Officer Masino!" she called and then laughed at me. "Hey, you got us into this shit."

"And you're a real laugh-getter, you know that?" I kept walking. Nicky pulled to the curb several feet ahead of us and jumped out, slamming the truck door. He marched over with all the lightheartedness of a charging bull.

"What in God's name did you girls think you were doing in there?" He gestured toward Paramount studios in the distance behind us. "And what the hell have you been rolling in?"

"Hey Nicky, what's doin'?" I asked with a carefree tone that suggested we were headed to a church picnic. I wouldn't let him know that, deep down, I was still feeling lousy for risking Addy's life.

"What's doin'?" he mocked in an incredulous tone.

"It means what are you doing here?" I said flatly. Nicky was in street clothes, dark grey pants and a starched white shirt which meant he was off duty.

"What am I doing here?" he bellowed.

"Jeezers, Nicky, if you're going to repeat everything I say we'll be here all day."

"I was sent to stop you before you got yourself arrested or... or killed! You seem to have no regard for your own personal safety, Miss March, but it's gross negligence to enlist your friend and your employee in this constant, unfailing damnfoolishness!"

Already wallowing in my own self-loathing, my cup runneth over. It was one thing to recognize your own glaring faults and another when someone else scoops them up and throws them in your face.

"Now wait just a minute! I'm perfectly capable of taking care of myself, as well as my best friend! We certainly don't require a nursemaid or a hot-tempered police officer who likes to over-step his boundaries. Do we Addy?"

Addy sighed. "Well, we did almost..."

"Aw shuddup!" I snapped.

Nicky started pacing and carrying on about the high level of ignorance of our plan and our audacity to think we could pull off such a stunt. Never mind that I thought he was right, or that we had escaped death by the skin of our teeth. We wouldn't receive an ounce of credit for our troubles, only heaps of guilt for worrying Pop. And Trudy Mae, who apparently gave Bud a good tongue lashing when he returned the truck to Bunker Hill instead of the office as I had instructed. Trudy Mae had had no recourse but to call Nicky to rescue us.

"Aren't you overreacting a bit?" I drawled, crossing my arms over my gooey chest. That might've been the wrong thing to ask.

"I thought you learned your lesson at the precinct!" Nicky yelled. "Getting arrested on purpose, and now you go sneaking into Paramount. Do you have any idea how ruthless the movie industry is? How ruthless those people are? Well? Do you?"

"Jeezers, it's not like we rushed in with guns blazing," I said.

"How the hell should I know?" he demanded. "When Bud told me what you'd done I... I didn't know what to expect." He looked me over. "I certainly didn't expect to find you walking down Hollywood Boulevard in pallbearer's clothes and reeking like a stockyard."

"Oh, for crying out loud, we're fine. Now if you'll excuse us, we have a long walk home. Come on, Addy."

"As much as I hate to say this," Nicky said, blocking my path. "I'm taking you girls home."

"Amen to that!" Addy cried. I shot her a *don't you dare* look. She walked directly to the truck and sat down on running board.

"We can manage on our own, thank you very much," I said. This whole fiasco was embarrassing enough and my only consolation was that Nicky hadn't laughed in my face. I'd heard enough sniggers from folks passing by and I didn't care to hang around to hear Nicky whooping it up. I'm sure the boys down at the Kettle would get their turn, when word got around.

"You don't have to be so stubborn *all* the time. Do you?" Nicky asked.

"No, she doesn't," Addy said, swatting the flies circling her head. "C'mon, Kate, I'm taking on passengers."

I stared at Nicky. For the life of me I couldn't understand why he kept interfering, and with such anger.

"Your pop truly is worried," Nicky said quietly, making things worse. Memories flooded back: Nicky telling me I couldn't tag along because I was too little and Pop would worry. Lawrence and Edward sending me home before dark because Pop would worry.

I sighed. "Well... only because Pop is worried," I said for the umpteenth time in my life.

It was nearly six o'clock when Addy and I descended the stairs. She wore the buttercream frock she had given me for Christmas. I was sporting some of my newest wardrobe, soft lavender lounging pants and a thin middy blouse the color of candlelight. They were cool and felt delicious against my freshly scrubbed skin and fluttered when I walked. I felt more light and feminine than I ever had before. Miles apart from how I'd felt a few hours ago.

Addy and I had washed ourselves three times in lilac water and carried the soft fragrance with us into the dining room. The four tall windows along the east wall were thrown open to accommodate the cool evening breeze. Sheer curtains snapped and tossed like gossamer hair and stirred up the delicate scent of roses from next door. It gave the illusion that Mrs. Masino's clipping garden had softly invaded our home.

The polished mahogany dining table had been lavishly arranged with Mama's special occasion Noritake bone china, crystal Waterford goblets, and polished silver utensils under starched white napkins. Overhead, the electric chandelier sparkled and threw diamond shadows along the walls. Aside from all the unusual fanfare, I also noticed there were too many place settings.

"How lovely. What's the occasion?" I asked Addy who was grinning like she had swallowed a secret. Before she could confess, voices filtered through the front door, and then Pop entered followed by Eugene, Detective King, and Nicky.

The men hung their overcoats and fedoras on the coat rack while Eugene tossed his Bakers Boy hat in a chair. They meandered into the dining room where Pop gave me an easy smile and a peck on the cheek. I startled and eyed him suspiciously as he took his seat at the head of the table.

Had he already forgiven me for sneaking into Paramount? For nearly killing myself and my best friend and for ruining his funeral tails? He had been so upset when I explained the unfortunate outcome. So why the *laissez-faire* attitude?

"Would someone explain what's going on?" I asked. No one answered. They mingled around the table, Eugene dropping heavily into a chair, Detective King glancing around for the ash can, and Nicky shifting restively.

"Oh, Kate!" Addy laughed. "Did you honestly forget?" She motioned behind me and Trudy Mae stepped forward with her famous triple-layered chocolate cake. Addy clapped her hands and shouted, "Happy birthday, you boob!"

I flushed with embarrassment. We had been so busy almost dying that I had forgotten my eighteenth birthday.

Pop called out, "Happy Birthday, my dear," and Eugene banged his knife and folk on the table, playfully demanding a piece of cake. Detective King offered gruff congratulations and Nicky passed off something of a compliment for living to see eighteen.

I lowered myself onto a chair and took a gulp of water. I suddenly felt feverish. Trudy Mae showed off her lovely creation and then returned it to the kitchen for later. She had been all day preparing my favorite meal of lamb chops in wine sauce which I'm sure she must have purchased from the hidden market.

Dinner proceeded politely enough and with the customary amount of chit chat. But I knew my birthday couldn't be the only reason for the occasion. Nicky and Detective King would not have been invited otherwise so that left the Taylor case.

"It's time we had a meeting of the minds, so to speak," Pop said, confirming my assumption. I set my knife and fork down

235

and looked expectantly at him. "Kate, I've briefed Ed and Nick on what you discovered today, and—"

"Yeah, she discovered a new use for cow crap," Eugene piped up. Detective King chortled. Nicky reached for his goblet and took a sip of water if only to hide a smile.

"Actually, Eugene, it was a fresh pile of donkey poop. Seconds, Addy?" I smiled pleasantly, offering her the dish of mashed potatoes. She stuck her chin in the air and looked down her nose.

"Don't mind if I do!" she said and then dramatically smacked a huge pile of potatoes onto her plate. We grinned at each other.

Pop cleared his throat. "Er, let's focus on the information gathered, not the way in which it was uh—" He choked on a laugh, and then Eugene started braying like an ass. Trudy Mae slammed a dish of buttered green beans onto the table so hard it made the utensils jump.

"Well, don't that curl your liver!" she retorted, jamming her hands onto her hips and shooting blistering looks around the table. "These here girls get up at the crack of dawn, doll up in marywalkers for all to see, play johnny-at-the-rat-hole to get some facts while y'all sit around like stumps-in-a-row, clatter whacking about the way they done it!"

No one spoke. There hadn't been such a shamefaced crowd since Moses brought down the Ten Commandments. Were they actually humiliated or just busy translating Trudy Mae's ripping reprimand?

I grinned and cut into my lamb chop. Trudy Mae turned on her heel and marched back to the kitchen. The others timidly returned to their food. After a few bites, Eugene leaned over and whispered like a frightened pupil under the teacher's watch.

"What's marywalkers?"

"Men's clothing," I murmured. Everyone breathed, "Ah," and nodded.

Detective King reopened the conversation by sharing new information about the case. On the day of the murder, Mr. Taylor spent the morning with his accountant, Mrs. Berger, from two o'clock until four. His chauffer, Howard Fellows, drove him home and then left with the car. Taylor and Berger would speak later on the phone. Without his car, Taylor walked to his dance lesson at five o'clock. Later at home, he had a phone conversation with Antonio Moreno, a colleague needing help with a Vitagraph contract. This was around seven o'clock and about the time Miss Normand arrived. It had been a very casual day, nothing unusual insofar as Detective King could see.

"So, you didn't find the murder weapon at Miss Normand's apartment house? In the basement as the anonymous letter stated?" I asked.

"We found two revolvers," Nicky answered. "They had nothing to do with the murder, and Miss Normand fully cooperated."

He was giving me a statement-of-fact for the paper, nothing disputable. Very professional and formal but hardly insightful. Probably a prearranged statement every other newspaper would run. Anyhow, it came to a dead end as I had suspected. Only worth a line or two in print.

I asked what they made of our findings at Paramount but Detective King said there wasn't much to do about gossip.

"We keep track of it, of course," he said. "Looking for patterns and that kind of shit, er, thing. Anyway, so far, everybody agrees that Minter was sweet on Taylor and not shy about it. That love letter leaked to the paper said as much."

"And, what about Addy's gossip overheard in the costume tents? All that business about Mr. Taylor making frequent trips to hop houses for research?"

"Yeah, I guess consorting with the lower elements of society could've meant trouble for the director. That drug angle is more disturbing than an infatuated starlet."

"And that Wallace Smith fellow," Pop said, shaking his head. The whole town had heard about Wallace Smith, the reporter whose columns in the *Chicago American* were charging that Taylor didn't attend hop parties for research so much as supplying drugs to several Hollywood starlets. His last column went so far as to allege that some starlet—an unnamed film queen—killed Taylor in a drug induced rage.

I reminded Detective King about one of my columns. "Henry Peavey stated that Miss Normand and Mr. Taylor had argued the night he was murdered. He didn't know what they had argued about, but it certainly contradicts Miss Normand's account of an innocent visit. To my knowledge, she hasn't changed her story." Like my column, I omitted the part about Henry hearing Mr. Taylor arguing about Mary earlier in the day. I couldn't see that it would make any difference toward the case. At least that's what I told myself.

"Miss Normand hasn't changed her story," Detective King grunted out. "And, I wouldn't expect her to."

To my surprise, Pop revealed that he had been trying to reach Wallace Smith, hoping he would elaborate on this drug accusation. Or at least reveal his source. Chicago was a long way from Hollywood, and Pop was curious as to how Mr. Smith had come by the information. Wallace Smith never returned his calls.

"Suppose there isn't a source," Nicky mused. He pushed his empty plate aside and leaned back. "Everyone's reporting on these hop parties or claiming drug pushers have been seen on Paramount's movie lots. Some say Taylor supplied the drugs, others swear he was anti-drug and known to chase them away.

This Smith fella is probably riding the gossip. He didn't outright accuse anyone by name, so no harm no foul. Legally, speaking."

"That's what we need," Detective King said. "Someone to find out who Smith is talking about. We need Taylor's closest friends to start squawking. Woolwine's got the Flying Squad poking around but they aren't getting anywhere. An amnesia epidemic, if you ask me."

Trudy Mae returned with slices of birthday cake and home-made ice cream. I took a plate and set it aside.

"Well, what about that party Friday night at the Cocoanut Grove?" I said. "Mr. Taylor's closest friends and colleagues will be there, and I have a personal invitation. I could rub elbows and eavesdrop for a while."

Eugene, who had stuffed his mouth with an enormous slice of cake, nearly choked on it. "The Cocoanut Grove!" he bellowed. "Are you joshing? You'd never get past the maître d. The Grove is high class now, Kate, not like the old days when it was first built. Them hoity-toity flappers and slick dandies roll up in custom touring cars dressed to the nines in rocks and dead animals. The Ambassador Hotel doesn't want locals rubbing elbows with their well-to-do clientele at the Grove. You gotta be *somebody* to get in and last time I looked, you ain't *nobody*."

"She's got an invitation!" Addy retorted. "She just needs a date."

Eugene licked frosting from his fingers. "Yeah, but that means *she* can't wear the pants." He laughed and then caught Trudy Mae's sour glare and collapsed like a wilting daisy.

"Aw, go stick your head in an ash can, will ya?" Addy grumbled in my defense.

"That's enough, Eugene," Pop murmured.

"Well, what do you think?" I smiled brightly, hoping Pop's *laissez-faire* attitude would extend beyond my latest fiasco.

239

He flinched in surprise. "What? Of course not!"

"But we can't miss this opportunity! We need to hear from Mr. Taylor's own friends. Detective King said so himself."

Detective King suddenly had the spotlight. He had been quietly contemplating things but one glance from Nicky and the game was over. Nicky didn't approve, thereby making up King's mind for him. This chain of command was a conundrum. One of these days, somebody was going to answer for it.

Pop set his coffee cup down and folded his arms on the table. "Kate, as I told you earlier, I believe you girls were foolhardy to sneak into Paramount the way you did and darned lucky to escape without being arrested. Or killed. So-called accidents happen all the time on movie lots. I've told you the movie industry is a billion-dollar game now. Morality bills in Washington could shut them down. Do you think for a minute those show folks would let you leave the Cocoanut Grove if they discovered you were a reporter taking notes on their private conversations? If they knew you were there to collect damning secrets that would harm them personally, not to mention help destroy their livelihood? They wouldn't buy that hogwash you fed the security guards down at Paramount about wanting an autograph from that Valentino fellow. You were lucky they released you unharmed. Don't think it will happen again."

Addy and I exchanged smiles. We had been rather proud of that spontaneous fib. Why, if it hadn't been for the future Mrs. Valentino's desperate attempt to break through the gate, I'm not sure what cock-and-bull story we would have come up with.

I was highly aware that Pop's common-sense lecture mirrored the one I had given Addy when explaining the dangers of sneaking into Paramount. Now on the receiving end I felt just as undeterred as she had felt. Perhaps even eager to take up the challenge. It was a spectacular opportunity I wasn't going

240

to toss away. Plus, I had full confidence that there would not be a pile of donkey manure within miles of the place.

Pop might not accept the idea now, it coming on the heels of my most recent disaster, but in the end, he would realize a break like this was a gift.

"'S okay, Pop." I smiled. "We'll think of something else."

Addy lowered her eyes so as not to give anything away. She knew I had no intention of squandering this opportunity, and I knew that falling out of a three-story building and landing in a pile of donkey poop had not suppressed her enthusiasm to stir up trouble. I could count on her like an abacus.

No more was said about the Taylor case. We retired to the parlor where I was seated in Pop's favorite chair and handed birthday gifts. Pop presented me with a new Kodak camera! I was over the moon! I'd always wanted a Kodak. Addy snatched it up and immediately began clicking pictures.

"Hey, Kate," she announced, "let's go Kodaking at Santa Monica Peer this Friday night! I'm sure I can wiggle out of work early."

I grinned. The seed of deception had been planted.

I moved on to Eugene's present, a black Waterman fountain pen. I suspected Trudy Mae's hand in this. Something so elegant and personal was beyond Eugene's imagination. The fountain pen went nicely with my gift from Trudy Mae, a soft moleskin cover for my reporter's notepad. She crushed me in a bear hug and announced that she was happier than a cat at a mouse show because I was turning into a fine newspaper gal. I blushed terribly.

Addy had, for the time being, given up on buying dresses for me. Her gift was a stylish fedora. It was ivory with a pale-yellow flower tucked inside a brown lace hatband. I suspected the flower had been Addy's touch. It was lovely. I hugged her and thanked her. She promised never to borrow it.

241

There were no presents from Nicky or Detective King which I hadn't expected, and would have been embarrassed to receive. It was perfectly fine that they stood apart with Pop and discussed the Taylor case without me. They could speculate all they wanted; I already had my next plan. Eugene cranked the Victrola and placed the needle on the recording of "Wang-Wang Blues" by Paul Whiteman and the Ambassador Orchestra. Addy and I lounged on the divan and carelessly flipped through a couple of *Smart Set* magazines until it grew late and she was due home. She threw out a careless goodnight to all, and then I walked her onto the porch. Once I had closed the door behind us, she whirled on me.

"You're doing it? The Cocoanut Grove, I mean?"

"Sh-sh-sh." I pulled her away from the door. "We'll talk later."

"But you can't go like... what'll you wear?"

I wasn't exactly a fashion failure but I knew what she meant. As lovely as my new wardrobe was, I couldn't stroll into the Grove in a middy blouse and trousers.

"I have no idea. It'll take some work to—"

"I'm here to tell ya!" Addy said, pulling a face. "We'll need help if you're gonna be putting on the Ritz so let me think on it." She went quietly down the steps, already deep in thought.

"Tomorrow, then," I called from the porch. "Meet you at the Flight. Don't be late!" I could hardly make her out under the grey moonlight. Damp fog had ushered in a chill. I shivered and hugged my arms, watching her disappear like Marley's ghost.

Infiltrating the Cocoanut Grove was a staggering idea and not the smartest decision I had ever made. It was one thing to picnic inside Paramount Studios with the extras and another to mingle with Hollywood's finest at the Grove. Pop had been right.

There was a certain element of danger to it. But that was another kettle of fish. My deepest concerns hit closer to home. I would need more than a passable wardrobe, I would need a willing date and a personality change. I wasn't exactly a carefree Modern who could flit from one party to another. I didn't have that 'it' quality that turned men into lesser beings to grovel at my feet. I was no Clara Bow. Jeezers, I already felt like a fraud and I hadn't set foot inside the Grove yet.

The front door opened and Nicky and Detective King strolled out. King cut a matchstick across his pant leg and a flame burst to life and then shrank. He cupped his hand around it, lighting a ciggy.

"G'night, Miss March. Stay out of trouble," he said. He pulled hard on his smoke, caving in his cheeks. He shook the matchstick to death and tossed it aside. He seemed to want to repeat himself and make that casual request an order but he must have changed his mind. He squinted into the foggy night and then grumbled something to Nicky as he clomped down the steps.

Nicky tipped his fedora back onto his head, slipped his hands into his pockets, and looked at me.

I sighed. "This the part where you tell me to say away from the Grove?" I asked, not bothering to hide my irritation.

"I'd like a clarification, if you don't mind," he said.

"Shoot."

"It seems on every occasion when you are told not to do something, you go right out and do it. Is that a fair assessment?"

I folded my arms over my chest. "That's about the size of it."

"So, if I were to tell you to stay away from the Cocoanut Grove Friday night, you'd show up with bells on?" He cocked an eyebrow, and I shrugged with indifference. "I'm going to say it anyway."

"Save your air," I said. "Addy and I have other plans. Besides, we both know you couldn't stop me *if* I wanted to get in. Which I didn't say I was doing."

"Someone needs to stop you, Miss March—"

"And lay off the Miss March stuff, while you're at it. I've known you all my life, Nicky Masino. It's just you and me standing here. I don't know what authority you have over Detective King, or anyone else down at the precinct, but you don't have a plugged nickel's worth over me."

I don't know why I was feeling so hostile toward him. Maybe I hadn't cared for the way he had laughed at me during dinner. Everyone else had. So why had it rubbed me the wrong way when Nicky did? It was one thing to laugh at something someone had done but another to laugh at the person themselves. Maybe I thought Nicky saw me as a joke. And, why should I care, anyway?

It could have been plain exhaustion from a long day and I was taking it out on him. Either way, I continued for another few minutes, throwing out every complaint under the sun. Funny thing was, Nicky didn't throw anything back. He just stood there taking it and grinning.

Near the end of my tirade, a small, out-of-place voice brought me to a halt. Nicky and I looked out into the yard and found Mrs. Banning standing on the sidewalk with Livingston in her arms. Fog hovered at her back but it didn't hide the scowl on her soft fleshy face.

"Pardon me?" Nicky called out.

Mrs. Banning raised her voice irritably. "I said, I've solved your murder!"

CHAPTER 16

I smiled, secretly thanking Mrs. Banning for her insight. Of course, she had no idea how much she had actually helped me, if tonight's plan was anything to judge by. But how to explain it to Detective Cahill?

"So," he said knowingly, "this neighbor of yours solved the murder, huh? And, we have her to thank?" He scoffed and flipped his pad to a fresh page.

"Not so fast," I warned. "Mrs. Banning had her part to play."

"If she's a friend of yours, I have no doubt about it," he said, chuckling and shaking his head.

"What do you know, anyhow?" I shot back.

"You're not seriously telling me that some old busybody from Bunker Hill knows who killed Taylor?" Detective Cahill asked sitting forward.

I smiled again, happy to have lured him further into my

Nicky was leaning against the front porch column while I was perched on the railing. The cool foggy night had turned down-right chilly and I shivered, rubbing my arms.

Mrs. Banning waddled up the sidewalk cuddling Livingston in her arms. Ten pounds overweight, the cat took every bit of strength she had.

"Listen up, you two," Mrs. Banning went on in the firm and familiar tone she had used in our youth when warning us to stay out of her garden. "I'm telling you I had the most astonishing dream last night. I dreamt that Livie, here, was dead but he came back to me as a spirit. He was yowling and floating about the house like a giant, spiritualistic balloon. Then, you see, he revealed the killer of that poor director fellow. It's none other than his chimney sweep." She snuggled her cheek against Livingston's furry grey head. "Just like that, didn't you Livie, dear? You revealed the killer in a dream. You're such a smart kitty. Even when you're dead." She lifted her face and grew serious again.

"Thought you'd like that for your column, Katharine dear. And, maybe you too, Nicola. Tell your little officer friends at the station that the killer is the chimney sweep. Well, we're off. Don't want to catch a chill. 'Night all!" With a job well done, Mrs. Banning dumped Livingston on the ground and tugged his leash, guiding him back up the sidewalk.

"Should we have told her Mr. Taylor had no fireplace?" Nicky asked, amused.

"And destroy her theory with annoying things like facts?" I laughed lightly and then yawned. I was ready to put this day to bed. Nicky blocked my path to the door.

246

"You will stay away from the Grove?" he asked. I gave him a perturbed look. Nothing I loathed more than being forced to lie. I much preferred not being asked in the first place. And Nicky was aware he was doing just that. Forcing me to lie.

"I believe I have already told you. Addy and I have something better to do this Friday night." Speaking of lies, I thought. "Your turn. Who were those two fellas we saw at the precinct the other night? You know the ones, those pasty-faced bucks in the motor pool? I asked you about them that night and have been waiting for an answer ever since."

"Couldn't say," he replied coolly.

"You and Angelo got pretty heated when you saw them."

Nicky shrugged and stepped back. "Probably a couple of swells looking to bail out their buddies on account of those anonymous tips you called in."

I smiled. That was load of horseshit and we both knew it. One lie was as good as another. Nicky had never been one to rattle easily. But that night by the motor pool he had been silently provoked somehow. Arguing with his brother was one thing but to lose his composure so completely due to a couple of strangers had me curious. They had made no threatening moves but Nicky and Angelo had reacted as though they were targets for an attack.

"Why won't you answer me? Truthfully," I said.

"Good night, Miss March," Nicky said brushing past me and walking down the porch steps.

"Do they have anything to do with the Taylor case?" I called. Nicky simply raised his hat as a final farewell and turned on the sidewalk, heading home.

* * *

247

My concentration during school the next day was generally lacking. Any answers I offered when called upon were vague and perfunctory. I wasn't bored, just highly diverted. I had a fair amount of emotions vying for my attention, fear ranking highest among them. Fear about Friday night at the Grove. *How could I possibly fool the elite masses who could spot shoddy acting a mile away? Fear about the gossip regarding Mary. If she had been involved with Mr. Taylor and he had been killed out of jealousy, was Mary in danger, too?*

My stomach burned and I rubbed my side.

What if Mary knew who the killer was? What if Paramount was forcing her to lie about what she knew? Could I gain Mary's true confidence and pry out her secrets?

Somewhere deep down, my real fear was brewing. I was afraid to know Mary's secrets. I hadn't wanted to look too closely and I hadn't wanted to believe Fannie Baker's gossip. I always thought of Mary as being fragile with bursts of recklessness. Anger towards her mother had driven her into fits of rage. It was completely understandable. Other times Mary seemed utterly lost. For years she had been a child trying to survive in an adult business. As a young woman of nineteen, Mary was about as stable as a dog on roller skates.

I wondered if Mary had a truly good friend as I had in Addy. I couldn't recall her ever mentioning one and I pitied her for it. I don't know how I would have survived without my Addy.

As always, she was sitting next to me at the lunch table surrounded by the usual Star and Crescent members. It suddenly occurred to me that I might just miss these times after graduation, although I hadn't heard a word anyone had said since I sat down. They had been deep in conversation while I had been dissecting my concerns.

"So, it's all settled then!" Addy announced, beaming at me.

"What is?" I asked.

"Jeezers, Kate, weren't you listening? You have a driver and a date for Friday night! You really should pay attention, I mean, this is only the biggest con you've ever played."

The stage had been set: Dewey Deets would play the part of my driver because he'd had actual driving lessons from his father. Abner Felts was voted to be my date because everyone agreed he'd been the keenest actor in the school production of King Lear. Also, because Abner had offered his father's touring car on the stipulation that he got to go along. I wasn't sure he was up to the task of rubbing elbows with shimmering starlets and dashing male leads but I didn't want to seem ungrateful. Both were being awfully generous with their time.

"You understand it might be dangerous?" I looked at each one respectively. "If the movie folks find out who we are and what we're up to, they might take us on a one-way drive, if you know what I mean. In the very least we could be arrested or barred from the Hotel and restaurant indefinitely."

"I'll have the car ready for a fast getaway," Dewey said importantly. "You can count on me."

"And I'll develop a character whose tormented past keeps him withdrawn, and quiet, but not too much. Wouldn't want them to think I'm off my nut or anything."

I groaned inwardly but forced a smile. This had all the potential success of the *Titanic*.

"That's swell!" Addy said, overenthusiastically. "Kate's real grateful for your help, aren't ya, Kate?" She elbowed me.

I perked up and graciously agreed. Never mind the bad feeling roiling in my gut. Two giant hurdles had been conquered in one fell swoop. All that remained was the transformation of me.

My time after school was spent down at *The Messenger,* hashing out possible murder theories with Pop and the staff. Occasionally, my mind wandered off course and I found myself conjuring horrific scenarios of being pummeled at the Grove by burly security guards. I had quite the imagination and gave serious consideration to becoming a scene writer for the picture shows.

Somewhere between being tortured and being tossed broken in a ditch, I heard Mrs. Hazeldine comment in favor of the jealously angle. Mr. Handle was keen on the newest accusation passed around by Wallace Smith, that midwestern reporter horning in on our Southern California calamity.

"A Chinese opium den?" I gaped at Smith's latest column. According to Chicago's illustrious reporter, a Chinese opium smuggler informed the authorities of a secret cult in which male members pledged their loyalties and secrecies to each other and swore to have no association with women. In the cult, the men would paint their faces, don silk kimonos, and assemble in various dens around the city where they would wallow in opium to their hearts' content. The informant claimed that Taylor was not only a member of the cult, but a leader. He had broken the code and was killed. Sounded to me like this so-called informant had broken the code as well.

"It's been less than two weeks since the murder and the papers have accused Taylor of attending hop parties for research, being a drug addict himself, supplying drugs to friends, being killed by a friend in a dope frenzy, and now killed by a homosexual member of a Chinese drug cult!" I wadded the paper and tossed it in the can. No such scenarios had appeared in my columns. The last thing I needed was some trumped up theory coming back to haunt me. But sooner or later I had to fit the pieces together. In no particular order, I needed to discover *why* Mr. Taylor had been killed and who had benefited from his death. Answer one and the other should follow.

Trudy Mae had taken an unexpected evening off but left a nice pot of stew on the stove. I hadn't much appetite for food or conversation. While Pop escaped in one of his books I wore a path around the library for a solid hour trying to think like a killer. *What kinda fella has the nerve to walk into another man's home and shoot him in the back when he wasn't looking?* I'd long thought it was someone cold and heartless rather than a random frightened burglar, but I hadn't decided if Taylor knew his killer. Had he welcomed him inside? Had Taylor turned his back on him without a second thought for his safety?

No. I firmly believed the killer had been waiting in the alleyway smoking those ciggys until Taylor bid farewell to Miss Normand. Then the killer had crept inside the bungalow and waited for Taylor to return. I couldn't say if there had been any sort of conversation or if Taylor ever knew he wasn't alone, until he was shot. Nothing in the apartment had been overturned. No evidence suggested they'd had a tussle and the gun went off accidentally. But why was Taylor lying face-up when Henry Peavey found him? When you're shot in the back don't you topple forward? Maybe he staggered around a bit first. Wouldn't he have reached out for support, maybe slid a hand across the desk? Knock things to the floor? If so, had the killer picked up the place and then turned Taylor over to make sure he was dead?

Doubtful. There had been no blood smeared on the carpet to indicate the body had been moved. Perhaps Taylor had spun around in shock when he'd been hit and then fell backward. The killer didn't have to do any clean up. He just walked out and pulled the door shut as Mrs. MacLean had reported seeing.

"Don't think too hard on it," Pop offered as he took a break to light his pipe. "You'll think you've solved it and your reporting will be tainted."

I sighed and rubbed my temples. "That's exactly what I was doing. But I just can't figure it any other way."

"There are a million options and yours might or might not be true. You're a reporter, not a detective."

I smiled and felt my mood lift. Pop had called me a reporter.

"But it doesn't hurt to think like a detective," I said.

"No, it doesn't." Pop winked and returned to his book.

"Well, I'm off to bed. Maybe I'll have a dream like Mrs. Banning and wake up knowing who the killer is," I joked and kissed Pop goodnight.

I clicked on my desk lamp, curled up in bed, and cracked open my favorite book for the umpteenth time: *Ten Days in a Mad-House* by my hero, Nellie Bly. Reading her story about time spent in a woman's insane asylum on an undercover assignment had often given me fantasies of my own journalistic career. Miss Bly was far more daring than I was but revisiting her story these past few nights had given me something more than idle fantasies. It had given me courage to trust myself when I was so often plagued with doubts. And nerve to push onward even after wearing animal dung down Hollywood Boulevard.

I was deep into chapter three again when I heard thumping against the house and a couple of Addy's favorite swear words. I crawled out of bed and opened the widow.

"Addy?" I whispered down the side of the house. She was grunting up the trellis, thick with vines, and eventually climbed through the window and threw herself onto the bed.

"Hiya!" she said, breathing heavily. She leaned over with a stitch in her side. "I ran all the way!"

"What's doin' with you?" I asked, picking leaves from her hair. "Hiding from your mama?"

"And how! Is Trudy Mae back yet?"

"Huh?"

Just then we heard the back door open and close. Trudy Mae's familiar footsteps moved through the kitchen below us.

"Say, what are you up to?" I asked, closing the window against the chill and climbing back into bed.

Addy sat up and tucked a leg beneath her. Her eyes were bright and her cheeks pink from running in the cold night air. "It all started because of Mama. She sent me to work as an usherette down at the Hollywood bowl tonight. I swear that woman's gonna run me ragged. Anyway, I got to talking with some chickpeas working a double shift and—" She stopped when Trudy Mae walked in. She was carrying a brown sack and puffing like a steam engine. Without a word, she went straight to the desk chair and sat down heavy from exhaustion. I curled my legs beneath the covers and hugged my knees. They had my undivided attention.

Trudy Mae removed various items from the paper bag and set them aside: a can of Old Dutch Cleanser, a tin of Coleman's Mustard, a bottle of Mulsified Cocoanut Oil Shampoo. I was baffled. Nobody offered an explanation for all this late-night monkey business.

The paper bag was empty but for one last item which Trudy Mae gently lifted out and held like a sacred offering. It was a long, narrow black box. I stared, first at the box and then at Trudy Mae's solemn expression. She moved to the end of the bed and set the box between her and Addy. Carefully, she removed the lid.

Addy and I peered inside. There were several thick oblong forms that appeared to be stuffed cotton bandages.

"So, it's true, then," Addy whispered.

"What's doin' with this stuff?" I asked nonplussed.

"Say, don't you know anything?" she retorted. "Trudy Mae's just a genius, that's all. Go ahead, Trud, tell her what she's gawking at like some low-brow palooka who don't know from nothing."

"Y'all might have heard about them," Trudy Mae said, "whispered behind hands because decent folk won't speak of it in public. Well, they're real and they're called cotton textiles. During the Great War, the Kimberly Clark Company sold special gauze bandages to the war department. When the war ended, they had warehouses full of unused medical gauze. Sure as I'm sitting here, a load of sensible nurses put them to good use." She gave me a pointed look, but I hadn't caught on yet. "When Kimberly Clark Company got wind of this idea, they took it a step further and developed the cellcotton napkin or what folks are calling cotton textile."

Addy picked one up and fiddled with it. "The chickpeas down at the Bowl called them Kotex. They gave me a hot tip and I sent Trudy Mae to track down a supplier. Most stores aren't brave enough to carry them and women are too embarrassed to buy them. We got these on the hidden market down on Central Avenue."

"But what's it all mean?" I asked, still unsure what I was looking at.

"It means, we don't have to use rags anymore," Addy said. "Leave it to a World War to invent the sanitary napkin."

"You mean... you're gonna put this thing... down... there?" I considered the long narrow bandage for a moment and then shrugged. "Kinda makes sense, if you think about it. It was made to stop the bleeding." Not that my monthly curse had been on my mind lately but the pads seemed like a swell idea.

I just wasn't as enthusiastic about them as Addy and Trudy Mae were. It could have waited until tomorrow. "So that's what all the uproar is about?"

"Heck no!" Addy said, changing rails like a train engine. She swiped a few cotton textiles and stuffed them down her bodice for later. Trudy Mae shoved a few into her pocket and left the remainders for me. "While we were making good on the Kotex, Trudy Mae ran into an old pal of hers. That's when we hatched our plan! It was all so serendipitous!"

"What was?"

"We found a way to doll you up for tomorrow night!" Addy's enthusiasm exploded all over again.

"Turns out my old pal, Injun Pat, still peddles costumes for the studios," Trudy Mae said. "He's gonna give us pick of the racks. And I'm talking top drawer rags, the kind the movie folk wear in the picture shows. When the time comes, you'll be so hoity toity, nobody'll recognize you."

"That's swell but... what about, you know..." I gestured to my face.

"That, too!" Addy said. "I'm telling ya, Trudy Mae's got more connections than Bell Telephone! It'll be the works!"

Trudy Mae stood and replaced the sundry items into the bag. "We'll get ya started first thing after school tomorrow. It'll take every minute you've got so don't mosey about. Hightail it home, ya hear?"

"Yes, ma'am."

"Can you believe it, Kate?" Addy grabbed my hands excitedly. "Final exams tomorrow, and then we're finished with high school! By this time on Saturday, we'll be officially graduated!"

Addy's enthusiasm was contagious and I felt my own excitement bubble to the surface. We hugged and laughed like we were getting away with something. I was more than ready to be finished with high school. Even though Addy and I hadn't the courage to go Modern yet, I felt a was change coming. Lord help us, but I knew something dramatic awaited in our future.

I was unusually focused for final exams on Friday, and whizzed through the morning challenges without hesitation. During lunchtime, Addy and I rehearsed the details of our upcoming escapade with Dewey and Abner. The boys were besotted with nervous energy, and I counseled them as best I could. Most importantly, they must concentrate on their final exams first. Everything after school would take care of itself. I had complete and utter confidence in them.

In a terrifying sort of way.

Three hours later, we were suddenly finished with school. Addy and I completed our last exam, said our farewells until graduation tomorrow, and left the halls of Los Angeles High for the last time. Addy was as giddy as a bride on her wedding night. I was relieved, but had moved on from giddy to apprehensive. Just what had Trudy Mae arranged for my transformation?

We bypassed our usual stop at the office, and headed straight home. Trudy Mae was waiting at the top of Angel's Flight with a picnic basket and a taxi. She looked around as though we might be followed, and then opened the door for us. Addy and I quickly climbed into the back seat, and settled in without a word. It was all very clandestine and I had the feeling we were about to do something quite nefarious.

The taxi sped down the winding hills of Los Angeles while nerves nipped at my heels. I was no Nellie Bly and had no qualms about dolling up for the story. It certainly couldn't be worse than wearing a donkey poop suit. I just didn't like being in the dark about the details.

"How long is this going to take?" I asked Trudy Mae. She was seated in front with the driver, some fella she'd introduced as Jenson. Another old pal of hers.

"It'll take as long as it takes," she said over her shoulder.

"Chin up," Addy said, digging into the picnic basket situated between us. "Even ol' Mata Hari was able to transform herself from a frumpy school girl into a wild sexual creature."

We'd heard stories about the infamous lady spy of the Great War. But I had no intention of trying to impersonate a wild sexual creature.

"You *do* know her last performance was at the wrong end of a firing squad?" I said.

"Not before she hypnotized audiences and tossed away lovers like yesterday's garbage." Addy stuffed an apple between her teeth and swirled her arms in mock seduction. "Don't you want to be a wild sexual creature, Kate?" she asked, drooling around the apple. I laughed and snatched it from her mouth.

While Addy and I munched on apples and grapes, Jenson navigated us into Hollywood and eventually pulled alongside a busy sidewalk. We climbed out at 5335 Melrose. The sign out front read *Western Costume*.

"This place is run by a dear old friend," Trudy Mae announced proudly. "Injun Pat gave me my first job when I rolled into Los Angeles. Of course, back then he sold authentic Indian goods. Old Pat outfitted *Squaw Man* nearly ten years ago. He's been costuming the movies ever since. If Injun Pat can't help us, there's no hope to be had."

Injun Pat turned out to be a swanky fella in a fashionable three-piece, pinstriped suit with necktie and collar pin. He wore a long black braid draped over his shoulder, shapely eyebrows arched like a couple of questions, stylish tan moccasins, and an eagle feather raised at the back of his head like a white flag. As spectacular as he was, it was nothing compared to his place of business. The spacious store held racks and racks of the most colorful clothes Addy and I had ever laid eyes on. I stood there gawking while she threw herself into shimmering silks and glorious satins. All around were plumes of ostrich feathers in every color imaginable and bouquets of bright-eyed peacock feathers. Rhinestones glittered like tiny suns in earrings, bracelets and bobbles from glass display cases. The costumes varied from practical to vampish to virginal to downright scandalous. They seemed to have a life of their own with daring hemlines, peek-a-boo lace, plunging necklines, strapless bodices, gloves longer than arms, headbands sporting feathers two feet tall, heeled shoes with sparkles, and enough beaded necklaces to choke a horse. The back of the shop held scores of men's costumes: bandits, cowboys, Indians, Civil War uniforms, train engineers, police officers, jail birds, and more. I wished we would have known about this place before sneaking into Paramount.

For the next two hours, Trudy Mae and Injun Pat went to work on me. He understood the delicate situation and brought out a slew of dresses and corresponding paraphernalia. They poked and pinched, stitched and ripped, tightened and stretched, fluffed and smoothed, raised and then lowered until they got their wish. All the while I stood on a dais, turned on command, munched an apple, and buried my nose inside *Life Magazine*. The cartoons of John Held sure could tickle my funny bone.

Addy had disappeared some time ago, and I hadn't heard a peep out of her beyond an occasional squeal of delight. I assumed she had died and was rolling around in heaven. When Trudy Mae finally pronounced me finished, Addy reappear. She stumbled from the racks wearing a bright yellow flapper dress with a peacock feather on her banded forehead that stared out like a third eye. Her neck was adorned with thirty pounds of beads and her shoulders were wrapped in a fluffy white boa as though she had plucked a ghost. Addy sported a lethargic, gin-soaked grin that had nothing to do with alcohol.

We gaped at each other and cried, "Look at you!" in unison.

We laughed and hooted like a pair of hillbillies. It was awful. I told Addy she looked marvelous in a tawdry sort of way. She laughed and spun me around to face the mirror. My mouth fell open and I dropped my apple and my *Life*.

It was a shock seeing myself put together. I had purposely avoided the mirror so I could enjoy the surprise afterward, but I had not expected this! My wardrobe staff had selected a red silk flapper dress etched in a dazzling modern art design with brilliant rhinestone flowers. Sleeveless with a low waist, the hemline barely reached my knees. The flesh-colored stockings I had allowed Trudy Mae to wrangle me into had been rolled to the knees. I felt utterly self-conscious and fought the urge to cover myself. But where to start! My bare arms or half-naked legs? Mama use to say a lady should never show her ankles, as if men didn't know we had any. And just look at me now! Could I really show all this scandalous flesh in public as I'd seen so many Modern girls doing?

"You know, Addy, if we lived in Utah I'd been arrested walking around like this!"

"One more thing," Trudy Mae said, undaunted. She slid a glittering headband on my head. It sparkled with clusters of rhinestones that copied the flowers on my dress. Altogether, it complimented the rhinestones on my heeled shoes perfectly. I hated to admit it but I thought it was perfectly sensational and very unlike me. I swished left and right, inspecting each angle and delighting in the silk against my skin. Who knew a dress could feel so luxurious?

"Whaddaya think, Addy? Is it too—"

"And how!" She clapped her hands and gave a bawdy laugh—a sure sign of approval.

"Best disguise I've had yet."

Trudy Mae and Injun Pat did not share our enthusiasm. They circled me with arms crossed and faces frowning. Injun Pat's eagle eyes felt positively invasive but he was too professional to cause embarrassment.

"You know she still needs work on the um—" He waved a hand toward my face.

"Already put the call in," Trudy Mae murmured, deep into her scrutiny.

"You called..." Again with the wave to finish his thought.

"Of course," Trudy Mae said. She instructed me to walk around to get comfortable in the high-heeled shoes. Addy helped me down from the dais and off I went, wobbling like a flamingo with broken knees.

"Aw, she'll get the hang of it by tonight. Won't ya, Cinderella?" Addy teased. I teetered and gave her a helpless smile.

"Well, Kate, you ain't Sarah Bernhardt but you'll do." Trudy Mae smiled with satisfaction.

"Do?" I cried, wind-milling my arms as I spun around. "You just watch! I'll fit in perfectly!"

Injun Pat tossed his measuring tape onto a chair. "Yes. Like a duck in Arizona."

CHAPTER 17

Detective Cahill gave me a pointed look. *"So, you had no intention of obeying your father when he specifically told you not to go to the Grove that night?"*

He sounded awfully parental but I let it slide. *"Look-it, I don't worry my Pop for kicks, you know. I was serious about taking advantage of the opportunity. The movie industry had closed ranks. No new information was getting out by this time, as you and the Flying Squad know perfectly well. And, it wasn't an easy assignment I'd given myself. Sacrifices were made. Just so you know."*

"What kind of sacrifices?"

I tucked a strand of hair behind my ear, hesitating. *"Well, all right. If you must know..."*

After our fitting with Injun Pat at *Western Costumes*, we hopped back into the taxi and sped toward Central Avenue. I thought we might stop at Addy's house where she and Trudy Mae had stashed a wig or something. Instead, we arrived outside a storefront on South Central Avenue and climbed out.

The sign out front read "Max Factor's Antiseptic Hair Store." I hesitated, suddenly wary. Addy guided me to the door and pronounced, "Icing on the cake." She was suspiciously eager to get me inside.

Although the shop was closed, we entered to find a pleasant older gentleman waiting. He had short wavy hair with traces of grey, a small mustache to match, round wire spectacles, and wore a pale blue smock. He smiled warmly and greeted Trudy Mae as old friends. While they reminisced, Addy and I strolled around like visitors in a circus sideshow.

Everywhere we looked were heads. Shelves and shelves of heads with blank faces sporting various wigs in a variety of colors. Labels on the shelves represented the corresponding wig: Blondes Only, Redheads Only, Brownettes Only, and Brunettes Only. Dressing tables lined the room, each with square mirrors framed in Edison's bright lightbulbs and containers of brushes, combs, strange tonics, and hand-held mirrors. Every dressing table held twelve jars filled with brown gunk in shades from light to dark and neat rows of tubes marked 'Greasepaint'. A number of barber chairs were situated throughout the room and equipped with various steel implements resembling a surgeon's tray. On the back wall hung anatomical drawings of faces divided into sections and a sign that advertised, "Made-To-Order-Wigs, Only The Finest Human Hair Used."

Addy and I looked at each other in wonder.

"Katie Ann, this here is Mr. Factor and he'll be fixing you up," Trudy Mae said, grinning broadly.

262

"A pleasure, my dear," the nice little man said, bowing slightly. I smiled tentatively, making him chuckle. "Please do not look so frightened, my dear. It will still be you, underneath it all." He guided me into a barber chair where the square of bright light around the mirror made me squint.

"Underneath all what?" I asked.

"Now listen, Max," Trudy Mae jumped in. "It's like I told ya; we want her done up right. None of that old theater junk. Let's have that new stuff you're peddling at the studios."

"But of course. The flexible greasepaint." He selected a jar from the neat row on the dressing table and held it next to my cheek. "Nooooo cracking. Nooooo caking," he crooned like a dove.

"Yeah, that'll be it. She'll need a heavy dose of the cosmetics, and I mean the kind that ain't for polite society. She's in disguise, see?"

He tutted at her. "Ah, ah, ah. I am calling this *make-up* now. Not cosmetic." He wrinkled his nose in a cute sort of way and then adjusted his little round spectacles and got busy with his instruments.

After removing my rhinestone headband, Mr. Factor tied a scarf around my head to keep my hair from interfering. Then he began by studying my face: skin, nose, cheeks, forehead, eyebrows, and lips. Using a modified wooden ruler, he tipped my chin one way and then the other, measuring my features and humming under his breath.

"What beautiful eyes!" he cried, a bit too enthusiastically.

"Thanks," I murmured. "They came with the face." I squirmed around to catch Addy's attention. She was lost in a row of heads. Mr. Factor was making me more self-conscious than Injun Pat had, and that was saying something.

"And excellent cheekbones," he remarked. "A fine chin, yes,

263

strong but delicate." Pleased with his findings, he threw his hands open and gushed, "How I wish I could use your face to make my model heads! The proportions are exact!"

"Oh, well, thanks anyway, Mr. Factor, but I'll be using my face this evening, if it's all the same to you."

Addy snorted a laugh. "Don't look till you're all done, Kate. I want to be there." She had abandoned the heads and went back to admiring herself in one of the dressing table mirrors. She was preoccupied because Injun Pat had loaned her the yellow flapper dress and she couldn't take her eyes off herself.

Mr. Factor turned me away from the mirror and got down to business. He selected a one-inch artist's brush, dipped it into the jar of brown gunk, and brought it to my face. I flinched. He withdrew and looked at me over his cheaters.

"I dare not cover such beauty with paint, but as I do for Mary Pickford, I do for you." He smiled softly, and I relaxed. He began painting my face in light, fluttery motions.

After he finished smoothing me out, he floured me with light powder, outlined my eyes with black liquid, shadowed them in smoky grey, combed something black onto my eyelashes, plucked a few eyebrows and then penciled them back in. He dusted my cheeks with color, painted my lips red, and then stood back to admire his handiwork.

"Beautiful!" he exclaimed.

"Jeezers, Kate! I wouldn't know ya!" Addy said.

"And now for the hair," Trudy Mae said.

"What *about* my hair?" I asked, fighting the urge to look in the mirror. It wasn't easy because my face tingled and my eyelashes felt like awnings.

Mr. Factor gestured toward the shelves lined with assorted wigs. I had my pick of the litter.

"Or," Trudy Mae said. "You could do with a trim." Her voice

was low and meaningful, and I realized she was asking if I wanted to bob my hair.

"Oh." My heart jumped and my eyes shot to Addy.

"Do it, Kate!" she cried, all wound up. This is what she had been anticipating all along. "For your story! For the paper!"

"But, Addy—"

"Oh, Kate! You've just gotta do it! If now's not the perfect time to go Modern, then when? You do it and I'll join ya! You know I will!"

If not now, when? Was this the moment I'd been waiting for? Was it time to choose sides? Honest to God, I couldn't think of a better reason to go Modern. It was ironic, though, sacrificing eighteen inches of my hair for a story. When I really thought about it, it seemed silly that a hairstyle should determine so much about a person. Wasn't it just hair? Wouldn't it grow back? Somehow, chopping off your hair had become a symbol of defiance or a statement of freedom from parental constraints. It was one of the few things a person my age could control for themselves. Maybe I didn't have the devil-may-care attitude Addy or real modern girls had, but I wouldn't mind a good time now and then. But more than that, I wanted to make something of myself. I wanted to do something useful.

I just hadn't allowed myself to truly want it. Sometimes you have to give yourself permission to want to be different. It's hard leaving the status quo where it's safe and comfortable. Courage isn't something they hand out during lunch break. Not until this very moment did I know if I truly had the guts to admit I was ambitious. It wasn't just about saving the paper. Maybe that had been a great excuse to get involved in a murder case, but I knew deep down I wanted more. I wanted to *experience* life, not shuffle down the same old road my mother and grandmother had taken. The first step on *my* road was making a change.

265

I looked at Addy. She was radiating with a let's-take-life-by-the-tail attitude. Addy had a different sort of ambition than I did but she was right. It was time for a change. I breathed easily and smiled back. I finally had the courage of my convictions. After graduation tomorrow, I would inform Pop I would be working full time at *The Messenger*. I'd be a real newspaper gal. When the Taylor case faded, I wouldn't be hobbled to the back pages writing obituaries or the rising cost of scripto ink. I'd hunt down another story, something with meat on it. It was time to choose sides all right, and the side I chose was mine. Maybe I didn't share the beliefs of a true, carefree Modern, but I could damn well take the first step to freedom.

"Okay, Mr. Factor, you can... bob my hair."

Addy hooped and hollered around the shop and then rushed back to clutch my hand as though I was ready to give birth.

Mr. Factor began sharpening his scissors on a long steel rod. The screeching sound of metal against metal made Addy twitch. I felt like a lamb before the slaughter. When he was ready, Mr. Factor stood behind me and gathered my long, innocent braid in his hand. He pulled it tight, opened the scissors, and made three smooth chops. I felt gnawing and tugging against my scalp and then I was free, my head tipping forward. Addy gasped.

"Oh, Kate!"

Hair cascaded around my chin. I touched it gently with my fingers. It felt thick and jagged at the edges.

"Now for the styling," Mr. Factor called cheerfully. He was clearly a man who enjoyed his work. He hummed and trimmed with sure and efficient strokes. Then he poured slick oil onto his hands, rubbed them together, and patted down my hair.

"You did it!" Addy cried. "Oh, Kate you look marvelous!"

Mr. Factor turned my chair to the mirror and I was suddenly

266

face-to-face with a vivacious flapper. I gaped in utter astonishment. Mesmerized, I slowly lifted a hand and touched my creamy cheek. My blue eyes were bright and heavily lashed and seemed to glow like sapphires. I arched a dark eyebrow and instantly became mysterious and provocative. My lips were red and full, and made my teeth look even whiter. Every detail of my face was exaggerated with color and contour, and it put me in awe of Mr. Factor's talent. But possibly it was my hair that proved the most dramatic change. Cutting off eighteen inches had removed nearly all of the auburn streaks. I was a brunette with a sharp curtain of hair below my jawline. I tossed my hair and watched it shimmer under the lights.

"Whaddya think?" Addy whispered as our eyes met in the mirror.

My heart was racing. I was in shock but it felt good. I nodded and said, "Yes. Definitely yes!" We grinned and then hugged.

"Your turn," I said, laughing at her eager expression.

No need to ask her twice. I moved out and Addy climbed into my chair and made herself comfortable. She was much calmer and more mentally prepared than I had been. She'd been waiting months for this. The forthcoming transformation seemed to add years to her age. She sat taller, straighter, and her face took on an air of sophistication.

While Addy became Modern, Trudy Mae pulled me aside for some last-minute preparations. She had brought along a beaded handbag stuffed with my notepad and pencil, which she slipped around my wrist. A gorgeous grey fox stole she draped around my bare shoulders. Then she slid the rhinestone headband in place and stepped back for a final look.

"Well, if you ain't the duck's quack now, I don't know who is," she said, smiling. I thought I saw moisture gathering in her eyes.

"I don't know how to thank you, Trudy Mae," I said. "Honestly, this was so much more than I expected and—"

"You can thank me by getting some solid quotes. Maybe even some clues to the murder," she ordered, blinking back her emotions. Trudy Mae was so rough around the edges and downright practical that the slightest sentimentality was enough to put a lump in my throat. She had been more than a mother to me over the years, something constant and reliable when so many things had been ripped away. I don't know what I would have done without her.

"You're starting to sound like me," I said, laughing softly.

"Do me proud, silly girl. But for Pete's sake, be careful. Anyone gives you the all-overs, why, you sock them right in the bread bag, ya hear?"

"Yes, ma'am."

Addy jumped down from the barber's chair and twirled around the shop. Mr. Factor had painted her lips bright red, and she laughed and cooed and fluffed her bob with utter delight. She was so happy you'd think she was the one attending a fashionable party tonight instead of me. I wondered what Addy's mama and all of her guardians of morality friends would make of Addy going Modern. I didn't dare ask now and spoil her glorious mood.

We took a moment to thank Mr. Factor for his time and attention. He said if I ever changed my mind about loaning my face or even my profile, to stop by anytime. I told him to keep peddling his colored creams and he might just make a name for himself.

The electric street lights had come on hours ago. It was getting late. Addy and I stepped onto the sidewalk, feeling positively woozy from our transformations. We were busy fussing over each other when Trudy Mae pointed out a spectacular Revere Five-Passenger Touring Car parked at the curb. It was blood red with gleaming black fenders, whitewall tires, and lush cream interior. It was so long and glorious it seemed to take up the whole block. Two spiffy young gentlemen were lounging against it but startled to attention when they saw us.

Abner was dandied up in black tails with a white bowtie while Dewey sported the black uniform of the well-heeled chauffer. It was hard to say who was more shocked by the transformations, us or them.

"Say, you been holding out on us, Abner?" Addy said, eyeing the splendid machine. She climbed into the open backseat and threw her arms across the leather, striking a dramatic pose of one of her favorite film stars. "If lip color is good enough for Clara Bow, it's good enough for Adelaide Wells," she said in a deep sultry voice.

Dewey's mouth fell open, and Abner dropped the pipe he was pretending to smoke.

"Oh, that's just Addy being herself," I said, laughing.

Abner retrieved his pipe and then strolled around, giving me the works. "Well, I'll be a monkey's uncle," he said. "That you, Kate?"

"That you, Abner?" I said. "You clean up swell."

"Hellzapoppin', Kate!" Dewey said, ripping the driver's cap from his head and bowing.

"Why, Dewey, that's the nicest thing you've ever said to me." I laughed, pleased they approved.

"You look absolutely continental," Abner said, offering a smile and an arm.

"How debonair. Don't mind if I do." I took his arm and climbed into the backseat next to Addy. "You gotta scoot now. Your mama's gonna have kittens when she gets a load of you. No point in being late, too."

Addy pleaded for a quick jaunt down Hollywood Boulevard

but Trudy Mae said she was "dead in the shell and needed some shut eye." We all hugged goodbye as though I was embarking on some grand overseas adventure. They climbed into the taxi and sped away. Abner joined me in the backseat and Dewey climbed behind the wheel. We were off to the Cocoanut Grove.

CHAPTER 18

Detective Cahill slipped off his suit coat and hung it on the back of his chair. Then he rolled up his white shirt sleeves, all the while staring intently at me, a look that said he was finally getting down to business. I dropped my hands into my lap and risked a peek at my wristwatch. It was getting late and I was getting nervous. I'd give anything to know what was happening outside our door. I could hear the occasional telephone ringing and faint typing and the low hum of chatter but nothing distinguishable. Nothing that suggested my plan had worked. It was torture.

"So, you were in disguise and under cover," he said unimpressed. "And, this fancy party, it's the one where you met up with the man in the alley?"

"Oh, not just him but both of the men. Those pasty-faced fellas. They come in pairs."

"And?"

"And that's where things got really interesting. At the party. See, I hadn't forgotten that Nicky seemed to know them and that he was tight lipped about it. But what I discovered that night was that they knew Nicky as well. They were... well, let me back up to the beginning of the evening..."

For as long as I could remember, the land around Wilshire and Vermont had been half grazing pasture and half dairy farm. Twenty-three acres of in-one-end-and-out-the-other. But time must yield to progress and so the cows were ushered out and the brick and mortar trucked in. Two years later, the Ambassador Hotel was born. I used to sneak around the construction site when I was a kid but hadn't been inside the giant H-shaped monstrosity since its completion. We'd all heard stories about the wild parties at the hotel's premiere club. That was another reason for my nerves. Looking the part of a sophisticated Modern was only half the bluff. I had to behave like one.

Abner casually slid his arm across my shoulders like a bona fide cuddle cutie. His trembling hand suggested he'd never been alone with a girl. With Dewey up front, we weren't exactly alone, anyhow.

"Bank's closed," I said, lifting his arm and placing it back in his lap.

"Well, now that we've gotten that off my mind," he muttered. "I was only getting in character. We've got to put up appearances and all."

I told him there was no need. "I won't be sitting too long in one spot. My plan is to gravitate around the Grove and eavesdrop on any pertinent discussions. Possibly strike up conversations and ask questions."

"Then what am I supposed to do all evening?" he asked disappointed.

Dewey twisted around and exclaimed, overzealously, "Dance, old sport! What else?"

"Who's going to dance with me?" Abner asked, sulking. He looked sideways at me but I was no help. I had more important matters to deal with than keeping my date occupied. "I can't get over the change in you," he murmured.

I patted his knee. "Well, you probably should."

"Say, kids!" Dewey called again. "You know the Grove has theme nights, right? My father says you never know what to expect when you walk in. Could be Frolic Night or Desert Rose Night. Hey, maybe you should ask someone famous to dance, Abner. Maybe Gloria Swanson or Clair Windsor? Or how about that Edna Purviance! She's some dish!"

I had met Miss Purviance outside Taylor's bungalow on the morning his body was discovered. If she was at the Grove tonight, I could only hope she wouldn't recognize me.

No, if I couldn't recognize myself in these swanky glad rags and new face, I hardly think a passing acquaintance could.

"Listen Abner, dance if you like but my biggest concern is for us to be tactful so as not to draw attention. We want no spotlights on us, right? We should be cordial of course but utterly inconspicuous."

Two giant barrels shot beams of light into the night sky over the Ambassador hotel as though searching for a lost plane. As we left Wilshire Boulevard and turned down the long gravel drive, we joined a line of fashionable autos stuffed with patrons nattily turned out like ourselves. It was a rambunctious crowd with tooting horns and boisterous laughter from open autos, grandiose limousines, and smart roadsters. The business was wheel-to-wheel combat with no road rules to speak of. Savvy chauffeurs gunned their machines to the delight of their enthusiastic passengers.

Dewey hollered at a spiffy two-seater blasting its horn. He stood up behind the wheel, gave a swift military salute to the irritated driver and shouted, "Down with socialism! Liberty or Death!" He plopped back into his seat and swerved around the two-seater, kicking up dust and sparking an outrageous cacophony of horns.

"What's doin' with him?" I asked Abner as we jostled along.

"Spiked his cream soda with his mama's cooking sherry," Abner said.

So that explained Dewey's rambunctious behavior this evening. The uptight President of the Star and Crescent Society was corked.

We finally came to a halt beneath a white awning stretched over the hotel's main doors. Dewey hopped out to open our door with an exaggerated bow. Abner climbed out first and then offered his hand to me, more for physical support than manners. I wobbled on my heels as though I was already boiled as an owl. I instructed Dewey to park the auto as close to the entrance as allowed and to stay awake should we be forced to leave unexpectedly.

Once inside the hotel, we followed the guests to the maître 'd stand which stood just outside the entrance to the Grove. Folks around us produced a white invitation card and were admitted without delay. When our turn came, I gave my name to the maître 'd and explained that we were with Fanny Baker's party. He sniffed loudly and checked the private list, looking down his long bony nose. He disapproved of my unrecognizable name. Or maybe he was constipated; it was so hard to tell.

Against his better judgement, he called over one of his captain ushers and waved us on as though shooing away kitchen mice.

We were escorted through the lovely Moroccan style doors trimmed in gold leaf with palm trees etched in the glass. A swell of music and a blast of energy greeted us and then suddenly, Abner and I were standing on the impressive plush grand staircase of the Cocoanut Grove in all its spectacular glory. A white banner arched over our heads reading; "WRITTEN IN THE STARS: A Salute to Hollywood's Finest Writers!"

The décor was a blinding display of white on white. The famous palm trees from the set of The Sheik where Rudolph Valentino made a name for himself had been transported to the Ambassador Hotel and lent the Cocoanut Grove its name. For this evening's occasion, they had been powdered with imitation snow and draped with celluloid ice cycles. Mountains of snowdrifts were pushed against the walls and piled on white-clothed tabletops. Guests fluttered about as though it was the most natural thing in the world to have a blizzard indoors.

Giant ice sculptures of fantastical literary creatures were on display: Pegasus with a ten-foot wing span, a seven-foot-tall kraken, a life size Medusa with her snake-ridden head, and a bust of Shakespeare. High on an ivory pedestal rested a live albino peacock with its splendid white tail poised above the heads of Hollywood's supreme stars. Several snow owls had perched among the trees. A sultry woman glided by in a white satin negligée with a snow leopard on a diamond-studded leash. Another woman cradled an arctic fox in her arms which was drowsily eyeing an arctic rabbit nibbling on cocoanut shavings at the next table. I guessed the animals had come straight from Selig Zoo and were loaded with enough tranquillizers to make them friendly.

Further into the room, the dance floor resembled a slick sheet of black ice and was congested with elegant dancers. On stage was a full orchestra costumed in white top hats and tails. They were performing "I'm Just Wild About Harry" a surprisingly proper arrangement for a night at the Grove. It was early yet.

Abner leaned to my ear again and said, "What an ungodly display of excess!" He was sporting his typical highfalutin expression that suggested he was above such nonsense.

"I thought you fancied yourself an actor?" I said, raising my voice over the music.

"A serious actor. Yes! Not for this nonsense." He flung his arm toward the madness.

I warned that he'd better get over it and get along. If we were discovered as frauds, the ungodly excess would be the last things on our minds.

Dolled up shebas in sleeveless gowns and backless dresses slinked by with foot-long cigarette holders and long-stemmed champagne glasses. I hadn't seen so much flesh since Ringling Brothers and Barnum & Bailey Circus came through town.

I was thankful Abner had dressed for the occasion as he fell right in with the majority of the gentlemen in formal tails. But honestly, my fear about drawing undue attention had been unfounded. We could have strolled through buck naked and nobody would've noticed.

The captain checked his seating card and motioned for us to follow. Down a few steps and into the throng we went, shouldering and squeezing and slipping through. Waiters in white waistcoats, black ties, gold buttons, and silver trays laden with champagne made like contortionists to maneuver around us. From the pungent aroma, it seemed the boundaries of prohibition had been rerouted around the Grove.

We stopped at a banquet table draped in a white cloth and overloaded with snowdrifts and crystal candelabras that resembled jagged stalagmites. Nearly every chair was occupied. I spotted Fanny Baker at the far end. She, of course, failed to recognize me.

"Charlie Chaplin... from Paramount," I whispered in her ear and watched her eyes balloon with understanding. She leapt to her feet and shook my hand.

"Lord have mercy, kid, but don't you clean up!" Fanny yelled over the rising music.

"Thanks so much for the invite!" I yelled back. "This is my escort, Abner Felts!"

They shook hands and then Fanny made room for us at the table. She explained the occasion for the spectacular event. It was not a Paramount affair but an industry wide party to celebrate the one-year anniversary of the Screen Writer's Guild.

"Around our table are some of the best writers and directors in the business," she said proudly, gesturing down the table where ladies sipped champagne and talked respectably over the music. "Cleo Madison, Ida May Park, Ruth Ann Baldwin, Lule Warrington, and that one there is June Mathis. First female executive at Metro. You remember *The Four Horsemen of the Apocalypse*? That was her baby. She discovered Valentino, you know. Some say she's the most powerful woman in the business. Alongside Mary Pickford." She smiled at my shocked expression.

"Jeezers, I had no idea so many women were writing or directing."

"Half of what hits the screen is written by women. Don't think otherwise." She twisted around in her chair. "Now look-it, there's Mary Pickford and Doug Fairbanks having dinner with Frances Marion and her husband Fred Thomas. Frances is a fabulous writer and director. Fred's an athlete. And over there is Carl Laemmle, Mr. Universal. He's dining with Lois Weber, another fabulous writer and director. Oh, and it looks like Grace Cunard just joined them for a chat. She's a director, too.

Now, over in that corner behind the ice sculpture of Shakespeare's head, is Anita Loos and John Emerson. She's the writer, he's the husband. Next table over is James Kirkwood, director. Say, you should speak to Mr. Kirkwood. He directed Mary Miles Minter in *Adventure*. He's sitting with Marshall Neilan and Antonio Moreno. All were good friends of Bill Taylor." She gave me a severe look and leaned closer. "I heard Taylor had been right here at the Grove on the Saturday night before his murder. Had a date with Clair Windsor. There was a lot of talk about Taylor and 'the boys' having a strange meeting that night."

"The boys?"

"Marshal Neilan and Anthony Moreno. But like I said, if you get the opportunity, talk to James Kirkwood. He gossips more than my Aunt Sadie."

After instructing Abner to be polite to his tablemates and steer clear of the champagne, I manufactured an accidental meeting with Mr. Kirkwood. I bumped into him while looking up at one of those wide-eyed owls. It was clear by his sputtering apology and wandering hands that Mr. Kirkwood was already soused. He could hardly stand up but that didn't stop him from asking me to dance.

Mr. Kirkwood was tall and lanky with dark hair and fabricated southern manners. If he was from the south, I was from Timbuktu. He slobbered across my hand and introduced himself as James Kirkwood, Director. Just like that, as though director was the exclamation point to the fine title that was his name. I fell into character as an excitable actress and allowed him to lead me onto the dance floor. A new song began and on cue, Mr. Kirkwood's face became intense and serious. Dare I say smoldering? I choked back a laugh, and then he slammed himself against my chest as we began the tango. His hand roamed my back and his heavy liquor-soaked breath begged me to call him James.

I had only danced the tango once when Addy insisted we learn after watching Valentino's famous tango scene in *The Four Horseman of the Apocalypse*. Mr. Kirkwood was no Valentino and I raced to keep up with his clumsy whipping and flinging movements. Side by side we danced, and then up and down, across the floor and back again. Mostly I danced on my toes in the high-heeled shoes to avoid twisting an ankle. Basically, I hung on for dear life. Thankfully, the music ended and we finished without injury. After a short applause for the orchestra, they struck up something more civilized, and Mr. Kirkwood pulled me back into his arms. I took advantage and coaxed him away from my neck by starting a conversation. It was an easy guess that flattery would be the elixir to which Mr. Kirkwood would succumb. After a few choice compliments, he began bragging about his prowess in wooing the opposite sex. This was not the topic I wished to discuss until his list of accomplishments included a description of "that pretty lil' thang, Mary."

"Of course, Miss Minter." I batted my eyes and smiled. "Tell me, are the rumors true about her and the late Mr. Taylor?"

I don't know where that question came from. I had made up my mind that nothing untoward could have happened between Mary and Mr. Taylor. He'd been too much a gentleman and she... well, I refused to believe Mary would go that far. She might fling herself at a man in a desperate plea for attention but I just wouldn't believe she had slept with him. Or anyone.

What Mr. Kirkwood revealed stopped my blood.

"Ah was first in line thayer, buleeve me," he slurred in his fake accent. "Old Neilan and Taylor just followed mah lead."

I opened my mouth to spit out objections to his vulgar lie. How dare he imply such a nasty thing! How dare he... I caught myself and looked away. I wanted to argue, to call him a south-ern-soaked drunken liar. That's what I would have done had we been in a regular juice joint and I hadn't been working a story. I reminded myself why I was here and wouldn't I feel just awful if I got us kicked out so soon. I thought of all the work Trudy Mae had gone to, and Addy and the boys. And, I thought of Nellie Bly in that insane asylum, and I steeled myself for the work ahead.

"You don't really believe Mr. Taylor would... I mean to say... well, Mary is so young and all."

Mr. Kirkwood eyes were floating but he took another stab at that smoldering expression. Mostly, he looked ready to doze off.

"Mah dear," he garbled, weaving back and forth. "It is the delicate flower that so draws the bee."

I tried to giggle and hold him up at the same time.

"How ev'ah," he continued while his sweaty hand roamed my back, "I cannot say with all certainty that Bill had sampled the nectar. But why plan a secret rendezvous with the flower if not for the promise of its sweetness?"

"Secret rendezvous?"

He gave me a slippery smile. "They planned to run off the day befor-ah he was done in. Uh 'course, that'll never happen now, will it?"

I smiled tightly and said, lightheartedly, "Why, surely you're mistaken. Mary, er, Miss Minter would never have—"

"On the contrary. Miss Minter *would* have. And Ah should know. Uh 'course she's outta control more than ev'ah since Mrs. Whitney was fired."

The name sounded familiar and I vaguely remembered Mary's mother had employed a secretary by that name. Mary had been awfully fond on her.

Mr. Kirkwood made another sloppy attempt at my neck but I squirmed out of reach. "I suppose that proves Mr. Taylor wouldn't have been involved in that Chinese opium den scandal that all the papers have been fussing about?" This made him laugh an obnoxious snorting sound.

"Ah should say not! Why, the very idea of Bill using drugs is preposterous!" His eyes raked over me as though searching for a safe landing place for his lips.

I managed to wrangle free and wag my finger at him. "Ah, ah, ah." Then I thrust myself into the crowd and escaped back to the table. I plopped down next to Abner who was having a polite conversation with the actress, Marion Davies.

"You okay?" Abner asked, taking in my harried expression. I didn't know what to make of Mr. Kirkwood's gossip—those horrible lies about Mary. Then again, he had sounded so casual about the whole affair.

Affair?

An outburst of shouting and scuffling caught everyone's attention. The music died and heads swiveled toward three men fighting near the entrance. Two were rough-looking thugs who probably worked for the hotel or maybe the studios. The third man was none other than Powder Pugsly from the *Los Angeles Times.*

Pugsly put up an awkward fight, flailing his arms and cursing about movie folk hiding information and obstructing justice in the Taylor case. He threw out stark accusations against DA Woolwine being in cahoots with the studio heads. One of the thugs socked him in the jaw. Pugsly went down and they dragged him out.

The crowd, momentarily stunned silent, exploded with bawdy laughter and then resumed as though nothing had happened. It seemed a game to everyone, even the death of one of their own. Abner and I were paralyzed with fear. I couldn't image what those men were doing to Pugsly in the parking lot. I only hoped Dewey wouldn't get scared and leave without us.

Abner moved to stand up but I grabbed his arm. "Sit down," I said, looking nervously around.

"But we should—"

"It doesn't concern us," I said. He considered and reluctantly eased back into his chair. I told him to go about his business and try to fit in. He took a nervous sip of champagne and then coughed. I spotted another pair of thugs standing near a waterfall that was pumping loads of bubbles into the room. It was the pasty-face men I had seen outside the 77th Street precinct. I hadn't time to wonder how or why they were here. Abner started whispering in my ear.

He had overheard a few conversations regarding Mr. Taylor. There had been encounters with drug pushers on the Paramount lot. Mr. Taylor had physically removed them himself, even threatened them with trespassing. Once, at the Ince Studios, Taylor ran off another pusher who was waiting to deliver drugs to some actors.

"Someone mentioned a possible hit on Taylor by gangland drug pushers," Abner finished. My mind was in a whirl. I had to write this down before the details faded. I would include Mr. Kirkwood's nasty gossip, as ugly as it had been. I knew the importance of staying objective.

"I gotta take a powder," I said, gathering my purse. Miss Davies lured Abner onto the dance floor. I left the Grove and entered an enormous hallway that seemed to sprawl for miles in either direction. Far to the left was a set of double doors. Halfway in the middle was another hallway leading to the hotel's rooms. To my right was an oak door marked Ladies. I hurried inside and collapsed onto a plush stool below a giant gilded mirror. I threw my purse onto the dressing table and fished out my notepad and pencil. I jotted down notes, reminding myself to track down Mrs. Whitney, and then the names of 'the boys' a.k.a Marshal Neilan, Antonio Moreno, and finally James Kirkwood. Abner's information would take some investigation; I needed witnesses or at least someone who could supply names of the drug pushers.

The door swung open and a stunning woman entered. She wore a white satin gown that shimmered as she moved and two bracelets coiled up her bare arms like silver snakes. Her wrap was grey mink that seemed to come alive when she tossed it onto the dressing table beside me. It was Gloria Swanson, and I nearly fell off my stool. She was even more beautiful in person than on the screen, those pale blue eyes, dark hair, and striking features. The kind of woman that made other women feel like frauds.

She caught me staring in the mirror. "A writer's work is never done?" she said. I'd never heard her speak before. Wouldn't you know it, she had a voice made of velvet money. When I didn't respond, her eyes dropped to my notepad.

"Oh." I clutched the pencil in panic.

She fussed with the kissing curls around her face and asked what story had occupied my thoughts on such an evening. She assumed I was a scene writer, and I didn't correct her.

"Well, it's about... drug pushers," I said, thinking fast. I looked at her in the mirror but she continued to toy with a disobedient curl.

"Go on."

"Oh, well, I'm at an impasse. I need first-hand knowledge of the effects of... cocaine. How it makes one feel and behave, you know? It should be authentic, don't you think?"

She gave up on the curl and retrieved her wrap. "Absolutely! Nothing I detest more in a story than a false bottom. You need an authority on drugs, that's for certain." She tossed the mink around her shoulders and flung open the door. "Check the sanitarium. Or better yet, ask Mabel. I hear she's back on the wacky dust." A wink and then she was gone.

I sat dazed for a full minute before I snapped out of it and jotted down Mabel Normand, cocaine. The connection with Mabel Normand to cocaine, to drug pushers, to Mr. Taylor was beginning to spark to life. Henry had said Mr. Taylor and Miss Normand argued the night he was killed. Could it have had something to do with drugs? Was the man seen leaving Taylor's that night a hired killer or the pusher himself?

I made a note to ask Henry if Miss Normand had seemed hopped up on the night Taylor was killed. Then I forced myself to make an additional note: *did Henry know if Mr. Taylor had plans to go away with Mary?*

I stuffed the notepad into my purse and made my way back to the hallway. It wasn't empty as before but scattered with couples that had escaped the pleasurable chaos of the Grove for more intimate conversations. One couple was talking in whispers and sharing a ciggy. Another was blotto and quarreling, and another was necking with wild abandon. They groped and groaned and squirmed against each other. I blushed terribly, never having witnessed such a scandalous display of fervor and determination. They had a job to do, and by God, nothing was going to stop them! Not even snickering or the occasional "attaboy!" from passersby.

The double doors at the far end of the hall opened and group of severe looking women entered. Their wide brimmed hats, long black dresses, and white sashes across their chests marked them as staunch Victorian supporters. Not the funeral procession one might think but a mother's league with a bone to pick. They were the self-appointed guardians of morality, defenders of prohibition, and custodians of the wayward younger

set. They were known to picket various establishments throughout Los Angeles. Their resolute vow to keep women chained to
the hearth and home where they belonged was downright
frightening. This was not the genteel breed of yesteryear; these
women had suffered greatly from The War. They had lost sons
and husbands. And they were hell-bent on stopping the train
loaded with juveniles headed toward Mr. Fitzgerald's side of
paradise. It had been two years since his book opened the eyes
of American families and still the train barreled onward. It
wasn't as though *This Side of Paradise* had started the younger
set's moral revolution. Mr. Fitzgerald had only pulled back the
curtain on what most of my generation were already doing.

As the group of women drew nearer, they made no attempt
to hide their disgust, not only for the necking couple, but for
anyone dressed in party rags. Their sneering, self-righteous
contempt was palpable. I assumed they had business somewhere inside the hotel for the Grove would surely bar them entrance. Nevertheless, the woman leading the herd halted with
a loud huff and began to chastise one half of the necking couple. The man she left alone because he was, after all, only male
and not responsible for his lack of moral fiber. The female, on
the other hand, was fully accountable for her own tragic fall
from grace.

"You ought to be ashamed!" the woman said to the flapper
whose bare back was pressed against the wall and left leg
wrapped around the waist of the immoral man. The flapper
broke their lip-lock and blinked tipsily.

"Aw, but there ain't no rooms left."

The woman bristled. I snorted a laugh. The herd looked
sharply at me as though I had been caught laughing in church.
That's when I saw her. The woman standing next to the
speaker. Her piercing blue eyes bore right through me with such

285

contempt that I caught my breath and took an involuntary step backward. Her eyes raked me up and down with utter revulsion. I was a disgusting specimen, part of the flaming youth who were destroying this fine country.

My throat closed up and I couldn't breathe. The only word in my head wouldn't come out.

Mama.

CHAPTER 19

I could feel Detective Cahill's eyes on me as I stared at my hands. I don't know why I told him about seeing Mama. It just sort of... came out, I guess. I hadn't even told Addy or Pop or Eugene. I hadn't been able to tell anyone I saw Mama that night.

Detective Cahill remained respectfully quiet as he lit another ciggy and waited for me to continue. Gotta hand it to the guy, he knew when to shut up and let me do the talking. It had been five years since Mama walked out on us, a lifetime ago. But seeing her that night, so unexpectedly, changed the course of the evening...

Mama, with her condescending scowl and dog pack mentality, hadn't recognized me standing in the hallway of the Ambassador Hotel. She was looking at a vivacious flapper, not the gangly school girl in braids I had been when she abandoned me. I couldn't expect her to see through my recent transformation, but the raw hatred in her expression hurt to the bone.

I had failed to call out to her. The urge never really came. It was shock, I suppose, seeing her so unexpectedly. I felt sick inside as though I had eaten rancid meat. All I could do was watch the group of women march by and disappear around the corner like a synchronized black cloud.

I don't know how long I stood there, trembling. By the time I reached for the door my whole body felt flushed with fever. I was numbed inside and unaware of my surroundings for several minutes. When I realized I was seated back at the table, I grabbed the nearest glass of champagne and downed it.

As my stupor faded I slowly became aware that the sophisticated affair celebrating the Writer's Guild had taken a dramatic turn in my absence. It was Babylon. The atmosphere snapped with electricity sparked by champagne and music that had elevated to barbaric heights. Just the antidote I needed. Seeing Mama had chased away all thoughts of the Taylor case and I decided there was nothing left to do but get stinking drunk. If only to stop my body from trembling with shock. Abner was getting primitive on the dance floor which left me to my work. I had never had champagne before tonight and found it sufficient for my current needs. Rather like a phosphate soda with a mule kick to the head. It didn't take long to relax, and hate myself for not speaking to Mama.

My head swam with scenarios of chasing her down and making her look at me, making her truly see me. I would be yelling, of course, because when your mama abandons you I figured you had a constitutional right to yell at her. Unfortunately, I couldn't think of anything to yell. Nothing was coming because there was too much to say. I began to think there had been too much hurt to even bother. Alcohol, it seemed, not only relaxed my limbs but had dumbed down the hurt I felt and turned it into anger. I was suddenly furious that Mama would count herself among those staunch self-righteous women who preached about morals and the sanctity of family. She was a charlatan selling something she had deliberately thrown away.

My tablemates came, and drank, and left, and danced, and repeated the whole thing over while I finished their half-empty glasses. There was no shortage of drink, and I was suddenly worshiping at the altar of bootleggers with secret caves.

"On your way to getting embalmed, are ya?" Fannie Baker asked. She and the ladies had returned to the table.

"Already there," I hiccupped. She extracted the glass of champagne from my hand before it reached my lips and nodded toward the dance floor. I twisted around and found Abner ossified up against Miss Davies. He was allowing her to run her fingers through his perfectly coiffed highfalutin hair. It would be a miracle if he didn't pull Daniel Boone all over her fancy shoes.

I wanted another drink but Fannie insisted I eat something first. She and the others ordered dinner for the table. I tried to flag down a waiter for more bubbly but suddenly caught sight of the pasty-face men. I asked Fanny if they worked for the studios. She had never seen them before. But why else would they be here and hovering in such a menacing fashion? Clearly, they weren't enjoying themselves. They couldn't crack a smile with a hammer and chisel.

A high-pitched squeal snapped my attention from the men. Miss Davies threw her hands in the air and wailed, "Claire darling! Over here!"

Claire Windsor was a soft radiant creature, the very definition of a woman. She practically floated toward us while gathering hugs and compliments along the way. The ladies at our table stood and welcomed her with open arms. This afforded me the opportunity to steal Ida May Park's champagne on the sly. Everyone insisted Miss Windsor and her date join us. They were ushered into seats directly across from Abner and me.

Her date was introduced as Mr. Michael Meeks, and I nearly choked bubbly up my nose. Mr. Meeks was just as handsome as his date, formally turned out in black tails with smooth blond hair and warm brown eyes. He had an engaging smile and an unhealthy share of confidence. And why shouldn't he? Mr. Meeks was Mr. Morgan, my playboy pal from the *Los Angeles Times*.

I stared through fuzzy eyes, astonished that he was here incognito. What's more, he had failed to recognize me. I would have burst with laughter if I hadn't felt so crummy. I couldn't get over seeing Mama. I had assumed when someone ran away from home they actually left town. Had she been living in Los Angeles all along? Had she ever tried to see us? Had she ever wondered how I was doing?

Lousy. That's how I was doing. Everything had been jake until I saw her. Now I couldn't chase away her image, those hate-filled eyes boring into me.

I flinched when my tablemates burst with laughter because I had been too busy feeling sorry for myself to pay attention. Mr. Morgan—or rather Mr. Meeks—had been entertaining the troops with a satirical yarn I had missed. Miss Windsor gushed adoringly at her date's brilliant mind but it was lost on me.

"I'm afraid some don't share my sense of wit," Mr. Morgan teased. I looked up and found myself the center of attention.

I shrugged and said, "Wit is the lowest form of humor."

"What'd she say?" Ruth Warrington called from the far end.

Mr. Morgan loudly repeated my quip and added, "A quote by Alexander Pope." Our eyes locked momentarily and then I swiped a glass of champagne from a passing waiter and took a deep gulp.

"You don't agree with Mark Twain who said, 'Humor is mankind's greatest blessing?'" Mr. Morgan challenged. He had everyone's attention but I didn't want to be drawn into the conversation. As far as I was concerned, my night was over. I was perfectly willing—even eager—to drink myself into a pleasant state of stupefaction.

Then again, I had a weakness for Mr. Morgan's games.

"Humor is merely tragedy standing on its head with its pants torn," I threw out and was rewarded with a smattering of favorable laughter.

"Who said that?" Clair asked.

"Irvin Cobb, American journalist," Mr. Morgan said, eyeing me with sharp interest.

I tipped back my glass and drained it. Abner returned and I tugged on his sleeve. Now was as good a time as any to leave, I thought. But Abner was busy fawning over Miss Davies. He would have one helluva story to tell at graduation if he wasn't too blotto to remember.

"That's a very contorted view," Mr. Morgan continued. "Would you have us believe that all humor comes from pain? Are we better not to have humor or the need of it?"

I chewed my lip, contemplating whether he had seen through my façade. Did it truly matter? Mr. Morgan was hardly himself this evening. Wouldn't we both be safe from the studio thugs if we kept our job descriptions to ourselves?

I raised my glass in a toast and announced with utmost certainty, "Why, Mr. Meeks, if I had no sense of humor, I would have long ago committed suicide!" This sparked a rousing blast of hoots and laughter and toasting around the table. I clinked glasses with Fanny. She smiled with approval.

"Sure are something, kid," she said.

"She is indeed," said Mr. Morgan. "And very well read to quote Gandhi so casually. Some kind of writer? Perhaps a—"

"Oh no!" Fanny jumped in to save me. "This little lady's an actress. Look at that mug. Why, she'll be the latest craze in no time. She's an actress, I tell ya."

"Is that true, my dear? Are you an actress?" Mr. Morgan asked with that familiar sexy grin.

I fluttered my lashes and smiled coyly. "Why, don't you know, sir? Every woman is an actress."

The women at the table burst into cheers and wails of agreement. They clapped and banged the table, making the snowdrifts jump. I was an unqualified success. Mr. Morgan threw back his head and laughed with utter delight. Then he jumped to his feet and raised a glass.

"And thus, I clothe my naked villainy—" His eyes flashed knowingly to mine as he awaited my response. I felt secretly exposed. Oh, what the hell. I stood, raised my glass, and finished his quote.

"And seem a saint when most I play the devil!"

"Shakespeare!" our tablemates roared, causing a spectacle. They fell over each other in amusement and praise of their own cleverness. They shouted for more quotes, wanting to continue the game. I clutched the table as the room began to spin. Was I hallucinating or had it begun to snow, right here inside the Grove? All around us, fresh snowflakes sprinkled down. I held out a wavering hand to feel the cold. It wasn't cold and they weren't snowflakes. They were tiny white letters. Mr. Morgan made the discovery as I did.

"Of course, it's snowing letters!" he announced. "Letters from heaven! It's a party for writers, isn't it!"

The entire room was in a flurry as guests jumped up to

snatch letters from the air. Those properly spifflicated stuck out their tongues, tickled to discover the letters were made of pressed sugar. Hollywood's most glamorous and sophisticated swells were walking around with their tongues hanging out and squealing like children. It was a scene most bizarre. I wished I had my Kodak to document high society at its best.

Desperate for fresh air, I stumbled from the table in search of the door. I smacked into Mr. Kirkwood who was downright zozzled with the alphabet decorating his dark hair like dandruff. He was more manipulative than our first encounter and finagled me onto the dance floor without asking.

"Please, mah sweet young thin'," he slurred across my ear. "Won't you relax for me?"

"If I were any more relaxed I'd need a pallbearer."

"Let us depart. Mah room is juss upstairs."

"Mr. Kirkwood, please!" I yelped when he grabbed my bottom. And then he was suddenly jerked backward and held at bay. Nicky Masino had him by the collar.

"Don't mind if I cut in," Nicky said, his voice tight and controlled. It wasn't a question but a warning. I couldn't decide if Nicky knew it was me he was looking at or just some flapper needing to be rescued. Mr. Kirkwood shirked out of Nicky's grasp and made a sloppy attempt to smooth his lapels.

"Don't care for the way you go about it, old pal," he said, sobering up somewhat now that competition had arrived. "Say, Ah know you. You're that police officer who's escorting Edna this evening. Ah told Edna it was wise for the studios to have policemen here. Already one troublemaker's been tossed. Ah hear there are a few more reporters who've sneaked in." He threw a contemptuous look around the room. "Damned Yankee snoops if you ask me. Ah understand some fingers shall be broken to make it difficult to type, but Ah think they ought'a be strung up... if you ask me."

"Nobody asked you," Nicky said, coolly. "Now I'll be dancing with the lady, and you'll be returning to your table."

Mr. Kirkwood bristled. "Now see here, Ah was working on this one. You cannot just..." He reached for me but Nicky backhanded him so hard against the chest he sputtered and coughed.

"You will return to your table, Mr. Kirkwood. Now."

My old pal Kirkwood tried to pull himself upright but he was careening sideways when he left us. I felt pity for whomever he pounced on next.

Nicky offered his hand and I took it, moving into his arms. I was still unsure if he knew me. There was a slew of women here. Could he have selected me by chance?

"So, you showed up with bells on," Nicky stated matter-of-fact.

"*Excusez moi?*" I asked, smiling innocently.

"You heard me."

"Aw, Nicky, didn't I fool you at all?"

"Not for a minute."

For some unknown reason that pleased me immensely.

"What are you doing here, Kate?"

"Just fulfilling your high expectations of me, I guess." I looked around and pretended I had something better to do. Really, I was ready to crumble. I wanted to tell Nicky about Mama. I wanted someone from the old days to know I had spotted the thief who had stolen my confidence, or that thing Dr. Freud called self-esteem. I wanted to say, *hey look-it, there goes the rottenest mother in town!* Nicky would understand, wouldn't he?

I sniffled and blinked back tears. Why was I so emotional all of a sudden, anyhow? Nicky was so hardened by The War he probably wouldn't care that I had seen Mama for the first time in five years.

"Well," I said taking a deep, shaky breath. "Can't say I expected to see you here. You're escorting Miss Purviance, then? I haven't recognized any other officers inside. Did the studios really hire police to—"

"No, they didn't. They have their own men posted at the doors for troublemakers like yourself. Miss Purviance and I are just friends."

"Sure," I said, wondering why I should care.

"I used her to gain an invitation," he added, looking down at me. "I'm here to see you don't lose any fingers for your troubles."

"These old things?" I scoffed, holding up my hand. "I got plenty to spare. Besides, I can take care of myself."

"Yes, I saw how well you were taking care of yourself with that snake charmer."

"Mr. Kirkwood? I had his number. He was harmless. Just soused and looking for a little horizontal happiness, if you know what I mean?"

"I know exactly what you mean," he said, tightening his grip around my waist. "And he isn't harmless, Kate. No one here is harmless."

I stared into his midnight blue eyes wondering if he were truly here because of me or maybe he was working the case. I understood the dangers in coming here, but honestly, I *could* take care of myself. I blinked drowsily from the effects of my champagne tantrum. Then I smiled, thinking how handsome Nicky was, I mean, really beautiful. I wanted to tell him but I suddenly felt like crying.

"I'm starting to think there's something wrong with me, Nicky," I said, sounding pitiful. He slowly shook his head.

"There is nothing wrong with you, Katie Ann," he whispered. We were too close for polite company. I could feel his warm breath on my lips.

"You're not gonna kiss me, are ya Nicky?" I asked softly. "I can't have you getting goofy over me just now. I've got things to do, ya know. I've decided, I'm gonna be somebody."

"I'm sure I've never been goofy over anyone in my life," he said.

"You're not blushing, are you, Nicky?" I smiled and laid my hand on his cheek. Even in the dim light I could see that he was.

"I'm on the job," he murmured. "Blushing is not allowed."

"That so?"

Nicky grinned and started to say more but just then a man tapped him on the shoulder and we parted. One of the pasty-face fellas asked to cut in. It was cold water splashed in Nicky's face. He froze and his face went blank, same as the first time we had seen this guy and his pal.

"May I?" the man repeated. He had a foreign accent, French maybe. It was hard to distinguish with just a few words. He was dressed appropriately this time, in black tails like everyone else, and he looked more American than before. He had patent leather hair meticulously parted down the middle and shel-lacked with pomade and intense dark eyes. He had an arrogant expression as though he was accustomed to the finer things in life. Or at least accustomed to getting his way. But it was that sly, knowing grin that told me he and Nicky knew each other. I got the feeling he was testing Nicky, the way they stared at each other.

The Frenchman shifted his attention to me by way of a slight bow. He reached for my arm but Nicky shoved him into the crowd nearly bowling over a handful of dancers. I gasped. The

Frenchman righted himself before he could fall. None of the dancers complained, it was the Grove after all.

The look of triumph on the man's face was undeniable. He had no interest in dancing with me; he had only wanted to provoke Nicky. Some unasked question had been answered. I felt like a pawn in a chess match.

Nicky pulled me from the dance floor and roughly maneuvered us through the crowd while surveying the room. He was looking for the man's partner, same as I was. We found him standing next to Shakespeare's bust. He was watching us.

Nicky swore under his breath. "You need to get out of here," he said, glancing around.

"Do those men work for the studios?"

"Don't talk to them, Kate."

"They do, don't they?"

"Do you understand me?"

"Yeah, yeah. I got it."

"They'll break more than a couple of fingers."

"Oh." I gave the man by the Bard a closer look.

"There's no way out through the kitchen," Nicky said. "It'll have to be the main entrance. I'll take care of them, one at a time. We don't want to draw attention."

"What do you mean 'take care of them'?"

"Go back to your table and stay there until I come for you," he said, urgently. "Please, Kate?"

Nicky's plea had me worried. I looked across the sea of crowded tables and found ours. Abner was ensconced in an inappropriate conversation with Miss Davies. She was sloshing a glass of Happy Sally in one hand while the other was playfully lifting her hemline. Her knees were exposed, showing off a pair of fancy European garters. Abner, who was positively liquefied, and had probably never seen a woman's unmentionables before, gaped in unpretentious shock. Across the table sat Mr. Morgan, his eyes firmly planted on me. His wide grin was an invitation to trouble which, under the circumstances, I happily accepted.

Our food arrived shortly after I left Nicky and slipped back into my seat. Five efficient waiters danced around the table in swift choreographed harmony. They were a well-rehearsed ensemble serving a variety of scrumptious entrees including several lemon meringue pies. My plate held spaghetti with meatballs but I hadn't an appetite. I made small talk with Mr. Morgan while trying to remove any alcohol within Abner's reach. Nicky had been too serious not to be taken seriously. If we were in danger, Abner and I needed to sober up immediately. I flagged down a waiter and ordered a pot of coffee.

The orchestra took a break and the room fell to soft voices and clinking china. The pasty-face man had abandoned the Bard and stood guard by the entrance. Unlike the two thugs pacing the upper level and scrutinizing party guests, the pasty-face man only had eyes for me. Nicky had not admitted the men worked for the studios. But if not, then who did they work for? And why was Nicky so scared of them?

The Frenchman from the dance floor had disappeared. I swiveled around, looking for Nicky. He had disappeared as well. The pasty-face man guarding the entrance seemed worried. He stepped up to the rail and urgently scanned the room. I assumed he was looking for his absent pal. I threw an arm around Abner and hissed in his ear.

"Listen up! They're on to us. We've gotta make a break or it'll be lights out for you and no more bendable fingers for me! And, whatever you do, don't—"

Abner jumped up and wailed, "Gawd'a'mighty! I knew we'd be found out! Let's run for it!"

Our tablemates startled in surprise. Everyone stared. I faked a laugh and yanked Abner back into his seat. He started whimpering something about the inconvenience of dying tonight on account of the commencement speech he had to deliver in the morning. The two studio thugs headed over, and so did the pasty-face man. There was only one thing left to do.

I stood up, grabbed a handful of spaghetti, and hurled it down the table at June Mathis. She had just opened her mouth to speak when the pasta slammed into her face and forced her head back. It landed with a wet slap and sent red sauce flying like blood splatter. There was a collective gasp and then stunned silence. I was absolutely horrified and fought the urge to rush over and explain. This was a swell bunch but the thought of losing my fingers and getting Abner pummeled had me going.

"That ought'a shut up your braying laugh!" I yelled at June and then winced. *Sorry, sorry, sorry.*

Mr. Morgan's mouth fell open.

Claire Windsor yelled, "What the hell?"

And then warm mashed potatoes hit me square in the forehead. I rocked back on my heels.

"No one talks to June like that!" Ruth Warrington said, livid. I scooped potatoes from my bangs. My rhinestone headband was mushy, and I felt bad for it. It'd been such a lovely touch. A thick splat of Chicken a la King casserole splashed across my shoulder. June Mathis had recovered.

I dug my fists into spaghetti and bombarded one end of the table with flying pasta. I yelled for Abner to step up to the plate, literally, and he dove into his Creole rice and kidney pie. His collateral damage included Miss Davies who promptly socked him in the eye and stormed off. Everyone was on their feet slinging food at us. I hurled my entre with fury, missing most of my targets and striking innocent bystanders. This spread the

299

fighting across the borders. We were inundated with mush-rooms and risotto, tom turkey in a lovely raisin dressing, fresh caviar, bits of a spring chicken, a stuffed tomato surprise—which lived up to its name—globs of chutney and even jellied consommé. When an English mutton chop conked Abner on the head, he fell to his seat and dropped his head in his hands, wailing like a soused seal washed up on the beach.

I pounced on unsuspecting waiters and striped their trays of culinary delights. Shrieks of laughter and foodstuffs filled the air. The orchestra struck up a lively tune without a care in the world. Just another night of bombastic merrymaking at the Grove.

All the ruckus stirred up the medicated animals, and a zoo suddenly arose from the mounds of fake snow. The albino pea-cock spread its enormous tail and fell from its perch to chase anything it found offensive or perhaps alluring? It was so hard to tell with peacocks. Owls wheeled overhead and the snow leopard hissed and broke free of his diamond-studded leash as a flurry of white rabbits darted by. Several arctic foxes leapt onto the tables and pounced on any food that wasn't airborne.

This was our chance so I dragged Abner into the fray. We raced through a tunnel of seafood shrapnel, slipping and sliding across the floor on our way toward the upper level. The studio thugs were coming down the grand staircase so we veered to the right, searching for another opening along the railing. Almost there, and then Mr. Morgan stepped into our path. His spiffy black tails were a smorgasbord. He smiled magnani-mously and raised a lemon meringue pie.

"Don't you dare!" I warned and then ducked as he hurled it at me. It hit Abner square in the face. He flailed like a man wrestling a spider web. The pie pan fell away, leaving a thick white and yellow concoction. Abner scooped out two eye holes

300

and blinked. I fell over myself laughing. Then I grabbed two more pies from the dessert table. I spun around and bumped into Mr. Morgan. The first pie flipped back and hit me in the chest. I gasped in cold surprise. Mr. Morgan roared with laughter. I reared back and flung my second pie at him. Unfortunately, he jumped aside and I hit Nicky square on the chin. Lemon meringue pie splattered across his neck and down his lovely black tuxedo.

"For chrissake, Nicky!" I yelled over the maelstrom I had created. "What are you doing standing there?"

Nicky looked down at his shirtfront smeared with yellow and white confection, and then up at me. Mr. Morgan doubled over laughing so hard I thought he might crack a rib. I half expected Nicky to sock him, seeing how he'd lost his sense of humor these days.

"This is what you do when I say *we don't want to draw attention?*" Nicky yelled over the noise. I shrugged and smiled hopelessly. Nicky rolled his eyes, contemplated for a moment, and then grabbed my hand and pulled me up the side stairs. I had just enough time to snag Abner on the way. The entrance was a bottleneck as the more conservative guests fled the pandemonium. We shouldered in with the crowd, right under the noses of the two thugs and the pasty-face man who seemed more concerned for his missing partner. By the luck of the stars we made it out alive.

CHAPTER 20

"The two men, did you get their names?" Detective Cahill asked with a measure of urgency. He quickly flipped to a fresh page in his notebook again. "There was no identification on your man in the alley so it would be a great help if you had their names." His pencil was poised to take down my answer.

I shook my head. "Sorry. Never got their names."

"But he asked you to dance," he urged. "Maybe Officer Masino mentioned the man's name? Or a nickname?"

"The man who asked me to dance was not the man in the alley," I said. "It was his partner or friend or whatever. The man who asked me to dance has disappeared. As far as I know. But both men were French, of that I'm sure."

As Detective Cahill jotted things down, I continued, recalling just how awful I'd felt the next morning...

It was the day of my graduation and I had some explaining to do. Not only was I suffering from the effects of last night but the aroma from Trudy Mae's elaborate breakfast was tempting fate. It would be saintly intervention if I didn't upchuck all over the lace tablecloth. I had never been keen on big breakfasts, a quick bowl of Kellogg's cereal had always been sufficient, but I understood the ceremonial obligation Trudy Mae had felt. It wasn't every day I graduated from high school.

While Eugene and Pop enjoyed eggs, ham, biscuits, gravy, and fried potatoes, I took my time nibbling dry toast and sipping black coffee. It seemed to do the trick, although I smiled tightly and told my stomach to lay low. There was too much on my mind and I wanted to consider things without heaving. Stumbling in last night in such a condition had not been the opportune time to tell Pop and Eugene I had seen Mama. Watching them happily enjoy the spread of breakfast bolstered that decision. I was grateful they had been in bed when I'd come home. I could imagine myself in a sobbing alcoholic induced confession had they greeted me at the door.

I had no problem explaining my adventures into the wild society of the Grove when I'd been explicitly told to steer clear. Pop would understand, especially if I was confessing from home and not a jail cell or hospital ward. But I simply couldn't cause Pop pain about Mama. Sometimes being so wrapped up in one's grief, you forget others had been hurt, too. Pop had lost a wife, and I knew it hadn't been easy for him. I couldn't say if he still loved her after what she did but I knew he had been lonely on occasion. As for Eugene, I couldn't guess what his reaction would have been. He had never asked about Mama apart from the day she left. Eugene wasn't one to share or show his emotions. Too much like Pop, I guess.

303

"So, you gonna tell us what happened to the rest of your hair or what?" Eugene asked a second time. I had been so busy thinking about Mama I'd forgotten his question.

I took a deep breath and began. When I got to the part about the Grove, Pop's fork stalled over his plate and he stared at me.

"But... I assumed your hair was for graduation or... didn't we have an agreement about the Cocoanut Grove, Kate?"

"Jeezers, Kate," Eugene said through a mouthful of biscuit. "Why can't you go out joy riding or necking like normal girls?"

"Eugene," Pop snapped, scowling at the idea.

"When I thought about all I could learn at the Grove, I just couldn't stay away. You understand, Pop." He shook his head and put his fork down. I hurried on. "It was fine. Really. Nothing happened. And, Nicky was there, too. Not that he was needed."

"Nick was in on this?"

"Well, no, I wouldn't say that. He suspected I would be there and he came to, you know, make sure I was alright. I guess. Don't go blaming him. It was my idea and it worked out perfectly. The only real danger was falling over in my high-heeled shoes." It was in Pop's best interest that I omitted the pasty-face fellas, the studio thugs, the champagne consumption, and the food fight that had helped our narrow escape.

Pop was not appeased so I offered details from my notepad, who 'the boys' were, and their curious night with Taylor on the Saturday before his murder. I included Mary's possible rendezvous with Mr. Taylor. And there was the drug pusher angle to consider.

Pop's face grew dark with concern. I reached over and squeezed his hand. "Listen, Pop, I'm sorry for always disobeying you. I don't mean to be obstinate, it's just... I want to be treated like a real reporter. And a real reporter would not have missed such an opportunity."

304

"She's got you there, Pop," Eugene said.

"But, Kate, you're only—"

"Eighteen. I'm eighteen now Pop and finished with school by noon today."

"If you ask me," Eugene said, sitting back and rubbing his full belly. "She's already chin deep in things. And not a bad writer. For a *girl*," he teased. I threw a napkin at him.

Pop considered things for a moment. Perhaps he hadn't wanted to admit I was growing up. I was ready to take on more than class essays and school exams. He eventually nodded, settling something in his mind. He didn't smile so much as relax to the inevitable.

"I understand."

"Thanks, Pop. Now tell me, what do you think of the drug angle?"

He sighed and set his napkin aside. "Well, I suppose it makes more sense to me that Taylor would be *against* drugs. I never bought into Wallace Smith's columns that accused Taylor of being a hophead or taking part in the Chinese opium dens. You said the murder scene hadn't been disturbed, apart from Taylor's dead body? It seems unlikely to me that a drug pusher would leave without stealing valuables."

I nodded, guessing where he was going. "You're thinking someone was hired to kill Mr. Taylor. Someone walked into Taylor's bungalow, fired a single shot, and left without hesitation because he was being paid elsewhere."

Eugene folded his arms on the table. "Ain't that the way the MacLean dame described it? The killer strolled away like nothing doin'? I say he was a cool customer because it wasn't his first murder."

I agreed but something was nagging me about it. I got the same feeling when the answer to a test question was poised on the tip of my tongue, just out of reach.

The back door swung open and footsteps hurried through the kitchen and into the dining room.

"Morning all!" Addy rushed in with cheeks aglow and arms loaded with mounds of material. She looked vibrant in her new bob. Eugene agreed by letting out a whistle. "Thanks ever so much!" She beamed, swirling around and fluffing her hair. Pop laughed at her enthusiasm and Eugene whistled again. Addy sure was enjoying her new look. After she'd had enough spotlight, she got busy hauling me up the stairs where she demanded to hear all the particulars about the Grove.

Once we had settled on the bed, I unrolled last night like a red carpet. "Abner got happily molested and then socked by Marion Davies. Mr. Morgan showed up incognito with Claire Windsor, and Gloria Swanson gave me writing advice! And then there was an outrageous food fight orchestrated by yours truly." I even described James Kirkwood's groping hands and Nicky being there with Edna Purviance and then the heated altercation between Nicky and the pale Frenchman. Addy smiled dreamily as though it had been a spectacularly and thoroughly Modern adventure.

"And, then—"

"Yeah?" Addy said, eagerly leaning forward as though I had saved the best for last.

I couldn't bring myself to tell her about Mama. I desperately wanted to but the words stuck in my throat. Addy was so happy and it was our graduation day I just couldn't ruin things.

"Nothing, I mean, I got some very interesting information that might lead somewhere but... that's all."

I knew shoving Mama aside for now was the best course for everyone even if Addy looked a little disappointed.

"So, what's all this?" I asked picking at the material in her lap.

"Golly, I almost forgot!" She hopped up and laid out five dresses with shortened hemlines and a pair of fashionable shoes. They were Addy's old dresses, remade and modernized. "Now Kate, I figured since you were willing to bob your hair, maybe it was time for a little feminine persuasion. I stayed up all night altering them. Well, what do you think?"

I looked doubtfully at her. I hadn't planned on changing my appearance beyond my hair style. A pale peasant blouse with tight, two-inch cuffs had been my morning selection. It was fitted around the waist and tied at the side. Loose trousers and low-heeled shoes were perfect for an outdoor graduation. Besides, it didn't matter what costume we chose; we were expected to wear our customary white graduation blouse and long black bow tied down the front.

Addy had a way of begging with her eyes and not her mouth. I sighed.

"'S'okay, I guess. You pick one for me. But it'll have to fit under my graduation blouse, you know."

She squealed and dove for her favorite, a beautiful blue concoction with a drop waist and sailor neckline. "You'll have to wear one of these to flatten your chest." She held up a short, camisole-looking garment with laces up the sides. "It's called a Symington Side Lacer. Trudy Mae and I bought a couple on the hidden market after we left you last night. I've got mine on already."

While Addy helped me into the lacer and laced up the sides, I asked how her folks had reacted to her new look. Her face grew dark and she muttered that her mama had called it crude and unladylike.

"Daddy said he'd better not find me sneaking cigarettes or going around with men in raccoon overcoats."

"You okay?" I asked. She shrugged.

307

"Don't let it get to you." I turned and gave her a hug. "You gotta live your own life, Addy. Isn't that what you're always telling me?"

"Thanks, Kate. I don't know what I would've done without you all these years."

"You'd have gone Modern a long time ago, that's what."

I studied myself in the mirror. Mr. Factor's make-up had been removed this morning so I could see myself again. The sailor dress was lovely with an air of fun but I still felt a little modest about showing my bare legs.

"Anything I wear going forward will be tame compared to last night's costume," I said smiling.

"You ain't talking hooey!" Addy said. "Wonder if you'll ever have occasion to wear it again."

"I doubt it. I plan to return it to Injun Pat as soon as possible. But these I plan to keep," I said holding up the silk stockings.

While I wormed my way into the stockings, Addy dug inside her pocketbook for some cosmetics she had purchased from the druggist earlier this morning. She applied a soft kohl liner to her eyes, shadowed them in soft pink, rouged her cheeks, and then added a rose color to her lips. All made up, she presented herself to me for final approval. This would be Addy's debut wearing society makeup, a new bob, and a flapper dress in public.

"Sensational!" I cried.

"*Femmes du monde!* Kate!" She sashayed around the room.

"You're right. You really are a woman of the world. A completely Modern woman."

We grinned with the unspoken understanding that it wasn't exactly true. We may look the part but we had yet to earn the title of being truly Modern.

"Well, this is it, Kate. Our final day at Los Angeles High School. By noon we'll be set free on the world."

"Lord help us," I breathed.

"And how! Now, powder your knees and get a wiggle on, or we'll be late."

In no time at all, we were standing among our fellow classmates on the football field of Los Angeles High School. Over our dresses, we girls dutifully wore our white graduation blouses with loose black bows hanging down our chests. Our male classmates were trussed up their best Sunday suits and ties. Those of us in the club had just received our Star and Crescent pins, attached to our collars. Next came poor Abner who stumbled through his commencement speech, wincing at the applause afterward. I suspected he had a humdinger of a headache.

After receiving our coveted diplomas, Reverend Shay was called forth to offer a closing prayer. At the Reverend's 'amen', the winter class of 1922—in unison and without further delay—threw up a resounding cheer. My high school career was over and I felt light and free. The school band struck up our fight song as the crowd migrated from the bleachers and surrounded us.

What followed was a flurry of hand shaking, endearing congratulations, and tearful hugs. Addy and I were inundated with classmates gushing over our dramatic makeovers. Who knew going Modern would cause such shockwaves. Addy lapped up the compliments. She truly looked sensational and carried it off like a seasoned Modern. Young fellas we'd never spoken to before came strolling around. Flies to honey, I thought.

Pop had tears in his eyes and Eugene shoved a bouquet of flowers at me. Trudy Mae was openly weeping. She hugged me so tightly I couldn't breathe. Mrs. Hazeldine came to my rescue with a gentle hug and warm congratulations. Addy's parents and grandparents offered their sincerest regards. I had the distinct feeling they were surprised I had spent enough time within the school walls to earn a diploma.

As the crowd slowly dispersed, I felt Addy at my elbow.

"What's *she* doing here?" she grumbled. Mary Miles Minter was standing at the edge of the field, a white-gloved hand shading the sun from her eyes. She wore her customary virginal white frock with her golden hair spiraled into a youthful style. A look that said she should've been skipping around in a pinafore, not zipping about Los Angeles in a spiffy roadster.

"I left a message with Mary's housekeeper earlier this morning. I wanted to speak to her about some things I'd heard last night. But I never expected her to show up at graduation."

What's more, I hadn't expected to see Nicky or Detective King here, either. By the look of Nicky's street clothes and glasses, he was off duty. Detective King was his usual disheveled self.

"I told Ed I'd be here this morning," Pop said, waving them over. "In case anything came up."

I declined several graduation party invitations from fellow classmates, insisting I had made other plans. I hated being a stick-in-the-mud, but honestly, I was too curious about what had brought Nicky and Detective King to my graduation. Something that obviously couldn't wait. I insisted Addy run off and enjoy herself, which she happily agreed to do.

"Afternoon, Miss March," Nicky said, as we met up in the middle of the field. "Congratulations on your graduation." He was back to his stuffy formalities as though we hadn't recently danced at the Grove and I hadn't covered him in meringue pie. I wished to heaven he would stop jumping back and forth over the fence. He was harder to read than a Chinese totem pole. Pop thank him for helping me last night, which I quickly pointed

310

out hadn't been necessary in the least. Nicky's response? A raised eyebrow and a cockeyed grin.

Detective King shifted restively and seemed put out to be in such an unlikely place. He did a double-take at me and then frowned. "New look? Not bad." His compliment went down like a flat phosphate. The fact that he had even noticed was something. Then he turned his attention to Pop with a scowl that could stop a train. He explained that District Attorney Woolwine had sent him to Santa Ana where a witness claimed to have seen Taylor's killer the night before the murder. The witness, a farmer named Mr. Cock, said he gave some fella a ride that night. The fella dropped his .38 Smith and Wesson break-top revolver in the mud because he was so nervous. Detective King thought it was a load of horseshit but decided to head south with Mr. Cock and check towns along the border. Sure enough, Mr. Cock pointed out his man down in Mexicali.

"The old boy was Red Kirby," Detective King grunted.

"That dewdropper they hauled in on suspicion?" I asked, surprised.

"The same. Only then Mr. Cock claims he might be mistaken. And Red's got solid proof it wasn't him so we're back to square one." Detective King removed his fedora and wiped a sleeve across his sweating forehead. "Now Woolwine's sending me up north to Folsom prison. Couple of mugs there confessed the murder to the warden. Of course, any half-wit can see that a pair of two-bit convicts confessed to the murder just to get hauled down here and make a break for it along the way. Either Woolwine's getting played for a fool or he's playing me for one." His face was heated from more than just the afternoon sun.

"Why would Woolwine play you for a fool?" Pop asked.

Detective King patted down his pockets, playing hide-and-seek with his cigarettes. "For appearances. It's got to look like he's following up leads. I'm no fool about Woolwine, I'll tell you that much. Wouldn't trust him further than I could chuck a cow. He wasn't accused of bribery back in '19 for nothing. Don't think he's not up to something." King won the game and lit up.

"Doesn't Woolwine figure Sands for the murder?" I asked. "That's what he's selling and some of the rags are buying."

Detective King scoffed. "Sands didn't kill Taylor any more than I did. And Woolwine knows it. Only he's not saying it freely like I am."

I didn't disagree. I never figured Sands for the murder. "Say, I've got Mary here. Maybe she can clear up some things I learned last night." I waved her over but Mary turned and fled with the strangest horrified expression.

"How interesting," I said, watching her go. I would definitely make a point of talking to her later. I explained to Detective King and Nicky what I had learned from my adventures at the Grove. "You see, I had wanted to leave Mary's name out of all this but after the implications of multiple affairs, I can't. That puts Mr. Kirkwood and Mr. Neilan on the list of men with possible motives if they knew Mr. Taylor was planning to run off with Mary."

"That's assuming they were in love with Miss Minter in the first place," Nicky mused doubtfully. He slipped his hands into his pockets and considered me. I couldn't read his eyes behind those dark lenses.

"I'm curious of this possible *hit* by a drug pusher," Detective King grumbled.

"It seems plausible to me," Pop added. "It was a clean hit, if you don't mind my saying."

"Single shot. No muss," King agreed.

I offered to interview Mable Normand about possible dealers but Detective King and Nicky said it was a lousy idea.

"Why?" I demanded.

"Say this was a professional gunman hired by a pusher," Nicky said. "What's to stop him from gunning you down for sticking your nose where it doesn't belong?"

"Where it doesn't belong?" I shot back. "Did I not prove myself last night?"

"Oh, you proved quite a bit last night, Miss March. For one thing, you drink like a fish. And for another, you have forgotten you are a *civilian*. Overstep your boundaries again, and it's called interfering with police business."

I could feel Pop's eyes on me. The reference to drinking, I suppose. I shook my head at Nicky, letting him know where I stood. "We'll see about that."

Detective King sighed. "Too dangerous anyhow. We can't have you tipping our hand. If the murderer is still around I don't want him running off. We'll look into it."

"Kate," Pop said sternly, "they're giving you sound advice. It's a fine line reporters must walk. Nick is right. We are civilians. We're after the story but they're trying to find a killer.

I untied my black bow in hard angry jerks and then slipped my graduation blouse over my head and flung it aside.

"Well then, if hunting down a drug pusher is out of the question, don't suppose you have any objections if I follow the jealousy angle, Officer Masino?" I asked sharply.

He pretended to mull things over. "Knock yourself out," he said, sporting a sideways grin. I seemed to amuse him to no end.

"You bet I will," I said, turning on my heel and walking away.

313

CHAPTER 21

"That was the beginning of things," I told Detective Cahill excitedly. I sat forward and rested my arms on the table. He had been leaning back in his seat, taking few notes for the past several minutes.

"What was?"

"Don't you see? If Nicky, um, Officer Masino, and King hadn't come to my graduation, we probably wouldn't have disagreed about the motive to kill Taylor and I wouldn't have gone off to follow the jealousy angle. Oh, it might have happened later on but that was it for me. I was a bloodhound on the case. And let me tell you, I was stumped! But not for long." I grinned. Detective Cahill sighed with irritation. Before he could complain and try to lure me back to the man in the alley, I said, "In case you're wondering, I was a complete sensation back at the office."

I went there straight after graduation and was met with a standing ovation from the entire staff! Boy, was I bowled over! Not only were they happy I had graduated (apparently there had been a running bet) but they loved my fashionable metamorphosis. The newsies let out whistles. Rico collected his winnings from Mr. Handle who cried, "Well done!" around the ciggy dangling from the corner of his mouth.

Mr. Fink and Mr. Dysinger leaned sideways to peruse my legs and then laughed as I blushed.

"Aw, you're nothing but a load of time-wasters," I said, smiling as I dropped the bouquet Eugene had given me into an old coffee tin. "Now get back to your hunt and peck machines and crank out something worth printing."

Bud was still gaping when I waved him over to my desk. He snapped out of it as I flipped open my notepad and gave him the low-down on my notes from the Cocoanut Grove. I asked that he hunt down information regarding everyone on my list: James Kirkwood, Marshall Neilan, Antonio Moreno.

"And Howard Fellows, too," I threw in as an afterthought. Something had been pestering me about Mr. Taylor's chauffeur but I couldn't put my finger on it. Perhaps it would come to me in time.

When Bud left to do my bidding, I rang up Mary and told her to expect me in thirty minutes. She was reluctant but I was adamant. My stomach had settled down and I felt the stirrings of hunger pangs. A quick bite at the Kettle might do, and then I would head to Mary's.

Mr. Morgan turned on his barstool and opened his arms in a grand welcome as I entered the Kettle.

"Behold! The Graduate!" he announced to a handful of startled diners. I laughed and strolled over.

"'Lo there, Mr. Morgan. What's doin'?"

He made a show of dusting off the neighboring barstool and presenting it to me with a flourish. I sat down and gave him a sly look. "Say, you on the sauce?" I teased.

"Oh!" He clutched his heart dramatically. "You wound me, my dear. I am but a humble servant from the East here to serve the intelligentsia of the West. In fact, I shall treat you to a brilliant lunch!" He turned to Bessie the waitress. "Madame! Your finest cuppa Joe for the Lady a la Graduate. And a thick slice of lemon meringue pie, perhaps?" He shot me a devilish grin.

I laughed and revised the order to a phosphate soda and turkey on rye. Then I gave Mr. Morgan the once-over. "I see you survived the night."

He returned the once-over with an approving smile and then propped an elbow on the counter and gazed dreamily at me. "And you completely overwhelmed me last night, Miss Kate. This conversion to the *femmes du monde* aside, I never expected to see you there. It was the night before your graduation, was it not?"

"Aw, you know what they say, 'Education is an admirable thing, but it is well to remember from time to time that nothing worth knowing can be taught'." I flashed my eyes knowingly because I had learned plenty while gallivanting around the Grove. Mr. Morgan collapsed onto the counter, rolling his head across his arms in despair.

"Oh, sweet lady, but to speak Oscar Wilde to me! It is my undoing!"

I laughed and nudged him playfully. "Oh, please sit up. Now tell me, why all this buffoonery?"

Mr. Morgan smiled lazily under a crop of blond hair that had fallen across his forehead in what Addy called a 'rakish manner'. "Such buffoonery should have a *raison d'être,* I suppose. And so, I do. I've been waiting here, hoping to catch your lovely attention." He lowered his voice. "You see, I didn't flee the party as quickly as you did, Cinderella. I thought perhaps you might enjoy the fruits of my labor?"

I narrowed my eyes. "And why would you share your information with the competition?"

"Never mind that."

"You wanna know what I found out?" I stated flatly.

"Forever distrustful of dear old Mr. Morgan." He pouted affectionately.

"Fine. Lemme have it. Just remember, there are only a few serious rags in this town. We can't all write the same story."

Bessie served my lunch and I started in on the turkey and rye while Mr. Morgan explained the aftermath of the ruckus I had created.

After the food fight had simmered down, the few remaining guests huddled around a quiet table in the far corner of the Grove. They were served coffee and left alone while the inebriated and the animals were returned to their proper habitats. The topic of Mr. Taylor's murder soon rose like Hamlet's ghost. The crux of their conversation went as such: a pal of Taylor's by the name of Arthur Hoyt was interrogated by detectives. He was reluctant to speak, having promised secrecy to Taylor, but Mr. Hoyt eventually complied due to Taylor being dead. He spoke of a particular evening he had visited Taylor at home. Taylor was highly agitated and, after some diligent coaxing, confessed his troubles. He said a dear friend was infatuated with him. In love, she claimed. Desperately in love. And Taylor was at his wit's end to deal with her. It was flattering and whatnot, but he was old enough to be her father. Well, she showed

317

up a few days before the murder—at three in the morning—demanding to stay the night. Taylor insisted she leave. She threatened to raise a ruckus and wake the neighbors. He became frantic, knowing how many friends lived nearby. Taylor finally convinced her to leave and walked her to her car.

I set my sandwich on the plate and looked warily at Mr. Morgan. "And the name of Mr. Taylor's infatuated 'dear friend'?"

"Mary Miles Minter."

I sighed with enough force to knock Mr. Morgan off his barstool. Reluctantly, I shared the gossip I had heard at the Grove concerning Mary and the planned rendezvous with Mr. Taylor. Mr. Morgan considered things.

"You think Taylor got rid of Mary that night by promising to go away with her?" he asked.

It sounded plausible. It also sounded as though Mary was up to her neck in lies.

"Taylor hadn't the appearance of going anywhere, had he?" Mr. Morgan asked. "Hadn't packed. And his valet, Henry Peavey, hadn't mentioned it."

"And, Mabel Normand was over for a visit that night."

"Maybe Mary showed up and saw them together."

We fell silent, thinking. I confessed that the drug pusher and hired gun theory were preoccupying Nicky and Detective King. Mr. Morgan nodded thoughtfully as though it made better sense.

"It was a clean shot after all. And there was a general understanding from my newly acquired friends last night that Mabel Normand was back on cocaine," Mr. Morgan said with a sympathetic smile. "For all we know, Mabel visited Taylor that night to warn him trouble was coming."

"Yes, and remember Henry Peavey said they had argued that night. Sure would like to interview Miss Normand again," I said, sourly.

"Pugsly had the same idea but Woolwine won't allow anyone to harass Miss Normand."

"But Woolwine doesn't work for the studios! Why would he—"

"He might be the DA but don't think he's not chummy with folks in the movie industry. There's a lot of money to be made there."

That reminded me of Eugene's account of those actors in trouble with the authorities and the payoffs that got them released without charges. It ran like clockwork, indicating that senior officers must be involved. Who was to say it didn't extend all the way up to the DA's office?

I rubbed my temples, feeling a headache coming. "Please tell me why you're doing this?"

"Something needs to change," Mr. Morgan murmured, his eyes emptying of their usual amusement. I took measure of his mood. I'd never know him to simmer in a philosophical stew. Had he picked up a sword and gone into cahoots with the competition to fight for justice? Had the playboy from the East grown a vigilante's heart?

"Just who did Claire Windsor and the others at the Grove think you were last night, Mr. Michael Meeks?" I asked.

He smiled wistfully. "An aspiring novelist. Miss Windsor and I were introduced by a mutual acquaintance. An older gentleman who owed me a favor. He went along with my crude thespian plot, as he is a veteran thespian himself. I manipulated an invitation out of Miss Windsor and... well... there I was."

I felt a pang of empathy for him. The sadness in his voice was no act. Mr. Morgan's deep desire to write novels had been stridently and routinely discouraged, if not forbidden, by his father and grandfather, both prominent lawyers in New York.

"You are a fine journalist," I said, squeezing his hand.

"I am notably substandard because I don't care for the profession," he murmured, patting my hand. "Haven't cared for months. You, on the other hand—"

"Love it," I confessed.

"It suits you. You are very intuitive, Miss Kate. I envy you that." We exchanged polite smiles. "Will this be your chosen profession, now that you've graduated?"

"I believe so. Don't mind a little sleuthing on the side."

"Which side?"

"The inside."

He chuckled. "Then do me a favor? With all the clues from the Taylor case buzzing about your pretty little head... trust that intuition, will you? No matter where it takes you?"

"I will, but... say, why do I feel like you're telling me... goobye?" A peculiar sort of panic hit me. Mr. Morgan was the most entertaining man I knew. I couldn't imagine life without his razor-sharp wit and cutthroat quotes. He offered an engaging mental challenge that I had come to rely on.

"It's all well and good, my sweet," he stood and kissed the back of my hand. "Keep this simple truth in mind... 'Journalism will kill you, but it will keep you alive while you're at it'." He smiled, tipped his fedora, and then was gone.

"Bessie," I said as I watched Mr. Morgan walk out. "How could a man so effortlessly quote Horace Greeley, king of the newspaper business, not have an ounce of desire for the profession itself?"

Bessie the waitress set her pot of black coffee on the counter, rested a hand on her hip, and shook her head. "Don't make a lick of sense," she answered as though greatly concerned herself.

Mr. Morgan was a puzzle but I appreciated his advice about trusting my intuition. Pop had given me the same guidance on more than one occasion. Problem was, I had a tendency to ignore my intuition when I feared the outcome. I had recognized this late last night when my inhibitions were swimming in champagne. Like it or not, my instincts were leading in the one direction I hadn't wanted to go.

I left the Kettle and went in search of Mary.

When I arrived at the house on Hobart Street, the maid informed me that Mary had gone out. Furious, I insisted on waiting for her and was led into the parlor. Less than an hour ago, I had telephoned and informed Mary I would be stopping by. Clearly, she was avoiding me. Hadn't she enough common sense to know it didn't look good?

After ten minutes or so, Mary's grandmother came down and graciously invited me to join her on the back porch. I was happy to keep her company. Mrs. Miles had always been kind to me. We settled ourselves onto wicker rocking chairs and chatted about the weather, this month's strawberry harvest, and various mundane trivialities. She never mentioned my new look, and I offered my condolences regarding Mr. Taylor.

"I know how much Mary thought of him," I said.

"Mmm hmm," Mrs. Miles replied, rocking back and forth.

"Sure hope they find his killer soon," I added vaguely, keeping an eye on the back door for Mary.

"Oh, yes, seems everybody's eager to solve it," Mrs. Miles said in her soft southern accent, reminding me that the family originated in Louisiana. "Why, the police have been round asking for our help, don't you know? Course, we can't offer any. We were all home that night. Mmm hmm." She tilted her head thoughtfully and gazed out at the yard.

"You mean everyone was home here? Not with Mrs. Shelby

on New Hampshire Street?" I asked to be polite. I didn't have an afternoon to waste waiting for Mary. If she didn't arrive soon, I might be forced to try the house on New Hampshire. I would welcome the black plague before encountering Charlotte Shelby. Either way, Mary would get a tongue lashing next time we met.

"Why, yes. Margaret, and Mary, and I live here now. Charlotte lives on New Hampshire. She was at a Swedish bathhouse in Hollywood that dreadful night. She frequents it occasionally. Helps her nerves. Mmm hmm."

"I see," I murmured distractedly. I had heard an auto engine round front and jumped to my feet. "Might be Mary. You'll excuse me." I rushed inside and left Mrs. Miles rocking back and forth, humming, "Mmm hmm."

By the time I reached the foyer, Margaret had walked in. I deflated.

She stopped abruptly, eyeing my sailor dress and bobbed hair until she finally recognized my face. "Pleasure to see you, too," she said acerbically. "Gone Modern, have you?" Margaret was wearing an unfortunate dress of brown chenille with pale yellow flowers. She removed her driving gloves and tossed them onto the entry table. Peering into the mirror on the wall, she patted down her mousy brown curls.

"Waiting for Mary," I explained.

"Obviously."

I tucked my hands behind my back and watched her thoughtfully. "It must be hard on you Margaret, playing second fiddle to Mary and all. I think you're a fine actress, myself."

That was a lie. I hadn't the faintest idea whether Margaret had any forte for acting. My information came from Mary who told me the Monster always included Margaret in Mary's contracts. If the studios wanted Mary for a moving picture, they had to find a part for big sister as well. I don't believe this enhanced

Margaret's career, only the household income.

Margaret put on a familiar sulking face, the one I had seen Mary use when trying to finagle money from her mother.

"Thank you. I've been told on occasion that I have real talent that goes beyond outward beauty. Ya know?"

I smiled politely. "Oh, certainly. But you must have your hands full with male callers."

She studied her plain features in the mirror, contemplating. "Not so many," she confessed. "Men can be so shy at times."

"Mmm hmm," I said, picking up where Mrs. Miles had left off. "And, then there's Mary." I sighed forlornly as though I knew her most intimate business and disapproved.

"Mary's so aggressive with men," Margaret sniped. "I think it's vulgar. And, so does mother. Why, if the public knew—" She stopped and looked at me in the mirror.

"You don't have to censor yourself around me, Margaret. I am perhaps one of the few people Mary trusts with her private secrets. You know she and I have been quite close for a while now, and well, she's always shared her feelings about Mr. Taylor. That's why I made arrangements for her to see his body before the inquest. To say goodbye and all." The tension in her distrusting eyes softened enough to encourage me to continue. "And, Margaret, I'd like to be honest with you. I'm here to help Mary. The police are looking into anyone who dated Mary and might have been jealous of Mr. Taylor."

"I'm aware of that fact," she said crisply. "They questioned Tom Dixon but the man wouldn't hurt a fly."

To my knowledge, the police no longer considered Tom Dixon a suspect. The pencil heir from the East had withdrawn from social circles due to being utterly humiliated when Mary's love letter to Taylor went public. Tom Dixon had been chasing Mary for quite some time.

323

"What about Marshal Neilan?" I said.

"Old Mickey Neilan? Jealous?" She snorted unladylike. "He wouldn't have the time. Not when there are so many—shall we say—feminine opportunities to chase down in Hollywood. You know he divorced his wife to marry Blanche Sweet. Quiet the smoother talker, and I ain't whistling Dixie."

"So, he lost interest in Mary? I forget, how did it end?"

She meandered into the parlor and offered a lemonade. I declined and she called for the maid to bring one for herself. Then she flopped onto the sofa and crossed her legs at the ankles. I took the chair opposite.

"Or perhaps it hasn't ended?" I prompted.

Margaret shrugged indifferently and flipped through the *Ladies Home Journal* magazine.

"Let's just say Mr. Neilan was persuaded to lose interest. Like they all are."

Poor Mary. I could imagine how men might see her, a young wealthy woman unhappy at home. They might have thought she was easy pickings. Mary must have suspected their motives and forced them away, especially when she saw through them. She had a hot temper on occasion, and the papers dogged her endlessly, making real relationships impossible.

"And then there was James Kirkwood," I said. Margaret's hand froze while turning a page.

"How—" she began and stopped herself. She tossed the magazine aside and stared at me through narrow brown eyes.

"I'm sorry," I said. "That's probably not a name you'd like mentioned around here. It's just that—"

"He's vile! A vile predator who should be locked up!"

I was taken aback. Such hostility! I wouldn't argue about the description either, having barely escaped his advances myself. Margaret's reaction gave weight to Mr. Kirkwood's tawdry gossip about Mary. "I-I couldn't agree more. But, do you suppose he could've been jealous of Mr. Taylor? Jealous enough to—"

"She was so young!" Margaret continued as though I hadn't spoken. "So very young and naïve and..." She stared across the room, a sad painful memory glazing her eyes. For the first time since I had known Margaret, she showed genuine sympathy toward her sister. Whatever happened with Mr. Kirkwood, Margaret had not blamed Mary.

"No," she finally answered. "No, that man is the lowest of God's creatures but he wouldn't have been jealous. Not of Mr. Taylor and Mary."

"I heard they planned to go away together. Mary and Mr. Taylor. Before he was murdered."

Margaret's eyes snapped to mine. She shook her head in pure disbelief. "How in the world could you possibly know that," she whispered. "Was it Mary?"

I opened my mouth but couldn't speak. Everything had been confirmed in one fell swoop. I tried to mask my shock while Margaret complained about Mary's behavior as though I were truly Mary's closest confidant. The sordid details would be no surprise to me. Margaret unknowingly confirmed Arthur Hoyt's account of the night Mary showed up at Mr. Taylor's, demanding to stay the night. And it had not been the first time. On Mary's most recent visit, Taylor had convinced her to go home, promising they would find time to go away and talk things through. Mary had been elated. The time and day never got settled because he was killed.

"Yes, I'm aware," I said quietly. "Poor Mary. And of course, you're right about Mr. Kirkwood. Now that I think about it. But if Mr. Neilan and Mr. Kirkwood had no designs on Mary, I wonder who did? Possibly someone Mary had rejected in the past? Oh, Margaret, I would hate for some thwarted lover to hurt Mary."

Margaret blinked stupidly.

325

"Who else knew of their plans? Antonio Moreno? Arthur Hoyt? Who would be jealous enough to want Mr. Taylor dead?"

"Why, I—"

The front door opened and Charlotte Shelby strode in. She wore her customary black lace dress, black stockings, black shoes, and hat. She removed the hatpin and hat. Her face was drawn and colorless, her mouth sagging in a permanent scowl. She hesitated upon seeing Margaret with company. A moment of intense study and then she recognized me in my new clothing and hairstyle. I stood up to greet her, putting on a pleasant smile just for the occasion. Mrs. Shelby grew icebergs for eyes.

"What are you doing here?" she demanded. The icebergs swept the room for Mary. Without a word, she yanked the door open and motioned for me to leave. I thanked Margaret for keeping me company while Mary was out. Stalking past Mrs. Shelby's petite frame, I had just enough time to cross the threshold before she slammed the door on my heels.

I gathered my thoughts on the drive back to the office. Margaret had been a fountain of information and I had much to sort through. A few notable and surprising facts I had documented in my notepad for safe keeping. Overall, I had come to the sad conclusion that the Mary I knew in friendship had only revealed a thin slice of her true character.

Unfortunately, Margaret's helpful insight had shortened my list of possible suspects. As much as Margaret hated Mr. Kirkwood, she refused to implicate him. And it seemed that Mr. Neilan's high opinion of himself wouldn't allow the excess of jealousy. So where did that leave my jealousy theory?

Upon entering the office, I was immediately overcome by a deafening rumble emanating from Belching Bertha. The printing room's double doors had been flung open, and Pop and Eugene were silently arguing at the top of their lungs over the racket. Eugene's overalls were smeared with grease, and he was flailing his arms at Bertha to make some point to Pop. No doubt they had differing opinions as to the cause of the grey smoke rising from poor Bertha's innards.

Across the room, Mr. Handle held up a phone to gain my attention. I made my way through the maze of desks to take the call. Meanwhile, Bud was ready with the results of his errands and thrust a notepad at me as I snatched up the phone.

"Hello!" I yelled into the receiver. "Hold on a minute, will ya!" I pressed the phone into my chest and hollered over the cacophony as Bud tried to explain his notes. "What? Bud, I can't hear a word you're saying!"

"It's all there!" he shouted, jabbing his finger at the notepad. "But, what about Arthur Hoyt! Should I—"

Bertha's loud rumble had shifted to an odd clacking noise that made us flinch. The grey smoke turned black, which must have meant something terrible because Eugene disappeared into the back and Pop stormed to his office, rubbing a very red neck.

Back on the phone I shouted, "Yes! Hello! Who is this?" I scrunched my face to better hear. "Addy?"

"And what about this one!" Bud cried, pointing at the notepad again. "Who's it?"

"You'll have to speak up! I can't hear a word you're saying!" I wailed to Addy. I squinted at the notepad in Bud's hand. "It says Mrs. Whitney! Whitney! Mary's old—oh, never mind! What, Addy? Who? Who's dead?"

Belching Bertha's clacking and rumbling had been working toward a discordant, mechanical crescendo. She rumbled like an earthquake and then backfired with a resounding BOOM! Nuts and bolts shot across the newsroom like missiles. Everyone hit

327

the floor. I crouched safely behind my desk while Bud curled into the fetal position with arms over his head. His doughy, collegiate eyes stared at me full of fear; it was his first time at the front after all. The seasoned staffers waited patiently while Bertha had her say. Bertha's smooth chugging rhythm could be deceptive. She was a capricious old gal and had been taking random pot-shots at us for years. Bertha was another reason why the paper needed money. Replacing her was costly and long overdue. Eventually, she returned to the familiar clicking, and tapping, and whirling noise of a well-oiled engine on the Southern Pacific rails. As she picked up speed, her smooth belts and black ink barrels spun without fuss. Heads appeared over desktops and life went on.

I was situated back in my seat and still clutching the telephone when Nicky Masino slowly rose from behind the front counter. He must have stepped inside at the point of Bertha's attack.

"Repeat that again please," I told Addy, keeping an eye on Nicky. He and Detective King had been deliberately avoiding our office to prevent suspicions from the DA's office. Nicky's presence here must be important. Rather than head to Pop's private office as I would have expected, Nicky lowered his chin and crooked his finger, beckoning me over.

"Got it," I said into the mouthpiece. "Thanks." I placed the earpiece in its hook and set the telephone back on the desk. I told Bud to take a moment to recover himself and then I walked to Nicky. "Is it true?" I jumped in before he could speak. "Is Red Kirby dead?"

Nicky's eyes flickered with surprise and then looked past me to Bertha. "Is that going to happen again?" He pointed toward the back. I shrugged. Less than satisfied, Nicky opened the front door and I preceded him onto the sidewalk.

It was late afternoon and the sun no longer shone between the giant grey buildings of commerce lining Broadway. The sidewalk was cast in cool shadows and thin on foot traffic. The business directly next to *The Messenger* was Mr. Calhoun's Hardware Store which sold everything from windowpanes to paint and varnish, to Champions sparkplugs and roofing asbestos. I waved at Mr. Calhoun through the window. He squinted, not recognizing me, but waved all the same. Nicky and I stood under Mr. Calhoun's awning opposite a line of black autos parked along the curb.

"I am here to formally *advise* you to stay away from the family of Charlotte Shelby, of which includes her mother, Mrs. Miles, and her daughters Margaret and Mary," Nicky said efficiently.

I squinted up at him. "By order of Woolwine?" I was refused an answer. The last thing the DA needed was a newspaper claiming that a Hollywood starlet was being protected by the Los Angeles Police Department during a murder investigation. There had been enough chin wagging when the picture of Woolwine escorting Miss Normand to the inquest hit the papers. I let it go and pressed him for news of Red Kirby's recent demise.

Nicky considered for a moment and then his face lit up. "Addy! She does filing for her Aunt Alice; she's the one feeding you information straight from the precinct. Yes, now, don't deny it. Your source has been revealed, Miss March."

I smiled. "I will neither confirm nor deny your charges, Officer Masino. But it would be wise to remember I was born and raised here, just like yourself. I know Los Angeles like the back of my hand. I have a plethora of sources at my disposal. Now, am I right about Red?"

"Yes. But don't go snapping your garters about it—and yes, I know you wear garters now." He laughed as I blushed. "Unfortunately, Red Kirby had absolutely nothing to do with Taylor's murder. But, then, you knew that already, didn't you?"

I shrugged. "Yeah, I've gone off that angle."

"And, so, after your interrogation at the home of Mrs. Miles—which I'm sure you would classify as a friendly chat—," he rushed on as I was preparing to deny it, "Which of your jealousy suspects fits the bill?"

He was humoring me but I took it on the chin. While he and Detective King had been chasing the hired gun angle, I had taken my jealousy angle just as seriously. I refused him an answer, choosing not to give anything away. Least of all the fact that I had no clue as to which of Mary's many admirers or lovers or discarded whatnots were capable of murder.

"No confessions of jealously then?" he asked.

"No. How about you?"

"Me? Jealous?" he said, growing flustered. I had meant to ask if he'd had any confessions regarding his hired gun theory but Nicky had taken my question the wrong way. Before I could correct him, he stumbled awkwardly through his thoughts on jealousy.

"It's a strange thing, that jealousy business," he said quietly, staring down at his shoes. "All kinds of jealousy. Makes a man do all kinds of crazy things sometimes."

I let out a small gasp. Nicky looked up sharply as though he'd been caught at something. "All kinds of jealousy," I repeated softly. "All kinds of jealousy." I turned away to consider something. Why had that sounded so familiar? All kinds of—

My scattered thoughts suddenly condensed into an epiphany that made my stomach jump. "Oh, my God!" I swung around and nearly blurted everything out. Thankfully, I caught myself. I couldn't possibly tell Nicky yet, but he had opened my eyes to that thing nagging me for so long.

"What?" Nicky demanded.

"I-I can't say! Not until I have proof."

I had to find Bud. I had to check my notes. I started for the office but Nicky clutched my arm.

"Where are you going?"

"What? Oh, I have to get back. To work. The office. Bud." I pulled and he released me.

"You're not cooking up anything silly, right?" he asked.

I grinned and opened the door. "Why, don't you understand, Nicky? 'If people did not sometimes do silly things, nothing intellectual would ever get done'." It was my favorite quote from Ludwig Wittenstein. Mr. Morgan would have roared. Nicky simply rolled his eyes. I threw out a laugh and hurried inside.

Belching Bertha was humming nicely, having succumbed to Eugene's tinkering. The office was busy again and Pop seemed pleased if not a little flushed from the excitement. He and Eugene had already moved on to their latest fascination, wireless receivers. I was happy to see them fiddling with Pop's new Crosley radio. It would be a great distraction for Pop and give me more uninterrupted time for sleuthing. I had yet to formally reveal my post-graduation plans to Pop regarding my career as a bona fide newspaper reporter.

With Pop busy, I maneuvered to my desk and gathered Bud. In hushed whispers, we poured over my notes, the timeline, and his photos from the crime scene.

"So, what do you think?" Bud asked after a fair amount of head scratching. He had failed to put the puzzle pieces together as I had.

I closed my notepad and sat back, feeling a mix of shock and excitement. "I-I think I know who killed Mr. Taylor. And why."

CHAPTER 22

I didn't want Detective Cahill to interrupt me with annoying things like questions so I kept going at a steady pace...

Late in the evening, Bud and I hopped a Red Car to Wiltshire and South Union and then walked over to 1622 Shatto Place. The residence was dark but for a dim light in the upstairs window. I knocked on the door and we waited. After a prolonged, discomforting moment, the door opened a crack and a wild eye blinked at us. What little I could see was recognizable as Mr. Taylor's chauffeur, Howard Fellows.

"Howard?"

"Who is it?" he barked.

"Kate March, here. From *The Messenger*. We met at Mr. Taylor's bungalow on the morning his body was discovered. I have one question to ask, if you don't mind."

"Why so late?" he demanded.

"Why not?" I inquired in what I hoped to be a lighthearted tone.

He pushed the door ajar to scrutinize us and then poked his head out, scanning the street in either direction. He was jumpy as a frog but I assured him we were alone and harmless.

Howard probed me with distrusting eyes. "I ain't never seen you before," he grumbled and threatened to close the door.

I couldn't blame him. For my evening out in the cold night air, I had changed into black trousers and a deep purple velvet tunic. My fashionable dress coat was black wool with a velvet shawl collar. A stylish black cloche topped my head. It was no wonder Howard hadn't recognized me. Even as I explained the recent death of my auburn braid, Howard was not moved.

"I'm not talking to reporters," he said. My hand shot out and stopped the door before he could slam it in our faces.

"Don't you think it's time, Howard? I mean, you're awfully young to be playing hermit the rest of your life."

"Huh?"

"She already knows," Bud said importantly. "You can trust her to do you right."

I was pleasantly surprised by Bud's confidence in me and more so that his influence had changed Howard's mind. Reluctantly, Howard resigned himself to the inevitable and swung the door open.

At nineteen, Howard Fellows had accumulated the usual luxuries of a young man living on his own: a second-hand sofa, a battered kitchen table pitted from overuse, a single wooden chair that doubled for a coat rack, and chipped dishes piled in the sink. What I found unusual was the generous amount of newspapers strewn about. Bud and I waded into the living room where I nudged aside the *Los Angeles Times* with the toe of my shoe.

"Keeping up on the investigation?" I asked casually.

Howard set a coffee pot on the stove to percolate and made a half-hearted search for clean mugs. "I should call Harry," he muttered.

I remembered his brother, Harry, had also been Mr. Taylor's chauffeur until Taylor hired him as assistant director at Paramount. The last thing I wanted was Harry telling his brother to roll over and play dead.

"That's not necessary, Howard. Like I said, I only have one question." I was eager to begin before his nerves got the better of him so I cleared a spot on the lumpy sofa and perched on the edge. Bud remained standing, his eyes scanning the place like photographic lenses. I appreciated his intuitiveness. Bud knew when to speak up, and when to stay quiet.

Howard dragged the wooden chair closer and sat opposite me. His knee began to vibrate. I tilted my head and smiled softly.

"Howard, it was you, wasn't it?"

Howard blinked rapidly and lowered his chin. He leaned forward and rested his forearms on his knees, hands clasped in a death grip. White knuckles appeared. He stared at the floor for a long minute, slowly rocking back and forth as he simmered with rage. His cheeks grew red. I glanced at Bud should I need backup, then I braced myself for an outburst.

Slowly, Howard lifted his face. His eyes were wide and moist with despair, fear, and pent-up anger.

"Oh, Howard," I said gently and placed a hand over his. He must have been suffering terribly these past weeks. "It was *you* on Mr. Taylor's porch the night of the murder. It was *you* Faith MacLean saw leaving. *You* pulled the door shut and walked calmly away."

He exhaled a shaky breath and nodded. "But I didn't kill

him! I swear! I had the car like always that night. I come up to the place just as I was told to. Mr. Taylor, he said he might go out later on. Said I should ring him by seven-thirty."

I nodded, recalling my notes. "You remember speaking to me at Mr. Taylor's, Howard? While your brother and Mrs. Ivers removed items from the bungalow? Good. Well, you told me you had tried to reach Mr. Taylor several times by phone within that hour."

"Yes, ma'am. I did." He brushed the emotions from his eyes. "You've gotta believe me, Miss. Please!"

"Yes, Howard, I believe you. Now, tell me the rest. Tell me what you didn't tell me before."

He sat back to collect himself. "Well, I was at a friend's house early on. That's where I was when I called Mr. Taylor. But he don't answer, see? So, I left my friend to go around to Mr. Taylor's about five minutes before eight or near enough. I come up about a quarter after eight. That's all the time it takes to get there. The door was open. And them lights upstairs, they was on. So, I knocked several times. Then I thought, maybe he don't wanna be disturbed or nothing, seeing how he didn't answer his phone and all. So, I pulled the door shut and left."

"Did you look inside when you pulled the door shut?"

"No, ma'am. I just grabbed it and clicked it shut. It was mostly dark anyhow, only them upstairs lights was on and a lamp or something dim downstairs. I swear I didn't see nothing. Jesus! I'd have told somebody if I had!" He jumped up and began pacing and running his hand through his hair.

"Were you surprised the door was open?"

He turned and thought about it. "No. It was a cool night and Mr. Taylor liked the cold."

"And, the police never suspected you were the man on the porch?"

"Well..." He returned to the chair and shuffled his feet a bit, looking cagey. "I overheard what that MacLean woman said to you, and sure, I knew it was me. I knew it looked bad and nobody'd believe me. Harry said I was right and that I shouldn't say nothing. The police never asked me directly. Just what time I rang up Mr. Taylor's phone and what time I put the car away for the night."

"And, did you walk in the direction that Mrs. MacLean indicated?"

"I did."

"Did you see her looking through the door?"

"Wasn't paying no attention."

"What were you wearing?"

"Coat with my collar up and my golf hat. It was kinda chilly."

"Where'd you go?"

"That way leads to the garage. Seeing how Mr. Taylor don't answer, I figured I should put the car in for the night."

"And did you?"

"I did. Took me a while. Big car, small garage. You figure it. And, I didn't want no scratches or nothing because it'd just been repainted."

I sighed and smiled at Howard. "Thank you," I said.

He fidgeted. "I'm... only telling you because... I cain't take it no more. Living like some outlaw when I ain't done nothing. I figure it's like you said. It's time for the truth. Even if it makes them police look like idiots. Them thinking it was that Edward Sands fella on the porch and all. Even if Harry and his bosses don't want me talking. It ain't them living like a... like a..."

"Hermit," I said. He was getting riled up again so I softened my voice. "Howard? Won't you tell me why Harry and his bosses don't want you to clear yourself?"

His knee began to vibrate again. "Don't rightly know," he lied.

"I bet my new garters you do," I teased. Howard blushed

336

and suppressed a grin.

"Miss March, I—" He stopped and shook his head. He just couldn't and wouldn't elaborate. "But you do believe me? You believe I didn't kill Mr. Taylor? Right?" He begged like a stray dog accustomed to being kicked.

"I *know* you didn't kill him, Howard."

"*How* do you know?"

"Because I know who did."

I hadn't felt this giddy since the National Council of Defense reinstated Christmas in the winter of 1918, allowing parents to buy reasonable presents for their children.

By the time Bud and I returned to the office, everyone had gone but Eugene. He'd taken apart Pop's radio to increase the inner workings and was reassembling it when we rushed in.

"He can probably reach Hawaii now," Eugene bragged, ignoring how Bud and I were flushed and out of breath. We had jumped off a moving Red Car and ran all the way from the corner.

"Oh, good! You're here!" I called out, panting. At my desk, I quickly rolled a crisp sheet of white paper into the Underwood and set off typing. "Get Bertha ready. I've got a sensational scoop that'll change the headline."

"Pop's not gonna like it." Eugene strolled over wiping his hands on a grease rag. He peered over my shoulder and squinted at my notepad. "So, what's it gonna... hellzapopping, Kate! You can't print that!" He stared at me. I smiled and didn't miss a stroke. "But, I thought—"

"So did everybody else," I said, sliding the return bar and typing feverishly.

He considered things and then shrugged. "'S' alright I guess, but you know this'll ruin Pop and the paper if you're wrong."

"I'm not."

"Didn't figure." He sauntered toward the back muttering, "Damnedest thing I ever heard."

We spent the next several hours reworking the front page, setting type, printing, binding, and finally delivering the paper ourselves. I drove Pop's truck while Bud and Eugene rode in back and dropped paper bombshells on every major street corner. Around five in the morning, one stack remained. I stopped at First and Broadway, home of the *Los Angeles Times*. I was particularly pleased that Mr. Chandler would receive a special delivery courtesy of *The Messenger*.

When Rico and the newsies arrived at the office, I sent them back out to find their bundles and start hawking papers. Satisfied and exhausted, I told Bud to go home and get some sleep, but he opted to sprawl across the back table instead. I settled into my chair to wait for Pop and the staff, and eventually fell asleep across my desk. Pop arrived at seven o'clock, read the shocking headline, and then shook me awake until I nearly fell out of my chair.

"What in heaven's name have you done!" he wailed. The tiny vein in his forehead that rarely showed itself had risen like the Nile. Only then did I consider that perhaps I should have consulted with him first. If only to spare him a potential heart attack.

"It's true, Pop." I sat up, rubbing my eyes. "Every word of it." Three of our telephones rang to life. And, then, the front door blew open and Detective King and Nicky stormed in.

"What in the hell is the meaning of this!" Detective King demanded. He thrust our paper in the air and then slapped it on the countertop. He was as red as a Hot House tomato. Nicky was rather subdued considering his partner's impending mental break.

"Kate," Nicky said congenially. No Miss March today for he was talking to an old friend who'd gone off her rocker. "Would you like to explain this?"

I sat back in my chair and took a moment to consider myself. Either I had been so far off the mark that my theory hadn't occurred, or even seemed plausible, to a seasoned special investigator like Detective King or I had seen what no one else had. I chose to believe the latter, coming to the conclusion that I had a real knack for sleuthing.

"I followed my jealousy angle," I said simply.

"And that led you to announce to the whole world that William Desmond Taylor was murdered by a *woman*?" Nicky asked incredulously. "Do you have proof? Or is this one of your games?"

"Games?" I stood and stared at them. Pop, Detective King, and Nicky looked expectantly at me. "You all think I'm playing fast and loose with the paper? That I'm in this for kicks?"

"Seems to me that everything's been a game to you. One harebrained scheme after another," Nicky said. "Trespassing into Mr. Taylor's bungalow the day of the murder, concocting raids to clog up the precinct to slip inside, sneaking into Paramount, and infiltrating the Grove to gather a load of nonsense from a bunch of drunken swells."

I looked at Pop. He was justifiably concerned. "My intention has never been to humiliate myself, or you, or the paper. You know I would never stoop to yellow journalism, especially when the blowback could shut down a small outfit like ours. Every so-called, harebrained scheme was devised to unearth the truth and every single one bore fruit that led to my discovery of the murderer. I *do* know who killed Mr. Taylor, Pop. I just haven't had time to prove it."

By this time Eugene had roused and was walking over,

scratching his belly. Ignoring the tension in the air, as was his habit, he offered to fetch coffee at the Kettle if he had any takers.

"You in on this?" Pop accused. He had not been completely soothed by my reassuring words.

Eugene shrugged. "She's on to something, Pop. Hear her out." He yawned and sauntered out the door.

Pop set aside the phones to stop their incessant noise. I suspected our shocked readers and advertisers wanted an explanation. He indicated chairs for Detective King and Nicky. King accepted while Nicky perched on the edge of a nearby desk and stared thoughtfully at me. Pop pulled up a chair and asked me to start from the beginning.

"I knew Howard Fellows must have been the man seen leaving Taylor's the night of the murder because of the timing; he began calling Taylor's home around seven thirty, or thereafter, and received no answer. That's about the time Taylor walked Miss Normand to her car and chatted for a moment while her driver cleaned peanut shells from the vehicle. Meanwhile, the killer had been waiting around back, pacing nervously and crunching gravel that Christine Jewett, Mrs. MacLean's maid, had heard. The killer had been smoking gold-tipped cigarettes which Addy and I had found the morning the body was discovered. The size of the pile indicated several minutes of waiting while Taylor visited with Miss Normand. The ciggys were the same brand that Fanny Baker offered to me on the Paramount lot when I had impersonated Charlie Chaplin. Fanny said most folks in the business smoked them because they were fancy and cheap in Europe. The ciggys, not the folks.

While Taylor escorted Miss Normand to her car, the killer took her chance and snuck inside the open door. When Taylor returned, he was immediately shot in the back. He probably twisted on the way down, flipping up the edge of the carpet. The only thing disturbed in the apartment. The killer probably stood over him to judge whether he was dead or if she needed to risk another shot. This was around eight o'clock, near the time Faith MacLean said they had finished dinner and heard a car backfire. While they discussed the possibility of it being a gunshot, Howard Fellows pulled the car around back of Taylor's and got out. He claimed he arrived a little after eight, went around to the front door, and called out, but got no answer. He pulled the door shut at the exact moment Mrs. MacLean peered out her door. Howard strolled away without a care because he never saw Taylor's body. Howard then spent a few minutes parking a large car in a small garage. He left on foot."

"The timing doesn't match up," Detective King growled.

"Not down to the exact moment, I agree. But if you'll check your notes, you'll find that Faith MacLean's account and Howard's numbers differ only by ten to fifteen minutes. That's a pretty narrow timeline for folks to know *exactly* when they finished eating dinner, heard a car backfire, discussed the possibilities of it being a gunshot, looked out a door, or traveled from a friend's house to the back of Taylor's bungalow, parked, walked around to the front of a bungalow, called out and awaited a response, pulled a door shut, and then returned to the car and pulled it into the garage."

Pop slumped back in his chair and rubbed his neck. Detective King stood and began pacing.

"This article says you know for a fact that it was Howard Fellows on the porch that night," Detective King said mid-stride in his pacing.

"Yes. Howard had been told to keep quiet but he admitted to me just last night that he was the man on Taylor's doorstep, not Sands. Howard pulled the door shut but hadn't seen Taylor dead on the floor. He could have easily denied it but Howard is young and scared. And before you ask, he had absolutely no motive to kill his boss. He's out of a job."

"That's all well and good, Kate," Nicky said, "if there *is* wiggle room in the timeline, but why does that mean Miss Minter killed Mr. Taylor?"

"Miss Minter?" I blinked at him. "Who said anything about Mary killing Mr. Taylor?"

Nicky startled. Detective King stopped and swung around.

"Well, who in blazes are we talking about then!" he bellowed.

"The Monster," I said simply, "Charlotte Shelby."

CHAPTER 23

Detective Cahill stared. "That headline... you mean it was... but nothing's come of it."

I grinned. "Oh, I wouldn't say that. But first I had to deal with the aftermath. You see, Pop didn't take my revelation particularly well."

"Jesus, Mary, and Joseph!" Pop groaned and thumped his elbows onto the desk, cradling his head in his hands.

Detective King was simultaneously glaring at me and frantically searching for his pack of ciggys. "Are you telling me you know for a fact that Charlotte Shelby killed Taylor?"

"A fact? Yes. With proof? No."

"I thought we agreed this was the work of a professional gunman," he growled as he stuffed a ciggy into his mouth and lit up. He glanced at Nicky who hadn't responded to my outrageous revelation. Nicky was staring at me, tense and thoughtful. No doubt contemplating my sanity.

"Personally, I believe murder stemming from jealousy rings far closer to the truth than murder by way of a professional gunman," I said. "I believe Mrs. Shelby was waiting inside when Taylor returned from walking Miss Normand to her car. I believe Shelby walked up behind him, maybe said a word or two, maybe he startled to hear someone behind him, and he lifted his arms. Then she fired a single shot. It would explain why the bullet holes in his clothing hadn't lined up. The angle of the bullet went upward at a sharp angle because Mrs. Shelby is a petite woman. I believe a professional gunman would have aimed for the back of the head to ensure a kill. Nothing had been stolen or disturbed because Charlotte Shelby hadn't gone there to do anything other than remove Taylor from her life. She had to stop him from running away with Mary. Once and for all."

"If the timing was that tight," Detective King said. "Mrs. Shelby would have passed Howard Fellows on her way out."

"Who's to say Mrs. Shelby left immediately after firing the shot? Perhaps she waited to ensure Taylor had died because he had seen her face. Perhaps he took a few minutes to expire. If Howard had knocked on the door and called out, she could have easily ducked into the shadows or hidden in the phone closet as I had. She could have waited until Howard had closed the door and went on his way. Mrs. Shelby had ample time to leave the crime scene on her own and without witnesses. No one had phoned the police. Sirens had not prompted her to panic."

Pop shook his head dismally and muttered, "I just can't believe a woman could be so cold-blooded as to—"

"Believe it," Nicky said abruptly. We looked at him in surprise. Nicky wore a dead expression and offered no explanation for his comment.

"But, why not Mary?" Detective King pushed. "She's wild and unpredictable. Could be she was jealous of Mabel Normand. Could be she came by Taylor's that night and saw them together."

"I agree. Mary can be impulsive and often erratic. But your theory suggests she had gone to Mr. Taylor's with a gun. Why take a weapon if she thought they were planning a rendezvous somewhere? Remember, she was in love with him. She knew, like everyone else seemed to, that Miss Normand and Mr. Taylor were only friends. In the end, Mary had no real motive to kill the man she loved."

"And what motivate have you assigned to Charlotte Shelby?" Detective King said irritably. "I hardly think she would've killed Taylor because she was jealous of her daughter's relationship with him. Unless you're suggesting Taylor and Charlotte were involved."

I looked at Nicky. "'Jealousy is a mighty strange thing. There's all kinds of jealousy that makes a man do all kinds of crazy.' Isn't that what you told me last night? On the sidewalk? Until that moment, I had been thinking of romantic jealousy between a man and a woman. But I tell you, Charlotte Shelby had plenty of reasons to be jealous. Say, about a million reasons.

She's a shrewd businesswoman. By Mary's own account, her mother has negotiated some of the most profitable contracts in the industry. Mary is only nineteen-years-old, and yet, she's worth millions. Thanks to her mother. Charlotte controls Mary's money until she turns twenty-one. Mary is allotted an allowance strictly controlled by Charlotte. If anything were to happen to Mary, say she ran off and got married to an intelligent older gentleman such as Mr. Taylor, Charlotte's financial empire would be in jeopardy. No more Mary, no more access to her money."

"She's supporting the entire family?" asked Detective King.

"As long as Mary remains single, she can be controlled," I said. "At least her money can. Charlotte Shelby was jealous of Mr. Taylor's hold on Mary. Taylor was a direct threat to Charlotte Shelby's livelihood. And, neither Mary, nor her mother, knew Taylor was already married. Charlotte Shelby felt Taylor was a legitimate threat."

"I don't know," Detective King mumbled, tossing his ciggy in the ashcan.

"What about that letter Woolwine received? The one who sent you looking for a gun at Mable Normand's apartment? Can you tell me what the handwriting was like? Can you describe it?"

Detective King's face fell. He looked sharply at Nicky and then muttered, "Well, I'll be a sonofabitch." He shook his head and then flipped open his notepad. "I can tell you how it was described by the experts. Here it is. The handwriting in question appears to belong to a lady of some refinement."

"There you have it," I said.

"You have interviewed Mary and her family?" Pop asked.

"Of course we have."

"And Charlotte Shelby and Mary have alibis for that night?" I asked.

"Mary was with her grandmother and her sister at that house on Hobart Street," he said knocking back pages in his notepad to catch up. "Charlotte Shelby was at her house on New Hampshire Street. Her alibi is a fellow named Carl Stockdale. They were having sandwiches in the kitchen about the time Taylor got plugged." He flipped the pad closed. "I say, if it wasn't a professional gunman—which I'm not sure it wasn't—

then Mary was more likely to kill Taylor than her mother was."

"But you just said Mary had an alibi as well. Why figure her for the murder?"

Detective King shifted uncomfortably. "While we were at Miss Minters, I took the liberty of, uh, extracting some hair from her hairbrush." He shifted in his overcoat, clearly embarrassed by his actions.

"Whatever for?" I asked, surprised.

"For analysis," Nicky answered. "In the crime lab."

"How interesting," I murmured. I had never heard of analyzing hair before. Fingerprint analysis, yes. But hair? "And what did you discover by analyzing Mary's hair?"

"Well, the hair I collected was matched against the hairs found on Mr. Taylor's clothing the day he died. Three blonde hairs were found under his lapel. You'll remember during the inquest that Mr. Taylor's valet, Henry Peavey, stated his employer was meticulous about his suits being brushed clean. Taylor was murdered in the suit he wore earlier that day. He must have been with Miss Minter at some point. I'm thinking he rescinded his offer to go away with her. She came over that night, packing heat. She found Miss Normand there and waited outside. All the while she was growing hot with jealousy. Once Miss Normand had gone and Taylor returned to his bungalow, he was shot. Just like you said, only by the daughter, not the mother."

As a curtesy, I considered his theory thoughtfully, as I hoped he would consider mine. The first problem was his lack of intimate knowledge of Mary's true character. He didn't know her as I did. She may be rambunctious and secretive, but underneath that celluloid facade, Mary was a passionate young woman desperate to escape her overbearing mother. Desperate to be loved by a man she could respect. A man who could, and had repeatedly, stood up to her mother. This had been no taw-dry infatuation for Mary. In a sense, Mr. Taylor had been Mary's ally. To his credit, Mr. Taylor had tried to remain a true friend to Mary, even as she had often embarrassed him with her late-night visits.

"Murdering someone in a jealous rage typically includes harming the third party when the lovers are caught together," I mused. "If Mary had seen Mabel as a direct rival, she would hardly have had the patience to wait outside and smoke a pack of ciggys while her beloved sat inside with his alleged lover.

When I spoke to Margaret yesterday about Mary's gentle-men friends, she said something very interesting, 'Mr. Neilan was *persuaded* to lose interest. Like they all are'. I had assumed Mary was the one turning away unwanted lovers but I see now that it had been Charlotte Shelby's doing. She had successfully pushed away anyone interested in Mary. I don't believe Mr. Tay-lor had any sexual designs on Mary but the poor man couldn't escape her intense infatuation. He had been forced to make a false promise to go away with her, if only to remove her from his home without rousing the neighbors. I'm sorry, Detective King, but I'm not convinced Mary would kill Mr. Taylor. Charlotte Shelby had all the motive in the world. *She* ultimately benefited from his death."

"The hair analysis is a solid lead," Detective King said, all but dismissing my argument.

"Hmm? Oh, that?" I waved it away. "You collected the three blond hairs after the autopsy, right? Yes, well, there's a simple explanation for finding Mary's hair on his lapel. I arranged for Mary to visit Mr. Taylor, or rather his body, at the morgue. The day after the murder, as a matter of fact."

"What!" Detective King wailed.

"Her hair could have easily been transferred to his clothing then. Mr. Taylor would have been mid-autopsy, naked, and covered by a sheet. Mary would hardly have thrown herself over his cold, stiff corpse. No, my guess is she gathered his things and hugged him goodbye that way." I realized that was a giant leap but stranger things have happened.

"Do you know what you've done?" Detective King said, his face swelling with rage. "You put Miss Minter in the room with Taylor *after* the murder! You have single-handedly contaminated evidence! If we wanted to make a case against her, those three blonde hairs wouldn't be worth a pile of dirt!" Rage had turned his face purple to the point I feared for his health. He ripped the fedora from his head and threw it into the chair.

"I'm sorry, but none of that matters in the least. Mary did not kill Mr. Taylor. She loved him far too much. I was with her at the morgue. She was truly and deeply devastated by his death. Mary had no reason to kill him. She has suffered greatly from the loss, not benefited from it. Charlotte Shelby, on the other hand, has come out on top. She has removed her most challenging rival. Someone just needs to prove it."

Detective King groused around and returned his hat to this head. "If you think you have the motive, you'll need the means. Most killers like to distance themselves from the weapon used in the crime. If we supposed—and I mean just *supposed*—that our suspects were ladies in the movie industry and not career criminals, my guess is the gun was dumped immediately after the murder. Weeks ago. The odds of finding a .38 caliber break-top revolver with any usable fingerprints are a million to one. We don't even know if Charlotte Shelby owns a gun."

"Not yet we don't," I said. "But her motive is clear, and that's half the equation."

"We'll have to place her at the scene of the crime," Nicky said. "We'll have to discredit her alibi while we're at it."

349

"Check your notes," I said. "You'll find that Charlotte Shelby gave two different alibis for the night of the murder. She told her mother, Mrs. Miles, she was visiting a Swedish bathhouse, which Mrs. Miles made a point of telling me. Charlotte Shelby told you she was at home."

"Maybe so," said Detective King. "But you'd better not print Charlotte Shelby's name in the paper." He gave Pop a severe look. "Don't doubt for a minute that she won't sue you for everything you've got, Thom. This is pure speculation and you know it."

"Yes, Ed. That much I do know," Pop said.

With that final warning, Detective King stalked out the door. Pop stood, patted me on the shoulder, and then went into his office and quietly closed the door. He might be on the fence now, but if I knew Pop, he'd come around. He just needed time to sort through things and possibly work on a statement for our advertisers once the phones had been returned to their hooks.

"Well, Miss March, I believe you're turning into a fine reporter," Nicky said as I walked him to the door. "That was quite a puzzle you put together. But you've stirred up a hornet's nest and every newspaper in town will try to build on your accusation or tear it down."

"Nothing I can't handle," I said lightly.

"I think you're in too deep this time," he said, growing serious. "Listen, Kate, if Mrs. Shelby is the cold-blooded killer you say, what's to stop her from shooting a nosy young reporter?"

I laughed. "Aw, you're just talking through your hat." Nicky didn't share my humor. I stepped closer and smiled up at him. "Are you worried, Nicky? Truly worried for me?"

His eyes flickered and he shook his head. "You're the damndest thing I've ever seen."

We grinned at each other, and a strange flutter tickled something deep inside me. I had the most unusual urge to kiss him.

350

"You'll worry your pop into an early grave, you know that?"

The strange fluttering and the urge faded as I thought of Pop. "He's a tough nut, my Pop. But seriously, Nicky, I could hint that it was Mrs. Shelby, couldn't I? Without actually printing her name?"

He shook his head again. "You've got to speak easy, Kate. I know it's not something you're accustomed to doing, but you have to *speak easy*, however you say it. And I don't want you interviewing anyone in Shelby's family. Especially Mary or Charlotte Shelby, herself. She's already noticed you sniffing around. Can I have your word on that?"

I mulled things over, already plotting other avenues for information. "'S'okay, Nicky. You have my word. I promise not to interview Mary or her mother."

I had the motive, of that I was sure. Now all I needed was the means—that damned gun.

* * *

Addy and I stood on the corner at 501 South Spring Street, home of the Alexandria Hotel, the first five-star hotel designed for our fair city. I was on the hunt for information about the Monster. Addy agreed to accompany me purely for the occasion of exhibiting her new bob and fashionable costume to the general public. School was one thing but to be a Modern in the world-at-large was quite another. Or, so I was told. Addy had been skimming money from the odd jobs her mama had been consistently hiring her out for. Little did I know Addy had been saving up for our grand metamorphoses as Moderns. This accounted for several new dresses she had recently purchased. Today, she had chosen a lovely drop waist daywear ensemble of soft floral print, a thin belt to accentuate her hips, and a short-sleeved blouse with a long, loose tie down the V-neck front. She looked divine and I told her so repeatedly. Because I was on the job, I preferred dark trousers with a black, white, and grey blouse of modern art design, and a white cloche over my polished bob. My desire had been the no-nonsense look, which was exactly what I was hoping for this morning. No nonsense. Just solid facts.

"Tell me again what we're doing here?" Addy drawled. She was practicing her bored, vampish voice.

"I told you. Rico has a friend whose cousin's brother's nephew works as an elevator boy at the Alexandria Hotel. Word on the street is that Mrs. Whitney has been staying at the Alex for the past few months."

"And, why do we need to speak to Mrs. Whitney?" she droned as though her jaw had come loose.

"Fanny Baker reminded me that Mrs. Whitney had worked as a secretary for Charlotte Shelby a few years back. I vaguely remember her myself. I'm hoping Mrs. Whitney knows if the Monster owned a gun."

Addy perked up and got serious. "I still can't believe Mrs. Shelby killed Mr. Taylor just to keep Mary's money. I thought my mama was keen on the green stuff. Boy oh, I tell ya, there's something peculiar about that cranky old generation. Since The War, Mama's been hoarding cash like the Kaiser's coming for it. Go figure."

The uniformed doorman opened the door and Addy and I strolled inside the Grand Lobby of the Alexandria Hotel. Two stories high, the lobby was a magnificent space of marble running 40 feet wide and 120 feet deep. Oriental rugs accented the length of the lobby and accommodated giant, potted plants and luxurious chairs and settees. Impressive marble columns reached the high ceiling and supported the women's balcony—

a lofty stone perch where the Greek goddesses of patent-leather could view the comings and goings below. Wainscoting ran six feet high up the walls, and made the mingling crowd appear small and insignificant. Usually they weren't. Studio heads, governors, royalty, and actors frequented the Alex. The place where Charlie Chaplain conceived United Artists, among other things. The rug beneath our feet had been dubbed 'the million-dollar carpet' due to the high dollar deals made there.

I surveyed the guests for Willie, my contact by way of Rico. No one matched his description so Addy and I situated ourselves in a chic sitting area deep inside the lobby. She lounged on a plush brocade chair, crossed her legs, and appeared to be someone of high distinction. I took the settee and flitted through my notepad. We waited. Guests strolled by in an assortment of fashionable costumes that quickly occupied Addy's attention. Soft classical music wafted through the air like money for your ears. Heavy perfume followed elegant couples like a wedding train. We were surrounded by the sound and smell of the wealth.

I noticed a red-headed, freckle-faced kid, around nine-years-old, in a short-waist uniform pretending to dust the potted fern to my right. His eyes darted nervously about the lobby as though he were being watched. I parted a couple of fronds and peered at him.

"Willie?"

"Sh-sh-sh!" he waved me quiet and then whispered, "Miss March?"

"You expecting someone else?"

He leaned closer and continued in a tiny, clandestine voice. "I cain't lose my job, see? Them house detectives been lurking around. Giving me the stink eye. Could be they's on to me."

He was laying it on a bit thick, but I played along. He was such a cute little fella after all.

353

"Rico said you know Mrs. Whitney," I whispered. "She's been staying here for a while now?"

There was a rustling sound as he slipped between the potted ferns and the marble wall. "That's right. Mrs. Whitney. I know the old bird. But it be a sticky situation, see? I ain't supposed to give out the private business of our guests." He started itching his palm. "I cain't lose my job. I gotta a paw what's sick and a maw what don't see too good."

"Yeah, yeah. And a cat with three-legs and a dog that don't bark." I rolled my eyes and dug into my pocket. I pressed two bits into his small, itchy palm. "Now, tell me what's doing with Whitney."

Two bits eased Willie's financial concerns and his apparent fear of the hotel management. He came out of hiding and hiked his hip on the armrest of Addy's chair.

"Every morning she comes down for breakfast at seven thirty and done by eight sharp. Timely old bird; on the dot if nothing else." He smiled against Addy's frosty glare unaware she loathed to be involved in something worthwhile and was biding her time until we wrapped up the story, and she could drag me into something petty and useless. Preferably involving interesting young men. "Say, you two ain't so hard on the peeps. What say we skip down to the tracks and throw some dough on the bangtails? See if we don't get lucky?" His little eyebrows danced like they had the jitters.

Addy scoffed. "Come see me in ten years."

Willie pulled a face. "'S only a joke, anyhow. Don't you laugh at the funnies?"

"I only laugh by appointment," Addy drawled, studying her nails.

"Aw, don't bother yourself—hey, wait. There's the old bird now. Just like clockwork."

An older woman across the lobby was just exiting the break-fast room. I recognized her immediately, having met her at Mary's years before. Mrs. Whitney wore a Victorian coif, tailored grey jacket, matching tweed skirt, and sensible Colonial Dame shoes. A brisk march was taking her toward the outer door.

Addy and I jumped up and waylaid Mrs. Whitney on the million-dollar carpet.

"Perhaps you don't remember me," I said. "I look quite different now." I touched the edge of my bob and smiled. "I'm Kate March, a friend of Mary's?"

Mrs. Whitney's shoulders eased and she exhaled a soft breath. She did remember me after all. At least by name. What little comfort she felt quickly vanished when I revealed my occupation and why I was there.

"Good day, then," she said, continuing toward the door.

"But, I only have one question," I called.

"I'm sorry. I don't want to be involved."

The doorman swung the door open.

"Please, Mrs. Whitney! For Mary's sake! She's in trouble!"

Mrs. Whitney stopped and scrutinized me and then Addy with a pair of sharp probing eyes. She would have made an excellent teacher. Mrs. Whitney considered things and then decided.

"How do you girls feel about canines?"

Fifteen minutes later, Addy and I were strolling through Pershing Square with Mrs. Whitney and three rambunctious dogs. A feisty terrier named Apple Jack who wouldn't stop licking Addy's new Mary Janes, a basset hound named Thomas Jefferson who kept stepping on his ears, and a tiny mouse-faced dog named Goliath who dribbled pee every time he barked. He barked at everything.

355

Addy and I held their leashes as they ran amuck around our ankles. Mrs. Whitney was forthcoming now that she understood the police considered Mary a suspect, and I was determined to prove her innocence. It might have been a slight exaggeration on my part but I offered something in return. I swore Mrs. Whitney to secrecy and then revealed the real killer.

"So, you're the one who broke the story in *The Messenger*? About Mr. Taylor's murderer being a woman?"

I nodded. "And what was your first reaction when reading the headline?" Mrs. Whitney raised her chin and gave me a knowing look. "You weren't surprised," I said. "You suspected Mrs. Shelby from the start?"

"My first thought went in her direction, yes. You see, I began working for the family back in '14. Over the years, I was aware that Charlotte had made numerous threats to men who showed interest in Mary. Of course, my work for the family ended late in 1920 but Mary and I have remained close ever since."

"So, you were around when Mary worked with... James Kirkwood?" I asked quietly. Mrs. Whitney bristled and looked away. I handed my leash to Addy and then guided Mrs. Whitney to a nearby bench for privacy.

"I know all about Mr. Kirkwood," I said, watching her fuss with her gloves and pocketbook.

"Yes, I was there," she said, sighing sadly. "And, I thought Charlotte would kill him after that affair. If Doc Hamilton had botched things up, I think she would have."

I stifled a small gasp but my blood curdled at the implication. Was Mrs. Whitney admitting that Mary had had an... abortion?

I looked away feeling nauseous. Mary had been so young back then! No more than fifteen when she worked with Mr. Kirkwood! That would certainly explain Margaret's strong reaction toward him.

I took a moment to rearrange my thoughts. Poor Mary. For the first time, I realized what a truly amazing actress she had been all these years. She certainly had me fooled. Mary was a far cry from the girl of childish innocence she presented to the public. Or to me. Her life was a lie. And that pretense had been forced upon her by Mrs. Shelby. I was beginning to understand the depth of despair Mary must have felt all these years. How desperately she wanted to be saved by someone as honorable and respected as Mr. Taylor.

"I suppose we can't blame Mrs. Shelby for wanting to protect her daughter," I said uncomfortably. It was all I could do to give the Monster any credit but my God, Mary had been little more than a child! No doubt she had been seduced by a vile predator.

"No, I couldn't blame Charlotte for that," said Mrs. Whitney tightly. "I firmly believed she was going to kill that man. Mary was terrified of her mother back then. And Mary, poor child, tried to defend herself. She explained how Mr. Kirkwood had taken her up in the hills and performed some sort of pretend wedding in the woods. He'd convinced her the ceremony had been real because they loved each other. But, I suppose you know all this."

"Uh-huh," I lied, rubbing the familiar ache that had sprung up in my belly. Part of me felt like throwing up. Another part felt like taking a baseball bat and making mincemeat of dear Mr. Kirkwood's man vegetables. "And how did Mr. Kirkwood take Charlotte's interference?"

"He was furious but what could he do? I suppose Mary told you Charlotte still has those love letters. She uses them to threaten Mary when she gets out of line."

"Love letters? From Kirkwood and Mary?" I tried to affect a faint recollection. "Oh, yes, of course. I'd almost forgotten about the love letters. And Mrs. Shelby's so cruel to use them to control Mary by..." I shook my head as though I couldn't finish the thought.

357

"Well, yes, my goodness. Mary was terrified that her gentleman Mr. Taylor would find out about her affair with Mr. Kirkwood. And naturally, about the pregnancy, and so forth. She felt he would despise her for it. Charlotte threatened, more than once, to reveal Mary's secret if she didn't stay away from him. Charlotte would ruin it so Mr. Taylor would never want Mary. Not that he really did. Poor child."

"So, Mrs. Shelby knew the full extent of Mary's affection for Mr. Taylor? I mean, I knew she suspected and all..."

"Of course, she knew!" Mrs. Whitney looked at me in surprise. "We *all* knew! I tell you, one night when Mary didn't come home for dinner, Charlotte called Mary's friends but no one had seen her. Charlotte was furious! Her chauffeur, Chauncey Eaton, drove us to Mr. Taylor's home. Charlotte was sure Mary was there. Mr. Taylor allowed her to search but Mary wasn't there. That was long before the night he was killed, mind you." She scooped up Apple Jack and began petting him in hard angry strokes.

"Did something happen that night, Mrs. Whitney?"

She took a deep breath, letting her eyes roam the park without seeing. "That was the night I realized how jealous Charlotte had become. How greedy and insanely jealous. You see, unbeknownst to me, Charlotte had taken a gun with her that night. She told me on the way home that if Mary had been there, she'd have killed Mr. Taylor."

"How interesting. So, Mrs. Shelby owned a gun? You're sure? You saw it? What kind was it?"

"I don't know one kind from another. But she had it. She pulled it from the sleeve of her coat to prove how serious, or brave, or whatever she'd been."

"What happened when Mary came home?"

"Oh, she came home much later, but I never heard where she'd been. There was lots of arguing behind the bedroom door.

I never did ask Mary and she never offered."

I clasped her hand and stared hard at her. "Mrs. Whitney, this is very important. Tell me, did you ever hear or see Charlotte Shelby threaten Mr. Taylor with a gun?"

"She threatened him numerous times at the studios but I couldn't say if she ever had a gun with her. I suppose no one there would admit that. They're probably afraid they'd lose their jobs if they talked to the papers or police."

"Could you identify the gun if you saw it again? Was it a .38 caliber break-top revolver?"

She shook her head. "I have no idea but it was the same one Mary used late in the summer of 1920."

"Come again?" I said hoarsely.

"Well, it was back when the family resided at 56 Freemont. Mary had come home late without telling Charlotte where she'd been. Charlotte was positively livid! She accused Mary of being with Bill Taylor in a... sexual manner. She threw a glass of water in Mary's face. Mary raced upstairs, ranting and carrying on that she couldn't take it anymore. That she wanted to end it all. We thought it was hysterics from an overwrought young girl. Until we heard the shots."

"Shots?"

"Chauncey and Frank Brown broke down Mary's door. When I arrived upstairs, she was sobbing on the bed. You see, she had fired shots into the floor and ceiling."

"Frank Brown?"

"He was a night watchman living with us at the time."

"What happened then?"

"Well, let's see. Charlotte took the gun and told Chauncey to get rid of it. Only he emptied out the shells and gave it back to her."

"How, Mrs. Whitney? Do you remember how he emptied the

gun? Did he snap the top apart like breaking the handle from the barrel? Or did he swing the cylinder out to the side? Did you see the chamber at all?" She looked taken aback. "I'm sorry Mrs. Whitney, but it's very important."

"But, my dear, I couldn't possibly recall those kinds of details. If it would help Mary I would certainly tell you, but... it was two years ago, you see."

"But you'll confirm that Mrs. Shelby owned a gun in the summer of 1920? You're sure?"

"I'm sure."

"Why haven't you spoken to the police?"

She shrugged. "Nobody has asked me. I haven't worked for the family in two years. But like I said, Mary and I have stayed very close." She gave me a pointed look and then proceeded with her story, revealing details that, I believed, could send Charlotte Shelby to the electric chair.

"You *will* tell the detectives when they come asking, won't you Mrs. Whitney?"

"Anything to help Mary."

"Yes," I murmured. "Anything to help Mary."

After thanking Mrs. Whitney, Addy and I parted company. She was due at the precinct to assist her Aunt Alice logging evidence into the evidence room. I ducked back inside the Alex and occupied one of their private phone booths. I had taken Nicky's concerns about Charlotte Shelby seriously. Because I believed she was capable of murder, I wanted to relay my interview with Mrs. Whitney directly to Nicky. It was important to gather as much damning and credible information before I wrote my next column. And perhaps I could persuade Nicky to be an anonymous source I could quote in the paper. It was a long shot, but worth asking.

CHAPTER 24

Poor Detective Cahill, he was still staring at me, unblinking, with his mouth slightly open. I hadn't wanted to reveal the killer to an outsider but with my current situation, well, it was my only move. Besides, I had the strangest feeling time was running out.

When I returned to the office later that day I was surprised to find Nicky and Detective King cloistered in Pop's office with the door ajar. These frequent visits led me to believe they no longer worried the DA would suspect them of feeding us information.

"What's doin'?" I asked casually, shutting the door behind me. The low energy in the room raised no internal alarms. Nicky was relaxed in a chair with an ankle crossed over the opposite knee. His department-issued hat rested in his lap. Detective King stood apart with a cigarette dangling from his mouth. He looked up from his notepad, the bags under his eyes suggesting little sleep.

Pop waved me over from behind his desk. "Where've you been? We've been waiting."

I fought off a smile and sat down, pleased that I had suddenly become so important as to be waited for. "I was tracking down leads. How about you guys?"

"I'll tell you what we've been doing," Detective King said sharply. "Thanks to your conversation with Mrs. Whitney, we interviewed Charlotte Shelby, *again*. Here's the gist of things."

According to Detective King, Mrs. Shelby was generous and cooperative in her explanation of the *single* incident occurring some time ago when she went looking for Mary at Mr. Taylor's home. It had been a foggy night and she was concerned for Mary's safety. After phoning Mary's friends, she became frantic as none of them had seen her. Mrs. Shelby then went to Mr. Taylor's on the vague possibility that Mary might have stopped there. Mr. Taylor had been very cordial and shared her concern for Mary's safety. Mary hadn't been there, and there were no threats exchanged by either Mrs. Shelby or Mr. Taylor. In fact, Mrs. Shelby had no ill feelings toward Mr. Taylor but found his formal manners very refreshing.

"She's lying," I said. "And what of the gun?"

"She does not own a gun," Detective King stated. "Not anymore. She had a small pearl-handled pistol for protection ages ago but lost track of it."

"She's lying," I repeated. "As I told Nicky, Mary fired a gun as recently as the summer of 1920. Mrs. Whitney was there. She heard it. She saw the gun herself. And she saw the gun Mrs. Shelby had on the night she went to Taylor's home. Mrs. Whitney was with her. By her account, they were the same weapon."

"What you have, Miss March, is the statement of a disgruntled employee against a powerful woman with powerful friends. It will be Mrs. Whitney's word against Mrs. Shelby's. Either way, it's not enough to arrest anyone. I'm not convinced that Charlotte Shelby had enough motive to commit cold-blooded murder."

"If Mrs. Shelby and Mr. Taylor were on friendly terms, why drive all the way to his home on a foggy night when she could have easily telephoned? She admitted to phoning Mary's friends. Why not phone Taylor? I'll tell you why. Because she fully expected to find Mary there. And, she fully expected to put an end to their relationship. Fortunately for Mr. Taylor, Mary hadn't been there. Not at that time anyway."

"Now don't go shooting around corners, Miss March. Tell me why you *know* she expected to find Mary there?"

"Because it had become something of a habit for Mary. She had gone to Mr. Taylor's several times over the past year. Arthur Hoyt's statement corroborates as much. He said that Taylor was distraught because Mary kept showing up at his home late at night. On one occasion, she had threatened to make a fuss and rouse the neighbors if he didn't let her stay."

"One incident does not make a habit," Nicky said casually.

"Hoyt implied there had been multiple times," I said. "Besides, I know for a fact Mary had gone before because I was with her on one occasion."

They stared in surprise. I shrugged it off. "I've told you. Mary and I have been friends for years. We've shared casual confidences now and then. The night I was with her, Mary had only wanted to show Mr. Taylor her new roadster. He was keen on autos. Besides, he hadn't been home that night."

Detective King fidgeted with his notepad. "You're assuming Mary going to Taylor's home in the past would cause Charlotte Shelby to go there on February first and murder him? Just out of the blue?"

"Not exactly," I said, grinning. "I had planned to save this part for my next column but here it is, the last tidbit shared by Mrs. Whitney. She knows Charlotte Shelby knew about Mary's plans to go away with Mr. Taylor. Mrs. Shelby had been at the house on Hobart Street where she overheard Mary and Mr. Taylor on the telephone, making plans to go to Santa Ana for the day."

"And just how does Mrs. Whitney come by such information?" Detective King demanded. "You said she hadn't worked for the family in two years."

"I'm getting to that. Now remember, Mrs. Whitney has remained very close to Mary, even after leaving their employ. Throughout her years of service, Mrs. Whitney came to love Mary and tried to protect her whenever possible. When Mrs. Shelby overheard Mary's plans with Taylor, she couldn't take such a risk. Her only recourse was to lock Mary in the bedroom. Mrs. Shelby then left the house. Sometime later, Mrs. Whitney got a call from Mary, pleading to come over and let her out of the locked room. Mrs. Whitney did just that. When Mary was freed, she probably went in search of Mr. Taylor, although that is purely speculation on my part. I haven't verified that yet."

I flipped through my notepad. "If we go from top to bottom on this, Arthur Hoyt claimed Mr. Taylor was desperate to talk some sense into Mary, desperate to stop her infatuation, and desperate to put an end to these embarrassing late-night visits. He made plans to go away and settle things once and for all. Now, then, we've all documented Mr. Taylor's last day; he ran errands with his chauffeur, Howard Fellows, throughout the day. He left his accountant, Marjory Berger, around four thirty. He went to Parker's Bookshop where he purchased a few books. Once he had returned home, Mr. Taylor instructed Howard to deliver the books to Miss Normand's apartment and then to have dinner, but to phone him around seven thirty because he might go out again. Howard left and did as asked. According to Miss Normand's maid, Mamie, Mr. Taylor had called to inform Miss Normand that he was sending over a few books but had forgotten one. Mamie told Mr. Taylor that Miss Normand was not at home, but she would get the message to her.

"This was just after five o'clock. Without a car, Mr. Taylor walked to the Payne Dancing Academy on Orange Street for a dance lesson. He was there for the next hour or so. That was about the time Mary was liberated from her bedroom. She might have gone to Taylor's home, but he wouldn't have been there. In any case, Henry Peavey never mentioned Mary stopping by that day. Remember, Henry told me that Mr. Taylor had been arguing with someone on the phone about Mary earlier on the afternoon of his murder. Quite possibly it had been with Charlotte Shelby, or Mary herself, although I doubt either would admit as much. After the dance lesson, Taylor returned home, had dinner, and, according to your notes, took a phone call from Antonio Moreno. Near the time Mabel Normand arrived at Taylor's for that forgotten book, Charlotte Shelby was on Hobart Street discovering Mary had fled. She called several places looking for her. No one knew where she was. Around seven o'clock, while Mabel and Taylor were chatting, Charlotte Shelby called Marjory Berger, who was not only Taylor's accountant but her own, as well. Mrs. Berger said Mary was not there. Forty-five minutes later, Mr. Taylor was shot dead."

Detective King struck a match and lit another ciggy. He puffed for a moment, eyeing me through the smoke. Nicky toyed with his hat. He and Detective King exchanged looks.

"That part about Mary being locked in her room?" Detective King said. "That came from Mrs. Whitney? Yes, well I'm still saying she'll be viewed as a disgruntled employee. One who's got it in for her old boss. Now before you go hollering at me, I didn't say I wouldn't follow up. It's just that... I'm not sure what to tell Woolwine."

"You can tell the DA I'm going with this story and would he care to make a comment," I said firmly.

Pop grinned and then removed his cheaters, fogged them, and cleaned them with his hankie.

Nicky smiled.

"How about it, Officer Masino?" I said. "Care to be my anonymous source?"

"Love to. Except I'm *not* your source. You did this all on your own."

Detective King sighed and clomped to the door where he stopped and turned back. "Oh, and yeah, not bad work for a... you know." He shrugged and walked out. I laughed.

"Well done, Kate." Pop came around the desk and patted my shoulder before walking out.

Nicky climbed to his feet. "You're sounding more like a detective than a reporter."

"If only I had the power to arrest."

"There'll be no arrests without a confession or the murder weapon," he said, sounding doubtful. I nodded. The gun was the key, and I had absolutely no idea where to find it.

I paced the office like a hophead in a sanitarium. Not a word yet from Nicky or Detective King regarding Woolwine's response to my evidence against Charlotte Shelby. Rico, I had situated on an orange crate outside the door to play lookout should anyone unexpected head this way. The last thing I wanted was Woolwine sending over a lackey to warn me off the story. I fully suspected some sort of blowback from the DA's office. Bud was over at the Kettle, firmly instructed to telephone should Nicky or Detective King show there. Addy was perfecting the art of eavesdropping down at the precinct. All bases were covered but the anticipation was excruciating.

Pop and Eugene were fiddling with the wireless again. Ever since the White House installed a radio, Pop had been keen on expanding his reach. Static whirled up and down the dial, grating on my last nerve.

"See if you can't tweak the thing, Eugene," Pop said. "Earl Williams over on Hope Street can reach Winnipeg, Canada and I can't even get Boise, Idaho."

Eugene unscrewed the back panel. "I keep telling ya, Pop, Earl receives from so far away 'cause he's got the Model XXV Crosley with the four tube set. Lemme add another tube like I wanted and see if we can't broaden the range. I swear I reached Hawaii the other night."

"Speaking of Hawaii," Mr. Dysinger called from the assignment editor's desk. "I got word that the State Department is using Pearl Harbor, Hawaii as a fueling station for our Navy's ships. Think we should front-page it?"

Mr. Fink whined loudly from behind his typewriter. "Aw, nobody'll care about that. Now look here, home prices have risen to $7,000! And gas-o-line is 11cents now!! Life is going to hell in a handbasket! *That's* the lead story!"

Mr. Handle squinted at the type on the white paper wrapped around the barrel of his Underwood. "Looks like this Hitler fella is gaining some traction with the Nationalist Party. Say, are there two m's in Germany?" I looked sharply at him, hoping to high heaven he was joking. Mr. Handle winked and I smiled with relief.

Mrs. Hazeldine peered over her cheaters with vague interest. She had recently become smitten with a new magazine publication called *The Reader's Digest* and was happy to while away her time until she was needed for copy. Her interest in

German affairs fell short and she went back to her *Digest*.

"Kate, please stop pacing," Pop said. "They'll let us know as soon as possible."

I plopped into my chair and waited. It was one thing to stop my feet from moving but my thoughts were another matter entirely. I picked up the telephone and clicked for the operator.

"Hello, Irene? Yes, hello. Get me Madison two, three, four, five and... of course I know it's the *LA Times* but... well, I don't care if they won't wanna talk to me... I'm not getting sassy with... yes, ma'am. My apologies. Thank you. Yes, ma'am, I'll be happy to wait." I sat back in my chair, tossed my white cloche onto the desk, and scrubbed a hand through my hair. I still had not gotten use to my bob.

A young woman's harried voice came on the line, and I sat up expectantly. "Mr. Morgan, please?" I asked. My dear friend's byline had been missing from the *Times* for a few days now. After our strange conversation at the Kettle the other day, I was on the verge of worrying about him.

"What do you mean he is no longer employed there? Was he fired? Well, then, where did he go? Has he taken up with another paper?"

The voice on the line became indignant and stated that Mr. Morgan had given his resignation last week. She was not privy to his current employment nor his whereabouts. I slowly hung up the earpiece and sat back in wonder. If Mr. Morgan had resigned last week, that meant he had been out of a job when he'd gone to the party at the Grove. It meant the information he collected was for *me,* and not his own story. But why? And why would he leave the *Times* so suddenly and not mention it to me?

The door flew open and Rico ducked inside with just enough time to announce that Detective King was headed this way. King, puffing like a steamer, headed straight for Pop's private office without so much as a hey or howdy. Pop and I hurried inside and shut the door.

"Fifty-six Freemont Street," Detective King said, dropping into a chair. "I verified that address you gave us as the previous home of the Shelby family when Mary fired those shots into the floor and ceiling in the summer of 1920. I wanted to dig the bullets out and compare them to our murder bullet but another family lives there now. Woolwine refused to investigate it." He gave me a dangerous look. "He will arrest *anyone* who disturbs the current occupants."

"Go on," I said, fascinated.

"That accountant dame—"

"Marjorie Berger, yes?" I prompted, knowing what was coming. I had spoken to Mrs. Berger myself after my interview with Mrs. Whitney.

"She verified that Mrs. Shelby called her office on the night of the murder, looking for Mary. She also stated that it was *Mrs. Shelby* who told *her* that Mr. Taylor was dead. Apparently, Mrs. Shelby called Berger's office between seven and seven thirty on the morning of February second."

"Ah." I lowered myself onto a chair, my mind unfolding what came next. "Henry Peavey discovered the body shortly half past seven. I arrived on the scene near eight o'clock."

"Are you sure?"

"Pos-i-lute-ly. I had learned about the murder through backstreet chatter and beat everyone to the scene. I was already there when the movie folk and the police came around. I was standing inside Mr. Taylor's living room when they discovered it was murder and not death by natural causes."

Detective King went back to his notes. "When I originally questioned Mrs. Shelby about how she learned of Taylor's death, she claimed that *Mrs. Berger* told *her*. Then this afternoon, I asked her again and she conveniently remembered that Carl Stockdale phoned her from the studio and told her."

"She's changing her story, again," I said. "Even so, that would mean Carl Stockdale would have known before seven thirty that Taylor was dead. And, Carl Stockdale is Mrs. Shelby's alibi on the night of the murder. She must be paying him off. Looks like it will all come down to the timing: *when* Mary was released from her room; *when* Mrs. Shelby went hunting for her; *when* she called Mrs. Berger; and *when* Mrs. Shelby knew Taylor had been murdered. Not to mention the timing of Mabel Normand leaving Taylor's home, and Howard Fellows arriving there on the night of the murder." I thought for a moment. "Did Mrs. Shelby say anything about a gun?"

"Still no gun. I told her about Mrs. Whitney's statement regarding Mary being locked in the bedroom. She says the lady can't be trusted. Left her employment as an unstable and unsatisfactory employee."

"You'll have to corroborate Mrs. Whitney's story with Mary, or her grandmother, or maybe Margaret, but—"

"Not a chance," said Detective King, snapping his notepad shut. "Woolwine was boiling oil when I presented him with these leads and the theory about Charlotte Shelby. He claimed Mrs. Whitney has her own agenda. He told me to sit tight and do nothing for now. And he ordered me to stay away from Mrs. Shelby and the family before she sued the department for harassment, which she has already threatened to do."

There was a knock on the door and Addy poked her head inside.

"What's doin'?" I asked, surprised to see her here.

"Hiya," she said to the room. I waved her over and she hurried inside and closed the door. "Jeezers, Kate, you won't believe it but I nearly missed out on the doing's down at the precinct. I was saying my goodbyes to the girls when I overheard one of them talking about evidence in Woolwine's private office. Now get this, Woolwine packed up some things he'd been keeping in his office bureau. Under lock and key. The girls say it was evidence. In the Taylor case. He was in a mighty big hurry, too."

"Where'd he take it?" Detective King demanded, struggling to his feet.

"Dunno. He and the Deputy tossed everything into his auto and raced off."

Detective King marched to the door and then swung around to Pop.

"Don't print that!" he barked and stalked out.

"We've simply got to find a way to expose Charlotte Shelby as the murderer I know she is," I told Addy over a late dinner. She was keeping me company as Pop had gone to the Men's Athletic Club to play cards and Eugene had gone to bed hours ago. I had devised several plots but none to my liking. Least of which was the risky plan to break into Mrs. Shelby's home and search for the gun like a pair of desperate burglars.

"Yes, stellar idea there, Kate. Thieves breaking in to a murderer's home." Addy rolled her eyes. "Or, shall we call her a murderess? Sounds more sophisticated."

"Okay, then, you think of something."

"Hang on a minute while I turn on my clever," she scoffed. "Suppose we ankle down to this blind pig I heard about? A few drinks might loosen our thoughts. Aw, come on, Kate. It wouldn't kill you to let the story take care of itself for once, would it?"

"Doesn't work that way," I said, pushing back from the table and standing.

"Yeah, well, if I'm not going to get stinking drunk and allow myself to get properly seduced by a beautiful stranger, I might as well head home. I'm due back at the precinct in the morning."

We strolled onto the front porch and caught Mrs. Banning passing by with Livingston.

"'Lo there, Mrs. Banning," Addy called. "How are you this fine evening?"

"Is that you, Adelaide? Why, you surely do look different."

"Yes, ma'am. Kate and I have gone Modern."

"Well, it's something to do, I suppose." Mrs. Banning smiled and then stopped. "Now Katharine dear, you let me know when you nab that director's murderer. Don't forget, Livi, here, was the genius behind it all. He should get the credit. Well, toot-a-loo girls!" She waved goodbye and went on her way.

"She talking hooey or into the cooking sherry?" Addy asked.

I explained about Mrs. Banning's dream where Livingston died and came back as a big fat spiritualist balloon and revealed Mr. Taylor's killer.

"The chimney sweep?" Addy scoffed. "Poor Mrs. Banning. Haven't you explained that Mr. Taylor had no chimney? Aw, well, she's probably gotten herself involved with one of those séance madams or palm reading charlatans. People will believe just about anything these days. Probably give me nightmares, too."

"You're probably right. She's just the sort to—Addy! You've just given me the most outrageous idea!"

"I have?" Addy, who was halfway down the porch steps, hurried back up with the first sign of excitement all evening. "Please tell me it'll put an end to this story once and for all."

"I believe it will. If I can pull it off. You're at the precinct tomorrow, right? Good. Ring me at the office when you arrive. I'm going to drop some bait in the paper and see if the Monster won't bite."

CHAPTER 25

"So, you think you've solved the Taylor murder," Detective Cahill said, matter of fact. "But, how does that get us to the man in the alley?"

"Luring out Charlotte Shelby put me in direct contact with the Frenchman in the alley. Not my doing, of course, but it was serendipitous, I suppose. Right place, but wrong time."

Because I had agreed never again to change the headline without Pop's knowledge, I rang him at the Athletic Club and quickly explained my idea. He wasn't as keen on it as I had hoped and gave me strict instructions on how to proceed. I had to tread very carefully, not only with our readers but with Pop. So naturally, it was full steam ahead.

I woke Eugene and dragged him down to the office to assist

me. A few hours later, the headline for *The Messenger* screamed: SPIRITUALIST NAMES KILLER IN TAYLOR MURDER! Below ran my story, asking readers if they could believe that a reliable spiritualist had contacted our office and claimed to have had a vision in which the apparition of William Desmond Taylor appeared. Taylor's apparition told the spiritualist that his killer was the mother of a beautiful young actress. The mother knew Mr. Taylor had been aggressively attentive toward her daughter. Fearing her innocent daughter would run away with him, the mother had been forced to kill him. The spiritualist added that she believed the mother was justified in her actions and knew the police, as well as the public, would sympathize. The spiritualist would give the mother until the evening to confess to the police. If not, the spiritualist would be forced to reveal the mother's identity.

"God awl mighty, Kate, you should write fiction," Eugene said, shaking his head at the crisp newsprint still warm from the press.

"I just did," I said with a flutter of excitement. I had been as persuasive as I dared, trying to entice Charlotte Shelby into believing all would be forgiven. This was sensationalized journalism at its worst but I had no regrets. No one had been named outright, and besides, I was luring out a killer, not provoking war.

The next morning, Addy phoned me from work. I asked her to be my eyes and ears and ring me the moment anyone responded to my story. She would also ensure that Nicky and Detective King read our paper and were in on the plan. After that was settled, the clock on the office wall turned into molasses.

I was too consumed with Taylor's murder to find interest in any other stories. Not the most recent civil war in Ireland, the election of the new Pope, or even miners trapped when a cave collapsed, God rest their souls. Let the staff run with those stories; I had blinders on. Closer to home, multiple headlines screamed about the nation-wide dragnet for Sands. *The San Francisco Chronical* and *Examiner*, the *San Bernardino County Sun* and others were running stories about love letters from Mabel Normand to Mr. Taylor, now in Woolwine's possession. I couldn't see the relevance.

Just past noon, Addy phoned to inform me that neither Nicky nor Detective King were pleased with my 'damnable scheme' as King had put it. I had expected as much.

As time passed, I secured my position in the office as an impossible nuisance. The biggest story this paper had ever covered was on the line and I couldn't sit still. I had single-handedly given Mr. Fink the jitters, and he could hardly be expected to digest his mother's rhubarb pie with such an affliction. Mr. Dysinger offered me part of his kidney pie if only to put something in my mouth to shut me up. I was too anxious to eat. Mrs. Hazeldine offered a book to occupy my mind. I couldn't possibly concentrate. By early evening, Pop was forced to send me away for dinner. I agreed only on the promise that he would phone me at the Kettle should any word come in.

Outside a storm was brewing. Had I been paying attention I would have worn something heavier than my thin V-neck middy blouse and drop-waist pleated skirt with a loose belt. Thankfully, I had thought to grab my wool cape on the way out this morning. I reminded myself to thank Trudy Mae for adding a few new winter items to my wardrobe. My former high school attire had fallen short for a career as a reporter. Pop had yet to receive the bill, but that was a bridge I would cross when it presented itself. In the meantime, I made my way to the Kettle in a lovely blue cloche and matching cape.

The Kettle was chockablock with the usual faces and chatter. The heady aroma of meatloaf, chili, and beef stew stirred my appetite, and I realized I was famished. Every hardboiled news-paperman gave me the once-over as I strolled through the maze of tables on my way to the counter. Our paper was the talk of the town, and I suddenly felt a heavy weight descend. I couldn't image what I would do if my scheme failed.

I ordered a cuppa Joe, a bowl of chili, and a square of corn-bread. A light rain had caught me on the last block and I shook out my cape and laid it across my lap. I shivered and hugged my arms. An unexpected flutter of sadness hit me. I suddenly missed Mr. Morgan's company.

"You're into it this time, ain't ya?" Pugsly the Ugsly said from down the counter. He was sandwiched between a couple of for-gettable smug mug colleagues from the *Times*.

"'The more I see of men, the more I admire dogs,'" I quoted Madame de Sevigne with a self-satisfied smile. Bessie the wait-ress poured my coffee, and I had just wrapped my hands around the warm cup when a soft chuckle emanated from behind me. I turned and there was Mr. Morgan brushing rain from his hair. He flashed a dazzling smile.

"'When a woman behaves like a man, why doesn't she be-have like a *nice* man?'" He quoted.

"Mr. Morgan!" I was elated but fought the urge to jump up and throw my arms around him. I had decided he must have left town. The gentleman next to me had finished his meal and stood up to leave. I patted the barstool for Mr. Morgan.

"I heard you left the *Times*," I said. "I was afraid you'd—"

"You were afraid? For *moi?*" He took the seat and leaned too close for polite company. "Do tell."

I grinned and shook my head, suddenly feeling shy.

"Very well then, by my calculations, if you fail to identify my quote, I shall be awarded one intellectual point and firmly take the lead."

376

I laughed. "Oh, it was that British stage actress... Ava... Eve... no, wait... Evans. Edith Evans." I smiled proudly. "Now tell me, did you escape the bowels of hell unscathed? And how is your novel coming? I assumed that's why you left the *Times*."

He sighed heavily. "A sensible deduction. But as you might agree, a writer can write anywhere. I shall be returning to New York."

"Oh. I see." I couldn't hide my disappointment. My fears were realized. "I suppose your father can be a very persuasive man, being the successful lawyer that he is."

"True. But I go with my dignity firmly intact, mind you. I'm returning on *my* terms. Not his." Mr. Morgan's serious expression spoke volumes. This meant a great deal to him.

"Good for you! And, well, perhaps it's for the best. Without the frustration of deadlines and interviews you could work on your novel. Find inspiration. Your muse, as they say."

"May I confess something?" he asked sheepishly. "You have been my muse for quite some time now. No, please don't look so traumatized. Have you not guessed how I might feel about you?"

I blinked nervously, caught off guard. "Well, I mean, no. I hadn't... I mean, we've always had fun talking about writing, and murder, and the business, but—"

He clutched my hand. "Come with me! Please! We'd have a grand time!"

"W-what?" I said. The newspapermen had gotten a whiff of something happening between us and looked our way. I leaned closer and lowered my voice to a whisper. "Are you asking me to go to New York?"

"Believe me, this is far from an impulsive flight of fancy. I've given this plenty of thought. I came here today to find you. You see, I'm leaving tomorrow." He laid two train tickets on the counter. "This one's for you. Please say you'll come."

I stared in utter disbelief. Train tickets. First class.

"But why? Why would I go to New York? I live here. I've lived here all my life."

"Exactly the point. Now that you're a free woman released on the world, wouldn't it be fitting to go out and explore it? You're young and intelligent and talented beyond all fairness. A Modern young woman must experience things, Miss Kate. You need some adventure in your life."

I laughed. "Apparently, you haven't been reading our paper."

He smiled affectionately. "I've read every word you've ever written. But keep in mind, this Taylor murder is just one story. Its twilight is coming."

"To be replaced by the next story," I said.

"Absolutely. There will always be a next story. I understand completely. You are a writer; you should write. As I've said, writers can write from anywhere. And, I offer the perfect solution— write from New York. You can send dispatches to your father. Hell, you could write from Paris. Rome. Anywhere. You could become a world news correspondent. Don't you see?"

"Mr. Morgan, I'm so very flattered that you want my company. Truly, I am but you must know I don't feel—" He cut me off, not wanting to hear anything that might dash his plans. He was undeniably earnest.

"Everything would be above board, I assure you. My family has apartments in New York and abroad. You could have your pick. We could travel first if you like. If not, you could write for the magazines. I have some old chums in New York, Harold Ross and his wife Jane Grant. You'd love Jane; she's a journalist for the *New York Times*. They're toying with the idea of starting up a new publication. They want to call it *The New Yorker*. Who knows, maybe in a few years, with some backing, they'll do it. I'm sure they would need as many experienced writers as they could find..."

"Fiction," I stated firmly.

"As I've said, I've read your latest edition." He cocked an eyebrow.

I smiled and waited politely as he rambled on. So many possibilities awaited. So many adventures. It did sound grand. I could see myself happily traipsing beside him. And, yet...

I laid my hand on his. "Mr. Morgan—"

"Monte," he said. "Won't you call me Monte? After all this time?"

"Monte, thank you for the most enticing invitation I've ever received. But I am exactly where I am supposed to be. At least for right now." I smiled softly against his frown.

"Think it over," he insisted. He stood and grabbed one train ticket, leaving the other on the counter. "Please? At least overnight. Until tomorrow." He kissed me on the cheek and then collected his hat and coat by the door. I watched him walk away with an ache in my belly.

Dear Mr. Morgan and his warm brown eyes and infectious smile. I would miss him terribly.

* * *

"Printer's ink has been running a race against gunpowder these many, many years. Ink is handicapped, in a way, because you can blow up a man with gunpowder in half a second, while it may take twenty years to blow him up with a book. But the gunpowder destroys itself along with its victim, while a book can keep on exploding for centuries."

I read the passage from Christopher Morley's *The Haunted Bookshop* aloud for a third time. Earlier this afternoon I had rejected the book from Mrs. Hazeldine, but now it was late, and, frankly, I was bored sitting at the office all alone. The day had passed without the slightest sign that anyone would respond to my column but I had refused to leave when the staff retired for the night. I was familiar with Morley's passage and thought it was ironic reading for tonight especially. The meaning weighed heavily on my mind. There was a certain amount of power in the press which gave me some comfort. My greatest fear was that Mrs. Shelby would pay Woolwine to ignore evidence that clearly pointed to her. She had plenty of money and he had plenty of greed. That left words. My words implicating her without directly naming her.

It was approaching nine o'clock and I'd heard exactly nothing from Nicky and Detective King. A tremendous rain had been let loose on the city for the past few hours. I had been enjoying a symphony of incessant pounding on the awnings and pavement. Honestly, the creaking of the old building was giving me the allovers. Thunderstorms were rare in the city and every crack of thunder put me on edge. I hadn't been this jumpy since the *Times* building was bombed a few years back. Perhaps reading about a haunted bookshop had been a poor choice after all.

I slowly turned a page under Edison's soft yellow lamp light while glancing around the dim room. Should I illuminate a few more lamps? My imagination was working against me, making lumpy creatures out of mute typewriters. A sudden clap of thunder convinced me, and I stood up too quickly, dropping the book. I stooped to retrieve it and when I straightened, a silhouette moved across the large front window. Instead of illuminating the room I froze and watched, hoping he was just another dewdropper on his way to Pershing Square or perhaps using our awning as an umbrella to get out of the rain. Nicky's repeated warnings about the dangers of investigating a murder came back to me. Had Mrs. Shelby sent someone around to shut me up?

The man hesitated, glanced around the street, and then

reached for the door handle. I flicked off my desk lamp and crouched down. Had I locked the door after Bud left? I couldn't remember.

The door opened slowly with a familiar squeak and I caught my breath. The latch clicked shut and then wet footsteps moved around the front counter. The man, clearly a stranger otherwise he would have called out, stood between me and my only exit. I squinted in the dark for some manner of weapon. Heavy breathing emanated from across the room. He was contemplating. Perhaps he had seen the light and wondered where I'd gone. A burglar wouldn't hesitate quite so long. This man was looking for someone.

I scurried over to Mrs. Hazeldine's desk. It was larger than my own and built with three oak drawers down each side. I hid on the far side and searched again for a weapon. The Underwoods were too heavy to chuck at someone, and the candlestick phones were useless. I was at a loss.

The wet footsteps squelched noisily across the floor. He was approaching Mr. Fink's desk. Ever so slowly, I pulled open the bottom drawer of Mrs. Hazeldine's desk and reached inside. Perhaps a heavy paper weight was hidden among those new colored pencils she was so fond of using? What I found was a small box that the dim light revealed as *Dr. Rose's Arsenic Complexion Wafers*. Next, I found a slightly heavier box of *Reliable Worm Syrup* with a bottle inside, and then a noisy box of *Dr. Worden's Female Pills*. I rolled my eyes and reached deeper inside the drawer. Ah, this time my hand found a long heavy bottle. *Vin Vitae: Wine of Life* the label said. It appeared my dear friend was in the habit of taking a nip of 'the Life' on occasion.

The man moved closer. His erratic breathing filled the intervals between distant thunder. He sounded as nervous as I felt. His hand must have brushed against something because papers

381

fluttered to the floor. I gasped and the footsteps halted. He was two desks away. Mentally, I mapped out my escape route. Lord have mercy but my heart was pounding furiously. My hands trembled around the tiny arsenal in my arms.

"*Mademoiselle?*" he called, unexpectedly. I sprang from my hiding place and pelted the man with arsenic wafers, worm syrup, and female pills! He threw his arms up in defense and stepped back in surprise. The barrage was all but useless. When he lowered his arms, we stared in shock at one another. It was one of the pasty-face French foreigners.

"I only want to talk," he struggled in a heavy accent. A knife glinted in his right hand.

"Uh-huh," I said and hurled the bottle of *Vin Vitae* at him. Caught by surprise again, it glanced off his forehead. While he staggered sideways, I raced up the aisle. A hand clamped around my arm. I twisted and struck him hard, elbow to throat. It was a solid, debilitating hit but hardly what I had been aiming for. I hurried toward the front, slipping on his wet footsteps. I reached the door and flung it open just as he caught the back of my blouse. He tugged and grunted. I yelled and flailed wildly. Then I looked back and kicked him right in the family maker. He released me so suddenly the force knocked me into the glass door with a violent crash. The door shattered around my head, cutting my scalp. I cried out as searing pain exploded across my forehead. Clutching my head, I stumbled dizzily onto the sidewalk where sheets of rain marred my vision. I saw wet hazy doubles of everything.

It seemed as though the city was under siege from punishing rain. Streets were clogged with autos caught in overflowing intersections and gutters. The wet concrete glared with headlights but I couldn't make out a single person in the mess. I careened along the sidewalk, unsure where to go. Businesses had locked up for the night, offering no help. I glanced warily behind me. The Frenchman was limping in my direction, one hand guarding the front of his trousers, the other clutching the knife. Blood seeped from his forehead where the bottle had struck.

I turned into an alley and stopped abruptly. This was not the shortcut I had expected. I knew this city like the back of my hand but I had gotten disoriented. I was two blocks short of where I wanted to be. The Frenchman had followed and blocked my exit. Only then did I realize I should have cried out for help. Not that anyone would have heard over the rain and traffic noise. We squinted at each other through the downpour. I took a clumsy step forward which prompted him to raise the knife. I braced a hand on the brick wall and tried to get my bearings. If only I could overcome this woozy circus in my head.

The man spoke, something harsh and demanding in French, and came at me. I wheeled backward, narrowly escaping the edge of the blade as he sliced it through the air. He was in worse shape than I was, and fell into the wall. The knife clattered to the pavement. I grabbed it and stood, my head swimming from the sudden movements. He pushed away from the wall, muttering and careening sideways. He yelled something again, some of which I thought I recognized from French class.

Oeil pour Oeil! Eye for an Eye?

I hesitated, confused. The Frenchman lunged at me, nearly knocking the wind from my chest. And then he stopped and grunted before hunching over. He looked down at himself and then raised his face to mine. I could just see his bulging eyes in the dim light. We came to the same realization at the same time; he had run himself into his own knife.

The man staggered back as I released my grasp on the knife handle. I stared down in horror and then looked back at him. His face contorted with rage and he lunged at me again, knocking my head hard against the brick wall. I grunted and squeezed my eyes shut. Blackness swirled in my head, making me nauseous. The man's knees buckled and the full weight of his bulky frame engulfed me. We slowly fell sideways, his cold, bloody face smearing across my cheek. We hit the ground with a painful, jarring thud.

"Ugh!" The air left me as a faint faraway noise penetrated my heavy head. Police and fire department bells rang up and down Broadway. "Help," I said and then slumped. No, they weren't coming for me but for folks stranded in the flooding. I was on my own.

I managed to roll the Frenchman's body off my bare legs, letting him flop against the wet concrete. I struggled to pull myself up but fell back against the wall, the wet world around me spinning. For a moment I just sat there, staring at my torn stockings and trying to catch my breath. I brushed aside the hair matted to my face, and forced myself to focus on something stationary. Through the pouring rain, dim street lights from Broadway cascaded just enough light to distinguish the shadowy, prostrate figure beside me, the knife protruding from his chest.

Rain had swept blood into my mouth, the metallic taste making me nauseous all over again. I spit and then grabbed my throbbing head.

"You okay?" someone shouted from the street. Beams of light ricocheted down the alley. Dark shadows made their way over and then a light shone in my face. I grimaced and raised a hand against it.

"Good God! Kate!"

It was Nicky of all people.

CHAPTER 26

"Didn't realize you'd been struck so many times," Detective Cahill muttered. It was almost as though he felt bad for not allowing me to clean up or even wash my face. The line of blood that had been trickling down my forehead had stopped some time ago and dried. "So, you're suggesting it was self-defense?" He finally looked up from his notepad.

"No, that's what I'm *saying*. I was attacked. First in our office and then in the alley. And I certainly don't own a knife. Not of that sort, anyhow."

"Did you ever get the man's name?"

"If I had a name I wouldn't have been referring to him as the pasty-face French foreigner for the past few hours. Ask Officer Masino."

Detective Cahill closed his notepad and sat back in his chair. A myriad of thoughts seemed to have overtaken him. For the first time since my interrogation began, the special investigator looked stumped.

"He... he was the officer who found you in the alley, Officer Nick Masino?" he asked. "And he brought you in, is that correct? You said, I mean the report states that the attacker was dead at the scene."

"Yes. Without any regard for my predicament, the evil little man expired and deprived me the pleasure of his name. But he was the same man I had first seen outside the station weeks back, and then at the Grove."

There was a knock on the door and Addy's Aunt Alice opened it before being invited in. She wore a policewoman's uniform, which I knew for a fact she had made herself, a long dark grey skirt and matching jacket. The badge over her left breast read POLICE WOMAN'S BADGE NUMBER ONE. She had a small towel and a bowl of water for me and a dark scowl for Detective Cahill.

"Sir, I must insist on taking custody of Miss March," she said, setting the bowl on the table. "She should have been under my care upon arrival. As you know, I am responsible for processing all juvenile and female prisoners. This interrogation, without a female presence, is against regulations. As you're well aware." She gently mopped up the blood on my face and the cut in my scalp.

"I understand, Officer Wells," Detective Cahill said. "But there's been a murder and the dead body is—"

"I'm aware of that," she snapped. "And the dead body will be just as dead tomorrow. Now, up you go." She took my arm and lifted me from the chair. "Can you stand?"

"Uh-huh," I said, feigning weakness. I offered Detective Cahill a smooth smile before Officer Wells steered me toward the door. He puffed up as though wanting to bark out an order to keep me here but eventually deflated without a word.

I was marched briskly down the hallway and through an arrangement of desks occupied by a handful of officers writing out late-night reports. Officer Wells seemed in an awful hurry so I slowed my pace to look around for Nicky or Detective King. Or possibly Addy.

"Quickly, now," she whispered, looking sideways at me and then, tightening her grip on my arm, guided me down another long hallway. I was in uncharted territory, the female prisoner's side of the precinct. We turned sharply down another hallway, passed through three doors, until I was suddenly standing outside in the rain and facing the motor pool.

"There," Officer Wells said, pointing to a police car waiting on the street. She nudged me down the steps as I had been too stunned to move. I had expected a hard seat on felony row, not an escape plan. Nicky opened the door and yelled through the driving rain.

"Katie Ann! Hurry! Get in!"

I raced over and climbed in across his lap. "What's happening? You busting me out?"

Nicky hit the accelerator, and I fell against the seat.

"You alright? How's your head?"

"Fine, fine. What's happening?"

"We got a response," he said, wheeling us sharply through the parking lot and onto the street.

"What?" I cried.

"Someone responded to your column."

"What!" I repeated. "Who? Charlotte Shelby?"

"Hold on!" Nicky growled, yanking the wheel to the left. I fell against the door as we crossed oncoming traffic and swerved around the corner.

"Hell's chariot! Where are we going?" I hollered. We raced around another corner, nearly riding on two wheels.

"That's him ahead. I can't lose him." We took another corner and then another, keeping several yards behind him.

"Nicky! Tell me what's happened!"

"That headline of yours! That's what's happened! I told you, *speak easy*, for chrissake!"

"That *was* speaking easy!" I said. "Now tell me what's happened!"

"That fella up ahead came into the office with a clipping of your column. Said he wanted to know exactly what the spiritualist had said about Taylor's killer. Claimed he was asking on behalf of a friend and wanted us to direct him to the spiritualist. We explained that we couldn't reveal the name of the spiritualist but if his friend would like to talk we'd keep an open mind."

"What's the man's name?"

"Wouldn't give it. So, I made him wait in the hallway. Then I sent every officer, court reporter, and file clerk I could find to stroll by the man, hoping someone would recognize him. An officer identified him as a lawyer he'd seen down at the Hall of Records. King tried to convince the lawyer to bring his friend in to speak to us. I've been waiting in the parking lot to follow him."

"Did you ask Officer Wells to help me escape?"

Nicky laughed lightly. "Not exactly. When she realized Detective Cahill had skirted around protocol to interrogate you without her presence, she cornered me in the hallway and demanded I get you out. I've already given a statement about the man in the alley. It was self-defense, right?"

"Yeah, about that man—"

"Later," he said, slowing down and taking the next turn gingerly. We were running too close behind our canary.

"You think this lawyer is headed to his friend's house?"

"That's the idea."

388

We followed the auto into a stately neighborhood and slowed as it maneuvered through the residential streets. Nicky and I glanced at one another. We were both familiar with the area. The lawyer turned onto Seventh Street and pulled to a stop outside the home of Charlotte Shelby. I grabbed Nicky's arm in anticipation. He pulled alongside the curb well behind the lawyer and cut the engine. We watched through the windshield, the rain little more than sprinkles now. The lawyer climbed from his auto, hunkered down over his satchel, and marched to the front door with his mackintosh galoshes flapping around his ankles.

"Lord a' mighty, Nicky, we got her!"

"*You* got her, Kate," he said, looking dumbfounded but pleased. I suspected we were both shocked the plan had worked.

I wiped fog from the side window and stared up at the giant mansion which had been purchased with Mary's money. She might've been happy there if not for the Monster. And possibly Margaret, too. Charlotte Shelby had wielded her authority over her daughters, and others, to the point of madness. It was no stretch of my imagination to believe she had killed poor Mr. Taylor in cold blood. She may have loads of power and influence, but that was about to change. I wanted to see Charlotte Shelby's face when her lawyer broke the news.

I reached for the door handle but Nicky grabbed my arm. "Don't," he said. "I know what you're thinking, Kate, but you can't. You'll spook her and she'll run off to Europe before Woolwine can bring her in."

"I just want to look in the window. I just want... I have to see her face." I jerked free and flung open the door. To my credit, I made it halfway across the slippery lawn before Nicky caught me.

"You are the most stubborn, impulsive female I've ever met," he said, marching me back to the auto.

"I simply wanted to put the cherry on top of this story," I said. "You could afford me that considering the night I've had."

We stopped on the lawn, Nicky looking down at me as though he had so much he wanted to say. Worry clouded his eyes as he shook his head. "If anything had happened to you tonight, I'd…" He choked on the thought.

"It didn't, Nicky," I said suddenly feeling awful that he should be so scared for me. He knew how dangerous that Frenchman was. He had warned me at the Grove. "I'm fine, Nicky, really. But I still don't understand who those men are. They don't seem connected to this case, so why would they come after me?"

Nicky reached out and cupped my face but we were suddenly caught in a pair of head lamps beaming from a police car just pulling to the curb. Nicky withdrew as Detective King threw open the door and clomped over, cursing the ungodly weather.

"Well, is he here?" he demanded.

I stared up at Nicky, wondering what he had meant to do before being interrupted. My mind was in a strange fog.

"Of course he's here," Nicky said. "Kate had it right all along." He looked down at me and we grinned like a pair of conspirators.

Detective King surveyed the home in the waning rain. "I'll be a sonofabitch," he muttered.

"It's over," I announced confidently. "Woolwine has enough to bring her in."

"You're right about one thing, Miss March," Detective King said. "It *is* over. After this lawyer left the precinct, Woolwine called me into his office. I'm off the case. *We* are off the case." He looked at Nicky. "He wants our notes. We're done."

"What about the evidence?" I demanded as a sour feeling stirred in my stomach.

"If you're referring to the only thing that might possibly implicate Shelby, that note sent to the station advising the police to look for a gun at Mabel Normand's apartment house, it's gone. Everything is gone from Woolwine's office. The three blonde hairs. Even Mary's letters to Taylor. The only thing left is Taylor's bloody coat and vest."

"That's what the file girls had seen being removed from his office and loaded into the back of his auto," I said.

"I'm sure of it," he said. "Your column to ferret out the killer must have spooked him and Mrs. Shelby. Woolwine was hotter than a pistol when you revealed the killer as a woman. He had everyone in town believing Sands was the killer. And then you went and got Howard Fellows to squawk to the world that he was the man seen leaving Taylor's that night. I figure Woolwine hadn't expected anyone to put it all together, but you did. That column this morning sure rattled him."

"Woolwine risked destroying evidence in a murder investigation because Mrs. Shelby is a powerful, rich friend," I said bitterly.

"I wouldn't exactly call them friends," Nicky clarified. "Sounds more like a business arrangement."

"Besides, what we call evidence he could see as nothing suspicious," Detective King said gruffly. "He's the DA. It's his call, and legally, he can release everything he claims doesn't pertain to the case. And that's just what he did."

"But it's an open case!" I wailed.

"Everything he got rid of was circumstantial," Nicky reminded me. "It's not as though he destroyed the weapon that connects Mrs. Shelby to the murder. We still haven't found the gun."

"But Nicky, tonight proves—"

"Nothing. In the end, tonight has satisfied *your* suspicions and convinced *us* but that's all. Your theory would hardly stand up in court, even if you could convince the DA to arrest Mrs. Shelby." Nicky held my shoulders and looked me in the eye. "You are a fine reporter, Kate—"

"A *damned* fine investigator," Detective King interjected. "I'd work with you any day of the week and twice on Sundays." He smiled around the ciggy he was lighting up.

I murmured my thanks, feeling grateful but heartsick. It wasn't as though I hadn't see this coming but I had hoped against all odds that Woolwine wouldn't prove to be so corrupt after all. It was so unfair, absolutely disgusting if you asked me.

"So, where does that leave things?" I asked sullenly.

"Mrs. Shelby may never be tried and found guilty in a court of law," Nicky said. "But you seem to have made a name for yourself. Your opinion and your evidence is out there for every-one to read in print. And they *are* reading it. There wasn't a single person who read your paper this morning who didn't know exactly who you were referring to. You've made a good case against her, and the court of public opinion matters a great deal in this town."

"Printer's ink," I said, thinking back to Christopher Morley's book. "That's what it's come down to after all. I have to outlast the Monster's gunpowder."

"How's that?" Nicky asked, frowning.

"I'll continue printing my suspicions until there isn't a person alive who doubts the identity of Mr. Taylor's killer."

"Atta girl," said Detective King, slapping me on the back. "I was hoping you'd say that. Every one of us down at the station who hates Woolwine will be cheering for you, kid. And who knows, maybe the next DA won't be so easy to bribe."

Nicky and I climbed into patrol car number thirty-three and sat for a quiet moment, digesting the outcome. Then he started the engine and maneuvered us through the wet streets. My mind was swimming with everything that had happened tonight. I had solved a murder but almost gotten myself killed in the process. This newspaper business certainly was risky and hard work. But that was half the fun, wasn't it? I smiled, remembering the excitement I'd felt chasing down leads and concocting theories. I couldn't wait to tell Pop and Addy that my plan had worked, mostly. Explaining the dead man in the alley was another issue entirely, especially when I hadn't a clue as to who he was, or why he'd attacked me.

While I had been reminiscing about my adventures, Nicky must have made up his mind to open up at last.

"Her name was Gabrielle," he said out of the blue. "We were working for the Allies. I'd trained as a spy and headed straight to France back in '17. She was working through a French and British spy network in Lille. I was told she was a dancer spying on German officers in the nightclubs. We were assigned to play a couple, both spies feeding information back to our contacts. We got... involved, and I fell in love. I mean, I thought I did. It was a few months later when I became suspicious of her. I hated believing she was capable of... I didn't really know her, I guess. One day, I confirmed my suspicions and reported them to my contact. I was told to continue my assignment but to track her every move. A few nights later, she must've realized I'd discovered her secret. We were lying in bed when she got up and... she came at me with a knife. She got me between the ribs first. I held her off and then..." His jaw muscle twitched and he looked out the window.

"I'm so sorry, Nicky," I said softly, remembering at least two more scars I'd seen near his stomach that night on the veranda.

That's why I couldn't identify them; he had gotten them in The War.

"When I went off to war, I never thought I would have to kill a... woman." He nearly choked on the words.

"But she was going to kill *you*," I said, scooting closer and laying a hand on his arm. "You did what you had to do, Nicky. Right?" He didn't answer but I suddenly understood so much more about the Nicky Masino I had known all my life. He had suffered so much guilt from what he'd been forced to do. "Did you truly love her?"

He wiped moisture from his eyes. "No. I think I got caught up in the danger and excitement of it all. At first, anyway. I was several years younger than she was. I didn't know what I was doing most of the time, but after she attacked me I... found my place. I turned pretty hard inside. And driven. I made a lot of connections with important people. Exchanged a lot of favors and had a lot of... monsters executed."

"You made a name for yourself," I said. "Is that why people at the station treat you differently?"

"They only know half of what I've done," he said bitterly. "Very few know my true rank and... it's not always a good feeling to be feared."

I let him sit quietly for few minutes before asking about his connection with the two Frenchmen who'd come after me.

"They were Gabrielle's brothers. Louis and Victor. They refused to believe she was collaborating with the Germans, even after all she did. They threatened to kill me. More than once. My commander had them arrested on trumped up charges so as not to interfere with my work. They'd been hounding me and threatening to expose me to the Germans. When The War ended, I traveled around, worried that if I came home they might find me. But I never really thought they would. When word reached us that they'd been released, Angelo begged me to return to France. To have them sentenced to life or executed. He was worried they'd show up here and hurt mother. I had no idea they would target you."

"But, why did they target me?"

Nicky took a deep breath, contemplating. "They must have thought you were someone... close to me. Someone I cared about."

"Oh." I clasped my hands in my lap, feeling my cheeks grow warm.

Nicky stopped the car and looked at me. "Kate, I... I'm so sorry. I never imagined they would take their revenge this far. I wished to God I'd gotten to you sooner tonight. I could have—"

"I managed just fine," I said, forcing a smile. "Well, at least that explains why the guy yelled 'an eye for an eye' before he lunged at me. He wanted revenge for his sister. And the other guy? The one that asked me to dance at the Grove? Where'd he disappear to?"

"I don't want to lie to you, so don't ask me that. Okay, Kate? Just leave it?"

I nodded and looked out the windshield. We were parked outside my house and rain was starting to fall again. "What'll you do now? Are you staying on the force?"

"For the time being. I've got some friends in Washington who want me on the inside. And that's all I'm saying so don't go looking for your next story." I laughed and agreed I wouldn't. "I should head back to the station. I've got quite a report to write up. And you should head inside... before you worry your pop." He grinned in that old familiar way.

I laughed softly. "Ok, Nicky, but only because I don't want to worry Pop." It wasn't exactly like old times anymore. So much had changed in the past few weeks but I was happy Nicky had finally opened up to me. With the two pasty-faced men gone, maybe he could put The War behind him and start fresh. I climbed out and looked back at him. Nicky was relaxed now and still grinning at me. Maybe Nicky Masino was goofy over me after all and he just didn't know it.

"Good night, Officer Masino," I said, smiling.

"Good night, Miss March," Nicky said, winking.

CHAPTER 27

Puffs of white steam shot from the underbelly of the Southern Pacific engine as it awaited passengers at the station. Addy
and I stood on the train platform, searching for Mr. Morgan. I
finally found him among the crowd, suitcase in hand.

"Miss Kate!" he called ecstatically upon seeing me. He shouldered through the throng of passengers bidding farewell to their
families and friends. Mr. Morgan clutched me in a fierce hug
and then threw his arms around Addy. "You've come to see us
off!" he exclaimed to Addy.

"Uh," Addy froze.

"Mr. Morgan," I said, coming to her rescue. "We came to
see *you* off. I'm afraid I can't leave now but I wanted to return
your ticket. It was very thoughtful of you, and I'm probably going to regret my decision."

"And how!" Addy retorted. She had made no secret of her

feelings on the matter. If it had been up to her, we would both be heading to New York with Mr. Morgan.

"Perhaps you could get your money back?" I said.

The light went out in him and he slowly reached for the ticket. "I see. I do understand. It was a long shot, I know. But it's an open invitation. Anytime you feel like seeing the world, just telegram, or even call long distance, and..."

"Of course. We just might take you up on that."

He pulled me into another hug and whispered his farewell quote from Emerson. "'Nothing makes the earth seem so spacious as to have friends at a distance; they make the latitudes and longitudes.'"

"'Sweet is the memory of distant friends. Like the mellow rays of the departing sun, it falls tenderly, yet sadly, on the heart.'"

He groaned and smiled down at me. "I shall take Mr. Irving's words with me. Farewell my friend." He kissed me on the cheek and then hopped onto the train. We waited until the porter made the last call and the giant iron wheels began to rotate. The whistle blasted and we waved goodbye. Mr. Morgan waved from the first-class window. And then he was gone.

"Are you sure?" Addy asked.

"I'm not sure of anything," I said.

The whistle blasted again and we strolled away.

A small crowd had gathered outside the office when Addy and I arrived on Broadway. Late last night, I had filled Pop in with the results of my scheme and the unfortunate tragedy of his glass door. I assured him that I was well and good, and that I had accepted the fate of my investigation. The story would remain an open case in my book, and I would remain vigilant with updates and covert accusations. It was the best compromise I could hope for.

"What's all the fuss?" Addy asked as we walked along the rain-washed sidewalks.

"Dunno," I said. "Let's have a look."

We came upon several workmen in overhauls I recognized from Calhoun's Hardware Store. They were sweeping up the broken glass inside and outside our office, some of which was smeared with blood. Another crew was handling a fresh pane of glass fit for the door frame. Mrs. Vandergrift, from the local shoe shop, was polishing the entire office window until it shone.

"What gives?" I asked Pop. He whirled around in surprise.

"There you are!" he cried. "Come and see. You won't believe it, Kate, but everyone has come to help."

Alongside *The Messenger's* staff I spotted Mr. Calhoun from next door, Mr. Rogers our mail carrier, Bessie the waitress, Irene the telephone operator, and tons of local shop owners I had known all my life, most who had advertised in our paper for years. They dropped their rags and brooms and began to applaud and cheer. They knew I had solved the murder. I was dumbfounded. I tried to explain that no arrest had been made but they wouldn't hear it. Somehow, they understood what had happened. I had fought against the corrupt machine of Wool-wine's police administration and outsmarted him. Every story I ran had chipped away at Woolwine's façade, allowing the public to see through their dishonest DA. I was told, in no uncertain terms, that Woolwine would hear their voices come election day.

"I don't understand," I said to Pop. "How could everyone know the outcome of my scheme already? I haven't written an update yet."

"I know, I know," he said, happier than I'd seen him in ages.

"An anonymous source reached out to every major news organization in the country and explained what had happened in response to your spiritualist ultimatum last night. I even heard Washington got wind of it. The papers ran the story this morning. Of course, no one named Mrs. Shelby outright but there's no need. You did an excellent job describing the situation. Everyone knows who killed Taylor and why. Now, I know you're disappointed not to have seen Mrs. Shelby arrested, but there's no doubt she's been found guilty. Everyone is so proud of you, Kate. Just look." He gestured to our friends and neighbors crowded on the sidewalk. "They came first thing this morning and volunteered their time and money to keep our office running."

Addy snorted a laugh. "Do they know you also killed a man last night?" she said behind her hand.

"Oh, yes, about that," Pop said. "Your Aunt Alice phoned our office this morning, looking for Kate. She wanted you to know there will be no charges brought against you for that man's death. Judge Simeon read Nick's report from last night, and then Detective Cahill's this morning, declaring it self-defense."

"Thank God," I said relieved. "I wasn't looking forward to continuing with Detective Cahill, poor fella. I'm afraid I bored him to tears. I practically told him my life story. When Nicky found me last night in the alleyway I begged him to take me down to the precinct instead of the hospital. That nasty conk on the head had me sideways. But I was hoping to be with your Aunt Alice and not Detective Cahill. He just happened to swoop in first. I thought if I hung around the precinct long enough, I might be there when the Monster came asking about the spiritualist."

"Easy peasy," Addy said lightly. "Well, I mean after you plugged that guy and didn't die from losing all that blood—"

I elbowed Addy to shut up and then looked at Pop. His smile dropped and he grew serious.

"It's jake, Pop, really," I said quickly. "Like I said last night, the man in the alley had nothing to do with the Taylor case. I know you're worried, but I'm fine. Really."

"Do we have any idea who he might be?" Pop asked, still upset.

"Yes, I do, Pop. Nicky explained things last night and... well, it's over. That's all I can say. We have to trust Nicky on this." I gave him a look that said it was Nicky's business, not ours. Pop took a moment and then nodded.

"But, they're gone now," Addy said, glancing around. "Right? You said one disappeared days ago and you ended the second one. So, that's *la fin?* The end?"

"Yes. They're gone. For good," I assured Addy. We heard my name called in the distance and swung around to Rico rushing up, distraught.

"Miss March! Miss March! *Gracias a Dios!* I found you! You must come with me. The sister of my uncle's best friend's cousin is missing! The police won't investigate! They say she ran away but she didn't! Please, you must help!"

"Rico, please," I said dislodging his firm grip from my arm. "You know I'm a reporter, not an investigator."

"*Si*, that's why *you* must come. *You*, they trust. They read your paper. They understand that you look at things differently. Plus, *I* told them I trusted you and they trust me. So please, will you help?"

I was taken aback. I hadn't had a chance to explain my career plans to Pop yet. And I certainly hadn't expected to find the next story so quickly or easily—if it *was* a story, which I doubted. I gave Addy a skeptical look.

"Well, I don't know if—"

Addy rolled her eyes and sighed. "Of course, she'll come. We'll both come." She slid her arm around Rico's thin shoulders and walked him up the sidewalk. "Now tell me, Rico, this friend of the family, the missing girl, has she gone Modern yet?"

"S' okay, Pop?" I asked. "You don't mind so much, do you?"

He wrapped an arm around my waist. "I expected as much. But if you ever feel college calling, you'll tell me?"

"Of course."

Pop returned to the crowd who was enjoying a round of hot coffee compliments of Bessie the waitress and The Kitchen Kettle. As I made my way up the sidewalk to join Addy and Rico, I noticed a woman in a high-collared Victorian dress and a wide brimmed hat staring in our direction. When I turned to face her, she disappeared so quickly I wondered if it had only been my imagination.

ABOUT THE AUTHOR

Lori Adams lives in Southern California. She is the author of the Kate March Mysteries, the Avalina Jones Series, and the Soulkeepers Series.

NOTE FROM THE AUTHOR

Speak Easy is based, in part, on the unsolved murder of Paramount Director, William Desmond Taylor. Scour the internet and you'll find many theories about the real murderer. I came to my own conclusion. As of this printing the murder remains unsolved.